T0286661

I'll Have
What He's
Having

I'll Have What He's Having

ADIB KHORRAM

FOREVER

New York   Boston

Forever
Hachette Book Group
1290 Avenue of the Americas, New York, NY 10104
read-forever.com
@readforeverpub

First Edition: August 2024

Forever is an imprint of Grand Central Publishing. The Forever name and logo are registered trademarks of Hachette Book Group, Inc.

The publisher is not responsible for websites (or their content) that are not owned by the publisher.

Forever books may be purchased in bulk for business, educational, or promotional use. For information, please contact your local bookseller or the Hachette Book Group Special Markets Department at special.markets@hbgusa.com.

Print book interior design by Taylor Navis

Library of Congress Cataloging-in-Publication Data

Names: Khorram, Adib, author.
Title: I'll have what he's having / Adib Khorram.
Other titles: I will have what he is having
Description: First edition. | New York : Forever, 2024.
Identifiers: LCCN 2023056640 | ISBN 9781538739518 (paperback) | ISBN 9781538739525 (hardcover) | ISBN 9781538739549 (ebook)
Subjects: LCGFT: Romance fiction. | Gay fiction. | Novels.
Classification: LCC PS3611.H667 I45 2024 | DDC 813/.6—dc23/eng/20231222
LC record available at https://lccn.loc.gov/2023056640

ISBNs: 9781538739518 (trade paperback), 9781538739525 (hardcover), 9781538739549 (ebook)

Printed in the United States of America

LSC-C

Printing 1, 2024

For Molly
Thanks for letting me borrow your backstory

For wine alone has power to part
The rust of sorrow from the heart.

—Abolqasem Ferdowsi, *Shahnameh*

I'll Have
What He's
Having

one

Farzan

Farzan was crying.

It was his own fault: he knew better than to let his knives get this dull, but he'd taken a job substitute teaching every day the last two weeks and hadn't made it out to the knife shop he liked.

Plus, this onion was aggressively potent. He'd started tearing up as he peeled the skin, even before he made the first cut. At least he didn't have to dice it. All he needed were some long strips.

Farzan wiped his eyes with the crook of his elbow, darkening the soft gray cotton of his Henley. He'd have to change before Cliff got here, but first he had to get the salmon marinating, plus wash the rice and get it soaking. This was going to be Cliff's introduction to Persian food, and everything had to be perfect.

He hummed along to Hikaru Utada—video game music was his go-to kitchen playlist—as he dropped the slices of onion into a wide dish. He added a good glug of olive oil, salt, and white pepper, then moved to his mortar and pestle for the saffron, red threads releasing their heavenly fragrance into the air as he ground them to a fine powder.

His mother insisted—as did many Iranians—that saffron was an aphrodisiac. Farzan certainly hoped it was true. This was his third date with Cliff, the make-or-break point. The first two dates—one at a coffee shop, the other a walk around Loose Park—had been pretty close to perfect. Cliff was fun, and interesting, and they'd had a good connection: laughing at each other's jokes, bumping elbows as they walked, sharing little smiles. The kiss they'd shared pressed up against the side of Cliff's Toyota had been full of promise, the kind of promise that set Farzan's stomach dancing.

Persian food and chill was the perfect third date. At least, Farzan hoped it was. Cliff had seemed happy with the suggestion, but there was always the worry that Cliff was just agreeing to spare Farzan's feelings. Sometimes dating was exhausting.

But Farzan was confident in his cooking. He'd waffled on whether to serve fish, given what he hoped might happen after, but taste had won out: saffron-marinated salmon, served over zereshk polow—basmati rice mixed with barberries, tart little rubies—was one of Farzan's specialties.

It was an unorthodox combination, one he argued about with his dad, Firouz, constantly. Firouz, like many Iranians, would've paired fish with baghali polow, fava bean rice, or at least sabzi polow, rice with lots of fresh herbs, especially dill. But Farzan loved the combination of sweet and sour, the lift it gave to the savory fish.

Farzan had learned everything he knew about cooking from his dad, who was in charge of the food at his parents' restaurant in the Northland. They called it Shiraz Bistro, even though their family came from Yazd. But his parents had insisted Shiraz was more familiar to Americans, because of the wine.

Not that they served much Shiraz at the bistro: Persis, Farzan's mom, was in charge of the books, and she kept tight reins on the booze budget. Farzan's brother and sister had taken after Persis in the math skills department, but somehow Farzan had missed out: math had been his worst subject in school, and every time he got a call to substitute for a math teacher, he seriously considered driving his car into the Missouri River instead.

"Shit!" he hissed, after bumping his elbow against the hot kettle.

His kitchen was smaller than he would've preferred, with not nearly enough counter space, but otherwise he really liked his apartment in the River Market. It had easy access to the farmers market on the weekends, a streetcar stop down the block, and countless restaurants nearby. Best of all, it was still rent-controlled, despite the intense gentrification all around. He'd moved in right after finishing his master's in education—fuck, that was more than a decade ago now—and he had no plans to move.

He grabbed the kettle to pour boiling water over the saffron; the red powder blossomed into liquid gold. He swirled it in his mortar before adding it to the marinade. But as he ducked into the fridge to pull out the salmon, his music suddenly cut out, and his phone started buzzing. He jolted upright, banging his head against the handle to the freezer door.

"Fuck," he groaned as he pulled out his phone, blinking at Cliff's photo on the screen.

Holy shit. Cliff was calling him.

Making the transition from texts to phone calls was a huge step, right? Maybe even bigger than Persian food and chill. His throat clamped for a second; his heart gave a happy flutter.

Farzan was definitely getting laid tonight.

He grinned, even though Cliff couldn't see him, as he answered. "Hey. I was just thinking about you."

"Hi. I catch you at a bad time?" Cliff had a mellow, throaty voice, not to mention nice lips framed by his well-manicured beard.

Farzan held the phone in the crook of his neck as he pulled on a pair of nitrile gloves. He always used them for this part; otherwise his hands would be stained yellow for days, and that was definitely not sexy. "No, I'm just getting dinner going. Can't wait to see you tonight."

"Oh." Cliff cleared his throat and went quiet for a moment. Then: "Did you get my texts?"

"No, sorry. I've been cooking. Everything all right? Oh shit, you don't have a fish allergy, do you?" Farzan mentally kicked himself. He should've checked before going to the grocery store. He should've—

"Nothing like that." Cliff's voice softened, in that way someone's did when they knew the listener wouldn't like what they were about to say. Farzan's shoulders hitched up. "Listen. I've been . . . Well, I don't think I can make it tonight."

"Oh." Farzan tried to keep his voice light, even though his sternum began to burn. "We could try tomorrow instead?"

But he was pretty sure he already knew where this was heading. His eyes began to prickle in the corners, and this time, not from onions.

Cliff cleared his throat again. "Listen. You're a nice guy, but . . . I'm not really feeling it. You know? I don't see this going anywhere. I didn't want to lead you on."

"Oh."

Farzan stared at the bowl of marinade. How many inches of liquid did it take to drown yourself in?

"I get it," he said. "Thanks for letting me know."

"I was hoping to catch you before you started. I can Venmo you for the groceries—"

"It's fine. Leftovers, right?" Farzan knew he sounded weird. His throat felt like it was closing up. Farzan didn't have any allergies (unless you counted how cantaloupe always made his tongue burn), but maybe he was becoming allergic to constant rejection.

Repeated exposure made allergies worse, right?

"I . . . guess I'd better let you go then."

"Yeah. Okay. Uh. Thanks, Farzan. Bye."

"Bye." But Cliff had already hung up.

Farzan jumped when Utada started singing again. He paused the song and sighed.

Thirty-seven years old and single again.

Thirty-seven years old, single, and about to drop a fifty-dollar salmon fillet on the floor.

"Goddamn it!" he spat. The salmon was a two-hand job.

He groaned and pulled it off the floor. A good rinse and it would be fine.

Farzan shook his head, blinking against the sting in his eyes. Did it count as a breakup if you were never officially together? It hurt like one. Not the sort of all-encompassing, black-hole-of-despair heartbreak he'd had with his last serious boyfriend, Jason (*fucking Jason*, he mentally amended), or even the jagged, knife-to-the-guts feeling of when he'd brought up being exclusive to Corey, who said he didn't see why they had to change their casual relationship to something more (that's what Farzan got for falling for a guy who *only did casual*) but still, this hurt enough.

What was it about him that drove men away?

Farzan knew he was fairly good-looking. His light russet skin was smooth and clear, thanks to a combination of good genes and good skin care. He had an elegant nose (if only a little largish—he was Persian after all). His thick, curly black hair wasn't thinning—Alavi men didn't usually go bald, though he had started finding salt in his pepper. Plenty of guys complimented his warm brown bedroom eyes.

Yeah, maybe he was headed toward a bit of a barrel chest, and yeah, he'd lost any trace of abs five years ago, but he was reasonably fit, even by the unrelenting standards of the gay community.

Farzan huffed. If it wasn't his looks, it had to be something else, something inside him, and he couldn't wait to hear his family's latest theories about *that* next time they interrogated him about his dating life.

Meanwhile, his younger sister was happily married, and his baby brother was in a long-term relationship. Everyone in the family was already taking bets on when he'd propose.

How had Farzan wound up as the one with no love life?

He finished rinsing the salmon and patted it dry with a paper towel. At least Cliff had called before he'd started cooking the rice. He could save the marinade for tomorrow—it would actually taste better after sitting overnight anyway.

Farzan didn't much feel like cooking anymore. Persian food was for sharing: for family gatherings, for date nights, for sitting together enjoying the warmth of a meal, lovingly prepared. It was not a food for breakups.

Thankfully (or lamentably), Farzan had a foolproof solution for heart-break: get drunk on wine and eat a bunch of french fries. He'd perfected the pairing in his twenties, commiserating with his best friends, Ramin and Arya, over the men they were seeing, and fucking, and loving, and losing.

Farzan paused his music and pulled his phone back out to text them. The only thing better for a breakup than wine and fries was wine and fries with friends.

> **Farzan**
> Guess who got dumped
> You guys free for wine and fries?
> We could check out that new wine bar.

His friends answered in less than a minute.

> **Arya**
> WTF
> Sorry dude

> **Ramin**
> Oh Farzan. I'm sorry.
> Are you doing okay?

> **Farzan**
> I'm doing okay.
> We'd only been on two dates anyway.

> **Arya**
> I'm working tonight
> I totally would otherwise
> You know mr

> **Ramin**
> Weren't you going to cook for him?

Arya
Me*
HE WAS GETTING FARZAN FOOD???

Farzan
Yeah but whatever
Arya no worries. Ramin you free?

Ramin
Dinner with Todd tonight. Our one year anniversary.
Sorry.

Farzan
Don't be! Have fun!
Is it already a year?

Fuck. How had Farzan missed that? And how come Ramin and Todd could make it a whole year, but he couldn't even make it to two weeks?

Ramin
See you Thursday then?

Farzan
For sure.
Love you guys.

Ramin
Love you

Arya
Love you doostammmm

Farzan flopped back on the couch. Looked like he'd be flying solo tonight. In more ways than one.

He pulled up the website of the wine bar. Aspire had opened over the summer in a vacant spot on Walnut. He'd been meaning to try it out—with Arya and Ramin (and Todd), in fact—but reservations had been hard to come by, and then he'd been super busy with jobs, and Arya always had a slew of end-of-summer events to plan, and Ramin had gotten a promotion, and now it was nearly fall and they still hadn't been.

But it was easier to get a table for one than for four.

Aspire didn't open for another hour. Farzan knew he should be doing his dishes, but honestly, he was content to lie on the couch and stare at the ceiling. There would always be more dishes. Turns out that was what his thirties had been about: endless dishes, knees that crackled when he went for a run, and graying hair. He'd even found a gray strand this morning while he was grooming himself down below, just in case Persian food and chill became . . . really chill.

He sighed. He should've left his poor balls alone. After all, they'd been more reliable companions than any man he'd ever dated. They hadn't dumped him after two dates, halfway through cooking for the third.

In the kitchen, his oven beeped that it had finished preheating for the salmon that it wouldn't be seeing tonight.

"Shit!" Farzan sprang off the couch and ran to the kitchen.

Maybe he'd better clean up after all.

two

David

David stared at the wineglass in front of him. The wine was a deep purple, nearly maroon, dark and mysterious. He gave it a swirl and admired the legs. Full-bodied, certainly.

Behind him, Dannon muttered hopefully, "You think you're going to stump him this time?"

Kyra scoffed. "Thirty bottles in, I've more or less given up on that."

"Do you mind?" David asked without heat. "I'm trying to taste here."

"So sorry." Kyra gave him a quirked eyebrow and mocking bow. She was the assistant manager at Aspire, a charming Black woman in her early thirties who treated David like a cranky old man even though he was only thirty-seven. She actually reminded David of his mom, but there was no fucking way he'd ever tell Kyra that.

She had warm brown skin, immaculate box braids, and kind dark eyes that turned up in the corners. Her signature pinstriped vest was buttoned up; a gray tie, still loose, dipped into her large bosom.

David huffed a laugh, rolled his eyes, and stuck his nose in the glass. Notes of chocolate-covered strawberries punched him in the face, joined by more subtle scents: fresh-roasted coffee, allspice, sagebrush. He swirled again, keeping the tasting grid in his mind, as he took his first sip.

The wine danced across his tongue and sang on his palate, a soft, sensuous mouthfeel he'd come to associate with Rhône blends, especially ones from the New World. This deep and dark, it had to be Paso Robles. Medium-plus acidity, yes, and high tannins, but they were nice and ripe. And the finish? Whew. Fuck him.

He took one more luxurious sip, as blackberry and licorice overwhelmed him. He closed his eyes and sighed.

"Saxum. James Berry Vineyard. Twenty..."

He caught Kyra's face. She was smiling, but she looked like she'd sucked on a lemon drop, too.

"Fifteen."

"Damn, I thought I had you that time."

David laughed as she started pouring more glasses. "Maybe next time. Come on, gather round."

One of David's duties as Aspire's wine director was educating the team—everyone from dishwashers to chefs to front of house. Every day, someone picked a bottle from the cellar, which he tasted blind to help him practice for his upcoming master sommelier test. After they tried (and failed) to stump him, everyone tasted a small pour of the wine, while David talked about it: who made it, what grapes were used, where they were grown, what foods it might pair nicely with.

He studied Kyra's face as she puckered her lips. "It's got a lot of tannins," she said.

"Juicy," David agreed.

"I could see this with a roasted duck," Brayan, their chef, said. He had cool beige skin, curly brown hair, intense dark brown eyes, and the sort of dimples that let straight guys get away with anything. Not that David could picture Brayan actually doing anything rotten—the guy was soft-spoken and kind. He kept trying to get David to hang out after work, but David had precious little time for socializing with his test looming.

It was set for December: just under three months away. David had spent pretty much every day studying for it ever since he passed his advanced somm last year. Well, every day that hadn't been given over to moving from Chicago back home to Kansas City when Jeri, Aspire's owner, had asked him to come on board as wine director.

It didn't hurt that it meant he'd be closer to his mom and dad. And he wasn't going to miss the Chicago winters, though the snowstorm that had blown through in late February, right as he was packing, had felt fucking vindictive. He wasn't sure if it was a "please don't leave" storm or a "good riddance" storm, but either way, he was happy to be gone.

It wasn't like he had many friends left in Chicago, either. Sure, he had people he sometimes hung out with, people it would be fun to grab a drink with after work, but ever since he started studying for his sommelier certifications, he hadn't had that much time for hanging out. There were only a couple people he'd legitimately miss, but that's what FaceTime was for.

And he certainly wasn't going to miss any guys back in Chicago. The Grindr pool had been feeling shallower and shallower the last few years as he inched closer to forty and had less and less time and patience for bullshit.

Granted, guys might've been just as bad at home, but David hadn't actually logged in since he moved back. He'd been too busy helping get Aspire off the ground, or studying, or spending time with his mom to make up for fifteen years of only being home at Christmas.

"All right, team," he said, as everyone finished their tastes. "Any final questions?"

Kyra raised her hand. David pressed his lips together.

"Kyra?"

"You sure you're not part mass spectrometer?"

David rolled his eyes. "All right. Back to work. Doors in one hour."

While the rest of the team finished their final checks before opening, David gave the wineglasses dangling above the bar one last polish. This was his favorite time: the calm before the storm.

Nah, that was bullshit. His favorite was being in the thick of things, on a Saturday rush, having to pick five wines for three different tables and seven different mains. He loved the magic of wine. He loved the challenge.

That part of him hadn't changed, at least, since switching careers. He hadn't gotten his bachelor's in econ in three years—or his master's in business analytics in eighteen months—by shying away from a challenge. Nor would he be putting himself through the grueling master somm test if he didn't think he was up to it.

"How we doing?" Kyra asked, sidling up to him and grabbing another polishing cloth.

"Good," David said. "Same old, same old."

Kyra laughed, a high, tinkly sound. "You got anything going on tonight? There's a new bar that opened in the West Bottoms. A couple of us were thinking of checking it out."

"I'm good," David said as politely as he could. Kyra asked him to go out with the crew nearly every night—it was sweet of her, if a little exhausting—but he had a stack of note cards waiting for him at home. "Thanks, though."

Kyra pursed her lips. "Okay, fine. What about this weekend? There's this guy at my gym..."

David held up a hand. "Kyra. I'm not—"

"Just hear me out." David suppressed an eye roll. He'd learned over the last five months that there was no stopping Kyra. This was attempted set-up number eight, and it was going to go just like all the others (with a firm "no thank you"), but he had to let her get it out of her system.

"His name's Anthony. He's only a few years younger than you, he's gay, he's handsome, and he's got a better ass than me."

David narrowed his eyes. "How old is 'a few years younger'?"

"Twenty-eight."

David sighed. That was nine years younger. Just because he'd started getting some salt in his stubbly goatee, that didn't mean he was ready to be an "older man."

"I'm good—"

"And don't worry, he's Black too."

David sighed. That *was* a point in his favor—if he had to hook up with one more guy who went on and on about how he'd "never been with a Black guy before..."

"Ah, I can tell you're thinking about it," Kyra said. "You need some dick to help you deal with all this stress."

"Okay, first off, you can't say that kind of thing at work."

Kyra rolled her eyes. Somehow, though they'd only met when David started at Aspire, she acted like they were old friends.

"Second..." This Anthony didn't sound...awful. David could almost picture him, imagine inviting him back to David's place to chill. He'd finished furnishing his new house—he'd spent too long in a cramped Chicago apartment to not want to indulge a little bit in having a house again—and the new couch was cozy. They could curl up, watch a movie...

"You're thinking about it?" Kyra asked.

David shook his head. He needed to be thinking about the stacks of note cards and piles of books and cases of wine blocking the TV.

"Second." David cleared his throat. "I don't have time to be dating right now. And for the record, I can get dick on my own just fine."

"First, I didn't say date him. Just meet him." Kyra's eyes sparkled. "And second," she said, sticking her nose in the air, "you can't say that kind of thing at work." With that, she spun around and headed back toward the kitchen.

David snorted. Outmaneuvered again.

Still, that didn't change things. Yes, he'd been in a drought since he moved back home, and yes, he could use some good dick. But his test had to come first. Once he got his master somm, he could get a job *anywhere*: San Francisco. New York. Austin. Seattle.

All places with way better dick than Kansas City, Missouri. He'd grown up here. He knew the score.

Aspire was great, but it wasn't permanent. He promised Jeri he'd help get it off the ground while he finished out his master somm, but that was it. This was a temporary thing, not a permanent move. He had big dreams, and he was so fucking close. No way was he going to get entangled right now.

Besides. He had two hands and a nightstand full of toys.

He would be just fine on his own.

three

Farzan

Farzan was running late.

At least, later than he'd meant to. It wasn't like he had a date. Or even a reservation. But cleaning up the kitchen had taken longer than he'd planned. He'd been overcome by the urge to scrub down the stovetop, imagining Cliff's face in the black metal as he worked. And then he still had to shower, plus the streetcar was running behind because some bozo had parked over the line and they had to wait for said bozo to move his car. It was either that or get towed, and despite the screaming, the guy clearly didn't want to get towed.

So it was past six when he finally pulled up at the Kauffman Center stop. Early evening light was streaming down 16th Street; uphill, the light caught the edges of the Kauffman Center's two silver humps, turning them golden. But Farzan was headed the opposite way, toward Walnut.

Aspire had a tiny parking lot (already full), and Farzan was relieved he'd taken the streetcar, because he was shit at parallel parking, especially if there were witnesses. If no one was watching him, he could do it—most of the time. But like Schrödinger's cat, as soon as someone observed him, his parking skills were dead.

A small patio took up half the sidewalk outside Aspire, dotted with two- and four-seat tables, hemmed in by a black metal fence and a few ginkgo trees with their leaves already fading toward yellow. The tables were full, though—no surprise—so Farzan stepped inside to see if he could get a seat at the bar.

Farzan had been to a lot of restaurants all around Kansas City—some amazing, some awful, and plenty mediocre. Aspire's vibe was immaculate. Warm, cozy lights shone on the gray tile floor; abstract paintings by local artists dotted dark wood walls; a long mahogany-topped bar was laden with black rubber mats and cocktail fixings; and right above the host stand a kitschy chandelier made of empty wine bottles cast a greenish glow all around.

The restaurant was packed. Even the bar was crowded, but Farzan thought he saw a free stool. Fingers crossed, he approached the host stand.

"Hi!" The host was a lovely Black woman with box braids. Her pinstriped vest had a little pin that said SHE/HER on the lapel. "Do you have a reservation?"

"No, sorry," Farzan said. "You have room for one?"

She glanced over her shoulder. "We've got a spot at the bar, if you want to wait until a table opens up."

"Sure. That'll be fine."

"Can I get a name?" She tapped at the iPad on her stand.

"Farzan Alavi. He/him."

"Sorry?" A group of four suit-clad lawyer-looking bros at one of the tables had just started arguing about last Sunday's Chiefs game.

"Far—" he tried again, but another one of the bros shouted, "No fuckin' way!" at the top of his lungs. Farzan sighed.

"Frank," he shouted. "Frank Allen. He/him." It was his default White Person Name.

"Great." She tapped away again. "I'm Kyra, by the way. Shout if you need anything."

"Thanks, Kyra."

She gestured toward the open seat at the bar, and Farzan hopped onto the high-top stool, though he could already tell it wouldn't be long before his ass fell asleep. He wasn't in his twenties anymore. Despite never missing leg (and glutes) day at the gym, his ass was no longer made for sitting on barstools. Hopefully a table would open up soon.

"What can I get you?" the bartender asked. She was a short, sepia-skinned woman (she too wore a SHE/HER pin) with her long black hair in a ponytail.

"Ah, glass of rosé?" Farzan asked. "Something you're excited about right now?"

"I got just the thing." On the counter behind her stood two glass-fronted wine dispensers filled with their by-the-glass offerings, one white, one red; above that, a ledge with top-shelf whiskeys and gins and vodkas and tequilas. It was a lovely bar, though crowded. While the bartender poured his rosé, Farzan scanned the restaurant. It was hopping, servers coming and going, topping up wine or dropping off beautiful square bowls of french fries. Farzan's mouth watered.

Wine and fries really was the ultimate heartbreak food.

Farzan raised his hand to try to flag down the bartender to put in an order (he could always take the bowl with him once he got a table, right?), but she still had her back turned, fiddling with the wine dispenser. And right next to her—

Farzan had to blink a few times, and then quickly duck his head before he got caught looking, because *holy shit*. In his panic, he'd gripped his water glass, smearing condensation all along his palms; he wiped them off on his jeans and risked another sly glance.

Ho. Ly. Shit.

Farzan had really liked Cliff. He'd been funny, a little self-deprecating, and really attractive: white, a bit taller than Farzan, with a dimple in his chin and one of those forehead veins that made a face interesting. He'd gone mostly gray, but the silvery kind that looked sexy.

But fuck Cliff. In fact, Farzan could barely remember why he'd found him hot in the first place.

Because the guy at the end of the bar had to be the most beautiful man

Farzan had ever seen. Dark, cool black skin that glowed where the lights hit his cheekbones; the most stunning pair of midnight-brown eyes, big and perfectly shaped, beneath thick eyebrows, one of which had a sharp slit on the outer edge; his lips were framed by a nicely trimmed goatee, and his hair, black with a few grays, was in short twists. And his suit: blue with lilac plaid, impeccably tailored to show off his lovely shoulders. Farzan tried to get a better look—a suit like that had to show off the guy's ass too—but the bar was in the way, digging into Farzan's ribs.

And then the guy turned, and fuck fuck fuck, did they just make eye contact? Farzan quickly straightened, looked back down at his hands, but sweet mother of crap.

Cliff who?

Farzan glanced up again, just in time to see what might've been a smirk. A smirk! Lips that perfect probably *should* be smirking. Full and oh-so-soft-looking. But maybe he'd imagined it. He was working, talking to his colleague. Farzan shouldn't read into it. But at least he could look.

Surreptitiously.

Don't be suspicious, Farzan repeated in his head. *Don't be suspicious.* Except he started humming the song from *Parks and Rec*, remembering the funeral scene, which made him chuckle, which definitely was suspicious, and fuck, the guy for sure caught Farzan's eyes before disappearing back into the kitchen.

Farzan was saved by the arrival of his glass of rosé, its sides already turning dewy with condensation. It was a light coral color, and Farzan could smell apple and apricot and strawberry as she placed it in front of him.

"Try this," the bartender said. "Gramercy Cellars Olsen Vineyard."

Farzan swirled his glass and inhaled and—fuck, it smelled amazing. Slate and, weirdly, a hint of cheese? But when he tasted, the finish lasted forever.

"Good, right?"

Farzan nodded. It *was* good. Nearly good enough to forget about the beautiful man he'd just seen, but not quite—he risked another glance. Still gone.

"It's amazing. It's got a little something…" Farzan rubbed his fingers together.

"Parmesan rind?" the bartender asked.

"That's it!"

She grinned. "It's from the Cinsault. This blend has a lot of it."

"Oh wow."

"Mr. Allen?" Farzan swiveled on his stool; Kyra, the host, was standing next to him. It took him a moment to remind himself that *he* was Mr. Allen.

"Yeah?"

"We've got a table ready for you, if you'll follow me."

"Oh. That was fast." He turned back to the bartender. "Cheers, uh…"

"Tonya."

"Tonya. Thanks. This is perfect."

Tonya gave him a luminous smile. "Enjoy!"

Farzan planned to.

He was ready to savor the wine, and the fries, and—if he was lucky—the view. The guy worked here, so surely Farzan would see him again. He had no idea if the man was into other men, or if he was single, or what.

But it never hurt to look. Right?

four

David

David was heading to table 12 with a Chablis when Tonya stopped him to check if the Gramercy was okay to sell by the glass, since they were down to their last case. As he assured her it was, he skimmed the bar, glad to see Aspire had a full crowd even on a Tuesday night. But something stopped him.

Well, not something. Some*one*.

He wasn't a regular, that was for sure. David had never seen him before. He had brown, sunset skin, silky black hair with a gentle curl to it, a bit of dark scruff that gave his chin some character, and—fuck.

The most beautiful pair of brown eyes David had ever seen in his life. Heavy-lidded, beneath a strong brow, and so, so warm. David was ready to drown in them before he realized he was staring, and shit, the guy saw him.

David looked away quickly, because he was absolutely not in the habit of creeping on their customers. He'd learned that lesson several times over back in Chicago: Michelin-star restaurants attracted Michelin-star assholes. So there was no fucking way he'd be anything other than professional, assuming he even talked to the customer.

But damn, those eyes. Lively and a little bit sad and so, so beautiful.

David shook himself and got his ass in gear; table 12 had ordered a bottle. He uncorked it and checked the scent (clean and crisp) before handing it over and pouring a taste. When the couple at the table—an older pair of femmes—approved, David poured them both full glasses, set the bottle in a marble chilling bucket, and took the back way through the kitchen to avoid the bar.

No sense tempting fate. His stomach gave an awkward little wiggle at the thought of seeing Mr. Brown Eyes again. He closed his eyes, took a deep breath—

And ran right into Kyra.

"Shit! Sorry." He steadied her with a hand on her arm.

"This is why you call corner, David."

"There's not even a corner." The back hall leading off the kitchen was a straight shot.

"Details." Kyra waved him off. "You need something?"

David shook his head. "I'm good, you?"

"Bio break." Kyra narrowed her eyes. "Why are you back here then?"

"Avoiding the crowd." David gestured down the corridor. "May I?"

Kyra gave a long-suffering sigh. "I suppose."

David headed toward the host stand, in case anyone came in while Kyra was in the back. And if he happened to glance over the iPad and the list of names waiting for a table, well, it wasn't like this was a doctor's office. They didn't have to worry about HIPAA compliance or anything.

He scanned the list, spotted the names of a couple regulars, but not too many party-of-ones. But then, there it was, on the wait list for a table: Frank Allen.

Why did that sound so familiar?

David leaned forward and peered around the corner, trying to see the bar, but he couldn't. He wracked his brain. Frank Allen...oh fuck!

Frank Allen was a food critic—probably the most notorious one in the whole metro area. Jeri had been trying to get him to visit Aspire ever since they opened, and now he was here? On her day off?

Sitting at the bar?

This was a disaster in the making.

David dashed back through the kitchen, narrowly avoiding Dannon, who was plating a pastry-wrapped Brie. He was white, short and stocky, with rosy cheeks and bright blue eyes that widened in surprise as David shouted a belated "Behind!"

He found Kyra right as she emerged from the restroom, tossing the paper towel she'd opened the door with into the trash can behind her.

She blinked at him. "What?"

"Frank Allen. At the bar," David said. "You need to find him the best table you can, right now. He's a critic. Jeri's been expecting him."

"Shit," Kyra hissed as they plowed back through the kitchen once more. "Behind!" she called before David could.

Poor Dannon nearly dropped his bottle of chipotle honey.

"Get him settled as best you can," David said. "Let me know once he's seated, and I'll take care of him."

Brown eyes or not, David had to get this right. No way was he letting Jeri down.

"Got it." Despite her constant teasing, Kyra knew when to get serious. "You go straighten your tie."

She left him at the host stand. David looked in the glossy surface of the dark iPad. His tie was already perfect: peacock-blue and gold paisley patterns against midnight black, tied in an impeccable trinity knot he'd been practicing for months.

"You straighten your tie," he muttered, though Kyra was out of earshot.

He did tug down the cuffs of his shirt, ran a quick thumb across his right eyebrow. He'd added a slit at his last lineup, and it was still crisp. His stomach did another uncomfortable flip, and his heart gave a little squeeze, but he was a professional. He was David Fucking Curtis, advanced sommelier, soon-to-be master sommelier. He'd handled critics before.

And he'd handled plenty of bedroom-eyed men before, too.

He knew what he was doing.

Kyra found Frank a two-seater in the corner—one that had technically been reserved, but they'd figure that out later. The table butted up against the window, with a view of the patio outside, the fading downtown twilight, and cars—plus those annoying electric scooters—zipping up and down Walnut. The ginkgo trees were fluttering in the September breeze; David could almost feel it.

Fall in Kansas City wasn't New England levels of gorgeous, by any means, but it was full of good memories: warm apple cider, his mom's pumpkin bread, trick-or-treating, going back to school. David was never that sad when summer ended. He liked his friends at school. Not that he'd made it to any of his high school reunions. The twentieth would be coming up soon.

But he had no time for reminiscing about the seasons. He put on his best smile—his secret weapon when it came to critics—and stepped up to Frank's table.

"How're you enjoying the rosé?"

"It's so good." Frank's voice was mellow, a low tenor that David felt in his sternum. His smile was bright and open, far less guarded than David was expecting. Maybe this was all part of his game. "Tonya was right."

"It's one of my favorites," David said. "Got a dozen cases of it this spring, and we're nearly out. But I've got something special for you to try, if you'd like."

He held out another glass of rosé, this one served in a Pinot Noir glass: the broader bowl would let it breathe more. It was a deeper blush, almost salmon colored. "Viña Tondonia Gran Reserva Rosado. 2012."

Frank's eyebrows raised.

"Twelve years in bottle?" he asked, staring into the glass. "I've never had one that old. And you sell it by the glass?"

"No, but I thought you'd like it. Don't worry about it."

"You sure?"

"Positive. Besides, if you don't like it, you can always spit."

David couldn't believe he'd said that.

Thankfully, Frank just snort-laughed, and then blushed, as if he was embarrassed. He blinked up at David, showing off his long eyelashes, and shook his head.

David felt a pinch right behind his belly button.

Frank was *cute*.

David's *no fucking patrons* policy absolutely extended to critics—if anything, it was even more forceful—but a little flirting never hurt anyone. Hell, he'd put himself through college on the generous tips he used to get flirting with any customer that moved.

There was nothing wrong with using a little charm to smooth an evening along. And if that evening led to a glowing review for Aspire? Well, there were worse things in life than flirting with a cute guy.

A cute guy who definitely licked his lips as David rested the glass on the table in front of him.

Worked every time.

"Is there anything else I can get you?"

Frank looked up, pink tongue still barely peeking out of the corner of his lips. He seemed to realize it, too, because he swallowed and cleared his throat. "Uh, I'd love to get some fries if I could."

"I'll get those started right away," David said. "They're the best fries in town."

David gave a little wink. Frank Allen had surely tried *all* the fries in town. But Aspire's were David's favorite, and he wasn't just saying that out of loyalty.

"I'm David, by the way," he added. "The wine director here. Just flag me down if you need anything. Anything at all."

Was that a lip bite? David blinked and dragged his eyes upward. A little flirting was fine, but staring at Frank's lips—his very pink, very arched lips, the surrounding stubble making them stand out—was too far.

Shit, Frank was talking.

"Thanks, David," he said. "I will."

David gave another confident smile and retreated toward the kitchen.

When he glanced back, Frank's head immediately whipped back toward his glass.

Was Frank checking out his ass?

David smirked as Frank swirled his wine, sipped, sighed with contentment.

Then Frank grabbed his phone and started typing furiously.

Jeri didn't need to worry about a thing.

This review was in the bag.

five

Farzan

> **Farzan**
>
> I think the hot sommelier might be flirting with me???
> He made a joke about spitting??
> And he gave me really nice wine?
> HELP!!!!!

Farzan took another sip of the new rosé. Flirting or not, David was right: It was special. A rich salmon color, sunset encased in crystal. Farzan swished the wine on his tongue. It was balanced, sharp, bright: sour cherry and blood orange and rosewater and this cedar backbone that brought it all home.

Farzan held back a moan, but only just. He swallowed, let the coolness soothe his suddenly dry throat. No way was he spitting.

"Holy fuck," he muttered to himself. What a wine.

"I see a smiling face."

Farzan nearly dropped his phone. He locked it and looked back up.

David was back, and Farzan could only pray he hadn't seen the group chat.

He cleared his throat. "This wine...what did you say it was?"

David smiled, a wide one that lit his whole face. His teeth were bright and even, a striking contrast against his midnight skin.

"Viña Tondonia Gran Reserva Rosado, 2012. My favorite vintage so far."

"It's amazing," Farzan said. "It's so complex, if I didn't know better I'd think it was a red."

David nodded. "Right? With those cedar-plank notes, and that finish..." His lips pursed tantalizingly. He closed his eyes for a minute, as if in prayer, as if he'd been transported to the slopes of Spain. "I love it."

Farzan was spellbound.

No wonder David was the wine director.

Farzan loved wine, and thought of himself as pretty knowledgeable, but David had to be on a whole other level. Especially to be wine director at a wine bar.

"Oh!" David snapped out of it. "Your fries are coming up, but I just wanted to check if you wanted anything else."

"Oh, ah. I haven't looked over the rest of the menu yet."

David smiled again and leaned in closer, giving Farzan a whiff of his cologne. Something woodsy that made Farzan's core tighten.

"Hmm. Do you trust me?"

"What?" Farzan fought the urge to swallow.

David's smile cocked a little higher; he leaned in even closer, resting a palm on the table, fingers splayed. David's hands looked strong but soft, nicely proportioned, fingernails trimmed and smoothed. Farzan wondered what they felt like.

"Do. You. Trust me?"

Farzan tried not to stare, but it was difficult. Arya frequently waxed horny about how hard it was to resist a man in a suit, and Farzan had to admit he had a point.

He had to be careful: if he stared too hard, he'd tip over into creeping territory, and flirting or not, Farzan wasn't a creeper. He'd spent enough time waiting tables himself—at places all over town, when he was still in university, or at his parents' restaurant when they needed help—to ever creep on a server. He always hated when old Iranian divorcées hit on him.

But it wasn't like David was an Iranian woman his mom's age. He had to be close to Farzan's age, with a perfect smile and a deep, honeyed voice and thick thighs.

And lovely brown eyes that winked at him. Winked!

David was still waiting for an answer.

Fuck it. There was only one thing to do.

"Yeah." Farzan was relieved his voice didn't come out squeaky—or worse, husky. "I trust you."

Trusting David was the best choice he could've made.

In addition to the basket of fries—crisp and golden and salty—David had also returned with a small wedge of baked Brie, wrapped in puff pastry and crusted with crushed pistachios. It was decadent, layered with honey and fig preserves, sweet and savory, and it went perfectly with the glass of Torrontés David dropped off.

"Whew, you've got to slow down," Farzan said. He was only halfway through the Spanish rosé. "I've still got to walk out of here, you know."

"You didn't drive, did you?" David asked.

"Streetcar."

"Perfect." David chuckled. "But I'll take care of you."

Another one of those winks. Farzan's heart hitched a bit.

"How about tasting pours instead? They're two ounces each."

"Deal," Farzan said. He could handle tasting pours. The Torrontés *was* a perfect pairing with the Brie, and he didn't want to miss out on what other wonders awaited.

While David disappeared again, Farzan checked on the group chat once more. Still no response from his friends; Arya was probably swamped, if he even had signal—if he was at the Kauffman Center, probably not—and Ramin always put his phone on do not disturb when he and Todd went out.

Still, he sent a photo of his spread so they'd know what they were missing.

After the Brie came a fennel and orange salad (David let him keep the Torrontés for that), sharp and fresh and tart, and then an individual chicken pot pie, the crust crisp and flaky, the chicken mouthwatering, the wine pairing—a French Chardonnay that tasted of brown butter and peaches and chalk—utter perfection.

Farzan took his time savoring every bite as night fell. Outside, the patio was lit with fairy lights; inside, wall sconces and hanging lamps gave everything a cheery, intimate vibe. If anything, David looked more beautiful in the warm glow, his smile a beacon, his cheeks gilded, the blue of his suit a balm.

"So?" David returned, resting his palm on the table once more, dangerously close to Farzan's own hand. He got another shock of David's cologne: vetiver, that's what it was, and Farzan was suddenly self-conscious. Did he smell like onions and salmon? Had he used enough deodorant? He blinked the worry away. Nothing he could do about it now.

"Amazing," Farzan said. "The crust, the chicken, the wine, everything was just..."

Farzan's voice failed him as he met David's eyes. They were sparkling, somewhere between amused and intrigued. He felt his cheeks burning as he realized he'd been leaning in toward David. He straightened in his seat.

"It was perfection."

"I'll tell Chef Brayan. He's awfully proud of those little pies."

"Brayan?" Farzan repeated, trying to match David's pronunciation.

"B-r-a-y-a-n. His family's from Mexico," David said. "Best chef I've ever worked with."

"Oh yeah? You've been at a lot of places?"

David leaned even more, putting his weight on his right leg, crossing his left to rest the toe on the ground. The move made the fabric of his slacks shift rather enticingly. Farzan tore his eyes away.

"At least a dozen, but this one's my favorite. By far."

"I don't blame you. Everything's awesome."

"Good. I've got my personal favorite, if you're ready."

Farzan's stomach was saying no, but his mouth wanted more. He didn't even realize he was licking his lips until he caught David watching him, that eyebrow with the slit quirked up. Farzan wondered what it would feel like to run his finger across it.

David smirked, like he could sense what Farzan was thinking.

Farzan swallowed and nodded. From behind his back, David produced a wide white plate with a hollow in the center, filled with a rich meat.

"Beef short ribs, braised in Amarone della Valpolicella."

Farzan's mouth watered.

"And I've got some more Amarone to go with it. Be right back."

As David retreated, Farzan couldn't help staring: Farzan had seen plenty of suits before, but never one that did as much for a guy's ass as David's seemed to. Or maybe he was just built differently.

Farzan shook his head and turned back to the short ribs. The meat fell apart as soon as his fork grazed it. The beef was savory and deep, but the wine had imparted a bit of fruit to it, too. Farzan closed his eyes as he tasted. It was so good. Everything was so good, he did what he'd been trying to refrain from all night:

He moaned aloud.

"Now that's what I like to hear," David's voice came from above, darker and closer somehow, and Farzan's eyes snapped open.

David was at his side, holding a glass of inky purple wine. He slid it onto the table, grazing Farzan's hand; Farzan gripped his fork tighter.

"I couldn't help myself," Farzan admitted.

"No shame in enjoying a good meal. How's the wine?"

Farzan took a taste: silky mouthfeel, concentrated raisin, leather, and vanilla.

"Wow."

"Good." David glanced at the plate, then back at Farzan. "I'll leave you two alone."

And then he withdrew, treating Farzan to another view of his backside, and fuck. Fuck!

Farzan's heart gave an annoying hammer against his rib cage. David was cute, and funny, and that wink had definitely been flirty, right? Farzan checked his phone again. Still nothing. He could imagine his friends' response though: Ramin suggesting restraint, Arya telling him to see if he could blow David in the back of the restaurant.

Neither felt right. He didn't want to hook up, and he didn't want to make David uncomfortable, but he *was* handsome, and if he *was* flirting then Farzan just needed to know how to respond. Should he leave his number on the check? Go the direct route?

What if he was just imagining it all in a haze of wine and food?

He ran a hand through his hair. What the fuck should he do?

As the night waned, the crowd thinned a bit. Aspire wasn't emptying, but it seemed the worst of the dinner rush was over. And still, David kept swinging by to check on him, always with a smile, or a quirked eyebrow, or a little wink. Always leaving behind a whiff of vetiver.

One time, Farzan glanced over at the bar, where David stood in profile, talking to one of the bartenders. With one hand, he poured a glass of white wine; with the other, he reached down and adjusted himself where the front of his suit pants seemed fuller than usual.

Fuck. *Was that because of me?*

Nerves rippled through Farzan's stomach, settling between his legs. Farzan was feeling warm all over, and not just from the wine.

David glanced his way, caught him looking, licked his lips. Was it unconscious or on purpose?

Farzan felt a twinge in his pants. He wished he could be sure.

Finally, dessert came: a tiny Bundt cake, with some sort of white glaze over top that set Farzan's mind racing. *Everything reminds me of him*, he joked to himself, then snorted.

"Problem?" David asked.

Shit shit shit. Flirting or not, jokes about cream pies were definitely off the table. Farzan could feel his cheeks getting redder as David looked down at him. That damned eyebrow cocked again.

Farzan blurted, "There's a hole in this cake."

The moment stretched so taut, Farzan feared it would snap. Sweet mother of crap.

Joking about holes was hardly any better, flirting or not.

Farzan became intensely aware of his sweaty armpits. Oh god, was it a flop sweat from bombing his joke, or meat sweats from the short ribs?

And David was still looking at him, eyes twinkling. Wait. How long had they been staring at each other?

"Uh." Farzan swallowed, noticed David's eyes track the movement. He was making it even worse. "*My Big Fat Greek Wedding*?"

David shook his head. "Never seen it."

"What?!" Farzan asked, way too loud. A couple people glanced his way. "Sorry. My family watches it like...every holiday." There weren't exactly a lot of movies about Iranians, at least not comedies. There were plenty of tragedies and action movies where the Iranians were all terrorists. But *My Big Fat Greek Wedding* was the next best thing. Every Iranian he knew had seen it, many on a yearly basis like the Alavis.

So Farzan got to explaining the whole Bundt cake scene, and how Toula's mom "fixed" it with a flower arrangement, and he was gratified to see David's eyes crinkle up in a genuine smile.

"I'll have to watch that sometime," David said, smoothing his goatee with his fingers. Farzan traced the movement and fought against the urge to invite him over to watch it that very night. *My Big Fat Greek Wedding* and chill.

Farzan restrained himself—barely—as David set down a flute of sparkling wine.

"Anyway. This is one of my favorite Champagnes. Le Mesnil Blanc des Blancs."

Farzan took a small sip, and holy shit. Crisp and bright, but it had these vegetal notes that reminded him of the stewed eggplant in his mom's khoresh bademjan.

"Wow." Farzan sipped again. It was the best Champagne he'd ever tasted. "This better not be off the bottle list."

David grinned. "What if it was?"

"You can't keep doing that. Won't you get in trouble?"

"Let me worry about that."

"But..."

"I just like seeing you enjoy it."

Well.

That was definitely flirting. Wasn't it?

Farzan bit his lip and rolled the stem of his glass between thumb and forefinger. He shuddered to think what this meal was going to cost, but it had been exquisite. Just what he needed.

He'd figure his finances out later.

"Everything tonight has been amazing. I don't know what I did to deserve all this, but thank you."

David cocked his head to the side for a second, like Farzan had just bombed another joke. "Are you kidding? It's been my pleasure."

"Really?"

"Of course."

David's smile was so warm. So was his body, hovering next to Farzan's table. His head was swimming with Champagne and vetiver.

"You want some?" Farzan blurted.

Shit.

David's eyebrow quirked.

"I mean. Not from this glass, obviously, but you could grab another..."

"Not in the mood to share, are you?" David's tone was light, teasing, but Farzan's heart hammered.

"Oh. I can share. I mean, my mouth has been all over it..."

David's grin turned wickedly triumphant. Farzan blushed.

"You're the devil," he muttered.

David laughed, and it was like a pressure valve burst. Somehow Farzan could breathe again.

More vetiver.

"You're sweet, but I don't drink on the job."

Farzan bit his lip. Of course. He was being a total creeper, anyway. All this weird tension was just in his imagination. There was nothing special going on here. No spark.

But then David grinned again.

"Lucky I'm in charge tonight. I can get off whenever I like."

Farzan blinked. David's eyebrows raised.

"Off of work!" he specified. Even with his dark complexion, Farzan spotted the flush in David's cheeks.

"I'd love to share some Champagne with you," David finally finished. "Lemme let the staff know I'm finishing up early."

"Great. Yeah. Cool." Farzan twisted the flute between his fingers and swallowed. "And then I thought, if you wanted, afterward you could...ah...come to my place?"

It was out of his mouth before he knew where the bravery had come from. He wasn't drunk—he hadn't actually had that much, and he'd balanced the alcohol with tons of food—but deep inside, he knew he'd regret it if he didn't at least ask.

Or maybe all that vetiver had gone to his head.

David was still looking at him. Farzan wanted to crawl beneath the table and hide.

Until David's eyes sharpened, and his nostrils flared.

"Love to."

six

David

The door to Frank's apartment swung open. David had a few moments to register exposed brick, and large windows looking out over the dark city, a comfy-looking couch and large television, before he closed the door behind him.

David had managed to keep his hands (and mouth) to himself the entire streetcar ride, from Aspire all the way north to River Market, where Frank's apartment stood, but his restraint was at its limit. Despite the dark, he quickly found Frank's belt loops, hooked his fingers through them, and smashed their lips together.

Frank tasted of limoncello cake and Champagne, salt and Amarone, heat and desire. David had finished his own glass of Champagne before convincing Kyra to cover for him as he ducked out early—he'd certainly covered for enough people over the last several months, and he never left a service early, but fuck if he was going to miss out on this.

David captured Frank's lower lip with his teeth, pulled gently, testing what Frank liked, and got a rumble from Frank's chest in response. He did it again, harder, pushing Frank farther inside, but Frank tripped over something, breaking the kiss with a "shit!"

"You okay?" David breathed against Frank's skin.

"Fine. Here." Frank reached behind David to turn on the lights and flip the deadbolt. David leaned in for another kiss, but Frank ducked away to untie his shoes.

Fuck, he'd been so distracted he forgot. If his mom knew…

"Oh my god," Frank gasped.

"What?"

"Your shoes!" Frank looked up from where he was kneeling, and David's dick twinged in his pants, because what a view. He'd been imagining Frank on his knees all night. Or on his back. Or any which way he liked it. David was vers. "These are amazing."

Shoes. Right. David gave a little grin. They were good shoes: high-top sneakers with crisp white soles and uppers of black jacquard with gold floral patterns.

"Instagram ad." David knelt, getting a heady whiff of Frank's citrusy cologne, and began unlacing them. "After years of showing me white twinks in underwear, their algorithm finally got my number."

Frank laughed, the sound so pure David wanted to lean in and kiss him again, but it would be way more fun if they could actually make it to the couch.

Frank stood, offered David a hand up—David hoped Frank didn't hear the pop in his knee—and then Frank's hands were around David's face, cupping the line of his jaw, and David put his hands at the top of Frank's waist.

Then they were kissing again, and it was Frank who took the lead this time, opening his mouth and letting his warm breath flow into David as he panted between kisses. Frank walked them steadily backward toward the couch, his lips never leaving David's, until he stopped and ground their groins together.

David wanted to make an "are you happy to see me" joke as he felt Frank's hardness against his own, but he couldn't think of an object that wouldn't be ridiculous. Wine bottles were way too large. It would be clownish.

Instead, David whispered, "All that wine and you're still thirsty?"

And felt Frank shiver against him.

He couldn't wait to make Frank shiver again.

"You have no idea," Frank said. He trailed kisses up David's jawline to his ear, licked and then nibbled on his earlobe. Now it was David's turn to shiver. "You're the most beautiful man I've ever seen."

David smiled and closed his eyes as Frank kept kissing his throat.

It had been way too long since he'd hooked up with someone, and despite what he told himself about his toys and hands, there was nothing like another man's mouth on him. And Frank sure knew how to use his: David's toes curled against the living room rug as Frank hit that soft spot in his clavicle.

When he went to work this afternoon, this is not how he'd expected his night to go, but he wasn't going to complain.

He needed this. And more than that: he *wanted* this. Wanted Frank. Fuck professionalism. He'd wanted Frank from the moment he saw those beautiful eyes and felt the hook behind his navel.

He moved his hands down to Frank's ass—that ass had driven him crazy, walking up the stairs to the third-floor apartment—and squeezed.

He was hoping for a moan, or more intense kissing. Even a little grinding.

What he hadn't expected was the sudden, loud fart.

Frank's lips paused from where they'd been caressing his pulse point. No one moved.

Awkward. But inevitable sometimes.

David tried not to laugh. He didn't want to embarrass Frank. David had certainly had his own misadventures with flatulence.

But he couldn't hold it.

He snorted, keeping his hands on Frank's ass.

Frank snorted too, and that got David going, and soon they were both laughing so hard they had to break apart so they didn't bump foreheads.

David didn't let go of Frank's ass, though.

When they could both breathe again, Frank sighed and muttered, "Sorry."

"Don't be. It's fine."

"This is what you get for feeding me all that food!"

"It's all good," David assured him, straightening up and smiling. He kissed Frank on the nose. His cheeks were getting red. "I guess no anal tonight, huh?"

"Not unless you want to bottom?" Frank asked lightly.

David enjoyed bottoming, but he was feeling self-conscious himself now. Normally he liked to take his time getting clean and ready, and he couldn't wait that long. "I'm vers, but I'm not really feeling anal tonight either. We can do other things, though."

"Works for me."

Frank leaned in for another kiss. David sucked on his top lip; it was soft and full and perfect, with a nice little bow. He traced kisses down Frank's stubbled jaw, relishing the texture. "Just so you know, though," David murmured against the warm brown skin. "I'm on PrEP. And negative across the board. And I haven't been with anyone since my last checkup."

An embarrassingly long time ago. Yeah, he'd had to study, but now that he could feel the heat of Frank's erection pressed up against his own through their pants, he wondered why he'd waited so long.

Well. It had been a long time since someone like Frank came along.

"Me too. All of the above." Frank was back at that spot behind David's ear, his breath sending tingles along David's spine. "Fuck, I want to blow you."

"Yeah?"

"Uh-huh." Frank sank to the couch, grabbed David's waist, and pressed his face into David's inseam. Even through his pants and underwear, the warmth of Frank's skin was heaven.

"I'm game if you are."

Frank grinned up at him and then went for David's belt. David started unbuttoning his shirt, but Frank stopped him. "Keep it on. I love a man in a suit."

"Yeah you do." David stuck his thumb in Frank's mouth for him to suck on while he dealt with David's zipper. He held his breath as Frank fought with the waistband of his boxer-briefs—his favorite pair, purple Savage X Fenty ones—and pulled his dick out.

David had been with enough guys to see the whole gamut of reactions to his dick. It was hard to be a gay Black man and not be aware of certain *stereotypes*, which led to certain *expectations*—expectations he didn't exactly meet.

His dick was beautiful, if he did say so himself, but it was average sized, not some Weapon of Ass Destruction. He waited to see Frank's reaction, fighting his nerves.

But Frank just made the same *mmm* sound he made when he tasted wine. He looked up at David with hunger, like he hadn't just eaten a full meal.

Frank wrapped his hand around David's dick and watched it intently as he pulled back the foreskin. But then he paused and looked back up, biting his lip. "Uh...should we do condoms for oral? I have banana and strawberry."

"I mean..." David shrugged. "It's up to you. I'm okay without, you know, since we're both negative and all, but I don't want you to feel pressured or anything."

"It feels better, though, right?" Frank asked. The question sent Frank's breath ghosting along his dick. David shivered. "With your foreskin and all."

It did. It fucking did. David nodded.

"Okay then?" Frank stroked him again, slowly, licking his lips. Fuck, that tongue. Stained purple and oh so pretty. David wanted to feel it. He ran a hand through Frank's sleek hair. He was sweating in his suit, even though the apartment was cool.

"Okay." David had been watching Frank's mouth all night—studying him as he sampled every meal, wrapped his lips around a french fry, or cradled a wineglass—but never in a million years had he imagined they'd wind up here, with those same lips just inches away from his dick. "Show me what that hot mouth can do."

So Frank did, leaning in to lick all over David's shaft, kiss the spot where his balls met his base, then finally, finally, taking David in his mouth.

David gripped Frank's hair tighter, not tight enough to hurt (he hoped), but tight enough to stay upright, because fuck. Fuck!

He'd missed this. The sex, yeah, but connecting too. That feeling when the guy you were with knew exactly what to do to make you feel good. That flame in your stomach, impatient to return the favor.

"That's right," David muttered. "Dig in there."

Frank's tongue was teasing the space between his foreskin and his dickhead, and David trembled.

"Fucking hot mouth."

He felt Frank give a little shiver and smiled to himself.

"Yeah, you like that," David said, thrusting a bit, trying to get a rhythm going, but then he lost it as soon as Frank's tongue found his frenulum, and his knees went weak. "Oh, fuck, Frank. Keep doing that."

Frank blinked up at him for a moment, a confused look in his eyes. Those beautiful eyes. David nearly forgot what he was going to say, he was so lost in them. But Frank's eyebrows shot up in a silent question.

"That thing with your tongue."

Frank did, over and over, sending tingles that radiated from David's dick straight to his core, lighting up his spine.

"Now suck it. Suck it hard."

And Frank did, without missing a beat, adding one hand to the action with a little twist-stroke, the other hand going for David's balls, cradling them gently while a finger stretched back to massage his taint.

How was Frank so good at this? He was reading David like a book: he knew every nerve, every bit of skin, every subtle move that could make David come undone.

David hadn't come undone in a long, long time.

"I'm close," he gasped. "Fuck, you've got a talented mouth."

Frank hummed, pushing David over the edge. His knees shook again, and he nearly lost his balance, burying himself in Frank's mouth, but

Frank held him up as the delicious, pinching pleasure took over and he came, his limbs quivering.

When he could think again, he straightened up, gave a little shiver, brushed Frank's hair off his forehead as he pulled his dick out.

"Oh my god," David breathed. "That was...fuck. Sorry. Was that okay?"

Frank ran the back of his hand over his smiling mouth and looked up at David. His pupils were dilated, his gaze heavy-lidded and liquid. "Yeah. For you?"

"Better than," David said with a smile. He looked down and saw Frank's own length, trapped against his left leg by his jeans. "May I have the honor of returning the favor?"

Frank blushed. "You don't have to."

Oh hell no. The fire in David's belly was nearly an inferno.

He wanted to unmake Frank the way Frank had unmade him.

"But I want to."

seven

Farzan

"Toss me that pillow," David growled.

Farzan grabbed the pillow to his left and handed it to David. He dropped it onto the ground, nudged Farzan's legs apart with his knees, and sank down.

Farzan's breath hitched as David's hands massaged his thighs. David looked up at him with a heated smirk. Farzan wanted to drown in those dark eyes. He'd wanted to from the moment he met them across the bar at Aspire.

This was absolutely not how he'd seen his night going.

His lips were still buzzing, remembering the way David's dick had felt in his mouth, warm and hard and slick. The way David's fingers had played through his hair. The way David had shivered when Farzan found a particularly good spot.

He couldn't remember the last time being with someone was so...effortless. Most times, he was at least a little worried: Was he making the other guy feel good? Did he look weird? Did he have to fart?

(Well, he'd already done that.)

But being with David was so easy. They were perfectly matched, like the short ribs and Amarone. Like everything tonight, really.

David's hands moved from Farzan's thighs up to his torso, slipping under his shirt to trace the sides of his rib cage—Farzan's skin tingled at the touch—before going back down to his belt. David pulled it loose, unbuttoned Farzan's jeans, and pulled down the zipper. Farzan sighed in relief—his dick had been trapped against his left thigh, throbbing and leaking as he'd gone down on David. He'd nearly come just from the pressure of the fabric.

"Cute," David said. Farzan looked down. He was wearing soft pink trunks with light gray leopards and deep pink cherry blossoms printed on them.

"Thanks," he whispered. They were his favorite pair, and he was glad David approved.

Farzan's breath caught again as David reached inside and finally freed his dick.

"Nice," David said, and Farzan blushed. His dick was pretty average, though it had a bit of a banana curve that gave it some character. David's thumbs stroked his balls. Farzan had shaved them this morning. Unlike David's, which were soft and silky, Farzan's had been covered in coarse and kinky hair.

"Thought you were getting lucky tonight, huh?" David asked, dragging his fingernails lightly along Farzan's scrotum. Farzan's back arched as chills swept up and down him.

"Not this lucky."

He figured he and Cliff would probably do something. But honestly? Fuck Cliff. Every moment had felt like a chess game, trying to figure out what they had in common, trying to act cool and fascinating and aloof enough to not seem desperate, but also interested enough to earn another date.

There'd been none of that with David. Instead, it had felt like a dance, easy banter and irresistible chemistry that meant they were always, inevitably, leading to this moment.

Farzan wasn't a hookup guy. He couldn't remember the last time he took a guy he'd just met home. Maybe in his twenties, if that. But how could he look at David's beautiful lips and soulful eyes and not want him?

And he did want David. Wanted him with a fierceness that scared him. He knew this was just a hookup; he knew the rules. He'd heard them from Arya often enough. Get in, get off, get out. But what if that wasn't enough?

He didn't have the brainpower to think about it, though, once David's tongue found his balls, rasped against the goose bumps that had risen. David's hands moved to Farzan's torso, pushing up his shirt to comb through his chest hair and reach for his nipples.

Farzan moaned, hands digging into the couch cushions as David kissed his way up his dick.

"Good?"

"Uh-huh," Farzan panted, before David took him in. *Good* didn't even begin to cover it.

David's mouth was so warm, so welcoming, so wet. His lips were soft but firm, his stubble tickling Farzan's skin every time he brushed against it. David was skilled, but that wasn't what set Farzan's mind whirring, his pulse racing.

David wanted him. He'd made that clear with every touch, every look, every sound.

It had been a long time since Farzan felt wanted like this.

The electricity between them was building, and Farzan was having trouble holding off. Pleasure mounted deep inside him, so sharp it made him clench for a moment. He tried to relax and breathe and surf the waves David kept unleashing on him, but he couldn't.

He couldn't.

He reached for David's hair, felt the soft twists, but then stopped himself. With a white guy, he wouldn't think twice about touching his hair, but with David he had to make sure. "Sorry."

David popped off his dick with a suck so hard, Farzan arched off the couch for a second. "What? You're fine."

Farzan swallowed, breathing hard. "I didn't mean to touch your hair without asking."

David's eyes crinkled up. "You're sweet. But I just had your dick in my mouth. It's all good."

"You sure?"

David smiled, grabbed Farzan's hands and placed them in his twists, showing Farzan how much pressure he liked. Farzan massaged David's scalp as David went down on him again, then started humming. The sensation nearly turned Farzan inside out.

"Oh, David," Farzan murmured, grasping at David as the soft twists caressed his palms. "David."

David's mouth was magic, his tongue and lips and hands playing a symphony across Farzan's skin. Farzan never wanted it to end.

But David's humming intensified, and his fingers went for Farzan's nipples again, gently but insistently pinching, pressing, kneading, and the electric circuit behind Farzan's balls completed itself, and then—

"Oh, fuck," Farzan moaned as he came, bucking his hips up off the couch in time with the contractions deep inside, until his core finally gave out.

Farzan breathed hard, like he'd just finished a workout at the gym. Like he'd just scored a home run at kickball, rounding the bases and sliding home.

"Fuck," he muttered again, caressing David's hair, tracing the soft, warm spot behind David's ears before his arms gave out, too, and he collapsed onto the couch.

David might've just ruined him.

"That good, huh?"

"Better."

"Good." David braced himself on Farzan's legs and pulled himself onto the couch.

Farzan tucked his dick away but didn't bother zipping his jeans back up. He was too content. Instead, he scooted until he could rest his head on David's shoulder, nuzzle his nose against David's neck to breathe in sweat and vetiver. Everything in him went quiet.

This felt right.

They breathed together for a moment, until David's voice rumbled.

"Guess you can't write about this in your review."

"Huh?" What David had said didn't make any sense. So much for post-nut clarity.

He must've heard wrong.

"For the record, I don't expect it to influence anything."

Okay, maybe not, but Farzan had no idea what David meant. He sat up straighter, furrowed his brows. David was looking back at him, head cocked to the side. Farzan stared at David's lips, still a bit puffy, and nearly lost himself before he remembered. "What are you talking about?"

"Your review of Aspire. Jeri's going to be pissed she missed you." David bit his lip. "By the way, not that she would mind, but you don't have to tell her about, ah, this part of the evening."

Farzan's head spun. "Wait. Who's Jeri?"

David blinked at him. "Jeri Talbott? Aspire's owner? She was the one who wanted you to review it for Frank's Finds?"

"Frank's . . ." Farzan bit his lip. David thought his name was Frank.

Oh shit. He had put that down as his name. Had he really never told David?

"Uh," he said. "My name's actually Farzan."

eight

David

My name's actually Farzan.

What the fuck?

"But—" David shook his head, as if that would help make sense of things. "Your table. It was for Frank Allen."

Farzan shrugged. "I give that name when it's noisy. Most people can't spell Farzan Alavi."

Farzan Alavi. David liked the sound of it, liked the way Farzan's lips shaped his name, but still.

"But Frank Allen's a restaurant critic."

"Oh shit." Farzan's cheeks reddened. "I forgot about him."

"You . . . forgot?" Was he getting catfished right now?

"Yeah. I've been using that name at Starbucks since I was in college." Farzan cocked his head to the side. "You know, that guy reviewed my parents' restaurant. They still have it on the wall. I don't know why. I mean, it was a good review, but it was also a masterclass in microaggressions if you know what I mean."

David snorted. From what Jeri had said, that sounded pretty typical. But that was beside the point. "Lemme get this clear," he said, eyebrows drawn. "You just call up restaurants in town and tell them you're Frank Allen?"

"No, most of the time I book online and it doesn't matter. I tried telling the host my name was Farzan, but she couldn't hear me and it was just easier to go with Frank." Farzan shrugged nervously. "I wasn't thinking."

David clapped a hand to his forehead. All that wine, all that money—he'd opened five different bottles, comped them all, only actually charged Farzan for his first rosé and the food.

But shit. All night long, he hadn't been the restaurant critic Jeri had been anticipating. He'd just been some guy.

No, that wasn't fair. Farzan wasn't a restaurant critic, but he was charming, and handsome, and gave great head. And to be fair, David had never actually asked, had he? Just assumed. Just went along with it, because Farzan was flirting with him.

David shook his head, but Farzan's nose crinkled up. It was so cute, David almost leaned in for another kiss.

"Wait," Farzan said, voice brittle. "All that time, were you only flirting with me because you thought I was a critic?"

David held up his hands. "I thought you were flirting with me! I was just flirting back!"

Farzan ran a hand through his hair, those soft, silky waves. David could still feel the ghost of them in the space between his own fingers.

This was all a big misunderstanding. Yeah, they'd both made assumptions, both read the situation wrong, but David was far from mad at the turn the night had taken. It had been damned good sex, and he wasn't just saying that because he'd been in a dry spell. It had honestly been the best head of his life, tender and enthusiastic in equal measures.

And more than that: being with Farzan had been…nice. David felt warm, content. Alive.

He reached for Farzan's hand, relieved when Farzan relaxed and let him twine their fingers together. He had to make him understand.

"Listen. Yeah, clearly I misread things, but I don't regret coming here tonight. Do you regret inviting me?"

Farzan's shoulders finally unclenched. "No."

David waited for Farzan to say more. He wasn't sure what: that he'd enjoyed the sex too? That he wouldn't mind a repeat some time?

Or that it had been fun, and a hilarious mix-up, but it was getting late and David should go?

Finally Farzan said, "I know I just had all that wine, but I think I need another glass."

That . . . was a good idea.

"You mind pouring me one?"

Farzan lowered his eyes. "It's cheap."

"Doesn't matter to me. Just don't tell me what it is."

Farzan went to the kitchen—pausing to button and zip his jeans—and David turned away to avoid seeing the wine's label.

(It was tempting to look, though. Farzan had a cute butt.)

When Farzan returned, he handed David a glass and sat farther away than before. David fought off a twinge of disappointment.

"So you're not mad?"

"After a blowjob like that? Fuck no."

Farzan laughed.

No, David wasn't mad. He could've done even the barest modicum of due diligence, but Farzan had been so handsome, he just dove right in.

David smelled the wine. Garnet red, medium bodied, jammy. "Malbec?"

Farzan's eyebrows shot up. "Yeah. It's—"

David shook his head, sipped, mentally went down his tasting grid. "Mendoza?"

Farzan nodded. But where else, really, would you get cheap Malbec? Cheap but good. It was lovely. Familiar, though young, probably the latest vintage.

"El Libre?" David guessed.

"Um. Yeah. Holy shit."

"I'm studying for my master somm. Need all the practice I can get." David shrugged and sipped again, but he appreciated the impressed look Farzan gave him.

"Anyway. No. I'm not mad. I could've asked, like, a thousand times tonight. Fuck, I could've even bothered to look at your credit card. And this was honestly really fun."

"Oh. Good." Farzan blushed, twirled his glass back and forth. "I really liked it too. I don't normally do things like this."

"Hit on waiters?"

Farzan choked on his wine; when he finished coughing, he looked back at David with rosy cheeks. "That makes it sound like I harassed you."

"All right, sorry. Here." David raised his glass, and after only a moment, Farzan clinked. David took a long sip.

"So. Farzan Alavi. Greek?"

"Iranian."

"But you said your family—"

"There aren't a lot of movies about Iranian families, and I swear, the aunts and uncles in *My Big Fat Greek Wedding* have literally said some of the same things mine do."

"Huh." David's own aunties had said some truly wild things to him over the years. Always well-meaning, and always cringeworthy.

"You've really never seen it?"

David shook his head.

"Here." Farzan leaned forward and grabbed the remote off the coffee table. In seconds he had the movie queued up, but then he looked back at David, a tentative smile gracing his lips. "You want to?"

David looked around the apartment, but there was no clock on the walls (not that he had any either). Still, it had to be getting late. Past midnight. And though this hookup had been fun, he didn't want to give Farzan the wrong idea. They'd already chilled, so what was the point of the Netflix?

Then again, the Malbec was good, and the streetcar had already stopped running, and also, David wouldn't exactly say no to another orgasm before going home. So he loosened his tie, stretched out, and slung his arm over the back of the couch.

"Sure."

nine

Farzan

Farzan was grateful for the distraction of the movie. With the TV as their only light source, David couldn't see the red flare of embarrassment that kept creeping up and down Farzan's neck and face.

Frank Allen. He should've remembered. But it was such a basic name, and it had the same initials, and he'd been using Frank as his White Person Name for as long as he could remember. At least since third grade, when one of their substitute teachers had bungled Farzan so badly, so repeatedly, that Farzan had given up and lied: "Frank is fine."

It wasn't fine, but it was better than giving his classmates more fodder for laughter. Ramin hadn't come out unscathed, either, though at least his was closer: the sub just read his name as "Ramón" and called it good.

Farzan sipped his wine and suppressed a sigh. What a fucking disaster.

The thing was, he really liked David. He liked their flirting at the restaurant, he liked David's sexy voice and beautiful smile, and he definitely liked the sex. But David had thought he was someone else, someone impressive. A food critic.

Not a substitute teacher who needed to pick up shifts at his parents' restaurant to make ends meet. Not the family fuckup.

Except, once David had gotten over his initial confusion, he hadn't seemed to mind that Farzan wasn't Frank Allen. He'd stayed.

And when Farzan kept a handspan between them, David scooted closer so their shoulders touched. His free arm, resting on the back of the couch, reached down to gently knead at Farzan's shoulders, before sliding up to glide through his hair. Farzan melted a little. David really seemed to like his hair, and Farzan loved the tender touch.

He sighed and settled in, half watching the movie, half watching David's reactions: the way he'd bite his lip to hold in a laugh, the way his whole chest moved when he couldn't anymore, the way his eyes shone as Toula fell in love with Ian.

Farzan had never told anyone, but John Corbett was one of his first crushes. He'd been a freshman in high school when the movie came out, and his parents took the whole family to see it three times in the theater. Not that Farzan was out then, even to himself, but looking back? Yeah. Total crush.

That was probably the start of his desire to be a teacher, for all the good that had done. He only lasted two years at the job before he burned out, hard. It had been a miserable couple years after that, too, going from job to job, doing his damnedest to avoid working for his parents. He'd spent enough of his childhood in that restaurant. And though he loved Shiraz Bistro, and he loved his parents, he didn't love *working* for his parents, much less needing their indirect help to pay his bills.

Fuck. He'd grown up wanting to be Ian, and now he was a Toula, wasn't he? No prospects, curly hair, and all.

Well. At least David liked his curly hair. But his wineglass was empty, and so was Farzan's.

"Want a refill?"

David pursed his lips. Was he worried about making it home? Farzan wouldn't mind if David stayed over. Or maybe he didn't actually like Farzan's cheap Malbec, maybe—

"Sure. This is nice."

"The movie or the wine?"

"Both." David grinned as Farzan reached for the bottle and refilled their glasses. "The company's not that bad either."

"Even if I'm not a critic?"

"Nah, that makes it better. Way less pressure to perform." David winked at him.

"You didn't have any problems in that area."

David chuckled, and Farzan rested his head against David's shoulder. They fit nicely, and Farzan could bathe in David's vetiver scent. Was it cologne? Moisturizer? Both? Farzan couldn't tell, but damn, David smelled good.

Farzan rested his free hand on David's thigh, kneading it, while David kept playing with his hair. When they got to the scene where Toula and Ian finally got caught, and Gus freaked out, he let out a full-on belly laugh.

"Your family's really like this?" he asked.

"Worse. But I love them."

David hummed, shifting on the couch, adjusting his legs, and the movement made Farzan's hand slide from David's thigh to his cock. Farzan didn't know if it was an accident or not, but if it was an invitation, he'd definitely take it up. One blowjob hadn't been nearly enough time with David's dick.

He let his fingers play around, gently tracing the warm shape in David's pants, and David didn't stop him, even as he began firming up. But he did look down.

"Should we pause?"

"I've seen it. You keep watching."

Farzan fought with David's zipper, and once David lifted his hips up a bit, Farzan dug his dick back out. The TV cast blue highlights over the dark brown skin and the lighter brown of the head as Farzan skinned it back. He'd been with uncut guys before, but not many, and he hoped it wasn't weird how much he liked it. All dicks were beautiful in their own way, but David's? David's was perfect. Perfect proportions, perfect balls below, perfectly warm skin, soft velvet wrapped around warm steel.

Husband dick, Arya would've called it. Farzan pushed the thought away. That was out of the question. Though it was hard to deny their chemistry. The little tingling in Farzan's skin. The flame in his chest.

No, he couldn't let himself think about that.

Farzan stroked David slowly, languidly, glancing between the movie and David's expressions as his nostrils flared and his breath sped up.

"I really like your dick," Farzan murmured, still resting his head against David's shoulder.

"It likes you too."

Farzan had never actually fooled around during a movie before. It seemed like the kind of thing you did as a teenager, but Farzan had been way too closeted to date in high school. It was kind of hot, though. Hot and fun, seeing what got David to react, even as he focused on the movie. What made him flex or clench up or sigh. He seemed to like it a lot when Farzan dug his finger in the folds of skin around his head.

"I'm getting close," David warned as the movie neared its climax, and Farzan couldn't have planned it better. He finished off his wine, set down the glass, and leaned in to finish David off with his mouth, shivering as David's fingers clenched in his hair. "Fuck," David moaned. "Fuck."

After, Farzan straightened back up and adjusted his dick in his jeans. It was aching hard again, but he ignored it, content to rest against David.

David had other ideas, reaching for him, a warm hand against his thigh, but Farzan stopped him.

"Watch the movie."

David huffed but acquiesced. He did lean in for a quick kiss, though. Farzan didn't let it go on for long. While he would've liked to make out again, the movie was getting to the best part. He broke the kiss with a sigh and cuddled up against David's side, enjoying the rise and fall of his breaths, and the vibration of his laughter, and the soothing hand in his hair.

He hated to say it, but he might actually owe Cliff a thank you. Because if Cliff hadn't flaked, he never would've met David. And this?

This felt like the start of something promising. Something real.

ten

David

Farzan was right: *My Big Fat Greek Wedding* was hilarious. And cute. His mom would love it; he'd have to suggest it next time he saw her. Though maybe she'd already seen it.

When the credits rolled, he waited for Farzan to grab the remote, but he didn't move. David reached for it, but Farzan still didn't shift. He finally looked down and saw that Farzan had fallen asleep against his side. David couldn't help a quick glance at Farzan's jeans, but it looked like he'd gone soft again.

It shouldn't have been disappointing—get in, get off, and get out was how David usually liked to handle hookups—but the thought that the night was more or less over left him feeling uncomfortably cold.

His feelings were all tangled, that was all. He was feeling cozy and domestic because it had been so long. He was out of practice. Yeah, Farzan was sweet, but it wasn't like tonight meant anything other than that they had terrific chemistry.

So why did he hate to wake Farzan up?

And why did he want to get Farzan off again before he left?

It was way past David's usual bedtime, and he barely stifled a yawn.

But also, he couldn't stay here, on Farzan's couch. He couldn't stay here in Farzan's apartment, period, though he didn't relish the idea of trying to find a Lyft this time of night. He'd left his own car at Aspire; he wasn't sober enough to drive, even if he could make it back there.

Farzan nestled into him more, soft and warm. David barely managed to catch Farzan's empty wineglass before it rolled out of his hand and crashed onto the floor. He supposed that was one way to wake up Sleeping Beauty.

"Hey," he whispered instead. Farzan's hair had fallen like a curtain over his forehead, and David switched both wineglasses to his left hand so he could play with Farzan's hair with his right, brush it off Farzan's brown skin. That hair was driving him crazy.

"Huh?" Farzan blinked.

"Movie's over."

"Oh. Sorry. I must've..."

"It's fine," David said. Well, maybe *fine* wasn't the right word. It was way off his usual hookup script, so far it might've actually switched genres. But if he *was* going to let a guy cuddle up against him, he could do a hell of a lot worse than Farzan.

"Should we go to bed?" Farzan cocked a head toward the dark bedroom, lit only by dim street lights flooding in through the window. "I've got a toothbrush."

David knew he should say no. First—again—no sleeping over.

Second, all his skincare was at home. So was his bonnet. And so were the tank top and shorts he liked to sleep in if he shared a bed with someone new, though he slept naked if he was alone.

Did Farzan sleep naked?

The thought sent warmth right to David's core. He wanted to drink in Farzan's brown skin, run his fingers through the chest hair that he'd gotten a glimpse of earlier, cuddle up and feel his legs tangle with Farzan's—

Good lord, he was drunker than he thought. That was not post-hookup behavior.

But fuck it. He'd already broken so many of his own rules tonight. What was one more?

"Sure."

David shot awake, startled to find himself wrapped around something. Something much warmer and softer and larger than a pillow, something that wriggled out of his grasp to smack a phone and shut off the horrible ringing.

"Sorry," a scratchy voice said, and it came back. Aspire. Farzan. *My Big Fat Greek Wedding.* David glanced at the windows—still dark outside. Either that or Farzan had the densest blackout curtains in the world. "I didn't mean to wake you."

Farzan grabbed the phone and slipped out of bed, and David missed the warmth right away, but more than that, he wished the lights were on because it would've been nice to see Farzan's ass in something more than the dim glow of a phone.

Turns out Farzan did sleep naked.

It certainly felt nice, snuggled up together. David hadn't cuddled with anyone since...fuck, what was his name? Derek. Yeah. Derek, this guy he met back in Chicago. They'd hooked up off and on for about six months, back when David was still working at JPMorgan. One time they'd gotten snowed in post-sex and stayed in bed cuddling watching the snow blanket the city. David's apartment had a great view.

God, that felt like a lifetime ago. He was so sure he'd been living the dream: the dream being, make enough money so his parents could retire. Make enough money so he'd never have to worry about bills.

Turned out that dream was fucking soulless—Derek worked in finance, too, and he'd also been pretty soulless in the end—but at least David made enough in those seven years to be set for a while. Long enough to figure out what actually made him happy, long enough to buy a house when he moved back to Kansas City.

Long enough to fall in love with wine and find a new dream of being a master somm. His finances were stable enough—*thank you, annual bonuses*—and once he got his MS he'd have his pick of any number of high-end restaurants, with higher salaries than Jeri could reasonably offer.

It had taken him a while, but he was back on track. His test was only three months away, and assuming he passed, he'd be ready to go wherever his life took him.

David stretched, stifling a groan, and reached for his phone. Five o'clock. They'd tumbled into bed only four hours ago. David pulled the covers closer around him. The bedroom was a little cold, now that he thought about it.

"Sorry about that," Farzan said softly, stepping back into the bedroom. He left the lights off, but David's eyes had adjusted enough that he could at least appreciate a little more of Farzan's form. The strong chest and arms, the little bit of belly, the hair covering his chest that David had enjoyed running his fingers through last night.

"Everything good?"

"Yeah. Got called in to work. I don't have to leave for a while, though. You can sleep in."

David groaned. "You get called in at five o'fuck in the morning?"

Farzan chuckled and leaned down to kiss David's temple. It was sweet and charming and definitely way too early for that shit.

"That's the life of a sub."

David turned to look at Farzan, quirking his right eyebrow as high as it would go.

"Oh god. Substitute teacher!"

David shook his head, stifling a laugh. The morning after was for making a quick exit, not for jokes and kisses.

"Want some breakfast? I'm a pretty good cook."

Breakfast was definitely off-script. Fuck. He never should've stayed the night. He had to get out of here.

"Nah, I better go. Still gotta pick up my car." He opened up his app to get a ride back to Aspire.

Unfortunately, his stomach picked the exact wrong moment to grumble. Breakfast did sound good, but that would mean staying even longer, and this *thing* between them would become a whole other kind of *thing*, and David couldn't deal with that.

"You sure?" Farzan asked, and it hurt to hear that little note of hope. He still sounded scratchy from sleep, and damn if that didn't make him even sexier.

This was dangerous.

"I'm sure," David said evenly. He didn't want to be a dick—Farzan didn't deserve that—but a little nonchalance might help expedite his exit.

"Oh." Farzan's voice was soft. David cringed inwardly at the hurt that flickered across Farzan's face.

Why was letting a guy down easy never all that, well, *easy?*

Thankfully Farzan seemed to be getting it because he straightened up. "Ah. Gotcha," he said, sounding a little too casual, a little too high-pitched now, but at least they were on safer ground.

Until Farzan clicked on the side light, and damn, seeing all that golden-brown skin in the warm glow of the lamp, highlights and shadows carving out every valley of Farzan's body, his dick hanging there with its morning fullness...

Abort! Abort! Abort!

David willed his dick to ignore his eyes as he rolled out the other side of the bed, grabbed his underwear, and started getting dressed.

Fuck, when did he get so out of practice at this? This wasn't his first blow-and-go. So why did his body want to crawl back into bed? Why did his mouth water at the thought of scrambled eggs—and Farzan making them naked?

Was it any wonder, after the end of a long dry spell, that he was suddenly thirsty?

But he didn't have time for distractions.

Even beautiful ones that gave amazing head.

Then again, last night had been...well, fucking amazing. For those few hours, whether it was swapping blowjobs or watching a movie, his whole body had unclenched. And though it had been cut short by Farzan's alarm, last night might've been the best sleep he'd had in years.

Maybe a little break, now and then, wasn't the end of the world. If he got a little stress relief every so often, he could study harder.

He wasn't looking for a relationship, not even close. But a reliable fuck buddy?

He wouldn't say no to that.

He put on his cockiest grin, turned back to Farzan, and tried to ignore how he was still naked.

"Hey. If you want to hook up again, I'd be down."

Farzan stared at him, and David wished he'd put on some clothes, because all that skin was distracting. Also, it was fucking awkward, standing here buttoning his shirt while Farzan stood there with his dick swinging.

Farzan swallowed, and he got this look in his eyes, like a kicked puppy. "Hook up?" he asked, voice soft and brittle.

This was not going the way David meant. He didn't want to hurt Farzan, he just—

"Is that all this was?"

"I mean, yeah. Wasn't it?"

Okay, maybe he could've put that better, because Farzan was blinking faster now. He really hadn't wanted to make him cry.

"Listen—" David began. He needed to explain. Farzan was a great guy, but David wasn't looking for *any* guy right now. He just didn't have time.

David's phone tried to buzz itself off the edge of the bed. He barely caught it in time.

"Shit, my ride's here." That was way faster than he expected. He slipped his socks on; his shoes were still in the living room.

Farzan stepped back as David hurried to the door and stuffed his feet in his shoes. He loved these high-tops, but damn they were hard to get on in a hurry.

"Uh. Get home safe." Farzan's voice had gone hoarse.

Please, please don't cry. David already felt awful.

"Thanks. See you around?"

"Sure," Farzan said.

But he was trying hard not to look at David. His cheeks and ears and neck and chest were all red.

And he was still naked.

Naked and beautiful, even when upset. David wanted to fold him into a hug, run his hands through Farzan's hair, make him understand...

His phone buzzed again.

His ride was about to take off without him. So he settled for grabbing his jacket and giving a little wave.

"Bye."

David pulled into his driveway, grabbed his coffee out of the cupholder, and let himself into his house. It was still dark out, though the eastern sky was beginning to brighten, and a few familiar crows were starting to caw.

David had forgotten how much he liked the sounds of Kansas City: mourning doves in the morning, cicadas in the afternoon, jazz wafting out of an open window. His apartment in Chicago's South Loop had made it easy to get to his job—he hadn't even needed a car; he could walk or take a scooter—but all he ever heard there were traffic and sirens.

David let himself in, tossed his keys on the table, and flopped onto the couch. At least as much as he could flop without spilling his coffee.

Fuck.

His house usually smelled somewhere between clean and slightly floral: his mom loved lavender and kept buying him candles. But something was off today.

His suit smelled. He gave it a sniff. Jasmine and citrus and cedar and *fuck*.

He smelled like Farzan.

David popped the lid off his coffee and inhaled the scent, just to reset his sinuses. He couldn't let himself get distracted. He had way too much to deal with.

If all went well, he wouldn't even be here come next year. Now was no time to get tied down, no matter that those brown eyes kept lingering in his mind. Eyes that had been full of heat and desire last night. Eyes full of hurt and accusation this morning.

But David hadn't promised anything. It had just been another miscommunication, like David thinking Farzan was Frank.

There was no point in wondering about what-ifs. He needed to focus on what was.

eleven

Farzan

"And then," Farzan said dramatically, dipping his bread in the bowl of must-o-musir, a dip of tangy yogurt and salty shallots. "And then, he was like, 'If you want to hook up again we can!' And I didn't know what to say—it was too early and I thought we'd had a really nice night and he was acting all weird. So I'm just standing there, naked, while he gets dressed and leaves."

Across the table, Ramin pressed his lips together, probably holding in a chuckle. Farzan's best friend was lighter-skinned, like a peeled almond, with bright green eyes, a large Iranian nose, and dimples that Farzan would've been jealous of if Ramin was a stranger instead of a brother in all but name. He kept his black hair short and parted on the right, sharp and professional. "That sounds like something out of a movie."

"Yeah, *Forgetting Sarah Marshall*," Arya said. "Kristen Bell broke up with Jason Segel while he stood there totally nude, thinking they were gonna have sex."

Farzan's other best friend was even darker skinned than Farzan, though his tended more toward a warm, ruddy copper. He had thick eyebrows, a long thin nose, dark brown eyes, and no hair at all: after going bald during college, he'd taken to shaving his head. He was rail thin, unlike Farzan, who was a little on the stocky side, or Ramin, who'd fluctuated over the years between fat and thin, but had finally (with the help of his therapist) found a healthy weight for himself. And, more important, a healthy body image.

Still, Farzan caught Arya sliding an extra piece of bread onto Ramin's plate, and Ramin nodding a silent thanks.

"So after all that he just bounced?" Arya's metallic teal nail polish caught the light as he swirled his wine, a cheap Washington Cab Farzan had convinced his parents to add to the wine list, because it was good bang for the buck and paired well with most everything on the menu.

"Yup." Farzan sipped his own glass. Must-o-musir was one of the few things the Cab didn't go with—too much acidity in the wine versus too tangy a yogurt. But all wines could be drunk with all foods, unless you were a wine snob.

Or even just an expert, like David, who'd been knowledgeable but not the least bit snobbish. Not to mention handsome, and a great cuddler, and he did this thing with his tongue where...

"I don't blame you, though," Ramin said, shaking Farzan out of his horny reverie. "If you're not looking for casual, better to tell him that, before either of you gets hurt. Especially after what happened last time."

"Ugh. Don't remind me."

The last time Farzan had tried doing the casual thing—a couple years ago now—he'd ended up with a broken heart and a round of antibiotics.

"Counterpoint: Hector was a lying asshole." Arya set down his wineglass and templed his fingers, leaning in to look Farzan in the eye. "But this guy doesn't sound like one. If the dick was good, you could've had a few more hookups before you canceled your subscription."

At the table to their left, an older Iranian gentleman began coughing on his rice, while his neighbor patted his back. Farzan recognized both of them: part of the crowd of older men who came in at least twice a month, sometimes only four and sometimes as many as twelve. They'd take over some tables in the corner right at opening, eat and play Rook, and go through pots of tea and plate after plate of appetizers. Farzan once asked his dad why he let them keep coming back when they took up so many tables but never ordered that much.

Firouz had just said, "If I tell them to go away, who will I play cards with when I retire?"

Which was a fair point, except Farzan wasn't certain either of his parents would ever retire.

When they'd moved to the United States after the revolution and settled in Kansas City, there hadn't been any Iranian restaurants in town, but they'd taken a chance and opened one. And despite Farzan growing up with them complaining, at least once a week, that they were only a single bill away from filing for bankruptcy, the restaurant had survived and even thrived for over forty years in its little corner of Gladstone. It had done well enough for Firouz and Persis Alavi to raise their three children.

And it had become a cornerstone of the local Iranian community: as more and more families moved to the Kansas City area, they found familiar food, familiar language, and familiar values at Shiraz Bistro.

Farzan had spent his childhood underfoot with Arya and Ramin by his side, as their parents and Farzan's played cards and reminisced about the Iran that no longer was, the dreams that had been stolen from their generation and the new dreams they'd created in the United States.

Dreams like seeing their children grow up and succeed in life, in love, in business.

Farzan was painfully lacking on that front, and David was just another in a long string of failures.

Once Farzan was certain he wouldn't need to call an ambulance, or do the Heimlich—though maybe they weren't supposed to do that anymore?—he met Arya's eyes.

Arya just snickered, though, and even Ramin couldn't stop a tiny smile.

When Farzan's parents found out he was gay, they assured him they loved him no matter what, and he'd always have a place in their home and a safe space at Shiraz Bistro. And they'd kept their promise, even if some of the older crowd got a little uncomfortable as Arya talked way too loudly about dick.

"Seriously, though," Arya said. "You know there's nothing wrong with hooking up."

"Of course I do." Farzan had done plenty of that in his twenties. But everyone in his life was settling down, and if he was honest, he wanted that for himself too. He wanted someone to come home to. Someone to complain about his day with, share a bottle of wine. Someone he'd get to know well enough that fucking each other's brains out would be a matter of earned skill and deep familiarity rather than luck of the draw and a bit of a banana curve. "But I'm tired of it. The games you have to play, apps, the coded language. It's exhausting. And I don't know, with David I really thought . . ."

But Farzan was too embarrassed to admit it.

Ramin nodded sagely, but Arya prodded. "Thought what?"

"I don't know. It felt real, you know? We had chemistry. The sex was amazing, but the kissing was even better, and the cuddling? Sitting together, watching a movie, laughing at the same parts? It felt right. It felt so right." Farzan reached for his wine. "But it was just me I guess. He didn't feel it. Or if he did feel it, it wasn't enough. He's not looking for anything serious."

"Hey." Arya reached across the table and took his hand, voice low. "You felt what you felt. And it's his loss, okay? Not yours. You're one of my favorite people."

"Thanks. You too."

"And I support you in your misbegotten quest for long-term dick."

Ramin rolled his eyes. Farzan snorted.

"Anyway. Whatever. Enough about me." Farzan turned to Ramin. "How was your anniversary dinner?"

"More important, how was the after-dinner?" Arya asked, waggling his eyebrows.

Ramin shook his head and blushed a deep salmon pink. With his lighter skin, every blush was super obvious. "Everything was really nice.

We walked around the Plaza afterward, and I don't know, it felt cozy." He bit his lip. "Do you think a year is too early to start thinking about moving in together?"

Arya gaped. "Seriously?"

Ramin blushed harder. "Maybe."

Truth be told, Farzan was only lukewarm on Todd. He was nice enough, but Ramin was the best person Farzan knew, and so it was hard for anyone to measure up. Todd was funny, handsome, and sweet, but also—and Farzan would never say this to Ramin—he came across a little milquetoast.

Every time Farzan saw him, he only wanted to talk about work and how much money the nonprofit he worked for had raised in their latest campaign, or the gym and the latest personal record he'd hit, all while Ramin pasted on a smile and pretended he liked hearing about it. Farzan couldn't even muster the will to feign interest anymore; he always tuned out or went to refill his wine.

And Todd had the whitest taste in music. Farzan's own tastes were pretty eclectic, but still, one could only listen to Taylor Swift so many times before wanting something a little different.

Worst of all, he had an Android, which turned the group chat (well, the one with him in it) green.

Still, Ramin liked him. A lot. And Farzan wanted Ramin to be happy, more than anything. Life had dealt Ramin enough blows; he deserved to be lucky in love.

Luckier than Farzan, anyway.

"If you feel good about it then go for it," Farzan finally said.

Ramin nodded and looked down, pressing his left thumb into the small tattoo he had on the underside of his right wrist. His mom's name—Nasrin—in Persian script. He had one for his dad, Sina, on the left.

"Hey, speaking of Todd," Arya said, nudging Ramin in the side. "Is he going to be all right for the game?"

"He says so." Ramin shrugged. "You know how he is."

Farzan fought the urge to roll his eyes. Todd had pulled his groin doing Bulgarian split squats, trying to "improve his dumpy," as he put it.

Arya reached for more bread. "That I do."

Arya was the one who'd introduced Todd and Ramin. Arya and Todd played together on a queer kickball team, part of Kansas City's growing community of grown-ass adults running a weekend kickball league. Arya had roped Farzan into joining the team as well, but Ramin had wisely opted out. Still, he came to cheer them on most games, and when Arya had noticed Ramin and Todd looking at each other, he'd taken matters into his own hands and introduced them, and they'd hit it off. Ramin had been smiles all year long.

Now here they were. Ramin was thinking about moving in with Todd. Their team, the Lions, was in the league playoffs. Arya was still enjoying a revolving door of dick.

And Farzan was the same: underemployed and single again.

Before he could wallow anymore, though, the door to Shiraz Bistro swung open, letting out an obnoxious electronic chime and letting in a brisk September breeze. Farzan glanced over his shoulder and did a double take.

It was his baby brother, Navid.

Navid was basically a miniature Farzan: a little shorter, a little less stocky, a little younger, but also way more of a know-it-all: he was an aerospace engineer, working for a company out in Lenexa.

All Iranian parents wanted their kids to be a doctor, a lawyer, or an engineer. Instead, the elder Alavis had wound up with a doctor, an engineer, and a homosexual. Farzan's sister Maheen was an OB/GYN.

While Arya and Ramin registered Navid's arrival with friendly waves, Farzan slid out of the booth to greet his brother, whose hands were linked with his girlfriend's. Gina was a graphic designer at SNK, the same advertising firm where Ramin was an assistant vice president, whatever the fuck that meant. She was pretty, round-faced and round-hipped, with auburn hair and plentiful freckles.

"Hey, Navid." Farzan pulled his baby brother into a hug. Ever since

Navid moved in with Gina—to a new place south of the river—Farzan hardly ever saw him. When they were young, Navid had looked up to Farzan, and Farzan always wanted to make his baby brother proud. They'd hit a rough patch while Navid was in high school, but things got better once Navid got to college and they could relate to each other as adults. Farzan had talked Navid through quite a few breakups before he met Gina.

Farzan turned to embrace her. "Hey, Gina."

She returned the hug. "Hi. Your parents around?"

"Back in the kitchen, like usual. What are you two doing here?"

Navid gave a nervous grin, and Farzan's had the strangest sensation of his stomach both soaring and turning over. He glanced down to Gina's hand. The new, simple platinum band stood out against her creamy skin.

"Oh my god," Farzan said.

"Shhhh!" Navid glanced toward the kitchen, as if their mother might be hovering just out of earshot instead of buried behind mountains of paperwork in the tiny office. "We wanted to tell Mom and Dad first. But I'm glad you know."

Farzan grinned and pulled his baby brother in for another hug, patting his back. "I'm so happy for you."

"Really?" For all his know-it-all-ness, Navid could be strangely shy sometimes, especially when it came to Gina, who he clearly adored.

"Really really." Farzan slung an arm over his brother's shoulder and gave a quick wave and a silent *be back soon* to Ramin and Arya. "Come on, let's go tell Mom and Dad."

twelve

Farzan

Shiraz Bistro's kitchen was an exercise in controlled chaos.

All Iranian kitchens were, one way or another; his own small apartment was no exception. Though thankfully, at Shiraz Bistro, there were no burning onions, no dropped salmon fillets, no canceled dates or one-night stands.

After the renovation five years ago, the kitchen had gone from a strange eighties-beige paint to plain white tiles, one wall given over to grills and stoves, the other to sinks and dishwashers, and a central island—which was really more like a peninsula—for prep. The familiar smells of basmati rice steaming, of hearty kabobs grilling, of onion and turmeric and saffron filled the humid air.

Firouz Alavi, Farzan's father, stood at the grill, his back slightly stooped with age—he had turned seventy-seven this past spring—but still attentive, rotating the skewers of kabob over the grill. He was bald, his remaining gray hair forming a fuzzy crescent from temple to temple.

Farzan's own hair was still thick and dark and curly, and he shoved away memories of the way David had played with it, but even as he neared forty, it was still growing strong. He vainly hoped he wasn't destined to go bald like his father. Arya looked fine with a bald head, but Farzan was terrified his would end up being weirdly shaped.

Firouz always joked that Iranian men could have either hair or brains, usually in earshot of Arya. But that was patently untrue, because Ramin had a full head of hair in addition to being the smartest person Farzan knew.

Still, there were days when Farzan looked over his bills, or rolled out of bed at five in the morning to fill in for a high school algebra teacher, or watched the most beautiful man he'd ever seen rush out of his apartment without looking back, and wondered if his dad had been a little bit right: if he'd gotten hair and not brains, and that was why his life was such a disaster.

And now his younger brother was engaged. Engaged, and in a stable job, and probably better off financially than Farzan, and Farzan was once again the gay fuckup of an older brother.

"Navid!" Firouz's eyebrows shot up. His expansive forehead wrinkled as he smiled. "What are you doing here?"

Farzan stepped aside so his father could embrace his favorite son, and then his future daughter-in-law, kissing Gina on both cheeks.

"Where's Maman?" Farzan asked. "Office?"

Firouz nodded absently and kept talking to Navid. "How's work? Did you get that project?"

Farzan slid through the kitchen, past Sheena—one of the line cooks who was testing the pot of rice with a wet thumb—and knocked on the doorjamb of his mother's office.

Firouz Alavi had always been the family chef, and Persis had been the family accountant. Farzan's mom had been the one to keep the lights on, the fridges stocked, and the staff paid, all while finding time to attend soccer games and choir concerts and piano lessons and whatever else her children got up to.

"Hm? Oh, Farzan-joon." Persis was short—a full head shorter than Farzan—her graying hair dyed a sunny blond and tied into a neat bun, her brown eyes keen and nestled between deep sets of crow's feet. Her ruby-stained lips quirked into a broad smile. "Is everything okay? Something wrong with the food?"

Thursday nights at Shiraz Bistro had become Farzan, Ramin, and Arya's tradition, especially as they all got older and busier. One night a week to eat Iranian food, catch up on life, be with the people who knew them best. And get spoiled by his mom and dad, who served up huge platters of food without ever actually charging them.

"No, everything's great," he said. "Navid's here."

"Oh!" Persis's eyes lit up as she pushed back from her desk. It was coated with stacks of paper, pastel Post-it Notes, and a few framed photographs of her children. One photo, of Farzan's sister Maheen, showed her at her wedding, smiling at her husband Tomás. Another, of Navid, was of him winning a big design award at work.

Farzan's was his senior photo from high school. He was young, pimply, and still dreaming of becoming a teacher.

Apparently that was the version of Farzan his parents liked best. Young enough that he hadn't actually disappointed them yet.

Farzan followed his mom out and stood back as she greeted Navid and Gina and tried to talk without stopping the flow of traffic through the kitchen. When Navid shyly raised his and Gina's linked hands, angled to show off the ring, Persis let out a cry and swooped in for more hugs and kisses.

"I'm so happy for you both," she said. "You two are perfect for each other."

"Proud of you, Navid." Firouz pulled Navid in and kissed his cheeks, then turned to Gina. "Welcome to the family."

"My son's getting married!" Persis cried again, and disappeared into the back, only to emerge with four bottles of Cava. It was Freixenet Cordon Negro Brut—Farzan had convinced his parents to switch from a semi-sweet California sparkling they got a good deal on but never sold because it tasted awful. The black-clad bottles were already sweating in the humid kitchen. "Farzan-joon, can you open these? Champagne for everyone!"

Farzan fixed a smile on his face, even as his mom's voice gnawed at his insides. *My son's getting married.* The successful one. Meanwhile, Farzan was just here to open bottles. He didn't begrudge his brother's happiness or success, or his parents' pride, but just once, he wished he could do something that made them proud.

While his mom cooed over Gina's ring, Farzan ran out to the small bar in the corner. Shiraz Bistro didn't actually have a bartender. The bar was mostly used to store glasses and display the wines they had on sale. Farzan started pulling down flutes as Ramin and Arya appeared at his side.

"What's going on?" Arya asked.

"Navid just got engaged."

Ramin elbowed Arya. "Told you."

Arya rolled his eyes. "Whatever."

"Give me a hand?"

Ramin helped Farzan pour while Arya started distributing glasses to all the tables, no doubt enjoying the chance to once again interrupt the card sharks. At least this time it wasn't about dick.

Persis, Firouz, Navid, and Gina emerged from the kitchen right as Farzan filled the last flute. He took glasses over to Navid and Gina, while Ramin followed with a pair for Persis and Firouz. They retreated back to the bar to grab their own flutes as Firouz grabbed a fork off the nearest table and tapped his glass for quiet.

"Everyone! Your attention please. My son Navid just got engaged."

Polite applause broke out over the restaurant, along with a few *shululululus*. Navid blushed but leaned in to kiss Gina.

"Let's hear it for the happy couple!" Farzan shouted before his dad could delve into a speech that would last until the Cava had gone flat, not to mention embarrass Navid into the next life. "Beh salamati!"

As patrons who knew Navid—like Farzan, he'd grown up underfoot at Shiraz Bistro—got up to congratulate him, Farzan retreated to his table with Arya and Ramin, tossing back his entire glass of Cava.

"It's kind of weird, isn't it?" Ramin said. "Little Navid getting married. I still remember when he was desperate to play *Mario Kart* with us."

"Ugh, and then he'd always play as Toad," Arya said disdainfully. "*Wahoo.*"

"As long as he's happy," Farzan said, and he meant it.

He loved his know-it-all brother. He loved Gina. They made a beautiful couple, and they'd make an even more beautiful bride and groom.

"Dude. You okay?" Arya asked.

Okay? Sure, he was okay. Jealous, but okay.

Navid had a wedding on the horizon. Farzan had an empty apartment.

"I'm good." He grabbed a radish and a few tarragon leaves out of the sabzi bowl. "So how's work going?"

Arya worked as an event planner at a production company called MME—Mitchell Murphy Events. It kept him challenged, on a weird schedule, and in constant supply of bizarre stories, which made for the perfect distraction.

Arya rolled his eyes. "Dude. Today I had a phone call with the densest client I think I've ever had. Like they did not understand the fundamental rules of physics."

Farzan grinned, and Ramin asked, "Which rules?"

As Arya launched into the story—apparently the client believed it was possible to "project darkness"—Farzan relaxed and sipped his wine. Yeah, he was single, and underemployed, and a perpetual disappointment. But he had his friends.

thirteen

David

Everything was going wrong.

"Where are those fries?" Andi, one of their servers, called over the service counter.

"On it!" Brayan called.

David crouched next to Jeri, holding his phone up as a flashlight, while she looked behind the broken fryer.

Aspire was getting a reputation for its fries (pommes frites, technically), and they normally had two fryers going nonstop throughout service. But today, one of them refused to turn on.

Granted, of all the ways for a fryer to break, *won't turn on* was definitely the preferred one, since the rest of the ways generally involved flying hot oil and the risk of grievous bodily injury and/or fire.

But one fryer was not enough to keep up with their orders. They were falling way behind. And while David helped Jeri try to diagnose the problem, he was neglecting his own wine orders.

"I think we've just got to call the technician," he finally told Jeri.

"I think you're right. Damn." Jeri wiped a hand over her sweating face.

No matter the season, Jeri always seemed to be sweating. She claimed it was because she swam so much and always ran hot, but two weeks ago, when they'd accidentally gotten drunk off a tasting with a new distributor, Jeri had admitted to David that menopause hit her like a ton of bricks. Or a ton of wine bottles.

David wasn't sure she remembered that conversation, so he'd kept quiet about it. Jeri *did* swim a lot: she was short, but broad-shouldered, with a strong back and chest and short legs. She kept her mousy brown hair in a no-nonsense short pompadour, and wore a black button-up shirt and jeans to work every day.

David had met her when he was in college and a bartender at Missie B's, Kansas City's most famous gay bar. Jeri was the assistant bar manager at the time. She'd mentored him, gave him extra hours when he needed it, and when she eventually left to manage a fancy steakhouse on the Plaza, she'd asked him to come with.

She'd been the one to introduce David to Marcus, who he stayed with all through grad school. And she'd been the one to cheer David up when Marcus said he wouldn't follow David to Chicago.

David had been so in love. That breakup had nearly destroyed him.

Even after he moved, Jeri checked in on him every couple months. When he'd burned out at JPMorgan, she was the one who gave him glowing referrals to some of Chicago's finest restaurants.

So when she finally realized her dreams and opened Aspire, David had agreed to come on board as wine director and help her get it off the ground. She knew it wasn't permanent, that she wouldn't be able to keep him after he got his master somm and was in high demand, but she insisted it didn't matter.

"You don't mentor someone to keep them shackled to you," she told him once. "You do it to see how far they can go."

So David said goodbye to the few good friends he still had in Chicago and moved home. It wasn't like he had a man keeping him there.

He wouldn't let a man keep him here, either.

While Jeri disappeared into her cramped office to call the service tech, David ran down to the cellar to pull some bottles. They had a modest but well-curated selection of first-growth Bordeaux, and some rich white yuppie trying to impress his date had ordered a bottle of Chateau Margaux.

David could clock a finance bro a mile away. The guy was even dressed like David used to dress, in a sleek silver suit, dress shirt with three buttons undone, no tie, and a hint of gym-raised pecs peeking out through the gap. In his twenties David had worked out hard, skipped meals, lived on stress and adrenaline, and had a body like that. Now that he was nearing forty, he was stronger and healthier, but also softer in spots. Not that Farzan had seemed to mind his thicker thighs or lack of a six-pack.

Fuck. He needed to stop thinking about Farzan. About silky black curls, and citrus cologne, and bedroom eyes, and—

David shook himself. He still had a service to get through, and he couldn't serve wine with an erection.

He poured the Chateau Margaux for the finance bro, who smacked his lips ostentatiously as he tasted. His date, a white girl in a slinky black number, flicked her gaze up for only a second before returning to her phone.

"Mm, nice," the bro said. "Top me up."

"Would you like me to decant it?" David asked automatically. It could certainly use it. He could smell the soul of France wafting out of the open bottle in his hands, but he knew with a decanting it would open up beautifully.

The bro's date looked up at that, but he shook his head. "We're good. You can just leave the bottle."

He left the finance bro and his clearly bored date to their wine, dropped off two plates of fries when he spotted Andi caught answering questions about dessert at table 11, then swung back to the office.

"Any luck?"

Jeri shook her head. "They can't come until tomorrow morning. I've got an appointment; any chance you can be in by eight?"

"Sure."

She sighed and slumped back in the mother of all ergonomic chairs, a huge red and black thing that was probably designed for people who gamed nonstop. Sometimes David missed his own gaming days—time spent staring into the tiny TV in his college dorm room, playing the latest *Final Fantasy* or *Tales* game—but he was way too busy now. He'd spotted a PlayStation in Farzan's apartment, had nearly asked about what games he played, but there'd been the sex and the wine, the movie and the revelation that Farzan was Farzan and not Frank Allen.

"I meant to ask, how'd things go with Frank Allen? Kyra said he came in Tuesday. Did he say when the review would go up?"

David's stomach sank. Was Jeri a mind-reader?

"Funny story," he said.

"Oh?" Jeri arched an eyebrow.

"It wasn't actually Frank Allen."

By the time he finished telling the story—omitting a few details, like how he spent the night—Jeri was in stitches, slapping her knee.

"You've got to be kidding me."

"I wish I was. That was a lot of wine."

Jeri waved it off; truth was, they wasted plenty of wine every night, and what David had opened for Farzan had been drunk and appreciated by the staff.

"So. When are you seeing him again?"

"Who?"

"This Farzan guy. Clearly you clicked."

But David waved her off. "I'm not. It was just a hookup."

Jeri frowned. "You're ghosting him?"

"Not ghosting! I told him I didn't have time for anything serious right now."

But Jeri crossed her arms. "Are you telling me you wasted a perfectly nice first date—and a great lay—because you're too uptight about your test?"

"It has to be my focus," David said simply.

"There's more to life than that damn test of yours. If you don't want romance, fine, but you're not even making friends."

"I have plenty of friends!"

"Name one person you hung out with for nothing but fun in the last month."

"Well . . ." David wracked his brain. Surely he'd done things. He had friends.

But he came up blank.

Jeri sighed. "I love you to death, David, but I swear to god, sometimes I think you were put on this earth to give me an ulcer."

"Someone's got to keep you on your toes."

"I have a wife for that." She stood with a groan David felt in his own joints. Restaurant life was not for the faint of heart—or the faint of body. "Seriously, though. I'm glad you met this guy, even if you fucked it up at the end. Life's short. Seize joy where you can."

"I didn't fuck it up!" David said. "It was a mutual thing."

"Mm-hmm." Jeri pursed her lips. "Sure, David. Come on."

David swung by finance bro's table. He was boring his date with (painfully inaccurate) trivia about Bordeaux wines; David thought about correcting him, but honestly, 90 percent of the finance bros he'd ever known had a terminal allergy to being wrong. So he just topped both glasses up and moved on.

As he passed by the host stand, Kyra flagged him down.

"Everything okay?"

"Aside from the whole fryer debacle?" Kyra shrugged. "Fine. Hey, you free a week from Monday? The thirtieth?"

"I'm not letting you set me up with anyone," David said automatically. But actually, maybe that's exactly what he needed: some meaningless sex with a stranger, to help him get the meaningless (but quantifiably excellent) sex with Farzan out of his mind. "Actually—"

"Oh my god, I know, I know," Kyra said, hands raised to ward off David's annoyance. "I got tickets to the new Wiley exhibit opening. You want to come with?"

"Okay, now you're just trying to set me up with you."

Kyra laughed, a high crystal thing that started in her belly and made her eyes crinkle up.

"David, I'm so far out of your league, I'm playing a different sport."

"Damn. You're really talking me into this."

On the one hand, Kehinde Wiley was incredible, and David loved his art. There weren't many queer Black artists at Wiley's level, and David had never gotten to see any of his work in person.

On the other hand, a day taking in the museum meant a day of not studying. Any break in his momentum now, no matter how small, could end up with disastrous consequences.

He was about to say no when Jeri walked past, nodding at him before sharing a long-suffering look with Kyra.

She was convinced David didn't have any friends. Well, she was wrong.

"Sure. I'd love to go. Send me the details."

fourteen

Farzan

"Farzan-joon, you mind taking out the trash?" Persis asked.

"Sure, Maman." Farzan grabbed the huge bag from the kitchen and hauled it out to the dumpster in the back lot of the strip mall where Shiraz Bistro stood. As soon as he opened the lid, he was assaulted by the smell of nail polish remover, courtesy of the Trans' nail salon next door.

The salon itself was already dark; they closed at seven p.m. As a child, Farzan had wandered into their salon when he got bored, admiring the wall of colorful nail polishes. Maybe that should've been an early sign of his nascent queerness, but his parents had a lifetime of gender expectations courtesy of their upbringings in Iran. It honestly hadn't occurred to them that their oldest son could be anything but straight.

Not that they'd been unsupportive in any way at all. Farzan knew how lucky he was. When Farzan came home from grad school one day and announced he was gay, his parents had accepted him without batting an eye. He was luckier than Arya, who'd gotten into a huge fight with his parents (though they'd since come around), or Ramin, who'd lost both his mom and dad before he even had the chance to come out to them.

Persis and Firouz had more or less adopted Ramin after that—though they'd already treated Ramin (and Arya) like extra sons pretty much from the first day Farzan came home, excited he'd made friends with other Iranians at school.

When Farzan stepped back inside, Firouz was giving the grill one last scrub, while Persis stood over his shoulder, talking in rapid Farsi.

"We should tell him," his mom said.

"We said we'd wait."

"We can't wait forever."

"Tell me what?" Farzan finally asked, making his parents straighten up like kids who'd been caught drawing on the walls. Firouz even hid the grill brush behind his back, as if that was the source of trouble. He seemed to realize it, too, tossing it back onto the grill and smoothing out his apron with an air of feigned nonchalance.

"Tell you what what?" Persis asked.

Farzan crossed his arms. "Whatever it is, just tell me."

His parents glanced at each other.

"If it's about the wedding—" Farzan began.

"We're closing the restaurant," Persis finally blurted out.

Farzan's head spun. He had to have heard wrong. He, Ramin, and Arya had only split the one bottle of wine, plus a glass of Cava each. Not nearly enough to get him drunk, not with a full meal.

"You're . . . what?"

"We're closing Shiraz Bistro," Firouz said. "It's high time we retire."

"But . . . but you're both still so young."

"And we want to enjoy our retirement while we're young. Travel some. Be ready in case we have any grandbabies."

Farzan gritted his teeth but kept quiet. Now was no time to indulge his frustration with his parents' constant passive-aggressive prodding about grandkids. Farzan and his siblings had all felt the pressure, one way or another, particularly Maheen, who'd been married for two years but was focusing on her career.

"But what about the bistro? It's the only Iranian restaurant in town. A pillar of our community." No, not just *a* pillar, *the* pillar.

Their place for gatherings. Their embassy to the rest of Kansas City. Their home away from home.

"Where are you going to go play cards when you retire?" he asked his dad. "Or gossip about whose kids have had nose jobs?" he asked his mom.

"The community is strong," Persis said. "Everyone will be fine. We've had an offer on the space, too. Not great, but…"

"Why close it? Why not sell it? Let someone take it over?"

Firouz sighed. "Navid and Maheen are much too busy to take it over. It's a full-time commitment."

Navid and Maheen. Apparently he wasn't worth even considering.

"And it's so much work. We need to relax. After her heart attack, your mother's doctor said—"

"Her *what*?" Farzan surprised himself with the screech he let out. He cleared his throat. "A heart attack, Maman? Really?"

How could she act like it was nothing? Ramin's dad had died of a heart attack at age forty-eight, when Ramin was still in college. It had devastated Ramin. Hell, it had devastated all of them.

"It was a very small one," Persis said, though she glanced toward the restaurant, like she was afraid Ramin might come in and overhear. "I'm going to be fine, I promise. I'm on a new medication, and without the restaurant, I can take it easy."

"But…" Farzan gripped his hair and pulled and looked around the kitchen.

It wasn't just a restaurant. Or a pillar of their community.

It was his heritage. His history. He didn't have Iran; growing up, visiting was out of the question. He had this. The bistro. Memories of running around underfoot with Maheen and Navid. Of curling up in a corner booth and playing endless games of Uno with Ramin and Arya. Of holidays and birthdays and graduations and a million other days marked within these warm walls.

All that would be gone. And they hadn't even asked him. They'd decided Navid and Maheen were too busy, and he wasn't even qualified. Just Farzan the fuckup. Again.

But he wasn't a fuckup.

"I'll take it over." He didn't realize he'd said it until it was already out of his mouth. "Don't close it. I'll run it."

Farzan's parents blinked at him.

"Are you sure?" Persis asked. "You know it's a lot of work."

"I know," Farzan said, fighting the urge to grit his teeth. She always asked that question: *are you sure?* She asked it when he wanted to become a teacher, and again when he decided to quit, and every other time Farzan made a decision she didn't like.

Why couldn't she just believe in him?

"But you always hated working here," Firouz said. "Any time we asked for help..."

"That was different," Farzan said. Yeah, he didn't like working for his parents. They'd always try to pay him more, or slip extra money into his pockets, and the constant well-meaning questions about the direction his life was taking were exhausting.

But he loved the bistro itself. He loved the smell of the kitchen, loved the quiet hours spent rinsing rice or marinating kabobs before opening, loved the way all the other Iranian families like his could come find a piece of home.

The more he thought about it, the more sure he felt.

"Maman. Baba. I can do this."

He didn't know how, but he would figure it out.

He'd prove his parents wrong.

fifteen

David

"A nything I can help with?" David asked his mom as she stood at the stove, simmering gravy.

His mom's kitchen was cramped, with the stove right next to the fridge. She had lived in the small house in Hyde Park ever since she and his dad got divorced, and though he'd been offering to bankroll a kitchen renovation for the last decade—the green Formica countertops had to go—she'd always said no, insisting David needed to save his money.

She wouldn't even let him help cook.

"I've got it, baby. You just relax. You look tired."

David laughed but left his mom to her cooking. His mom always thought he looked tired. Granted, Sunday mornings were rough, following as they did on the heels of Saturday service. But David was used to that.

The problem was, he hadn't gone to bed when he got home. He'd spent thirty minutes unwinding, reviewing his note cards, blind tasting a red wine from his stash (turned out to be a 2021 Languedoc). And then, instead of going to bed after, he'd found himself thinking about a pair of bowed lips, a set of soulful eyes, silky black curls of hair that felt so good between his fingers, and before he knew it, he'd had his dick in hand, his vibrating prostate massager fully charged and ready to go, and memories of Farzan's warm mouth to tip him over the edge.

And then he had to clean up and shower, too.

So yeah, he was tired. Tired of being horny, which was a weird feeling to have, but after going so long without sex, it was like his night with Farzan had unleashed months of pent-up desire. He hadn't felt like this since he was a teenager.

It was getting so bad, he'd been thinking about calling one of his old friends with benefits back in Chicago, just for some phone sex. Either that or giving in and downloading Grindr again.

At this point, David would do just about anything to get Farzan out of his mind. If only Farzan had been down for something casual. They'd had great chemistry. Amazing sex. Why did Farzan have to make it complicated?

"Baby?"

"Hm?" David shook his head. "Yeah, Momma?"

"Didn't you say there were mimosas?"

David laughed and poured his mom a drink. When it came to brunch, Kathleen Curtis was in charge of the food, but David was in charge of the booze. He could cook, yeah, but not nearly as well as his mom, who could've given Brayan a run for his money, and Brayan had gone to culinary school.

When brunch was ready—fluffy scrambled eggs, buttery biscuits with creamy, spicy gravy, bacon, and his mom's latest obsession, fried brussels sprouts—David pulled his mom's seat out for her as she sat at the table.

"Oh, stop," she said, swatting at him with a napkin, but smiling all the same. David's mom had beautifully high cheekbones, warm brown skin—David got his cool undertones from his dad—and large upturned eyes of the richest brown. David might've gotten his dad's skin, but he had his mom's eyes. And her nose, too.

As David sat, he raised his glass, clinked it with his mom's.

"Love you, Momma."

Her eyes crinkled up. "Love you, baby."

They ate in silence, for the first few minutes at least, which was fine by David, because his mom had an alarming habit of interrogating him about his social life. Or lack thereof, if one were to believe Jeri.

Thank god Jeri and his mom had never actually met. He wasn't sure he could handle them teaming up on him.

"These are good," David said, popping another brussels sprout into his mouth.

"They're made with love," Kathleen said, which was undoubtedly true—Kathleen made everything with love—but also, in the Curtis family, *love* was code for *butter*.

Lots and lots of butter.

"Hey, whatever happened to what's-her-name? The vegan?"

David scoffed but smiled. "Ayesha?"

She'd been his best friend in Chicago. They'd worked together at JPMorgan, and they'd stayed close after his escape. David had even gone to her wedding: a destination event in Napa, where he'd taken his love of wine to the next level.

That trip, riding a charter bus from Oak Knoll all the way up to Calistoga and back, wandering the vineyards and tasting the grapes fresh from the vine, he'd gone from *loving* wine to *living* it. Before, wine had been a thing he served at work. A drink he shared to unwind with friends.

After, he knew what it really was: Magic in a bottle. The kiss of the earth itself.

At the airport heading home, he'd started looking up how to get his sommelier certifications.

Last time they'd talked, Ayesha was still at JPMorgan, and she and her wife, Janine, had two babies and a pit bull and a quaint house in Oak Park. But ever since he'd moved back to KC, they'd texted less and less.

David cleared his throat. "Last I heard she was doing okay."

"Last you heard?" David's mom was a master of the raised eyebrow.

"You know how things get. We're both busy."

Still, he should probably send her a hello, at least. Hadn't one of her boys had a birthday recently?

"And when's the last time you talked to your dad?"

Last week? No, two weeks ago. David wracked his brain for details of their last conversation.

"It's been a little while," David admitted. "I'll call him. Why?"

"Just wondering," she said airily, polishing off her mimosa.

Kathleen and Christopher Curtis didn't talk much since their divorce, but they'd remained friendly enough to backchannel with each other when they felt their only son wasn't paying enough attention to them.

"Well, you know I've been busy," David finally said, reaching for his mom's flute to make her another mimosa.

"I know. I just wish you wouldn't push yourself so hard. You only live once."

David shrugged. He'd lived plenty when he was young and foolish, and he'd live plenty more once he passed his test. The world was just waiting to open up to him.

"Don't worry about me, Momma. I'm good."

Despite what his mom—and Jeri—thought, he wasn't lonely. He had hookups, like Farzan. And he'd even made a friend date with Kyra. What more could they ask?

So instead he said, "How's work?"

If there was one surefire way to get his mother off his back, it was asking her about her job. Despite her being well past retirement age, he was pretty sure his mom would never actually retire. She loved teaching high school French way too much to give it up.

His mom rolled her eyes and pushed her flute back toward David. "I do not have enough mimosa for that."

David laughed and topped her up.

"Which of these rosés is sweetest?" The patron asking was young and white—maybe midtwenties—with a cut-off jean jacket covered in trans pride enamel pins and a dyed-black bowl cut that belonged in an anime. David wondered who their stylist was.

The patron laid their hand on the table and pinned him with a wide-eyed gaze. "I literally just want to drink candy."

David laughed. He found sweet rosés borderline offensive, but to each their own, and it was his job to be knowledgeable about all types of wine, even the nasty ones.

"The Paso Robles is probably the sweetest, but if you're looking for candy, I've got a Moscato-Brachetto blend, a sparkling sweet rosé."

The patron's eyes lit up. "Fuck yeah. I'll do that."

"Me too," their friend, fatter and browner and a bit more femme, with long brown hair in a braid, said.

"Gotcha."

David retreated to the bar, poured out two glasses of Bigarò, delivered them and basked in the smiles of a perfect selection.

"Let me know if you need anything else."

He turned to head back to the bar and stopped in his tracks, blinking a few times just to make sure he wasn't hallucinating.

Because there, at the end of the bar, looking a little nervous and a little tired and still deliciously sexy, was Farzan.

Before David could react, Farzan locked eyes with him. Gave a little smile and a wave.

David smiled back, stepped up next to him at the bar.

"Hey. You came back."

"Yeah." Farzan swallowed, the motion of his Adam's apple impossibly tantalizing. "Can we talk?"

sixteen

Farzan

Farzan sat at the bar, drumming his fingertips against the counter, jiggling his leg against the barstool. What the fuck was he doing here?

It made perfect sense. Except the part where it was completely fucking ridiculous.

He'd spent the last three days alternating between panic (at his impulsive decision), anger (at his parents' doubt), frustration (at the state of the restaurant's bookkeeping), and, occasionally, this fluttery feeling it had taken him a while to identify as pride (as he talked to the kitchen staff, who seemed to trust him).

He was taking over Shiraz Bistro. His parents would finish out the month, help him get up and running, but then it would be his.

Well. It would still be in their names, technically; he wouldn't own it outright. He didn't have that kind of liquidity. Who did?

But he'd be the head chef *and* the general manager. He'd be in charge.

What the fuck did he know about running a restaurant?

When he'd told Ramin and Arya, they'd both promised to do whatever they could to help. But seriously, what were they supposed to do?

Ramin was a marketing executive, and Arya was an event planner. Neither knew anything more than him about running a restaurant.

They'd stayed up late into the night talking in circles, until Arya dropped his phone on his face, which seemed to signal it was time to go to bed. Farzan said good night, but then he'd stayed awake on the couch, nursing another glass of Malbec. Staring into the inky red liquid, wishing it would tell him what to do. It was another bottle of the wine he'd shared with David, and that made him think of David, of the amazing sex, of the even more amazing cuddling after, the sweet relaxation of watching a movie together and feeling just right.

David. Who helped run a restaurant.

It had taken Farzan a couple days to work up the courage. That, and he slept most of Saturday, after taking a high school sub call on Friday after only two hours of sleep. He wasn't in his twenties anymore, and if he didn't get eight hours (or at least six, for the love of god), he always paid for it.

But now here he was, at Aspire, and there David was, delivering two glasses of wine to a booth, and when he turned and caught Farzan's eyes, Farzan nearly wanted to bolt out the doors.

Because it was foolish. It was foolish to ask David to help him when they barely knew each other.

It was even more foolish to put himself back in David's orbit, when every cell in his body was desperate for David's touch. He'd told David he couldn't do casual, that he didn't want to hook up, but if David offered sex again—even meaningless, emotion-free sex—Farzan didn't think he could resist.

David's eyes lit up, followed quickly by a broad smile. And: nope. Farzan definitely couldn't resist.

"Hey. You came back."

Farzan thought he'd been imagining the things David's voice did to him, but no, that was real. Farzan's stomach flipped at the sound, deep and mellow and the tiniest bit breathy.

"Yeah." This close, Farzan's senses were overwhelmed by the musk and vetiver of David's cologne, the way his maroon-gray suit highlighted his shoulders and hugged his hips, the deep warmth of his eyes, framed by the faintest of laugh lines. He swallowed.

This was a mistake.

But he'd never been so glad to be the family fuckup.

"Can we talk?"

"That's . . . a lot," David said, when Farzan had finished sharing the most compressed version of his story he could muster. David stood behind the bar, stirring an Old Fashioned (made with a big sphere of ice, and no cherries, Farzan was glad to see). "But your mom's okay?"

"Yeah. She is." When Farzan called his mom Friday night—ostensibly to talk about logistics but really to check up on her—he'd been tempted to yell at her for keeping her heart attack a secret, but he'd managed to have a calm, adult discussion instead. Persis insisted it was mild, they caught it early, it didn't do any damage, she was lucky and taking new medication, and everything was going to be fine.

"I'm glad."

"Thanks." Farzan could tell David really meant it. Even though he'd never met Persis. Farzan's chest warmed. "Anyway, I just thought . . . well, I don't know what I thought. Except suddenly I'm supposed to run a restaurant and I don't actually know anyone else who does that. Except you."

David chuckled. He passed the Old Fashioned off to another server and topped up Farzan's Syrah (a nicely structured one from Walla Walla). "I don't technically run this place. That would be Jeri."

"Yeah, I know, but . . ."

"And your parents run a restaurant."

"Yeah, and they don't think I can do it. If I start asking them questions . . ."

"Gotcha." David sighed. "Well. I'm happy to help."

"Really?"

David nodded. "I've been in the hospitality industry for...oh god." David seemed to deflate a bit before he straightened out with a laugh. "Nineteen years now, off and on. And the last eight of them full time in fine dining."

"I've been around Shiraz Bistro all my life, but I have no idea what I'm doing. I mean, cooking wise I've got it covered. But all the business-y things? Spreadsheets and payroll and inventory and god knows what else?" Farzan's hand tightened around the stem of his wineglass; he made himself relax before he snapped it.

"Hey. Take a breath." David's hand brushed Farzan's; Farzan couldn't tell if it was intentional or not, but either way, they both jumped at the contact. "I got you."

"Thanks." Farzan took a deep breath. "And I'm not asking for free. I can pay you in Persian food, or more wine, or I can help you study for your test. Whatever works for you."

Farzan wasn't going to bring up sex. That would make it feel way too transactional. He sipped his wine as David studied him, eyes turning mischievous.

"What if I want to get paid in blowjobs?" David asked. "That works for me."

Farzan spat his wine out his nose, spattering the bartop and burning his sinuses. David yelped and narrowly dodged getting the wine on his suit jacket, but he was back right away with a towel.

"Sorry! Sorry. That was mean."

Farzan coughed and sputtered and drank his water. He should have been annoyed at how easy it was to fall back into flirting. How natural. He should have been annoyed that he *wasn't* annoyed.

But that wasn't what any of this was about. He cleared his throat. "It's fine."

"Yeah? More blowjobs?"

David was incorrigible.

"Ass."

"I'll take ass too."

Despite his resolve, Farzan started laughing, which seemed to be what David had been aiming for.

He gave Farzan a wide, toothy smile. "You looked like you could use a laugh."

"Laugh, yes. Wine out my nose, not so much."

"Point taken." David bit his lower lip. It was so full, and Farzan wanted to kiss it again. But no. That wasn't why he was here. "Anyway. I could really use a study buddy."

For a moment, Farzan wondered if David was thinking about kissing too. But then he glanced to his right, toward the kitchen. Farzan followed his gaze.

A short woman with broad shoulders and a shock of brown hair was studying David, arms crossed. No. Studying the two of them, her head cocked to the side and her thin lips pursed.

David sighed and lowered his voice. "Actually. I could really use a friend."

Farzan and David *did* have chemistry, but chemistry didn't have to mean sex. Or even romance. It could mean lots of things, including friendship, and Farzan liked that idea.

"Works for me."

David offered his hand. "So. Friends?"

Farzan shook it and tried very hard not to remember the way David's fingers felt in his hair, or pressed against the back of his neck, or wrapped around his dick.

"Friends."

seventeen

David

Friends.

He could work with that.

He *did* need friends. If for no other reason than to get Jeri off his back. Though friends with benefits would be better.

And if he felt a little twinge of something more, of being inordinately happy when Farzan had shown up at Aspire, well, he could tamp that down. Anything that might happen between them had a built-in time limit. Once David passed his test, he was out of here.

In the meantime, though, he had flash cards to study and blind tastings to do, and having a friend would help.

Helping Farzan in return would be good, too. The raw determination in Farzan's eyes . . . that was something new. Something exciting. David wanted to see where it led.

Monday morning—the day of their first friend date—David did a long-overdue house cleaning. Back in his JPMorgan days, he'd had a cleaning service, but he'd given that up when he moved back home, convinced he could handle it. And he had, up until he started living at the base of Mount Flash Card.

After lunch, he picked up his dry cleaning and dropped off his glass recycling. Thank god for Ripple Glass: he went through bottles at a terrifying rate. When he got home, he sorted out his wine fridge (separate from his wine cellar downstairs) and washed his spit bucket, throwing out the wine-stained photograph of Ronald Reagan at the bottom and replacing it with a fresh one. His old wine shop in Chicago had used a photo of a different, more tangerine-tinged ex-president, and yeah he had been awful too, but David loved getting to spit in the face of the president who'd let the AIDS crisis run rampant and killed off a generation of his queer elders.

Fuck that guy.

David showered and moisturized—hard to miss how much Farzan liked the smell of his skin—but waffled on what to wear.

One of his work suits was definitely overkill, though he hadn't forgotten the way Farzan had practically salivated over him. And he had a heather gray one that showed off his assets nicely. Then again, when it came to showing off his assets . . .

He settled on a soft Royals T-shirt (not that he cared much about baseball, but he liked the way it hugged him) and light blue sweatpants, sans underwear. He wasn't going to push anything, but he wasn't above advertising the benefits package.

David had just opened a bottle of Oregon Pinot Noir when the doorbell rang. He tried to play it cool, but as soon as he saw Farzan, holding a laundry basket laden with two huge pots, he broke into a laugh.

Farzan shrugged. "It's the Persian carryout system," he explained as he squeezed past. David was certain he saw an appreciative eye dart to his sweatpants.

While Farzan pulled off his shoes, David took the laundry basket into the kitchen. The two pots inside were wrapped in dish towels and tied at the top to keep the lids secure, but they smelled absolutely divine.

"What's all this?"

"Well, I had all this celery I needed to use, so I made celery stew. Khoresh karafs. I told you I would pay you in food."

David laughed and handed Farzan a pair of plates.

"Do you have a bigger plate?" Farzan asked.

"Sure, why?"

But Farzan didn't say anything. He just took the platter, put it over top of one of the pots and, with a practiced flick of his wrists, inverted the whole thing. When he removed the pot, a resplendent golden disc of rice sat on the platter, shining and perfect.

"Damn!" David said.

Farzan beamed and started dishing rice onto the plates, then ladling stew over it: green chunks of celery, brown cubes of beef, and verdant green herbs releasing their scent into the air.

"We can eat on the couch," David said. "I usually do."

"You sure?"

Yeah, David was sure. The couch was way cozier, especially since it was technically more of a love seat.

He shot a smile Farzan's way and took their wineglasses and the bottle through, setting them on the coffee table. Farzan followed with plates and silverware.

They settled in. David was normally opposed to manspreading, but he let his knee rest against Farzan's, and Farzan didn't pull away.

David poured their wine, handed Farzan his glass.

"Well. Here's to you, for helping me," Farzan said, raising a toast.

"Cheers."

The wine was simple but lovely: good spice, soft tannins, a lighter body, and a good undercurrent of cherries. But the food? The food was heavenly. Every grain of rice was distinct, soft yet toothsome. The golden bits on top were crispier than the best potato chip. And the stew was hearty but bright, with the subtlest hint of lime.

"Fuck, this is amazing," David said around a mouthful of food, manners be damned. He shoveled another bite in.

"Thanks." Farzan blushed and sipped his wine.

"Seriously. So good."

David had learned how to cook—his mom had made sure of that—but he'd never had the spark that made it special. Not like his mom.

Not like Farzan, either.

"I'm glad you like it." Farzan grinned but then looked away. David shifted so his knee pressed against Farzan's, which got a bigger smile and fleeting eye contact. Was Farzan allergic to compliments, or was he playing hard to get?

"Did you train anywhere?"

Farzan laughed. "Just at the restaurant. And at home. My dad taught me."

"Oh yeah?" David copied Farzan, breaking off a piece of the crispy golden rice and sticking it in his mouth, savoring the crunch and accidentally moaning at the heavenly taste.

"There's a familiar sound," Farzan muttered, but then his eyes went wide and his cheeks darkened.

The expression was so funny, David started to laugh, but instead he swallowed wrong and started coughing and hacking.

"Sorry! Sorry." Farzan set down his plate so he could pat David's back. "That was inappropriate."

David reached for his wine, took a sip and cleared his throat. Farzan's hand retreated, and he missed its warmth. "It's all good. Revenge for that blowjob joke I guess."

"I'm not that petty." Farzan gently nudged David's side with his elbow.

"I know." David leaned into the contact.

Even if this went nowhere—even if they were just buddies and not fuck buddies—he was surprised to realize how easy it was, just being with Farzan. Sitting and eating, casually brushing each other. Comfortable.

Maybe Kyra was right. Maybe he did need more friends.

When they'd both finished, David took their plates back into the kitchen, while Farzan topped up their wine.

"So what are we studying first?" Farzan called from the living room.

David returned with a pile of flash cards, all in neon colors, because he'd found them on clearance in five-hundred packs. They burned his eyes, but at least they were hard to misplace.

Farzan gaped as David handed them over. "These are . . . bright."

David sat back down, reaching for his wineglass, and if he settled a little bit closer to Farzan than he had been when they were eating, well, that's just how the couch cushions were.

Farzan reached for his own glass, then studied the top card. "Wait. Cognac?"

"Yeah, the master somm covers beer and spirits, too."

"Huh. Okay." Farzan straightened out, twisting on the couch to face David more fully. David tried not to be disappointed they weren't touching anymore; he really did need to focus. Farzan licked his lips and read the first card. "What are the departments where grapes for cognac are grown?"

They spent the next hour going through the flash cards, until David's brain felt fuzzy. He retreated to the kitchen to get them waters; when he came back, he was pretty sure Farzan was looking at his dick swishing back and forth in his soft sweatpants. He bit his lip to stop from smiling as he sat, splitting the last of the wine bottle between their glasses.

Farzan nodded absently and flipped over another note card. "What are the two—"

"Wait wait wait," David said. "I'm fried. I think that's enough flash cards."

"You sure?"

"Absolutely." David rolled out his neck. "We haven't even talked about what's going on with you."

Farzan groaned and ran his hands through his hair. David remembered how soft it was, how sleek the gentle curls felt when they tangled between his fingers.

Before he could stop himself, he scooted closer and reached for the nape of Farzan's neck. Just a touch.

Farzan didn't move away.

"If you couldn't tell by me licking my plate, I think you've got the food angle covered. What're you so worried about?"

Farzan let out a dry chuckle. David kept playing with his hair.

"Just...everything. I've got to manage a staff. Do inventory and pay-roll. Maintenance and overhead and budgets and..."

"Hey." David tugged on Farzan's hair, just enough that he saw goose bumps break out along the plane of Farzan's neck.

He wanted to play connect-the-dots with his tongue.

But they were here to work.

"Hey," he said again. "Let's take it one thing at a time."

"Okay."

"You know, before I was in hospitality I was in the finance sector."

"Wait, really?" Farzan twisted to face him, his whole face scrunched up in disbelief. "You were a finance bro?"

"Yup. So I know a thing or two about spreadsheets."

"Great." Farzan shifted, putting his hair out of David's reach, and took a deep breath. "Okay, first of all, my mom's accounting system hasn't been updated in fifteen years."

David winced. "Oof."

"Yeah."

Farzan actually knew more than he thought, often realizing the solution to a problem halfway through complaining about it. Where he could, David gave advice, or shared his own experiences. But mostly he let Farzan talk. Farzan talked with his whole body—hands gesturing, arms flailing. He was full of life, full of determination, and there was nothing sexier than a man on a mission.

"And then—" Farzan began, gesturing and nearly upending his wine-glass. "Fuck. Sorry. Sorry. I just—"

David grabbed Farzan's shoulder and gave it a firm squeeze. It was hard as a rock.

"Easy. You don't have to have everything figured out tonight."

"But—"

"I get that you're stressing out about all this, but you're only one guy."

"I'm not stressed."

David dug his fingers into Farzan's shoulder a bit deeper, and Farzan seemed to melt.

"This is *not stressed* to you?"

Farzan let out a low, satisfied grunt that David felt in his core.

What a sound.

"Point taken."

David dug his thumb into the tight cord along Farzan's neck.

"You know what's good for that," he said, low and soft.

Farzan went still. "I didn't come here for that."

"Sure." David chuckled. "As if you haven't been staring at my dick in these sweats all night."

Farzan hid his face behind his hands. "It's like a pendulum. You've dicknotized me."

David grinned. Yeah he had.

"You know, I still owe you an orgasm. I hate being in debt."

"Ugh, no more budgeting!"

David just laughed, tugging Farzan a little closer so he could get both hands on his tense neck. He kneaded the tight muscles, leaned in so he could whisper in Farzan's ear.

"No more budgets. Can't I just make you feel good because I want to?"

"I'm not sure..."

David clocked Farzan's jeans. "Your hard-on says otherwise."

Farzan chuckled and then sighed. He didn't say yes. But he did bite his lip.

"You really don't want this?" David asked, letting his hands fall away.

Farzan turned and finally looked at him. His gaze moved from David's eyes down to his lips, even lower to his sweats, and then back to his mouth.

David held his breath.

A second stretched between them, and David wondered if he'd misread things.

But then it snapped, and Farzan lunged, kissing him hungrily. David responded with equal desperation, pressing into Farzan's warm mouth. Farzan's tongue wasted no time in begging for entrance.

A whole-body chill swept up David's back.

Fuck. Why had he ever thought about downloading Grindr again? This was so much better.

Farzan's hands cupped his face, and David leaned in, pressing Farzan up against the back of the couch. But the shift in position made his stomach gurgle audibly.

Farzan laughed against his lips and broke the kiss. "I should've warned you. Khoresh karafs gives most people gas."

"We've got to stop eating these big meals and trying to fuck after," David said, licking the shell of Farzan's ear. "But I've got two hands."

And with that, he dug for Farzan's waistband, fighting with the belt, finally getting off Farzan to push him back. Farzan was wearing another cute pair of underwear, black with roses printed on them, but David yanked them down to get at Farzan's already-leaking cock.

"Fuck," he moaned appreciatively, wrapping his hands around the warm, smooth skin. And then: "Fuck. Lube."

He leapt off the couch, ran to his bedroom and grabbed it out of the bedside table. Back in a flash, he slicked Farzan's hard length, giving his balls a gentle scratch, before leaning in for a kiss as he started stroking.

Farzan's hands pawed at David's waist, gripped his hardening cock through his sweats, but David shook him off. "Let me take care of you," he whispered, lips brushing Farzan's ear, savoring the full-body shudder that followed.

Last time David got Farzan off, he hadn't gotten to study Farzan's reactions. See his face turn red, see him bite his lips, see him unravel. But this was a sight to behold.

Farzan's breath came in shorter and shorter gasps, in between bouts of kissing. David sucked on Farzan's tongue, nibbled on his lower lip, then released him again to enjoy the muttered *fuck*s and gasps of pleasure.

"Fucking hot cock," David muttered into Farzan's ear, relishing the way Farzan's neck arched in response. "You've been needing this, haven't you?"

"Uh-huh," Farzan grunted, and David grinned, but damn, he'd needed it too. Needed to feel Farzan's cock again. Needed to whisper dirty promises in Farzan's ear and watch him shiver and writhe. Needed to see Farzan come.

He brushed his nose against Farzan's jaw, ran his teeth over Farzan's pulse point, savored the way Farzan's cock swelled in his hand in response.

"Yeah you have. Been needing it so bad." He tightened his grip as Farzan squirmed and whimpered. The sound sent a lightning bolt straight to his core. He could feel himself leaking in his sweats as his dick flexed and strained. "You gonna come for me?"

And Farzan did with a gasp, coating David's hands and spilling onto his shirt and jeans. David almost came himself, the sight was so hot, but he didn't let up until Farzan flinched as his dick became sensitive.

Farzan turned to jelly, going all boneless in his arms and against the couch. David kissed him on the nose, then reached for a napkin to try to save his clothes.

As David wiped up the mess, Farzan breathed heavily. His head flopped over, showing off a languid, satisfied smile. His eyelids drooped, brown eyes shining, and David almost wanted to drown himself in them.

No. David shook himself. This had been about dealing with Farzan's stress. Not getting all mushy about his bedroom eyes.

David cocked a grin. "Less stressed now?"

Farzan sighed, then let out a low laugh. "Definitely."

eighteen

Farzan

"You sure you don't want me to—"

"Positive," David said, even though Farzan could see his dick tenting his sweats, a growing wet spot at the point. "I wanted to make you feel good."

And Farzan *did* feel good. His skin was humming. His shoulders had finally unclenched.

But his mind was racing. This wasn't supposed to be about sex. This was supposed to be about helping each other. Professionally.

About being friends. Not fuck buddies.

He and David had just blown past the boundaries Farzan had set in his mind. Well. Planned to set, at least.

Definitely intended to set.

But then David had opened the door in those damned soft blue sweats, that weathered tee clinging to his torso, and Farzan had gotten sucked into his gravity well. Drawn to him like a moth to a flame. Or to a dick print.

David drew his knee up, which mercifully covered his still-rampant erection. He crossed his arms over his knee, rested his chin on his hands, and smiled at Farzan. His midnight eyes were luminous.

"I can hear the gears grinding in your brain. Did I overwhelm you?"

"No." *Yes.* Every time Farzan blinked, the darkness behind his eyelids swirled with red and black numbers, white spreadsheets stretching to infinity.

David's smile faltered. "Do you . . . regret what we did?"

"No," Farzan admitted. But should he?

The more blood returned to Farzan's big head, the more of a mistake it seemed. David had made it clear, their very first night, that casual was all he was into. And Farzan didn't want casual.

It wasn't just because of what happened with Hector. That had been toxic, yeah, and the gonorrhea had been the worst possible parting gift. (Farzan had gone his entire life without an STD up until then.) But that wasn't the problem. Farzan trusted David.

But trust wasn't enough.

Farzan wanted romance. He wanted what his parents had, what Navid and Gina had, what Ramin and Todd had.

David's voice was low and smooth. "Talk to me?"

"This was supposed to be about helping each other, professionally. And about being friends. Not about getting off."

David was still right next to him, smothering him with the scents of vetiver and sex. He waggled his eyebrows. "I assume you've heard of friends with benefits."

Farzan sighed. "Yeah, but . . ."

David's smile changed, from teasing to something more serious.

"You and I are good together, yeah? I mean, the sex has been amazing, and we haven't even done any actual fucking yet."

True. Farzan had almost forgotten what good sex was like. But still . . .

David rested a warm, smooth hand on his arm.

"Just hear me out, okay? We've both got a lot of stress in our lives. And we've both got jobs that are taking a lot out of us. And I think we make good friends. I had a lot of fun, just hanging out, even before the sex. Didn't you?"

Farzan had. He felt lighter around David, the same lightness he got with Ramin and Arya. Someone who saw him.

"I did," he admitted.

"They call it 'friends with benefits,' not 'benefits with friends.' So let's be friends. And if we happen to fool around some, well, we're both adults. We can both handle it without things getting messy." David gestured at Farzan's stained shirt, eyes sparkling with mischief. "Well. Emotionally messy. Can't guarantee your laundry."

Farzan snorted. But what David said . . . did make sense. Sort of.

Could he really do it? Be friends and fool around and not catch feelings?

"And besides. Once I pass my test, I'll be moving away."

That brought Farzan up short.

"Wait. Really?"

"Yeah." David sat up straighter. "Once I've got my master somm, I'll have my pick of places all over. New York, LA, San Francisco. Chicago, too, though I don't know I'd want to go back."

"Nowhere in Kansas City?"

David shook his head. "Aspire's great, don't get me wrong, and Jeri is a ride-or-die for me, but it's no French Laundry. It's no Alinea. And it's never going to be."

"And that's what you want?"

"Yeah." David looked upward, a wistful smile curling his lips. Farzan could've sworn he saw little stars dancing in David's eyes as he imagined it. "No matter how well Aspire does, it's never going to pay what I can get at a place with multiple Michelin stars."

"And you want that?"

David bit his very full bottom lip. "I was on track to buy both my parents houses before I changed careers. I still want to do that for them."

Farzan could understand that. He and his siblings had never really talked about it, but it was kind of understood that, even though he was the oldest, he'd never be the one who could take care of their parents. Maheen and Navid were.

"That's cool," Farzan said. "When's your test, anyway?"

"Two weeks before Christmas."

Three months. A little less, even.

Farzan chewed his lip.

Three months to figure out how to run Shiraz Bistro his way. Three months to get David ready for his test.

Three months of possibly excellent sex.

Somehow, putting a time limit on it made it better. Even if Farzan did catch feelings, it wasn't like he'd go head over heels in only three months. Yeah, he'd be bummed when David moved away, but it wasn't going to rip his heart out.

He'd survived worse.

And like David said, they *were* good together.

He imagined a tiny Arya, hanging over his shoulder, whispering in his ear. "When good dick is on special, order as much as you can."

On his other shoulder, tiny Ramin warned him: "Guard your heart."

But Farzan could guard it for three months.

He studied David, who was still smiling at him. A small, soft smile that made Farzan feel like he could breathe again.

"All right," he said. "Let's be friends."

"Friends," David said, extending his hand. "With benefits?"

"With benefits," Farzan agreed.

"So. Same time next week?" As David asked, he tickled Farzan's palm with his middle finger. "I've got some gray sweatpants too, you know."

Farzan laughed and yanked his hand away.

And if he missed the warmth of David's hand, well. It was a little chilly out.

⁓

"You have to double-check every time," Firouz said, pushing hard against the refrigerator door. "It likes to stick mostly closed."

Farzan nodded, popping the door open and closing it again. It did stick about an inch before closing. Farzan wondered if the door not closing was in any way connected to the enormous (though thankfully shallow) dent on the front, made several years ago after an unfortunate "tahdig incident" his parents had refused to elaborate on.

Once Farzan finished helping his dad sort and put away the latest produce order, he ducked into his mom's office.

"Hey, Maman. How're you feeling?"

Persis glanced at Farzan over the top of her glasses. "See, this is why I didn't tell you about the heart attack. I'm feeling fine! Besides, I'm the one who's supposed to worry about you."

"You don't have to worry about me, Maman."

"You're my son. Of course I do."

"You've got two sons. But I've only got one mom."

Persis waved him off, but she had a little smile, too.

"Anything I can do to help?"

"No, just sorting things."

Farzan's mother seemed to follow the "everything where I can see it" school of organization. The office was a well-ordered maze of stacks of paper, files that needed to be sorted, empty cups of tea, piles of receipts. It gave Farzan hives every time he stepped inside. There was a reason his apartment was minimally decorated, and it had everything to do with dreams of being buried alive under an avalanche of paper.

Which, come to think of it, probably had to do with the time he *had* gotten buried under an avalanche of files when he was eight years old, playing with his Transformers in the corner of the office as his mom worked.

Regardless, the office would have to be sorted before Farzan could take it over, but his mother refused any help on that front. Even though Farzan would be the one who needed to know where things went.

"Actually, Farzan-joon, can you get me some tea?"

"Sure."

Farzan delivered said cup of tea, then joined Elmira, one of their servers, out front, wiping down tables to get ready for opening.

"So you're gonna be the new boss, huh?"

"Yup. I'm Mister Manager."

Elmira blinked at him behind owlish black plastic glasses. Maybe she was too young to have seen *Arrested Development*. At least he hadn't made a joke about blue-ing himself.

"Never mind."

As they wiped down the tables, and leveled one that had gotten a little wonky, there was a knock on the front door.

"We're still closed." Elmira sighed, but Farzan ignored her and let Arya in. It was pouring outside, their first proper fall thunderstorm, and raindrops dotted Arya's bald head. He never bothered with an umbrella.

"Hey. Thanks," Arya said, pulling Farzan into a very wet one-armed hug. "How goes the peaceful transfer of power?"

Farzan snorted. "Oh, you know."

"That well, huh?"

"You've met my parents, right?"

Arya arched his eyebrows. "Mm-hmm."

Arya's parents were a lot, too, or at least they used to be. They'd mellowed some, since Arya had been smart with his finances and became a partner in his event planning company. Now they were proud parents of a business owner.

It probably helped that Arya was the baby of the family, not the eldest.

"By the way, what are you doing Monday?"

"Huh?" Farzan was used to Arya's rapid changing of topics, but sometimes his mouth needed a moment to catch up to his brain.

"Monday night. You free?"

Technically, Mondays were when he was supposed to meet up with David. For study sessions. And possible *de-stressing*.

But David had texted asking if they could postpone this week's, due to a prior commitment, which Farzan tried very hard not to read too much into.

"What's with that look?"

"What look?"

"You've got this look, like…" Arya gestured. "Like someone burned your tahdig."

Farzan rolled his eyes. He never burned his tahdig.

"If you've got something going on, I won't be offended."

"I don't!" Farzan said. "I was supposed to, but it got canceled."

Arya raised an eyebrow.

"What, exactly, got canceled?"

"Nothing." Farzan stepped back.

Just because tiny devil Arya on his shoulder gave him advice, that didn't mean he needed real Arya knowing about his situationship with David.

But Arya stepped closer, eyes fixed on Farzan's. His whole face lit up with glee.

"Oh my god, you got some more dick, didn't you?"

"Dude…" Farzan glanced behind him, but they were alone in the front of house, Elmira having returned to the kitchen. Still, he didn't exactly want to talk about getting dick while at work. Especially if his now-employees could hear. His ears burned. "Keep it down, would you?"

Arya waved him off. "Was it Wine Bae?"

"We're not calling him that."

Fuck. That wasn't a *no*.

Arya gasped, his eyes widening comically. "Oh my god, it was, wasn't it?"

Farzan groaned but nodded. "He's helping me learn about the restaurant business. And I'm helping him study for his test."

"Plus you're fucking."

"We're trying out a friends-with-benefits thing."

"Huh." Arya's smile faded. He cocked his head to the side, staring into the middle distance.

Farzan expected Arya to be happy for him. He constantly extolled the virtues of a regular influx of Vitamin D. As if to punctuate that, Arya's phone chose that moment to emit the telltale sound of a Grindr notification.

But Arya ignored it and looked back to Farzan.

"You don't usually do casual."

"So? I'm trying something new."

"I just don't want you to get hurt."

"Thanks. But I'm a grown-ass man. I'll be okay. And besides..."

"Besides what?"

Farzan cracked a wicked grin. "The dick is good."

Arya's smile came back so strong, Farzan thought the sun had come out.

"Well, good, then. So. Monday?"

"What exactly are you asking me to do?"

"Nothing unseemly," Arya said, clutching imaginary pearls. "I got some tickets to the opening of the Nelson's new exhibit. You know we did that gala for them last month?"

Farzan nodded.

"Well, I got VIP passes as a thank-you gift. Want to come with?"

"Sure."

"Great. I'll text you the ticket." Arya's phone went off, a calendar alert instead of another Grindr bleep. "Fuck, I've got a client meeting. See you soon. Love you, dude."

Arya pulled Farzan into a hug, then bolted out the door, hunching against the rain. But then he ran back inside to grab the thermos he'd left on the table.

"Need this," he muttered. "And hey. I've got your back."

"Thanks."

The word was barely out before Arya was back in the rain, ducking into his car and pulling away.

Farzan shook his head. Arya was ridiculous, but he wasn't wrong. Farzan hadn't done casual before. But he could learn. This was a temporary situation, and once David moved away—and Farzan was more firmly settled at the restaurant—he'd get back out there and date for real. Find a partner.

Show his family who he really was.

nineteen

David

> **David**
> Where are you???

David paced outside the Nelson-Atkins gift shop, footsteps echoing off the slick gray concrete. The lobby was long and narrow, connecting the parking garage below to the Bloch Building at the far end. A set of marble stairs, which used to open onto the eastern lawn, now led up into the Nelson-Atkins building itself. David had only the vaguest memories of visiting the museum as a child, before the addition. Mostly he remembered the giant shuttlecocks outside.

David's phone buzzed. Finally. He swiped past the group chat—a few friends (and a dozen not-really-friends) from the Chicago restaurant scene he kept on mute because he legitimately only cared about two of the people in it—and pulled up Kyra's message.

> **Kyra**
> I'm so so sorry
> Family emergency

> My mom broke her tailbone!!
> DOING ZUMBA ☉
> I'll email you the tix, you can still go
> without me!
> sorry sorry

Fuck, that sucked. David's stomach gave an uncomfortable twinge as he imagined his own mom breaking a tailbone. Granted, his mom would no doubt walk it off, dust herself off, and still be at work at six the next morning. David could barely remember his mother even taking a sick day. Or his father, for that matter. Both of them had spent their whole lives showing David the value of hard work.

He'd had grand plans of buying them each a house—a mansion, even—with maids and butlers and whatever fancy shit they wanted. Plans he'd had to modify when he'd realized he couldn't keep going to a high-paying job that made him miserable. He wasn't hurting now by any means—he more than took care of himself—but he wanted to take care of them, too, the way they'd always taken care of him.

Like he'd told Farzan, that would be way easier on a salary from somewhere like Le Bernardin. Which is why he was studying so hard.

Shit. He'd only agreed to this museum thing to prove to Kyra (and Jeri) that he had a social life. But with no witnesses, he might as well head home, dive into his flash cards, maybe—

"David?"

David shook himself. "Farzan?"

"Hey." Farzan smiled, and David's stomach gave a different kind of twinge. He knew they were keeping things casual, but that hadn't stopped him being a little disappointed when he realized he had to take a raincheck tonight.

But now here Farzan was. Looking absolutely stunning in a black sweater with a V-neck that gave just a hint of chest hair, and dark-wash jeans that looked dressy yet also showed off his thighs and ass.

David snapped his mouth shut. He hoped he hadn't drooled. But *damn.*

"Fancy seeing you here," David finally managed, sounding totally awkward. He tried again. "If I'd known you were coming to this, too, I wouldn't have felt so guilty about canceling tonight."

He mentally kicked himself. Like that was any better.

"You look nice."

Farzan's eyes crinkled up.

There. Third time was the charm.

"You too." Farzan looked David up and down.

David had opted for charcoal dress pants, a hunter-green sport coat, and a white button-up with soft pink pinstripes. And though the lobby was cool, he felt Farzan's gaze like a heat beam.

"Thanks. So you got tickets to this, too?"

"Yeah. Arya—one of my best friends—did some work for the museum a while back, so he got tickets. He said he'd meet me by the gift shop." Farzan pulled up his phone and frowned. "Aaaaand he just texted me that he can't make it. Some sort of floral arrangement emergency."

David laughed, and the air between them didn't seem so thick anymore. "Floral arrangement emergency? Is that a thing?"

Farzan turned his phone so David could see. Sure enough:

> **Arya**
>
> Dude I'm so sorry, I got a call from
> Bitch
> *Mitchell omggggg
> There's a floral arrangement emergency
> I need to take care of
> Convention Center . . . could be hours
> Sorry dude. Go without me!
> There should be free champagne!!!!

"Your friend must lead an interesting life."

Farzan smiled, deepening the lines around his eyes. David couldn't help smiling back.

"He certainly tries to. Ramin—that's my other best friend—he's always been the calm one. Arya's the adventurous one. Last year he even got me to sign up for this queer kickball league. We're in the championships and everything!"

"That is... extremely random." David hadn't played kickball since fifth-grade recess. The thought of adults playing it was utterly ridiculous.

Then again, the thought of Farzan in some cute athletic shorts, his strong ass stretching the fabric, sweat glistening on that little patch of skin at the base of his spine... Did Farzan wear compression shorts? A jock?

David shivered the thought away.

Farzan blushed a bit. "I guess so."

"But it sounds fun."

"You know what? It weirdly is." Farzan cleared his throat and gestured up the lobby. "Anyway, I guess I should... I mean, you waiting for someone?"

"Nope. My friend bailed on me too."

"Oh. Sorry."

"Eh, it's fine..." David was about to suggest, since they'd both been bailed on, they head back to his place. But before he could:

"You want to look around some, then?"

He shouldn't. He should go home. Study.

Farzan gave him a sly grin. "You can practice your tasting skills on the free Champagne."

David laughed. "Now how can I resist an offer like that?"

"Damn, your friend got you the fancy tickets." David raised his flute.

"To Arya," Farzan said. "And yeah, I guess they were VIPs or something?"

David clinked and took a sip—pretty decent, though now that he tasted, it was definitely California sparkling wine, not Champagne. It

was good, though. He took another sip. Nicely crisp, but with a little but-tery hint from some malolactic fermentation. Fresh apple, warm bread...
"Schramsberg. Blanc de Blancs."

Farzan ran back to the bar, peeked over the counter, and gave David a thumbs-up.

Nailed it.

Farzan wound his way back, and they found a spot toward one of the corners of Rozelle Court, the enclosed atrium in the center of the Nelson. It was an acoustic nightmare: pink marble floors, columns, a gallery on the floor above, and a glass ceiling over the whole thing. David could barely hear Farzan over all the mingling people.

"I can't even think in here," Farzan said, draining his wine and then covering his mouth; his cheeks puffed out like a chipmunk as he stifled a burp. David nearly snorted out his own wine.

"Same." They dropped their empty flutes on one of the trays carried by circulating waiters, then made their escape, into a quieter hallway lined with statues.

"Where is the exhibit, anyway?"

Farzan pulled up his phone again, brow furrowing. David wanted to smooth out the little tense spot with his thumb.

Wow, that wine had hit him fast. He wasn't a face-massage kind of guy, even if Farzan's face was empirically beautiful, his lips pursed in thought...

"Don't be mad."

"What?" David shook himself. "Why would I be mad?"

"I read the ticket wrong. The reception was up here. The exhibit is in the Bloch Building. Back the way we came."

David just laughed. "Hey, we're VIPs, we've got to get some wine before we take in the art."

David led the way back to the lobby. When he sidestepped an older couple headed toward the reception, his hand brushed Farzan's. Some silly part of him—some primal instinct, maybe—told him to link his hand with Farzan's. But they weren't on a date. They were friends, looking at art.

He stuffed his hands into his pockets. He needed to get the night on safer footing.

"So how's things at the bistro?"

Farzan groaned.

"That bad?"

"No, they're fine, just... I get that I've got a lot to learn, but I'm not a child, you know? It's not like I don't know anything. But my dad won't let me work in the kitchen without hovering over my shoulder, asking if I'm sure I salted the kabob enough, or do I really think that the tahdig is done."

"Too many chefs in the kitchen, huh?"

"And my mom's even worse. Like, the washer—the laundry washer, not the dish washer—was leaking, and when I called a plumber to come fix it, she made me wait until she'd tried to fix it herself. And she ended up breaking it worse!"

David knew Farzan was frustrated, and it wasn't funny, but also, it really was. He tried to stifle his laugh, but it came out anyway.

Farzan shot him a sideways glance, trying to frown, but he ended up laughing too.

"God. Is it always gonna be like this?"

"Nah. Some days, it'll be worse."

Farzan groaned. "Maybe this was a mistake. Maybe my parents were right."

"Hey." David pulled his hand out of his pocket to grab Farzan by the elbow. "You've got this. You're an amazing cook. You're going to run an amazing restaurant."

"Thanks."

"Seriously. That celery stew you brought? I had it for lunch like the next three days. It only got better."

Farzan's eyes twinkled, and he seemed to relax. "Really?"

"Really."

"Well, I'll start thinking what to make for next time."

David's mouth watered at the thought. Still: "Just remember, we're not eating first."

He was pleased to see Farzan's cheeks darken. "I remember. Fucking first, then food."

twenty

Farzan

"T hat was amazing."

"It really was."

"Seriously, I've only ever seen pictures, but seeing them up close? I mean, you can read they're thirty feet wide, but then you see them and it's like, wow."

Farzan loved seeing David so enthusiastic. As they'd gone through the exhibit, David had stopped in front of nearly every piece, taking them in, getting as close as he could without setting off the little alarms.

(One time he even did set off an alarm—apparently he'd leaned too far forward and tripped a sensor—and a docent came over to warn him off.)

Farzan didn't have much of a head for art. That was more Ramin's thing. Ramin would've loved this. Arya, too; it sucked that Arya was stuck doing floral arrangements.

But still. It had been a nice surprise, this friend date with David. Chatting and admiring the paintings. Or sometimes just walking quietly next to each other. It wasn't weird; it was comfortable.

"What're you smiling at?" David asked as they joined the tide of people headed for the parking garage.

"Hm?" Farzan schooled his face. He hadn't realized he'd been smiling. But it was hard not to when he had that filled-up, floaty sort of feeling that he'd only ever got with Arya and Ramin before, whether they were crammed onto a couch watching a movie or shouting at a video game or laughing over mozzarella sticks. "I was just thinking. This is the kind of thing real friends do."

"I guess it is, huh?" David dropped a warm, relaxed smile his way. "I can't remember the last time I went and did something with my friends."

"Really?" David didn't seem like the kind of guy that had trouble making friends. Honestly, with a smile like that, Farzan couldn't imagine anyone *not* wanting to be David's friend. Clamoring for it, even.

"Yeah. I had a couple close friends back in Chicago, but most of the folks I knew were, as the French say, *toxique.*"

Farzan raised an eyebrow. David's accent was atrocious. "They say that, do they?"

"Of course." He waved his hand. "It was mostly finance bros. They're the worst."

Farzan could believe that.

"And what about here? Any friends *sans* benefits?"

"Not really." David shrugged. "I've been busy."

He said it lightly, like it didn't bother him. But there was something in his jaw, like he was trying too hard to keep his face neutral.

It made Farzan's heart ache, just a little, and he let his hand brush against David's for a bit of warm comfort. He'd be lost without his friends. Maybe David needed tonight more than he let on.

"Hm. Me and Ramin and Arya have dinner once a week. That's like... our BFF time. And I see Arya at the kickball games. Ramin comes sometimes, too, just to watch. His boyfriend is on our team, too."

"Oh yeah? Do you have uniforms and everything? With cute little shorts?" He waggled his eyebrows.

Farzan shook his head, fighting off a smile. "Wouldn't you like to know?"

"I might have to come to one of these games, then."

That... actually sounded kind of fun. "You should."

David waved him off, his voice light. "Nah, I don't want to cramp your style."

"You won't. It would be fun." Farzan held the door for David.

The parking garage was directly beneath a glass-bottomed fountain; rippling light danced across David's features.

"Seriously," Farzan continued. "You should come to one. We can add that to the benefits package."

"Kickball games?" David teased.

"No. Hanging out. As friends."

David's lips pressed into a flat line. Farzan wondered if he'd pressed too far. They'd only really agreed to help each other professionally. And sexually.

Nothing about just... hanging out.

The thing was, Farzan *liked* hanging out with David. He couldn't remember the last time he'd had this much fun. But David didn't want that. Of course he didn't. He'd made his goals clear: Study for his test. Have sex to relax.

Get the hell out of Kansas City and chase his dreams.

Farzan's armpits felt damp. He'd fucked everything up. Again. He'd asked for more than David was willing to give, and now everything was going to go up in flames.

But before Farzan could apologize and say never mind, David's lips relaxed into a smile.

"That sounds good."

Farzan kept his mouth shut and just nodded. If he said something, he was liable to ruin the moment.

He followed David until he stopped next to a slick black BMW.

"Well. This is me."

Farzan was glad they hadn't spotted his car first. Then again, David might've already seen his beat-up Honda when he drove to David's house to study. And get a handjob.

"See you, then?" Farzan asked.

"Yeah. See you."

But David didn't move to unlock his car.

Farzan's armpits felt wet now.

"This was nice," David said. "I'm glad I ran into you."

"Me too." Farzan's heart was hammering. How did friends say good night? If this was Arya and Ramin, they would've just waved at the entrance and split to find their cars. Or they would've carpooled together, in which case they'd have piled into whoever's car and headed to someone's house to split a bottle of wine and chill before calling it a night.

But then again, Farzan had never had sex with Arya or Ramin.

Farzan realized he was staring at David's lips. He looked up—

But David was staring at his, too. In the weird parking garage light, his rich brown eyes turned nearly black, shining like wet ink on fresh paper. And then David caught him staring. He smiled, but it was a small, tentative thing.

Farzan swallowed. His tongue felt too big.

"So." He swallowed again.

The car behind him beeped, the doors unlocking. Farzan automatically stepped closer to David, which pressed him up against the door of his car.

"So?" David asked, drawing the word out.

"So. Do friends kiss each other good night?"

David's smile widened. "Pretty sure that's one of the benefits."

So Farzan leaned in, grazing David's lips at first, feeling the soft stubble that surrounded them, before claiming them more firmly. He leaned in, pressing David back against his car, his hips suddenly pressed against David's, the heat between his legs noticeable even in the chill night air.

David's lips parted to let Farzan in, and he tasted like Champagne, and raspberries, and desire. Then David pressed back, angling his head, and suddenly it was David's tongue that led the dance, teasing first sweetly then aggressively, like he wanted Farzan to go down on him again right there, in the middle of the parking garage.

Farzan's skin was on fire, his heart hammering, but he couldn't stop kissing, couldn't get enough of David. That soft, familiar scent enveloped him, vetiver and skin and sweat.

Farzan was getting hard in his pants, could feel David's cock filling out too. Farzan surged forward once more, using his hands to pin David's wrists against the car's windows. He never wanted the kiss to end.

A sudden honk startled Farzan.

Fuck. The car next to them was waiting to pull out, the twenty-something yuppies inside looking scandalized.

Farzan gave a little wave, and he and David moved so they could leave.

David chuckled, his face lit red by the retreating taillights.

"I've got an early day tomorrow," he said, voice gravelly. "I better say good night."

"Yeah." Farzan's own voice felt rough. "Good night."

But before he could move, David leaned in one last time, planting a soft, lingering kiss that sent a wave of exhilaration down Farzan's spine.

Benefits, indeed.

David pulled back and smiled. "Drive home safe."

"Yeah." Farzan cleared his throat. "You too."

On Friday, to Farzan's surprise, his parents didn't come into the restaurant. His dad had texted him that morning.

Firouz
You can handle it

Farzan was stunned but pleased by the vote of confidence.

Firouz
Plus your mom has an appointment

There it was.

Farzan
Give her my love
Hope it goes well.

Shiraz Bistro was quiet in the early hours before service, when it was only Farzan and the kitchen staff in to prep. Sheena was cleaning and trimming produce, Spencer was marinating kabob for the grill, and Chase was rinsing the rice.

Farzan was surprised—pleasantly so—by the staff his parents had assembled in the kitchen. Sheena was Iranian, the daughter of a friend of a friend, and Elmira was Iranian too, though Farzan didn't think their families knew each other. But Chase was a Black guy who'd just graduated high school and was a wizard with tahdig, and Spencer was white and nonbinary, and his parents hadn't even batted an eye.

"In Farsi we don't even have gendered pronouns," Persis had said airily after mentioning Spencer, who used they/them pronouns, to Farzan. "I don't know why it's such a big deal."

Granted, Farzan's parents had handled his own coming out with barely a shrug.

"We love you no matter what," his dad had said, even though Farzan had grown up hearing both his parents make homophobic jokes from time to time. Granted, he'd grown up in the nineties, when everyone had made homophobic jokes all the time. Hell, Farzan and Ramin and Arya had made more than their share, and look how they ended up.

Farzan had never really doubted his parents would accept him. But he had just graduated college and was about to start his teaching career, and no matter what, he hadn't been able to get that *what if?* out of his mind.

But *what if?* hadn't happened. His parents loved him, and they loved Arya and Ramin just as fiercely. Maybe even more fiercely—though all three of them had, over the years, had to field the occasional "Are you *sure* you're not dating?" from one parent or another.

Arya and Ramin were both handsome guys, but *gross*. They were more than Farzan's friends, they were his brothers. In some ways, even more than Navid.

Farzan gave the kitchen a once-over: everything was going fine. He grabbed the spices he needed off the rack and retreated to his mom's office. No, not his mom's. It was his office now. Most of the mess had been sorted into two huge filing cabinets Farzan had stuffed into a corner. There were still family photos all over the place, but now there were photos of Farzan and his friends, too. In a place of pride next to the door, there was a photo of Farzan's parents, Arya's parents, and Ramin's parents, taken back in middle school, before Ramin's mom had died. It was a jolt to realize the smiling parents in the photo had been only a few years older than Farzan was now.

Fuck.

Farzan put on some music, pulled the spice grinder from the desk drawer, and got to work. Advieh—Persian spice mix—was essential to most Persian cooking, and the Alavi family recipe was a closely guarded secret. Farzan's father made his advieh the same way he'd been shown by his mother, Farzan's grandmother Safa.

Safa had insisted it never be written down, only transmitted orally, because she was afraid her sister would steal the recipe.

The advieh was a mix of cumin, fenugreek, cardamom, white pepper, dried rose petal, dried Persian lime, nigella, and golpar, though Farzan went a little lighter on the white pepper than his father, and a little heavier on the dried lime. Farzan ground the spices one by one, using a rolled-up sheet of paper from the old laser printer as a funnel to get them into the jar without spilling. The fragrance of each spice permeated the office; Farzan sneezed a few times as he added the white pepper.

The sweet fenugreek, on the other hand, made him think of David, of the khoresh karafs he'd made, of the sex that had followed after. And that made him think of the museum, of the kiss they shared, the few texts they'd exchanged, plans to meet up again Monday, and *nope*, Farzan absolutely could not daydream himself to an erection right now. Not on the job.

When he was done grinding, Farzan sealed the jar and shook it to mix the advieh. As he did, Spencer popped their head in. They had medium-length brown hair that was shaved on one side, and a small septum piercing that gave their round face a bit of character. "Hey, Farzan? Your sister's here."

"Thanks, Spence. Can you send her back?"

Farzan cleaned off his desk and tucked the spice grinder away as Maheen stepped in.

No one could look at Farzan and Maheen together and not see the resemblance. They had the exact same nose, though Farzan's was a tiny bit larger, the same rich brown eyes, the same warm sepia skin, the same full eyebrows, though Maheen's were a bit thinner from all the plucking she'd done when she was a teenager.

"Hey," Farzan said, standing to pull his sister into a hug. She was a full head shorter than him, something she'd complained about when they were teens. She had dreamed of playing competitive volleyball, but no one in the Alavi family had ever surpassed six feet tall.

"Hey. It smells good in here."

"Making advieh."

"Mm." Maheen eyed the jar hungrily. She was a decent enough cook, but not on Farzan's level: partially from lack of interest and partially from lack of patience. Maheen would rather microwave something than wait for it to stew on the stove. "So how's it going?"

Farzan swept his eyes across the office, and past the door, out into the kitchen, where everyone was quietly humming along, with Taylor Swift (Chase's choice) as their prep music for the day. Once the restaurant actually opened, they'd switch to Iranian music. Googoosh was on heavy rotation at Shiraz Bistro.

"Going okay," Farzan said, honestly. Thanks to David's advice, the payroll had gone off without a hitch, and the kitchen was working smoothly, and he'd only freaked out a few times, never with any witnesses.

He'd even been able to take joy in the time spent at the grill, or over the stove, seasoning a khoresh until it was just right.

So yeah. Going okay.

"What're you doing here?"

"I need an excuse to visit my favorite brother?"

Farzan snorted. That was patently false. Maheen and Navid were notorious for ganging up on him.

Maheen blushed. "Fine. I wanted to...I don't know...see the place. It's part of our family history, yeah?"

"Yeah."

"I'm glad you took it over. I wanted to, but me and Tomás just couldn't."

Farzan didn't blame his sister. Maheen would rather cut off her arm than give up her work as an OB/GYN. It filled her soul, and Farzan was glad for it. Maheen loved helping people, and Farzan loved that about her.

"But the thought of this place being gone..." Maheen shook her head. "Well. I'm grateful. But not surprised. You always take care of everyone."

"Nah..." Farzan scratched the back of his neck, where it was starting to heat up. He loved his little sister with all his heart, but the two of them didn't do earnest very often.

"Oh, come on. Like I don't remember what it was like growing up."

With their mom and dad busy at the restaurant, Farzan had been the de facto babysitter most nights once he was old enough—that being twelve years old—to take care of ten-year-old Maheen and seven-year-old Navid.

"You're always taking care of other people."

Farzan just shrugged. Yeah, he did like taking care of people. That's why he'd wanted to be a teacher. Watching his students grow, watching the little synapses firing behind their eyes as they made new connections, had filled his soul the way being a doctor filled Maheen's.

Or at least it had, until one day he'd woken up and dreaded going into work. Had felt an ache deep inside, like someone had scraped him out and poked holes in his soul until everything in it had leaked out all over the parquet floors of his rent-controlled apartment.

And that's why Farzan loved cooking so much, too. He lived for that look people got on their faces when they tasted something familiar, something that unlocked a memory. Like that scene in *Ratatouille* where the guy literally flashed back to his childhood from one bite of vegetables.

But now, taking care of people didn't just mean cooking. It meant taking care of the whole staff: managing schedules, and salaries, and benefits, and training. He did his best not to let that weigh on him every time he pondered an expense or signed a check.

"Besides," Maheen said, studying the photos all around him. "It's about time you finally found something stable to do. You can't keep subbing forever."

That stung. Maheen might've grown up in the United States, but she was a master of that Iranian classic: the backhanded compliment.

Maheen had known what career she wanted to pursue when she was sixteen years old. Had gotten straight A's in high school and a partial scholarship to KU, and now she owned her own practice. Farzan had just bounced from job to job after burning out on teaching.

He sighed. It wasn't Maheen's fault he was such a fuckup, but given how grateful she claimed to be, maybe she could've laid off the passive-aggressive digs a bit.

"Yeah. Well." Farzan gestured around his office. "I better get back to work. You want to hang around? Grab some tea?"

"I've got to get home. Just wanted to see you." She gestured to the office walls. "It looks good in here, Farzan. It looks like you."

"Thanks."

Farzan let Maheen pull him into another hug.

At the end of the day, he loved his sister, backhanded compliments and all.

"Love you."

twenty-one

David

"You've got twenty-five minutes," Jeri said, peering at David through a gap in the row of six wineglasses. "The clock starts when you touch your first wine."

She winked at him.

"Good luck."

David nodded. He shouldn't need luck, not with the way he'd been studying. Not with all the practice tastings.

The row of wines sat between him and Jeri: three whites, three reds, all in Bordeaux-style glasses. He took a deep breath: his sinuses felt clear. He'd spent a few minutes inhaling the steam off the espresso machine at the bar, and then sniffing coffee beans, to prep his palate. He reached for the first wine, and Jeri tapped her phone to start the timer.

Six wines in twenty-five minutes meant four minutes and ten seconds per wine. Ideally he'd be below four for most of them, that way if he went over on one, he'd still be good. He visualized the tasting grid in his head: clarity, brightness, intensity, color. Fruit, flowers/herbs, earths, oaks. Body, acidity, alcohol, tannin. Quality and climate. Grape, blend, country, region. Producer. Vintage.

He blocked out the sounds of pre-service prep, the tinkling of silverware, the rhythm of knives on chopping blocks, the clattering of plates being stacked. There was only him, the wines, and the clock.

He made his way down the line, confident in three, certain in two, but the last one was a challenge. The clock had to be winding down.

"Syrah, Grenache. Hm." There was something else there, something he couldn't put his tongue on. "France? No. Hm." He sipped again, spat. "This has Carignan, too. Spain. Oh." David grinned. He knew what it was. "Montsant. Can Blau. 2020."

Jeri tapped her phone; David leaned in to see he had two seconds left.

"Damn, I thought I'd stumped you with that one," she said. "Six out of six."

David beamed. "You almost did. After all the others, I wasn't expecting table wine."

"Hey, you never know. They could be tasting critter wines. Or Malbecs from the grocery store. Hell, even Boone's Farm. Be prepared for anything."

David chuckled. He hadn't tasted Boone's Farm since his college days.

"All right. Thanks, Jeri."

"Sure thing."

David took one last taste of the Can Blau, closed his eyes and tried to commit it to memory. There were so many wines in the world; he'd got all six right this time, but it was the test that mattered.

"So," Jeri said, emptying the other glasses into the spit bucket. Taking a page from David's book, she too had stuck a photo of Ronald Reagan at the bottom. "How was the museum? You and Kyra went, right?"

"No, Kyra bailed on me."

"Oh, because of her mom?"

David nodded.

"Boo. So what'd you do? Head straight back home and bury yourself in a pile of note cards?"

David arched an eyebrow. Maybe he deserved that, for the way he'd been in the past, but he was actually taking her advice for once. He deserved a little credit.

"For your information, I stayed and saw the exhibits. My friend Farzan was there too."

"Farzan? Like, Fake-Frank Farzan?" Jeri's eyes widened behind her glasses.

"Don't call him that," David said automatically. Technically he *was* Fake Frank, but if Farzan was going to have a nickname, that wasn't going to be it. David wasn't even sure why it bothered him, Jeri making fun of him that way. David had been the one to mix things up, not Farzan. "Anyway, we saw the exhibit, chatted some. It was fun."

Jeri blinked at him. "Who are you and what have you done with David Curtis?"

David rolled his eyes. "Despite what you think, I am, in fact, a grown-ass man capable of making my own friends. And having fun. So."

"I'm glad. You work too hard."

David waved her off.

"You do. I love that about you. But you deserve to have fun too." She waggled her eyebrows. "Just how much *fun* did you have anyway?" She drew the word *fun* out like an aged cork.

"I'm reporting you to HR."

It was an empty threat—like Aspire had an HR department—and Jeri just laughed.

"I'm happy for you, David. Really." She patted her thighs and stood. "Now come on, we'd better get prepping."

It was nearly one in the morning when David pulled into his driveway. A light drizzle coated his windshield as he parked in the little detached garage, cooled his face as he let himself into the house, carrying a case of wine. They were all wrapped in brown paper bags so he could blind taste them by himself, but as he set the box on the kitchen counter and flicked on the lights, he felt unsettled.

It had been a stressful service—two bridal showers and one rehearsal dinner, all for straight white people with the kind of money that conversely meant they tipped poorly. Thank god Jeri paid the staff fairly instead of doing the usual restaurant sub–minimum wage bullshit.

David wasn't angry, but he was annoyed. His skin felt too tight. He was too keyed up.

Usually he'd have a glass of wine before bed, to unwind and chill, but he found himself weirdly wishing Farzan was around. To talk to, share a glass with. Not even to *de-stress*, though that might've been fun. But he just . . . honestly liked Farzan.

Jeri had been right. His mom had been right. Kyra could never know, but she'd been right. He did need a friend. And now that he had one, it made the empty house feel that much emptier.

But whatever. He'd been on his own long enough; he could survive. And Farzan was only temporary, anyway.

David put on some music and took a long shower, let the water pound on his tight shoulders. Maybe he was just horny. He'd had fun with Farzan at the museum, but it had been sex-free fun. Well, not counting the kiss that nearly made him come in his pants.

David had plenty of toys, lots of imagination, and all the porn in the world. He didn't lack for gratification. But kissing was something he'd missed. And Farzan was a fucking good kisser.

He got half-hard as he washed his balls and skinned himself back to clean his dick, closing his eyes to enjoy the sensations, thinking of Farzan. But before he could take care of himself, his music cut out. Someone was calling.

"Fuck," he muttered, wrapping a towel around himself and grabbing the phone. It was Rhett, one of the few friends from Chicago he still talked to. Rhett had worked with David at Millennium, the pretentious lakefront steakhouse David had been at before he moved back to KC.

David tightened the towel around his waist and answered the FaceTime.

"Why are you all wet?" Rhett immediately asked. "Are you naked?"

"I was in the shower," David said. "You know what time it is, right?"

"Fuck, I forgot," Rhett said. "It's not even midnight here yet."

"Where's 'here'?" David asked, swiping water off his forehead with the back of his hand. Obviously not Chicago.

"Los Angeles, baby!" Rhett held the phone out and spun to show off his digs, but it was just an apartment like any other, hardwood floors, white walls, minimalist IKEA furniture, black curtains over the windows.

"What're you doing in LA?" David put his phone down so it faced the ceiling while he dried himself off, slipped on a pair of sweats, and flopped onto the couch.

"If you ever answered the group chat, you'd already know." Rhett raised his bright-red eyebrows at David. Rhett was probably the whitest guy David knew: ivory-skinned, freckled, with a button nose, square chin, and red hair.

"Sorry. I've been busy." And also, he had too much self-respect to wade through all the bullshit that happened in that group chat. Most of them were still in their twenties. David missed his six-pack, but he didn't miss all the drama that went along with it. "So what's the deal?"

Rhett grinned broadly, bringing the phone closer to his face and treating David to an oh-so-flattering up-the-nose view. "Guess who's gonna be GM for Shyla Thorne's new restaurant?"

David's jaw dropped. "Seriously?"

"Seriously!"

"Fuck! Congrats, man. That's amazing."

Shyla Thorne was a trans woman who'd catapulted to fame after a surprise victory in last year's *Top Chef*. David didn't realize she was already opening a new restaurant.

"Yeah, Shyla's amazing. She wants to hire an all-queer staff."

In which case, she couldn't have found a better GM than Rhett, a trans man who was probably the most competent assistant manager David had ever worked with.

"Which brings me to you."

"Me?" David quirked an eyebrow. "What about me?"

"Well, we'll need someone to lead our wine program, and rumor has it you're gonna be a master somm in a few months. And by rumor, I mean your constant reminders that you're too busy studying to join us for monthly game night."

It was true: David had missed all but one of them since moving; his PlayStation was covered in so much dust, David could have written his name on it with a finger.

"I can neither confirm nor deny," David said, but yeah, he was going to be one by the new year. As long as he passed. "Wait. Are you..."

David's heart nearly launched itself out his mouth.

"Are you offering me a job?"

"Fuck yeah I am." Rhett's face turned serious. "Even if you don't pass, I still want you on board, but if you pass I can get you a way better salary."

David whistled. He'd been expecting offers to come in once he passed, but not before. And the chance to lead the wine program at a new restaurant—in LA, no less—well, that was the kind of opportunity he couldn't pass up.

"Fuck yeah, man. I'm in."

This was it. Things were finally happening. And he hadn't even taken his test yet!

He'd have to tell his mom and dad. And Jeri, of course, so she could start thinking about replacements. And Farzan—

David felt a weird twinge at the thought of telling Farzan. But surely by January Farzan would be in good shape running his restaurant. And as for their situationship, well, David had made it clear from the start that there would be a time limit.

Plus he'd have access to dick aplenty in LA.

Though he'd miss Farzan's smile, and his silky hair, and the way his eyes lit up when he was excited, and the smooth confidence he exuded in the kitchen, and why the fuck was he fixating on Farzan right now? In the middle of the most important phone call of his life?

"Okay, great," Rhett said. "I've got some stuff to sort out on my end still, and we don't actually open until spring, but I'll keep you posted, yeah?"

"Sounds great. Thanks, man. Really."

"You can thank me by answering the damned group chat once in a while. Otherwise I might just show up on your doorstep one day to make sure you're alive."

"Okay, okay." David yawned ostentatiously. He really did need to get some sleep.

"Oh my god, you faker," Rhett said. "I'm hanging up. Bye."

"Bye."

David let his phone drop into the valley of his chest and stared at his feet, wiggling his toes. Holy fuck.

Holy fuck!

He leapt off the couch, sending his phone tumbling, did a quick happy dance he was grateful no one was around to see.

It was happening. It was really happening.

His dreams were finally coming true.

twenty-two

Farzan

And if you'll just sign here..."

Farzan nodded and added his signature to the contract.

One good thing about being Iranian: you knew plenty of lawyers, even if your firstborn son didn't end up being one.

Reza was about five years older than Farzan. They'd been friends in the sense that their parents had known each other back when there weren't as many Iranian families in town, and so they'd been forced into friendship through sheer lack of options. Farzan had vague but happy memories of being seven years old and terminally impressed with Reza's Power Rangers collection.

Along with memories of being terminally impressed with the boys in the *Power Rangers* show, who had definitely captured Farzan's attention in a way he wouldn't understand for years.

"Great." Reza grabbed the pages of the contract, straightened them out against the desk, and slipped them into a folder. A gold wedding band shone brightly against his brown skin. Farzan's family didn't really hang out with the Abbasis anymore—they lived out in Lenexa now—but Farzan had attended Reza's wedding five or six years ago.

"You're next!" Everyone kept telling him, but of course Maheen had beaten Farzan to it, and now Navid was going to as well.

"You're all set. I guess congratulations are in order?" Reza extended his hand; Farzan gave it a firm shake.

It was official. He owned Shiraz Bistro now.

The business, not the building: his parents still owned that, and the bistro would be paying them rent, which would supplement their retirement. It wasn't exactly ideal, but it was the only solution that really made sense. It wasn't like Farzan had money floating around to just buy a building.

Well, half a building, the part with Shiraz Bistro. The other half of the building was owned by the Trans, who'd been running their nail salon even longer than Shiraz Bistro had been around. The Trans were friendly, and Farzan had fond memories of growing up exchanging pots of saffron rice and skewers of kabob for steaming pots of homemade pho around the holidays. Two immigrant families, celebrating that most American of traditions: ignoring the separation of church and state to take December 25 off.

Farzan shook himself when he realized his parents were still talking to Reza in Farsi.

"They haven't set a date yet, but we think some time in the summer," Persis was saying.

"Well, give him my congratulations," Reza said, gently leading them toward the door, no doubt hoping to avoid a lengthy Persian goodbye.

If anything, his parents' inherited Persian goodbyes had merged with their adopted Midwestern goodbyes into hours of taarofing.

"We will," Farzan said, in English, ushering his parents out the door, but Firouz planted his feet and turned.

"Oh, tell your mom and dad hi," he said, and Reza nodded. He caught Farzan's eye for the briefest of moments, and Farzan stifled a laugh. One glance into the lobby told Farzan that Reza did, in fact, have other clients he needed to see, ones that probably paid him in money instead of pots of khoresh and guilt trips. "Khodahafes!"

"Khodahafes!" Farzan said for his parents, gently guiding them out the lobby and toward the elevator.

"Reza's new office is nice," Persis said as the elevator dinged. He'd relocated his practice to a new building in Overland Park. "He's doing well for himself."

"Mm," Farzan agreed noncommittally. Thankfully he and his parents drove separately, so he wouldn't have to hear them praising Reza on the drive home.

He walked his parents to their car and paused.

"Well," he said. "It's official."

His mom pulled him into a tight hug, kissed him on his cheeks.

"You're sure this is what you want?" she asked.

It was a little late for that, but—

"I'm sure."

And he was sure, more sure than he'd been of anything in a long time.

He could do this. He could keep Shiraz Bistro going, could make it better than ever.

With David's help, but still.

"Proud of you, baba," Firouz said, clapping Farzan's shoulder. "You'll do great."

Farzan couldn't remember the last time he'd actually made his father proud. Warmth bubbled up in his chest, pushing away the nerves that had settled over him after signing the contract.

It was all on him now.

But his dad was finally proud of him. He intended to keep it that way.

The Costco parking lot was a zoo. Why had everyone decided to go to Costco at noon on a Friday?

Farzan's car was filled to the brim with paper towels, toilet paper, and soap. Of all the things his parents had neglected to mention about running the bistro—that one electrical outlet that constantly threw the breaker, the correct color of paint to touch up the walls, the need to occasionally bribe their produce guy with kabobs—the bathrooms had to be the most alarming. How could a restaurant with three unisex stalls go through so much toilet paper in a single week?

He grunted, leaning his weight on the trunk to get it to close. Well, at least that was done. Now he just had to do . . . about a dozen other things before service tonight. It was fine.

Except as soon as he dropped into his seat, his phone rang. Maheen was FaceTiming him.

"Hello?"

"Help. Me," Maheen said through gritted teeth.

"What's wrong?" Farzan's heart immediately lodged itself in his threat. "Are you okay?"

"I've bitten off more than I can chew." She flipped her camera to show her kitchen table, covered with flour and bowls of almonds and baking sheets. "Help."

"What are you trying to make?" Farzan asked, trying to get his hammering heart under control.

"I promised to bring qottab to Elaina's baby shower." Elaina was Tomás's eldest sister. "And it's tomorrow."

Farzan sighed. Qottab were time-consuming and, though he would never say it out loud, beyond Maheen's baking skills.

But his sister needed help.

"I'll be right there."

twenty-three

Farzan

Maheen and Tomás lived in a nice house out in Leawood, an over-priced suburb in Johnson County, Kansas. Farzan had never understood why his sister chose to cross State Line. The rest of the Alavis were all in Missouri.

He pulled up to the curb, shot off a text to Sheena to let her know he'd be late getting to the bistro, and let himself inside.

"Help. Me," Maheen repeated. She was seated at the table, her hands in a bowl of almonds soaking in water. As he watched, she picked an almond out and peeled off its skin.

Farzan stifled a laugh.

"You bought whole ones?"

"I thought it would be easier," she said, as Farzan kissed her cheek and took another seat.

"You know you can buy them already blanched and peeled?"

The set in Maheen's jaw told him that she did not, in fact, know that.

So Farzan reached for the bowl, dug out a handful, and started peeling. Some he could squeeze out of their skins easily; others he had to scratch at. His fingernails were going to be wrecked.

He and his sister worked in silence, except for the occasional splish of water as they dunked their hands into the bowl to grab more almonds. Growing up, Farzan had spent many mornings—usually before holidays or birthdays—with his dad, helping make qottab, little almond-filled pastries that were a Yazdi specialty. Then again, most desserts were Yazdi specialties. It was a time-consuming process, rolling out and cutting the dough, filling all the little half-moons and sealing them just right so they didn't explode while they baked. Or fried.

Good lord, was Maheen planning on frying them?

"You're not frying these, right?" Farzan asked.

"No," she sighed. "Tomás promised to divorce me if I burned the house down."

Farzan nodded. That was wise.

"But they're not as good baked," Maheen said wistfully. "Not like you and Baba made."

"These will still be good. How's your dough looking?"

Maheen nodded ruefully at the bag of flour standing open on the far side of the table, surrounded by a white field.

"Ah. You keep peeling. I'll get to work."

It was past seven when Farzan pulled the last batch of qottab from Maheen's stainless steel oven. As far as fancy suburban kitchens went, it was aesthetically pleasing, but also really impractical. Her refrigerator door wasn't even magnetic.

"Okay. You dust these, then you should be good to go. Just remember to put parchment paper between each layer when you store them."

"I will." Maheen pushed her hair off her flour-streaked forehead with the back of her hand. "Thank you so much. Really."

"Hey. What are big brothers for?"

Maheen pulled him into a hug. "Seriously, Farzan. Thank you."

"You're welcome." Farzan kissed his sister on the forehead. "You good?"

"I'm good. Yes. Are you going to be okay getting in late?"

Farzan shrugged. "I'm the boss. Can't exactly write myself up."

He just had to hope the last few rolls of toilet paper had held out. Or that someone had run to the Target across the street to get a few emergency rolls.

"Love you," she said, following him to the door. He slid on his shoes.

"Love you too."

Farzan tried to sleep in on Saturday. Thankfully there had been no bathroom disasters, but the kitchen had been working hard to make up for his absence, so he'd sent everyone home early and stayed late to take care of cleanup himself. It seemed only fair. He'd gotten home past two and promptly collapsed in his bed.

Only to be awakened at eight-o'-fucking-clock by his phone nearly buzzing itself off his nightstand. It was Arya.

Arya
SOS
dude!! emergency!!!
oh are you sleeping?
sorry, i forgot
Hey call me when you get this
it's kind of important
like right when you wake up, before you make tea
okay sleep well dude
CALL ME

Farzan rubbed his eyes. His mouth tasted like cotton. He hadn't had anything to drink last night, not even a glass of wine when he got home, but he still felt like he had a hangover.

A hangunder. That's what it was. A hangunder.

Better than calling it what it truly was: the footsteps of his forties creeping steadily nearer.

Farzan wasn't actually too bothered by getting older. When he thought of all his queer elders who didn't survive to old age, he reminded himself that every day wasn't just a gift but a victory. Still, he wouldn't mind if his knees popped a bit less, or he woke up without feeling like a dried-out washcloth.

He pulled on a tank and shorts and chugged a glass of water before finally FaceTiming Arya.

"Hey. Hope I didn't wake you."

Farzan snorted. "You didn't. My phone buzzing twelve million times did."

"Good. Listen, we've got a situation." Arya sipped his mug of herbal tea—he never drank caffeine—and blinked as he processed Farzan's sarcasm. "Dude, sorry. I didn't mean to wake you."

"It's all good. I needed to get up anyway." Farzan scratched at his chest, where some of his salt-and-pepper chest hair was spilling out the top of his tank. "What's going on?"

"Bryce tore their rotator cuff."

Fuck. Bryce was their kickball team's third base.

"Are they okay?"

"Yeah, but they obviously can't play."

"Shit."

"Yeah. If we can't field another player we're going to have to forfeit."

"Abso-fucking-lutely not," Farzan spat. They were playing against their rivals, the Lawrence Gryphons, another all-queer team. Yes, they really spelled it that way, with a *ph*, because the Gryphons were a bunch of pretentious KU hippies. (Granted, Ramin had also gone to KU, but Ramin was neither pretentious nor a hippie.)

Worse, the Gryphons were a bunch of copycats: they had clearly borrowed the Lions' logo and stuck a pair of Jayhawk wings on it.

"Agreed," Arya said. "But I've already called every queer I know."

"Everyone?"

Arya rolled his eyes. "Everyone I know by name instead of dick."

"What about Ramin?"

Arya bit his lip. "He said, if we absolutely couldn't find anyone else, he'd try. But you know how he is."

Farzan did. Ramin came to their games to cheer for them (and Todd, who played first base), but he didn't like playing team sports. Probably some lingering trauma from high school, if Farzan had to guess. Hell, he *didn't* have to guess. High school was brutal.

Ramin had gotten into yoga about five years ago and insisted that was enough exercise for him.

"Fine," Farzan said. "Let me think. I'll let you know."

"Thanks, dude." Arya hung up on him before he could even say bye.

Farzan made himself scrambled eggs while he waited for his tea to steep, and texted people he knew: other queer folks on the sub circuit, friendly acquaintances, even Spencer from Shiraz Bistro. Everyone was either busy or uninterested or a KU grad.

"Fuck," he muttered, scooping his eggs onto his plate. He'd burned them a bit while texting, but whatever. There was still one person he could try, but he hesitated. It was kind of a big ask on a Saturday morning, especially for someone who kept the same hours as Farzan.

Then again, they were friends, right? And it was a casual, friendly thing to do, filling a hole in the roster. (Farzan chuckled to himself: *filling a hole.*) But after all, David said he wanted them to be friends. The fucking was just a bonus part. And friends helped each other out.

He finally texted.

Farzan

Good morning!

I have a weird favor to ask

twenty-four

David

David hadn't been to Loose Park in years.

When he was a teenager, with a fresh driver's license, he'd bring his grandma and stroll the path with her, taking in the trees and the sun and the "young folks canoodling," as she liked to say. Right before elbowing him and asking when he was going to get a girlfriend.

The area hadn't changed much: a few new houses had sprung up, and they'd redone the parking lot, but it was almost a relief to see it looked more or less the same as it had when he was a child.

He spotted Farzan waiting for him at the gate.

"Hey!" Farzan gave him a quick kiss on the cheek. "Thank you so much for doing this."

"No problem. It sounds like fun."

"You're just saying that because I wore those shorts you were so interested in." Farzan gestured to his pair of black athletic shorts which, sure enough, were nice and short, barely hitting midthigh. He wore them beneath a white raglan with green sleeves, with KC Lions over the heart.

Farzan handed over a matching raglan; David was already wearing his own shorts, but they were longer and looser, more for lounging around the house in the summer than for playing an actual game.

"Thanks." David pulled off his white T-shirt and pulled the raglan on; when he stuck his head through, he caught Farzan staring at his chest and gave him a wicked grin.

Farzan just shrugged. "I'm allowed to enjoy the show, too."

"You're a menace."

"Come on," Farzan said with a laugh. He turned to lead David toward the field, and damn, David's imagination hadn't done the sight of Farzan's ass in athletic shorts justice.

He wanted to tackle him right there, but this was kickball, not rugby, and also, there were still kids on the playground. It was one of those perfect October days: the sun gently warming him, a light breeze cooling him, the sky a rich blue and stacked with fluffy white clouds so tall they looked like they reached all the way to outer space.

He'd originally planned to spend the morning on his back patio, enjoying the weather and going through his Italian wine regions again. In fact, he'd been sorting out his note cards when he got Farzan's text. Even though he knew he needed to study, and even though he hadn't played kickball since fifth grade, the thought of getting out into the sun and seeing Farzan again had won out.

"Hey, everyone. This is David."

David gave a little wave. Farzan ran through the rest of the team—David forgot nearly everyone as soon as they were introduced—but he did clock Farzan's friend Arya, stringy and brown-skinned and bald.

"Nice to meet you," Arya said, shaking David's hand. "Thanks for filling in."

"Glad to do it."

As David stepped away, Arya said to Farzan, loud enough for everyone to hear: "You're right, he is hot."

David's dark skin didn't show a blush easily, but Farzan's did. David grinned when Farzan met his eye, his cheeks turning rosy. But then Farzan's eyes went past David and he waved.

David turned to see two more guys walking up: one, a white guy in a team uniform; the other, well, maybe white, but his nose was kind of like Farzan's, and he had piercing green eyes. Farzan jogged over and gestured for David to join.

"David, this is Todd, he plays first base." David offered a hand to the white guy. "And this is Ramin."

"Nice to meet you, David," Ramin said, shaking David's hand while having an entirely silent conversation with Farzan using only his eyes.

"You too."

"I'm going to grab a seat. Good luck." Ramin turned and kissed Todd; Todd reciprocated by goosing Ramin's ass.

Ramin just laughed, showing off an impressive set of dimples, waved toward Arya—who was already leading warm-up drills—and lugged his lawn chair over to the side of the field to claim a spot. He tugged the hem of his shirt down and took a seat.

"Hey, thanks for doing this," Todd said as they followed Farzan back to their team "dugout"—really just an area marked off with orange traffic cones. Todd was brown-haired and brown-eyed, with a round nose and a short, well-kept beard. "This is the championship."

David bit his lip as, ahead of him, Farzan pulled his ankle back and up into a quad stretch, which exposed more of his brown thighs. David wondered what Farzan had on underneath. Briefs? A jock strap? David had just gone with compression shorts.

Shit, Todd was talking.

"Say again?"

"You play much?"

David laughed. "Yeah, when I was twelve. Sorry if I'm not that good."

"Don't be. Neither are most of them," Todd admitted, gesturing toward the team. It wasn't just queer men: it was an all-gender team, cis and trans and nonbinary, white and brown and now (with David's appearance) Black. But everyone was smiling and laughing, even though it was clear, from watching the warm-up kicks, that most didn't have an athletic bone in their body. "The main thing is to show up and trash talk the Gryphons."

"That's the other team?"

"They're from Lawrence," Todd spat, and Farzan nodded sharply from Todd's other side, glowering.

"Oh, you a Tiger?" David asked. He'd been glad to leave behind the ridiculous rivalry between the Mizzou Tigers and KU Jayhawks when he moved to Chicago—only to wind up listening to his coworkers endlessly fight about the White Sox and the Cubs. He'd gone to UMKC himself, and he'd never cared much about basketball anyway.

"Technically," Farzan said. "But only really on kickball days. I wasn't into much of the sportsball when I was in college."

David snorted. "Same."

On the field—pitch? diamond?—Arya blew a whistle.

"Come on team, let's huddle up," he shouted.

Todd jogged out, but Farzan hung back with David.

"What did I just get myself into?" David asked softly.

"Come on," Farzan said. "It'll be fun. I promise."

Farzan kept his promise: David couldn't remember the last time he laughed so much.

When he was in school, kickball had been just another thing to do at recess: a game you could get in on if the tetherball courts were full and the hopscotch squares had been taken. He'd never given much thought to how utterly ridiculous it was.

But now, watching twenty grown-ass adults kicking an enormous inflatable red rubber ball, it was hard not to feel like a giddy kid again. When Todd took a blow to the face with said ball and dropped like a rock, David laughed so hard he got a stitch in his side (once it was established that Todd was all right).

Arya, as team captain, was the most serious one there, shouting encouragement, complaining to the referee about bad calls (even though David didn't know what calls there were to be made, other than if someone crossed the neutral zone illegally), and trash-talking the Gryphons. Farzan got in on some good-natured heckling, but when it was his turn at bat—at ball?—his face got deadly serious. Turned out he was a hell of a kicker, and a good runner, too, those legs of his pumping hard, those shorts showing even more of Farzan's delicious skin.

David made himself concentrate on the game instead of on getting Farzan out of those shorts, but fuck!

David wasn't half-bad himself. He at least consistently kicked the ball, getting on base more often than he got out, and doing a decent enough job chasing down balls in the outfield. Xavier, a burly nonbinary player with a shock of bright green hair, had filled in at third base, since ze was more experienced, much to David's relief.

In the end, the Lions won, twenty-one to eighteen. You'd think they won the Super Bowl, the way they shouted and cried and hugged each other, the way their friends and families and partners rushed the field to share in the euphoria.

For a moment, David almost wished he'd asked his mom or dad to come watch. They would've gotten a kick out of it.

No pun intended.

"Hey," Farzan said in David's ear, pulling him into a sweaty hug. Farzan's hair was wet and matted to his forehead, his upper lip dewy with perspiration, and he'd never looked sexier. "Thank you again. So much."

"Thank you for asking me. I had fun."

"Yeah?"

David pecked Farzan on the lips. They were salty and smacked of coconut from Farzan's sunblock. "Yeah. So what now?"

"Now, we usually do a team brunch," Farzan said. "Then work, I guess."

"What time do you have to be in?"

"Three or so."

It was just past eleven.

"We could go to brunch," David said, stepping close enough to speak low in Farzan's ear. "Or we could go back to my place."

Farzan only considered for a moment.

"I'll meet you there."

twenty-five

David

As soon as the door was closed and locked, David spun around, pressed Farzan against the wood, and kissed him hard.

Farzan's mouth opened right away, letting David's tongue in to tease him, and David pressed closer, smashing his chest against Farzan's, grinding his hips, until Farzan's groans turned into a yelp.

"What?" David asked, but Farzan just shifted over to the right.

"Doorknob."

"Sorry," David breathed.

But Farzan shook his head and kissed him again. His hands snaked under David's raglan, tracing the tender flesh along his ribs, making him shiver and moan into Farzan's mouth.

"Should we shower?" Farzan asked between kisses, panting hard like he'd just run the bases again.

"Fuck no." David pressed his nose into Farzan's collar. "I like the way you smell."

Clean deodorant and sweet grass, musky sweat and tangy salt. David dipped his tongue into the hollow of Farzan's clavicle, tasting the sun on his skin.

"Oh god," Farzan groaned, deeper than before. It went right to David's cock. "Me too. You always smell good."

"Yeah?"

"Mm-hmm." Farzan clenched his jaw as David trailed kisses along it.

Damn. If playing sports and getting sweaty got Farzan this worked up, he'd have to do it more often. Heat settled in David's core.

"I want you to fuck me," Farzan murmured.

That heat blazed up David's spine, made his head spin. He paused his kissing to rest his forehead against Farzan's, looking deep into Farzan's eyes. His pupils were dilated so wide, David could see his own reflection in them.

"How long do you need to prep?" he asked.

"Ten minutes?"

David nodded, pulling Farzan away from the door. He yanked Farzan's raglan over his head, exposing his hairy chest and stomach, his brown nipples pebbling in the cool air. He wanted to lick every inch of Farzan's skin, but if he started he might not stop.

He gently pushed Farzan toward the bathroom instead. David's house was a little older, and the bathroom, though spacious and recently renovated, was down the hall from the bedroom. David had thought about getting quotes on connecting it, so the bedroom became a true primary suite, maybe even installing a half-bath off the kitchen or something, but what was the point when he'd be moving next year? Though he supposed he could do it anyway, then rent the place out for cheap. There were plenty of queer folks who could use affordable housing.

David was still holding Farzan's raglan. As he headed toward his bedroom, he brought it up to his nose and inhaled Farzan's scent. Tingles of euphoria rippled along his neck and shoulders.

While Farzan cleaned up, David laid old towels across his bed. They were faded red, though they'd once been bright: relics of his brief but intense "everything black and red" phase when he'd gotten his first apartment back in Chicago. They were a little threadbare, some unraveling in the corners, but still serviceable as sex towels.

He rummaged through his nightstand, grabbing lubes and condoms and his favorite prostate massager, a little black silicone number that hooked just like a talented finger.

"Hey," he said through the bathroom door. This was such a ridiculous thing to have to ask about, but better safe than sorry.

"Uh. Almost done," Farzan answered.

"You're good. Just, you mind if I use a toy while we fuck?" Silence. "On myself, I mean?"

"No. Why would I mind?"

David sighed with relief.

"I once had a guy ask me—and this is verbatim—if his bussy wasn't tight enough."

The sound of Farzan cackling only stoked the fire in David's belly. Damn, he loved Farzan's laugh.

"I promise I have utmost confidence in the integrity of my bussy," Farzan said, though he couldn't make it through the sentence without laughing.

David left Farzan to it, stripped off, lubed up the toy and popped it in, savoring the delicious pressure against his prostate. His cock, already hard from all the kissing, leaked out a bead of precum.

He heard the creak of the door, turned, and forgot how to breathe.

Farzan stood naked before him, hair wild and skin flush. Yeah, he'd seen Farzan naked before, but that was at five o'fuck in the morning, when the light was dim and David was too sleep-addled to appreciate the sight. Now he could drink Farzan in like a fine Bordeaux.

Farzan's chest was strong, but a little soft, and tufted with black hair, though plenty of gray was visible in it. David wanted to drag his fingers down the valley between his pecs. Farzan didn't have abs, but David could tell he had a solid core. And speaking of solid, for all those shorts had shown off, they hadn't done his legs justice: thick and powerful, made for rounding bases, made for running a kitchen, made for fucking.

David couldn't wait for his turn.

"God, you're beautiful," David whispered, and Farzan's neck and shoulders turned a deeper red, even as a shy smile creased his lips. How could someone so delicious be so shy?

"You're fucking breathtaking," Farzan said back, and David's heart gave an extra thud, because yeah, Farzan was practically panting, eyes trailing up and down David's body.

"Come here." David held out his hand, and Farzan stepped into the bedroom, walking David backward until he fell over the bed. "Hey Siri, play my sex playlist."

Fazan's eyebrows quirked, and he leaned in for a kiss.

"Okay. Here's your Square Enix playlist," his speaker announced.

David turned away from the kiss in a panic. "No, fuck—"

"*WHEN YOU WALK AWAY—*" Utada started blaring the theme song to *Kingdom Hearts*. He'd fallen in love with the game while he was in college, had kept up with all the sequels (and interquels and prequels and fuck-whatever-quels) even as his life became increasingly chaotic. But now was *not* the time.

"Hey Siri, stop!" David called, but Farzan was already cracking up, his face buried against David's ribs. Way to spoil the mood.

"Don't make fun," David pouted.

Farzan looked up, resting his chin in the valley of David's chest, a warm weight David never wanted to go without. "I'm not. I love *Kingdom Hearts* too."

"Yeah?"

"I've never played a game that manages to be so gay and yet so painfully straight at the same time."

"Oh my god, right? The whole vibe between Sora and Riku..."

"Which Sora? There were twelve last count. Wait, you played the sequels, right?"

"All but the one on the phone." David had tried it a bit, but he hated playing games on his phone. His battery drained way too fast.

Farzan grinned and scooted forward to press a sweet kiss against David's lips. David had gone soft, but his dick started coming back to life, especially when he felt Farzan's own warm length against his thigh.

"Mm. So." Farzan leaned up again. "You have a sex playlist?"

"Oh my god." David wiped a hand over his face, reached for his phone, and turned on his actual sex playlist, some bass-heavy lo-fi beats that felt warm and erotic to him. "Better?"

Farzan didn't answer, just kissed him again, and David was so over-whelmed with the warmth of Farzan's skin, the sweet musk of him, that he thought he might get off right there. He rolled over, earning a brief huff of surprise from Farzan, then bracketed him with his arms as he pushed up to hover above him.

"You are so fucking sexy," he breathed, and Farzan only leaned up, his lips desperate for David's. David teased him a bit before giving in, drawing Farzan's tongue into his mouth to caress it, tease it, bite it just a little, drinking in the way Farzan purred under him. He broke off from Farzan's lips to make his way down Farzan's jaw and neck and chest, kiss-ing one nipple while he curled his fingers in Farzan's chest hair. Farzan bucked under him.

"You like that?"

Farzan gasped in assent.

"Yeah, you do." David kissed the other nipple, adding a few love bites, as his stomach heated and his skin tingled. Farzan moaned in time with the music.

David continued his journey down, licking the sweat off Farzan's stomach, his belly button, the valley of his thighs, before finally going down on Farzan's rigid cock. He used one hand to press his thumb against Farzan's taint, while his middle and ring fingers traced light caresses further back, toward Farzan's hole.

David's own dick was so hard his foreskin had pulled itself back, and his core kept clenching and unclenching, driving the prostate massager against his button in a delirious rhythm. He was dripping now—prostate play, whether from a toy or a partner, always had him leaking—but fuck, he couldn't think about that now, not when he had Farzan's dick in his mouth, twitching and flexing and warm against his tongue. Farzan's breath came in little gulps; his hips bucked up to meet David's lips.

He let Farzan out of his mouth with a pop and sat up on his knees.

"How do you want me to get you ready?" he asked, lightly scratching at Farzan's balls, enjoying the little shiver that wracked Farzan's body. He was desperate, desperate to touch, desperate to feel, desperate to plunge right into Farzan and feel that warmth and connection. He could feel Farzan's desperation too, the twitching of his dick against his stomach, the gooseflesh all along his thighs, the hunger in his gaze.

Farzan blinked and swallowed.

"Can I be honest?"

"We're totally naked."

Farzan chuckled. "I'm not, uh, super into rimming for some reason."

"Giving or receiving?"

"Either. Is that okay?"

"Of course." David was a fan, but he knew it wasn't for everyone. He kneaded harder with his thumb, gratified when Farzan ground back against him. "Fingers okay, then?"

"Yeah."

David reached for the lube, slicked his fingers and Farzan's muscle, and slowly, gently pressed his index finger in.

"Like this?"

"Yeah."

Farzan was warm inside, warm and tight, and David searched for Farzan's prostate, hooking his finger until he got another one of those hitches in Farzan's breath.

"You like my finger in you?" David asked. "Soon it'll be my dick."

Farzan's eyes widened, and David wanted to drown in them. The heat in his belly roared as he opened Farzan up, adding a second finger, whispering how good Farzan looked and relishing the way Farzan shivered and clenched around him before easing back up.

"Yeah, look at you," David said. "You've got goose bumps. You ready for me?"

"Fuck yes."

David reached for the condom, but Farzan got there first.

"Let me," he said, so David moved forward, straddling Farzan's chest. Farzan steadied his cock—his massager gave another delicious flutter inside at the contact—and rolled the condom on slowly, double-checking it was intact and secure. "Good?"

"Yeah. You ready?"

"Can we do a pillow?"

"Oh, fuck," David said. He wiped a lubed hand off on one of the sex towels, reached for a pillow, and tucked it under Farzan's hips. Once he sorted the towels out again, he said, "Better?"

"Much." Farzan's eyes bored into his. "Fuck me."

David had never wanted anything more in his life. His limbs were on fire, his face hot, as he lined himself up and pressed in. Slowly, smoothly, studying Farzan's face, as Farzan breathed and relaxed around him, staring at him with those beautiful eyes, a brown so deep David wanted to dive in and drown in them.

"You feel so good around me," David murmured, leaning down for another kiss, feeling Farzan clench and release around him. "Fuck yeah, keep doing that."

"Fuck me," Farzan insisted, so David did, his hips slowly but surely finding a rhythm before speeding up.

"Yeah, you're so tight," he said. "You been practicing your Kegels, huh?"

Farzan let out a little laugh, but it turned into a moan as David shifted his angle slightly.

"You feel amazing," Farzan whined.

"Yeah, I do. You want this dick?"

Something—the sex, the sweat, the sun—had him more fired up than he'd ever been, and seeing Farzan's eager responses, the little noises, the fluttering eyelids, only set David's engine running harder.

"Yeah you do," he growled, giving Farzan a hard thrust.

Farzan flung his head back, and David couldn't stand it. He leaned in, scraping his teeth along the tendon in Farzan's neck before tracing kisses up to his lips. He breathed into Farzan, let Farzan breathe back into him.

David was sweating, he felt it trickling down his temples, slicking up his stomach, with Farzan's leaking dick between them.

David slowed his pace and broke the kiss, leaned up to get better leverage, as Farzan wrapped his legs around his back, used his calves to draw David in closer.

Fuck, this was perfect.

"You're so fucking sexy," David said again, at a loss for anything else to say as Farzan looked up at him, and he looked down at Farzan, and the world was just the two of them, and nothing else mattered. He reached for Farzan's dick, gave a tentative stroke, as Farzan arched up toward him. "So fucking sexy."

He kept up a steady rhythm, both his hips and his hand, occasionally pausing to lean in for more kissing, or to drag his unlubed hand through Farzan's messy hair, but it was too much, and he could feel himself getting close. He didn't want to leave Farzan behind, not this first time, not until he got to know Farzan's body, know if he liked coming first or second.

"I'm close," David said, though he could barely concentrate enough to form words. Every brain cell, every nerve, was concentrated on the searing connection between Farzan and him. His mouth hung open as he repeated, "I'm close."

"Me too," Farzan breathed. "Go for it."

"Fuck." David had just enough brainpower to pull out and check the condom—still good—before slipping back inside. He gripped Farzan's cock tight and sped up his stroking until Farzan's eyes rolled back.

"Shit!" Farzan cried as he came all over David's hand. His walls tightened, setting David off too, and David ground himself against Farzan's ass until they had both rode out their orgasms. As the last pulses rocked David's core, he collapsed, lying chest to chest against Farzan, mess be damned, panting and happy and so, so peacefully quiet.

Slowly, David came back to himself, back to the rise and fall of Farzan's chest beneath him, the soft bass beat in the air, the smell of sweat and sex and Farzan, Farzan, Farzan.

David dropped one final kiss on Farzan's forehead, ran his fingers through Farzan's hair one last time.

"That was fucking amazing."

Farzan smiled, leaned up to kiss David once, twice, then let out a sigh and collapsed back onto the bed.

After—when they'd both cleaned up a bit—they lay atop the covers of David's bed, cuddling, Farzan trailing soft kisses along David's shoulder. He had to be at work in a little over an hour, and he needed a shower, but he couldn't bring himself to move. His skin still buzzed, and his dick still tingled from the mother of all orgasms.

David had had a lot of good sex in his lifetime. Plenty of mediocre sex, too, and even a few bad experiences—not traumatic bad, just unskilled bad—but nothing like this.

Not the kind of sex that set his soul free of his body.

He ran his fingers up and down Farzan's scalp. Farzan had a longer drive to work, plus he'd probably need to swing by his apartment for a change of clothes. But he didn't want Farzan to leave yet, either.

"Hey," David said softly.

"Hey."

"That was really good, huh?"

"Really good. A-plus stress relief."

David winced. He hadn't fucked Farzan to de-stress him. He'd fucked him because . . .

Well, because he'd wanted to since the first time he laid eyes on him at Aspire.

But stress relief was all this could be. He still had a pile of note cards waiting for him in the living room. A Saturday service, with a private party in the back room, waiting for him at work.

A life just about to finally, finally start.

"I talked to a friend the other day," he found himself saying. He hadn't told anyone about Rhett's offer: not his parents, not Jeri, not even Ayesha back in Chicago. But Farzan was a neutral outsider, he told himself. He felt safe to talk to about it. "He basically offered me a job."

"Oh yeah?"

"Yeah. You know Shyla Thorne? She won *Top Chef*?"

"Uh-huh."

"She's opening a restaurant in LA. My friend's gonna manage it." David shivered as Farzan's fingers gently twined through his twists. "He asked me to come be their wine director."

"Oh." Farzan's voice was soft. "Wow. That's amazing."

"Yeah."

"I'm happy for you." Farzan turned to smile at David. "You must be excited."

"Yeah," David said, but he didn't feel excited. He felt...annoyed. He tried to keep it out of his voice, making sure he didn't scrunch up his eyebrows, but damn.

He knew this thing with Farzan was casual and time-limited, but still, after a fuck like that, Farzan could've at least acted a little sad to be missing out on all this quality dick.

And more than that, missing out on their blossoming friendship. David couldn't remember the last time he'd had as much fun as at the kickball game. But then, Farzan had other friends. A community. He wouldn't be lonely when David left.

David prayed for a little post-nut clarity, instead of whatever post-nut funk had descended on him instead.

They were friends. Just friends. Friends with benefits, yes, but still, he didn't have a claim on Farzan, and Farzan didn't have a claim on him. And all this cuddling was just muddying the waters. He needed to get moving before he did something truly foolish, like suggest a second round.

David groaned but disentangled himself. "Shit, it's almost two. I'd better start getting ready for work."

"Me too." Farzan pulled on his discarded raglan, then glanced around the bedroom, brows drawn. "Oh, they're in the bathroom."

David chuckled. "Your shorts?"

"Yeah."

"I'll toss them to you. I've gotta shower. Can you let yourself out?"

Farzan gave a sharp nod and rolled to the other side of the bed, treating David to another great view of his back and ass. If he minded being shuffled out in a hurry, he didn't show it.

Clearly he was on the same page as David: time to go before things got weird and messy.

"Sure. Hey. Thanks for today. The game, and this. It was great."

"Anytime." David offered him a cocky wink. Farzan just shook his head.

David went into the bathroom, found Farzan's shorts and—yep—a red jockstrap. But he didn't have time to admire them. He tossed the clothes out of the bathroom and turned on the shower, standing under the warm spray, but he only relaxed once he felt the thud of the front door closing reverberate through the floor.

He needed to get his head back in the game. Focus on his test. Not on how good Farzan had felt. Not how nice it had been, cuddling up after.

Not the sting when Farzan hadn't batted an eye about David's job offer.

That wasn't the deal.

He couldn't afford it to be.

twenty-six

Farzan

Farzan made the drive home in a daze, his skin buzzing. He still smelled like David, like sweat and vetiver and warmth. It filled the car. His ears were painfully full, as if he was on a plane, but the only pressure crushing him was the thought of David leaving.

Yeah, they'd promised to keep things casual, and Farzan had told himself he could do that. He'd done his best to keep his voice bright and even while he imagined David jetting off to the West Coast, working in some fancy restaurant on the beach, getting a lavish condo overlooking the Hollywood sign.

Or whatever. Farzan had only been to Los Angeles once, when he was a child, despite it being the heart of the Iranian diaspora in the US. Tehrangeles, his mom and dad always called it, while also never wanting to visit.

"Too much traffic," his dad would say.

Now David would be stuck in that traffic, but he'd be living his dream, and Farzan could hardly begrudge him that. Hell, if they were really friends, then Farzan should be glad for him.

Even if he'd miss David.

Even if he'd just had the most amazing sex of his life, his core still occasionally shuddering with aftershocks.

Even if he couldn't get the look in David's eyes out of his head. The warmth, the gentle smile, the hunger that Farzan had only known how to give in to.

No, no, no. He'd promised himself he wouldn't do this. Wouldn't catch feelings.

And David had certainly made it clear that this had just been a fuck. Yeah, they'd cuddled as they came down from their orgasms, but then it was *I've gotta shower, you can let yourself out*, like Farzan was just some Grindr hookup.

Granted, Farzan *did* need to go home and change. He didn't have time to hop in the shower, lather David up, knead all those strong muscles that had gotten a workout at kickball and then in bed.

But it would've been nice to be asked.

Whatever. David had work to do and a life to lead, even if that life was leading him west. And Farzan had work to do, too. A restaurant to run. People counting on him.

He parked his car, adjusted himself—he'd let himself think about David in the shower just a bit too long—and ran inside.

Sunday morning, Farzan headed into work early. He liked the quiet hours before anyone else showed up, when the kitchen was all his, clean and gleaming and empty, before the chaos of the day consumed it. Sometimes, he'd come in and get a head start on making kabobs or pick a stew to make as a daily special, drawing from one of his dad's old recipes or else picking something from one of the stack of Persian cookbooks in his office.

His parents had a well-worn copy of *New Food of Life*, the dust jacket long since destroyed and the spine quite broken, that they had always referenced if they were making something outside the family's usual wheelhouse. Farzan had added his own books to the collection: *Salt Fat Acid*

Heat, which was by an Iranian author but had more than just Persian food, including a lot of excellent food theory; *Bottom of the Pot*, which was probably his favorite Persian cookbook; plus a complete collection of Alton Brown, for when he needed something science-y.

But he wasn't here to cook today. He had a week's worth of invoices and paperwork and little notes to deal with.

He sat at his desk with a heavy sigh, paired his phone with the little Bluetooth speaker perched atop one of the filing cabinets, and pulled up a *Final Fantasy* playlist. As "One-Winged Angel" blasted, he hummed along and did battle with his to-do list.

To be honest, he would've rather been impaled from behind by a ridiculously oversized katana than make one more phone call to their online reservation platform's tech support. Literally, not euphemistically, though after the fucking David gave him yesterday...

No, nope, not thinking about that, or the chance for a repeat tomorrow when they met up for more studying. He had vendors to pay.

A knock against the office's doorframe startled Farzan; he jerked up to find Ramin standing in the doorway.

"Oh. Sorry." Farzan paused his music. "Hey."

"Hey. Mind if I . . . ?"

"No." Farzan gestured for Ramin to step inside. Farzan really needed to get another chair in here, now that the space was slightly more organized. Instead, he came around and sat on the corner of his desk, which sent a stack of mail toppling.

Thankfully, Ramin caught it.

"You didn't come to brunch yesterday." Ramin handed the envelopes back. "Neither did David."

"Yeah. We . . . hung out after."

"Mm-hmm." Ramin studied Farzan. "David seems pretty cool."

"He is."

"And you're still doing okay? With this . . . situationship?"

Farzan chuckled. *Situationship* was very much an Arya word, not a Ramin word. Clearly they'd been talking behind his back.

"Yeah. It's going great. He gives good advice, and he gets along with my friends." Farzan couldn't stop himself from blushing. "And the sex is amazing. So, yeah. I'm okay."

Ramin nodded. "I don't want you to get hurt. You don't do casual."

"This isn't like Hector," Farzan said, waving a hand to swat the memory away. "We both know what we're getting into, we're communicating, and we're actually doing friend things, too. He and I hung out at the Nelson-Atkins when Arya bailed on me."

"Okay. I just wanted to make sure."

"I'm okay. Really. Anyway, how are you and Todd doing? Did you make a decision?"

A shy smile unfurled across Ramin's lips, his dimples making an appearance. He rubbed his right thumb against the tattoo of his dad's name. "Good. We went for a walk after brunch, just around the Plaza some, and..."

"And?"

Ramin's ears were turning pink. "And I asked him to move in with me."

"Really?" Farzan nearly fell over. Probably would have, if he hadn't been leaning against his desk. "What'd he say?"

"He said yes." Ramin's grin was so big, so infectious, Farzan had to mirror it.

"That's great."

If Ramin was happy, that's what mattered. Farzan pushed down the ache in his chest. He loved Ramin too much to be jealous. But he was allowed to be a little sad, right? Change could be sad, even if it was good, even if it meant his best friend was getting his happily-ever-after.

"I'm really happy for you," Farzan said, and he meant it.

"Thanks." Ramin tugged on the hem of his shirt. "Sometimes you have to take a risk, right?"

"Right," Farzan said, but he got the uneasy feeling that they weren't talking about Ramin and Todd anymore. He cleared his throat. "I need some tea. You got anywhere to be?"

Ramin shook his head, so Farzan led him out to the kitchen, where they leaned against the counter and sipped their teas. Farzan let Ramin tell him about his plans: converting part of the unfinished basement into a little home gym for Todd (and he could use it for yoga as well, instead of doing it in the living room), moving some stuff out of the bedroom into his home office so Todd could help decorate it, and maybe even turning the spare bedroom into a second office for Todd to use.

Ramin had a nice house in the Northland—not far from Shiraz Bistro, actually—that he'd bought with the inheritance from his dad. He and Arya and Farzan had spent many a night in their twenties curled up on Ramin's couch, playing *Mario Kart* and drinking terrible sweet cocktails and taking turns complaining about the men in their lives. As they got older, Ramin's house had somehow become the go-to house for gatherings, probably because it was on a suburban street with easy parking.

Now it wouldn't just be Ramin's; it would be Ramin and Todd's. The vibe would be different. They wouldn't just be a trio anymore; they'd be a trio plus Todd. Though perhaps cohabitation would help smooth off some of Todd's edges.

And who knew? Maybe they'd get married. Maybe they'd adopt a dog, or kids. Ramin would make a great dad—Farzan had no doubt about that—but fuck, that would be a change. Farzan had never much wanted kids, though he was looking forward to being a guncle if and when the time came. If Navid or Maheen had kids, he'd spoil them rotten.

Well, as best he could when he made a fraction of his siblings' salaries.

"Anyway." Ramin shook his head and poured more tea. "Enough about me. What about you? When do you see David again?"

"Who's David?"

Sweet mother of crap. Farzan needed to remember to lock the back door. If one more person snuck up on him . . .

Not that it would've thwarted Navid, since everyone in the Alavi family had a key.

"Hey, Navid." Farzan pulled his little brother into a hug. Navid was in a slick black rain jacket, damp and dripping onto the kitchen floor. Farzan hadn't heard it start raining. "What're you doing here?"

"You first." Navid sidled up to Ramin, leaning against the same counter and crossing his arms. "Who is this mysterious David?"

Ramin pressed his lips together, fighting a smile. Farzan sighed.

"Just a guy I'm seeing," Farzan said. "It's not a big deal."

But Navid's face lit up. "You've got a boyfriend?"

"Er..."

Emphatically not. Farzan loved Navid, but he was straight, and all his ideas about relationships were formed through that lens. While Farzan had been in the closet, Navid had been having his first kisses at middle school dances. While Farzan had borne the brunt of his parents' asking *When are you getting married?*, Navid had been, by all accounts, a bit of a player in college. He'd sown his wild oats, then met Gina and settled down, and now they were getting married.

It was all so beautiful and romantic and heteronormative, and that was nothing like Farzan's dating life: hookups and boyfriends and, now, a fuck buddy.

"We haven't really labeled it yet," he finally said.

Navid's smile only widened. "That's so great. Oh my god, have you told Mom and Dad?"

"No, and neither will you, or you can start paying for your own kabobs."

Navid held up his hands. "Okay, okay. But still. I'm happy for you. Hey, this means you'll have a date for the wedding!"

Farzan suppressed a scoff. David would be long gone by then. And even if the wedding was next week, filling in at a kickball game was one thing. Being a wedding date? That was definitely pushing the limits of his and David's arrangement.

"Have you picked a date yet?" Ramin asked, passing Navid a cup of tea. Farzan tried to telepathically thank Ramin for the redirect, and it must've worked, because Ramin gave him a subtle nod.

Navid took a long sip of his tea and winced. He usually let his tea cool before he drank, while Ramin and Farzan both liked theirs piping hot. Maybe that came with being the baby of the family.

Navid blew on his tea before taking another sip. "Yeah. Next summer."

In which case David would *definitely* be out of the picture.

"That's actually what I wanted to talk to you about."

"If it's about catering—"

"What? Fuck no. You can't cater my wedding."

Farzan was at once relieved and offended. Did Navid not think he could handle it? That was just typical. Farzan opened his mouth to argue, but Navid kept going.

"I was going to ask you..." Navid's voice petered out. He swallowed, dropped his eyes to his teacup. "I was going to ask you to be my best man."

"You...oh."

All the arguments Farzan had been formulating fell apart in his head.

Navid wanted *him* as his best man?

For some reason, the urge to cry hit him, so hard and fast it felt like he'd been swept underwater by the wave pool at Oceans of Fun.

"Really?"

"You're my brother," Navid said simply, finally meeting Farzan's eyes.

"Yeah, but..."

Navid had so many friends, from work and school and life. Plus Gina had brothers, too.

"You're sure?"

"Of course. You really think I'd ask someone else?"

Honestly? A little bit.

But Navid hadn't. He'd asked Farzan.

Farzan set down his tea and pulled Navid into a hug. Navid hugged him back tightly, more tightly than he had in a long time. It took Farzan back to their childhood, to games played in the backyard, movies watched curled up on the ugly orange sofa his parents used to own, to LEGO cities and Transformers battles.

"It would be my honor," Farzan said, giving his brother another squeeze before releasing him.

"Good. Good." Navid's shoulders relaxed.

"Why were you so nervous? Did you really think I'd say no?"

"Not really." Navid shrugged. "I don't know. This whole thing is just emotional."

Farzan's eyes cut sideways to Ramin, who was grinning silently and sipping his tea.

"You're invited too, by the way," Navid said. "Just so you know."

Ramin laughed. "Thanks. I can't wait."

"Okay. Well." Navid took a deep breath. "I've still got more errands to run. Gina's parents are coming into town, and we need groceries. Hey, you need anything from Costco?"

It was Alavi family tradition—maybe all Iranians did it, honestly—to always check before a Costco run.

"I'm good," Farzan said. "Unless they have that wine with the owl on the label?"

"Gotcha." Navid gave Farzan another quick hug, clasped Ramin's hand, pulled up his hood, and headed back out, letting a gust of rain-cooled air into the kitchen.

"And don't tell Mom and Dad!" Farzan reminded Navid as the door swung shut.

It was hard enough explaining his and David's deal to himself, let alone his parents.

He turned back to find Ramin giving him a wide, dimply smile, though his eyes were a little moist. Ramin was an only child, so he'd always treated Navid like a little brother, too. No doubt he was remembering little Navid chasing after them when they were kids. And now he was all grown up and getting married.

"So," Ramin said. "Best man, huh?"

Farzan shook his head. Him, best man.

At his little brother's wedding.

His little brother was getting married, and Farzan would likely be single again by the time it rolled around.

Fuck his life.

"I guess so." He set his teacup in the sink and stretched. Suddenly he just wanted to be alone for a while. That to-do list wasn't getting any shorter, and Ramin was too damned perceptive sometimes. "Hey. I've gotta get back to work. You don't have to leave, but..."

"But I'm in your way." Ramin drank the last of his tea. "When do you see David again, anyway?"

"Tomorrow, probably. I'm sure he's already got a stack of note cards ready."

"All right. Well." Ramin studied Farzan again, gave him a soft smile. "I love you, man."

"Love you too." Farzan pulled Ramin into a hug. "Say hi to Todd for me."

"You say hi to David for me, then," Ramin said. "And hey."

Ramin leaned back but kept hold of Farzan's shoulders, looking Farzan in the eyes. Ramin's green gaze was intense. "Just be happy. Okay?"

"You know me. I try."

twenty-seven

David

"H ey, son. Bad hair day?" David's father asked as soon as David answered the FaceTime call. Christopher Curtis had never been one to mince words.

David groaned and ruffled his beanie, but he didn't take it off. Bad hair week was more like it. Sunday was generally his wash day, but his twists had come out so badly, he'd kept his beanie on the entire time at Farzan's Monday night, and he'd been so self-conscious that when they finished studying (going through Sonoma AVAs for David, looking at different employee health insurance plans for Farzan), instead of going to Farzan's bedroom and fucking, they'd ended up on the couch playing Farzan's PlayStation. Farzan had a decent collection of co-op games, including a pretty fun one where you played wizards zapping monsters while collecting spell parchments and trying not to hit your teammates with friendly fire, which happened way too often.

In fact, all they'd done was kiss a few times. Well, more than a few—they'd kissed between every level—but they were quick, soft and sweet, not hot and heavy, and what's weirder, the lack of sex hadn't even bothered David. In fact, it had been a bit of a relief. After they'd fucked

Saturday, leaving David in his feelings, he needed a breather. Perspective. A moment to get his head on straight.

Friends. With benefits, but still, friends. Friends could hang out and play video games. That much, at least, was fun.

He'd called his barber first thing Tuesday morning for an emergency appointment. He couldn't go into Aspire looking like this.

So of course, his father had been sure to point it out.

"Little bit. I'm about to go see Ronni." Ronni was basically an institution. She'd cut David's hair growing up, and when he moved back home, she was still at it, though now one of her sons helped her manage the barber shop in KCK.

"Tell her I said hello." The camera spun and went dark for a moment; when the image returned, David's father was drinking what was no doubt his eighth cup of coffee for the day.

It was barely nine o'clock.

"I will, Dad," David said. "So what's up?"

"Can't I call my favorite son to catch up?"

David rolled his eyes. He was an only child.

"I talked to your mom the other day." David reminded himself he was lucky that his parents still (mostly) got along after their divorce. "She said you got a job offer? In San Francisco?"

"LA," David corrected.

"Huh. Well, it's been nice having you home, but as long as you're happy, I'm happy."

"I will be," David said. "It's a great opportunity."

"I bet. But you know there's more to life than just work, right?"

This coming from Christopher Curtis? The man who had worked seven days a week all David's life? The man who'd retired and immediately found four different volunteer gigs and was, somehow, even busier than before?

Apparently David needed to work on fixing his face, because his dad said, "I know, I know. Pot, meet kettle."

David snorted.

"Seriously, though." Christopher chewed on his lip. "I wish I'd made more time for you and your mom. Maybe things would've been different."

"Dad..."

"It's fine." Christopher waved his hand in front of his face, accidentally smacking his phone. The picture went chaotic and dark once more as he recovered. "You know, I always wanted to be a good provider. But I wish I'd known that meant being there, you know, physically."

David stared at his phone, stunned. Yeah, his dad had been a workaholic, but David had never felt he'd gone without when he was growing up. And he'd learned the value of hard work from both his parents, even if their marriage hadn't lasted.

"Anyway, enough of that," Christopher said. "I actually called for a reason. Two reasons."

"You mean other than kicking me when I'm already down?" David cracked.

"I'm sure it's not that bad."

David pulled off his beanie. At the look on his dad's face, he tugged it back on.

"I stand corrected." But Christopher chuckled, and David grinned. At least they were back on more familiar footing, teasing each other. "Okay. The first thing."

His dad's voice went all scratchy; David's hackles rose.

"Is everything okay?" he asked.

"Yes, yes, everything's fine. But I ran into Marcus the other day."

David nearly dropped his phone as his hand went temporarily numb. "Really?"

"Yeah. He asked how you were doing."

"What'd you tell him?"

"I told him you were doing well, that you were back home for a while but were moving to California soon. Is that okay?"

David puffed up his lips and blew out a long breath. "Yeah. It's fine. How was he doing?"

"Married! Can you believe it?"

David could.

Years ago, David thought *he'd* be the one marrying Marcus. He was the first man David had fallen in love with, and David had fallen hard. He'd dated some after coming out, but nothing serious, not until Marcus. He'd seen a future for them.

But then he'd gotten the job offer from JPMorgan, and asked Marcus to move to Chicago with him, and Marcus had said no.

No.

He couldn't leave his home, his family, no matter how much he loved David.

And that had been that. David had spent his first year in Chicago nursing his broken heart. And he'd never loved someone as hard as he'd loved Marcus. Maybe he never would again. But he didn't regret chasing his dreams. He'd make the same choice in a heartbeat.

That wound was healed. It was.

"I'm glad he's doing well," David finally managed. He wasn't sure why his dad was even bringing Marcus up, except that Christopher had really liked him. He'd been nearly as upset about the breakup as David—but at least David had long since gotten over it. "So what was the other thing?"

"Oh!" His dad cleared his throat. "I'm kind of seeing someone."

"You're joking."

"No! It's the truth." The smile that crossed his dad's face was unlike any David had ever seen before. It made him look like a shy teenager again. David looked a lot like his dad; he wondered if he ever smiled like that. What would Farzan think if he saw it?

David shook the thought away.

"And I wanted to ask if you want to meet her?"

"Of course I do."

"Okay. I know your schedule's hectic, but you think you can take off Friday?"

"I'll try. I'll let you know. All right?"

"Sure. Love you, kiddo.".
"Love you, Dad."

Jeri had been positively gleeful when David asked for Friday off and told her why.

"Oh my god, you're going to have a new stepmom!" she teased, as David restocked their WineStation, swapping out empty bottles for fresh ones and checking the argon tank.

"It's not like they're getting married," David groused, tapping the gauge, but it was empty. "Can you hand me another tank?"

Still, there was no denying that it was a big step. If David's dad had dated since the divorce—over fifteen years ago, now—David hadn't heard about it. And he'd certainly never met any of his dad's girlfriends before.

Not that David had brought home anyone since Marcus, either. No one he'd dated in Chicago had been worth it.

Friday afternoon David got a text with the address, a place up in the Northland. Something about it tickled David's memory—had he eaten there before?—but he didn't have time to look it up, not when he was knee-deep in the indigenous grapes of Italy.

When five o'clock rolled around, he took a sponge comb to his freshly rescued twists (no sense giving his dad any more comedy material), dressed in dark-wash jeans and a white sweater, pulled on his newest boots—these ones shiny wine-red jacquard on black—and headed out, bopping to his Square Enix playlist. Ever since the Siri mishap, he'd remembered what great driving music it made.

The overcast sky hung low over him as he drove north. He missed the long days of summer.

His phone's directions led him to a cluster of buildings and strip malls in Gladstone, with a bank, a Starbucks, a hairstylist, a Chinese buffet, a preschool, a nail salon, and—

Oh, fuck.

He pulled up right in front of a plain white building with large windows stretching across the front. The left side was taken up by the nail salon, but on the right side, huge red light-up letters spelled SHIRAZ BISTRO.

His dad had brought him right to Farzan's restaurant.

What the fuck.

twenty-eight

David

It wasn't like David could bail on dinner with his dad. And especially not on his dad's new girlfriend. But why didn't he bother checking where they were going?

He knew the address looked familiar—he knew it. He just hadn't put two and two together. And now here he was, outside Farzan's restaurant, and what if Farzan was there working? Would it look like David was bringing his parents for Farzan to meet? That was abso-fucking-lutely not the signal David wanted to be sending.

A light rain had started to fall, misting over David's windshield. His phone buzzed; he had missed a few Are you still alive? texts from Ayesha. He'd been meaning to give her a call for the last couple weeks, but between Aspire, and his test, and Farzan, he'd been too busy. He was typing out an apology when a familiar off-white SUV pulled into the spot beside him.

He could finish it later.

David checked his hair in his visor mirror before stepping out.

His dad shot a quick smile his way before scurrying around the hood to open the door for his girlfriend—a chivalrous move David couldn't remember Christopher Curtis ever pulling off before.

David got most of his looks from his dad: the same dark brown skin with cobalt underneath, the same high cheekbones, the same blocky hands. (He'd gotten his eyes from his mom, though: Christopher Curtis's eyes were small and spaced a bit too close to his nose.) David was the same height as his dad, too, though lately he'd seen the slightest of stoops in his father's shoulders. He refused to think about that.

The woman his father helped out of the car was lovely: dark amber skin, a broad nose, full lips painted a cool purple that matched her cardigan. She was short and plump, with a shy smile that turned the corners of her eyes up as she looked at David.

"David, this is Deb," Christopher said. "Deb, my pride and joy, David."

"It's lovely to meet you," David said, offering his arm as she stepped up onto the curb. Her nails were short, manicured, and the same lavender as her lips. "How'd you two pick this place?"

"My ex-husband's Iranian," Deb said. "We used to come here all the time. I still bring my kids when they come to visit."

"Oh yeah? How many kids you got?"

"Two daughters. Both in their twenties."

Christopher held the door open; after letting Deb through, he rested a hand on David's elbow. "I hope this place is okay."

"It's fine," David said, a little too quick.

"What?"

But David shook his head.

Deb was at the host stand, waiting next to a lovely fat white woman with her black hair pulled back into a ponytail. David followed them to their booth in the corner. A small, red-wreathed chandelier hung above, thankfully high enough David didn't have to worry about standing up and hitting it.

"Nathan will be taking care of you tonight," the host was saying. "Let us know if you need anything, Deb."

"I will. Thanks, Patricia."

David slid onto his side of the booth, crooking his arms out a bit because his pits were suddenly sweaty. Deb was a regular. At Farzan's restaurant. Did they know each other?

David's back was to the kitchen, so he wouldn't even have any warning if Farzan suddenly appeared. The restaurant was noisy, joyously so, with couples and friends and families talking in a mix of English and Farsi, many of them shouting over each other or cackling in laughter. It *did* remind him of *My Big Fat Greek Wedding*, come to think of it. He fought back a smile at the memory, but his dad caught it.

"You been here before?"

"No, but I've heard it's good." David was not about to get into his whole deal with Farzan. One, he didn't want to steal his dad's thunder (not that there was thunder to steal, since he and Farzan weren't dating). Two, his dad would undoubtedly make a way bigger deal of it than it was, and that would only muddy the waters even worse.

If he could just get through the night, he and Farzan could laugh about this later.

"Thanks, Nathan," Deb said as their server, a lanky boy with blond hair and wispy eyebrows that made him look surprised, dropped off their menus. Shit, was she on a first-name basis with Farzan too? Did she know he'd taken over? "It *is* good. Better than my ex-mother-in-law's cooking, but please don't tell anyone I said that."

David laughed. "Your secret's safe with me."

Deb offered a twinkly smile. "They do an appetizer sampler, and sharing platter if you want kabobs. But they also have amazing stews."

"I bet," David said, remembering Farzan's delicious (and gas-inducing) celery stew. Much too dangerous to have tonight. "Kabob does sound amazing."

Christopher leaned in close to look over Deb's shoulder at her menu, instead of scanning his own, and they made such a cute picture together, David was tempted to pull out his phone. He'd seen his dad in a lot of moods: joyful, exhausted, proud, angry, sad, even drunk once (just the once, and that was the night he learned why his dad didn't sing in public). Still, he couldn't remember ever seeing his dad so . . . flirty.

Had it been like this between his mom and dad when they were younger—when he was younger? Before the house turned into awkward silences and awkwarder conversations over the dinner table on Sundays? David got a strange pang in his chest.

"So a sampler and a platter?" Christopher said. "David, why don't you pick the wine?"

"Yes, please," Deb added. "Your dad says you're about to take a big fancy wine test?"

"It's for the Court of Master Sommeliers," David explained, flipping the menu to find the wine list. "Basically it means you're one of the most knowledgeable people about wine in the country."

Deb let out a low, pitch-perfect whistle.

"He hasn't even taken it yet, and he's already got job offers rolling in from fancy restaurants in California."

One offer—half offer, really—could hardly be considered rolling in, but David smiled and shook his head and studied the list. All were more or less table wines—he spotted Farzan's favorite cheap Malbec, the one they'd had their first night together—and with only 25 percent markup, too. David would have to mention that to Farzan: even Aspire, which prided itself on its low markup, did 33 percent.

They ordered their appetizer sampler (some sort of yogurt-cucumber dip, a salad of tomatoes and cucumbers and onions, and bread with feta cheese and herbs) and a bottle of wine to split (David went ahead and picked the Farzan-approved Malbec). Once Nathan left them, David steepled his fingers.

"So. How'd you two meet?"

Deb launched into a hilarious story, like something out of a movie, of them bumping into each other in the hallway of the food pantry where they both volunteered. Deb was carrying another volunteer's birthday cake, which smashed into Christopher's chest when they collided.

David wondered if it was a Bundt cake.

Their appetizers came, and David smiled as his dad and Deb swapped telling little bits of their history. David had never seen his dad so *happy*. There was no other word for it, was there?

He'd never seen anything like it.

Their flirting was interrupted by the heaping platter of meat that showed up to their table, along with three plates of white rice: two gleaming white, topped with yellow saffron; the third, Deb's, covered with little red jewels.

"You know how I like it!" she said. "Thanks, Nathan."

"What's that?"

"It's zereshk polow. Barberry rice. Here." She scooped some onto David's plate. "You have to try it."

"Thanks." He took a small taste, and wow. Sharp, sweet, and sour played across his tongue, along with the mellow, perfectly cooked rice and earthy-floral saffron. It was heaven.

"Good, right?" Deb's eyes lit up, even as she started piling pieces of meat onto David's plate. Before David could stop her—tell her to serve herself first—he heard a familiar voice and nearly dropped his fork.

"Hey folks, how's everything?" Farzan said, swinging around to the side of the booth.

David blinked up at him, mouth still full of rice.

Farzan's eyebrows shot up. "David?"

twenty-nine

Farzan

It *was* David. Sitting in a booth. In his restaurant.

Staring at him with a grain of rice stuck to the corner of his lip.

Two older Black folks sat across from him, one of whom had the same amazing cheekbones and midnight skin and perfect lips as David. That had to be his dad. Was the woman David's mom, then?

What were they doing here?

Farzan completely forgot what he was doing. And by the look on David's face, he'd forgotten what he was doing, too. He finally swallowed, slowly, his Adam's apple bobbing up and down, and Farzan pushed away flashes of licking along that stretch of neck and down to the hollow of David's collarbone, because now was emphatically not the time.

"Uh. Hey," David said softly, hesitantly, and fuck, how exactly were they supposed to play this? David meeting his friends was one thing: his friends were queer, and their age, and understood the whole fuck-buddies situationship, even if Ramin clearly had some unvoiced reservations about it.

But Farzan hadn't imagined a single scenario in which they met each other's parents. That was well outside the realm of friends with benefits. Distinctly un-casual.

"You two know each other?" David's maybe-dad said.

"Yeah." David sipped his wine and cleared his throat. "Dad, Deb. This is Farzan. My ... friend."

Farzan ignored the twinge between his ribs.

Friend. So that's how they were going to play it.

That was fine.

They were friends, after all. That was safe territory.

But then the woman, Deb, said, "David, your dad already told me you were gay. Is this your boyfriend?"

David's dark skin didn't turn red, but Farzan could swear his cheeks darkened anyway, matching Farzan's own blush.

What's worse, Deb had said it kind of loud, loud enough for—

"Boyfriend?"

Farzan's shoulders hiked up right next to his ears.

Farzan's mom swung around from the corner table where she'd been sitting with Arya's mom and a few other Iranian women from her book club. She came up, resting her hand around Farzan's waist.

"You have a boyfriend, Farzan-joon?" she asked, then spotted Deb. "Oh, Deb!"

"Hey, Persis," Deb said. "Sorry it's been so long. You know how life gets."

"How are your daughters?"

Farzan's head spun. His mom knew Deb, who was ... not David's mom, but seemed to be with David's dad, possibly romantically. David, who was here, with his dad and a woman. David, who had locked eyes with him at the first mention of "boyfriends," panic evident in his wide-eyed stare.

"Farzan?" His mom was staring at him. Had she asked him something? He'd been too busy trying to wrap his mind around the slowly moving meteor crashing down on his world like an end-game cinematic.

"What?"

"This is your boyfriend?" she asked, glancing toward David.

Farzan met David's eyes. What were they supposed to do now? David had made it clear they were not dating. He was moving away. He didn't want anything permanent.

"No," Farzan said, the same moment David blurted out "Yes."

That meteor blasted apart into something warm and glowing. David had said yes. Why had he said it? Just because he remembered Farzan complaining about his family not taking him seriously? He smiled at David, tried to silently thank him for that, but David's dad started laughing.

Persis, meanwhile, said, "You don't have to be embarrassed, Farzan-joon. He's very handsome."

Farzan's ears burned as he caught the heavy wink she threw David's way. He wasn't embarrassed by David. (And yeah, David *was* very handsome. The most beautiful man Farzan had ever seen in his life.) No, he was embarrassed from being tossed into this situation without any warning. And right in front of his mother, too. Which meant in less than five minutes, his dad would know, and his siblings.

By this time tomorrow, his cousins in Iran would probably be talking about it.

"Okay, I'll let you enjoy your meal," Persis said, reaching out to briefly clasp Deb's hand. Then she turned to Farzan. "Why don't you sit for a while, maman? The kitchen will be fine without you."

David's eyes went wide at that, and Farzan wasn't sure if it was in surprise or panic. He needed an exit strategy.

"I should really..."

But Deb cut him off. "Please, join us." She gestured to the open seat next to David. Farzan glanced back toward the kitchen. Yeah, they could probably handle things for a few minutes, though Farzan had been in the middle of seasoning the fesenjan. But surely Sheena could check on it.

He locked eyes with David one last time. David gave him a tiny nod.

"All right."

Farzan slid in, bumping his knees against David's.

"Wine?" David offered, but Farzan shook his head.

"I better not. What with all the knives and all."

Smooth. Real smooth.

"He's got a *point*, you know," David's dad said.

David groaned.

"What? You know you love my *sharp* sense of humor."

Farzan chuckled, relaxing his shoulders a touch.

"I'm sorry, Mr. Curtis, I don't think I caught your name."

"With a knife? A net would work better."

"Dad," David begged, and suddenly Farzan had a vision of what David's teenage years might've been like.

"Christopher," David's dad said, extending a hand.

"Farzan Alavi," Farzan said. "Nice to meet you."

"You too. So. You own this whole place?"

Farzan felt something weird in his chest; it took him a moment to realize it was pride. The last time he'd met a boyfriend's parents, he hadn't exactly had a steady job. But now?

"Yeah. Well, I own the business now. Though my parents still technically own the property."

"Was that always the plan? For you to take over?" Christopher scooped a few pieces of chicken kabob onto his plate.

"Not really. But when they wanted to retire, I knew I couldn't let it close, so I took it over." Farzan glanced at David. "David's been helping me, actually. Giving me advice and stuff. He's got way more experience with restaurants than I do."

"Yeah, but you're the better cook," David said. "You make all this?"

Farzan shrugged. He had prepped the spice mixes and marinades, but Spencer had done the actual grilling.

"You've got your father's touch," Deb said. "Maybe even a little better. Don't tell him I said that."

"I won't."

Farzan still couldn't believe Deb knew his parents. Was, apparently, a regular at Shiraz Bistro. He was still learning a lot of the usual crowd:

people who came in once a month, or a few times a year for celebrations. Families that came in every other week, or ordered takeout on Fridays. For as much of his youth as he'd spent in and around the restaurant, there was so much he still didn't know.

"So how'd you meet this handsome guy?" Christopher asked David.

"*Very* handsome," Deb corrected.

Farzan wanted to hide under the table.

David shot him a look. "At Aspire, actually. He came in for some wine and fries, we got to talking. Exchanged numbers." David shrugged.

He'd left out the mistaken identity and blowjobs, but that was definitely for the best.

"Aww," Deb said. Her own plate was piled high with rice and kabob barg, flattened filet mignon skewers, Farzan's personal favorite. She sprinkled a liberal amount of sumac on top, too. "Where was your first date?"

"The Nelson," David said without missing a beat. "The opening of the Kehinde Wiley exhibit."

Farzan grinned. Hard to call it a date when they'd showed up separately after both being ditched by their friends. But it had been fun.

"You two are too cute. Look at that smile." Deb winked at Farzan. "I think your son is in good hands, Chris."

Farzan shook his head, fighting a blush, but David grabbed his knee under the table.

"I am."

Another burst of warmth blossomed in Farzan's chest. "Thanks." He risked a quick peck to David's cheek. "Now, I better get back to work. But it was nice meeting you both."

"Same," Christopher said. "Don't be a stranger."

"Thanks." He met David's eyes again. "See you."

"See you," David said, cracking a small grin.

Farzan scooted out, swept a glance across the restaurant—everything seemed good—and retreated back to the kitchen. He checked the fesenjan, added a bit of salt, then retreated to his office and closed the door.

Farzan collapsed onto his seat, breathing hard, like he'd just chased a kickball halfway across the outfield. Bad enough to get ambushed by David and his family, but in front of his mom?

This was a disaster.

Had they played it off okay? David had seemed alarmed but not upset by the whole thing. At least they'd both panicked together.

Farzan's knee still burned where David's hand had rested on it. A friendly gesture, that was all it was.

They were just friends.

Friends who had both lied to their families.

Fuck.

Farzan's phone buzzed. A text from Navid.

> **Navid**
> You told them!!
> Happy for you bro!

Fuck.

Sure enough, the Alavi family network had propagated the news. Now they'd be expecting him to bring David around for dinners, and parties, and holidays. Now they'd be asking when he and David were going to *get serious.*

And when the whole thing ended and David moved away?

Well, they'd be *sorry* for Farzan. Yet another relationship that didn't work out. And then they'd all talk to each other, speculating about what went wrong, about why Farzan kept getting dumped, about how all the men he dated *seemed so nice* but ended up breaking his heart.

Wondering if maybe the problem wasn't the other men, but Farzan. After all, he'd been through this before. With Jason, who Farzan had dated for six months, but broken up with because Jason wanted to open their relationship while Farzan didn't. With Sean, who Farzan had dated for nearly a year, but who dumped Farzan because he found someone he *clicked with* more. With Omid, who lied to Farzan about being out to his family, and what a clusterfuck *that* had been.

With Brandon, who Farzan had dated for three months, and the whole time, despite Farzan's many attempts to correct him, he kept calling Farzan and his family Arabic. Not Arab, which was a people, but Arabic—the language.

And the Alavis weren't Arab anyway.

Fucking Brandon.

And now here Farzan was again, except this time the ending was already written. David was moving to Los Angeles. This all had an expiration date. And everyone wondering if this time he'd met *the one* were going to be disappointed—but not surprised—all over again.

And worst of all: Farzan would be disappointed, too. Because he really liked David. A lot.

Yeah, he told himself he could keep things casual. Yeah, he could say they were just friends who sometimes slept together.

Except they'd slept together their first night, and as Farzan had curled up in bed with David, a knot deep inside of him had finally unraveled. And every time he'd seen David since, he'd felt lighter inside.

He was falling for David. And that was strictly against the rules.

He needed to call this off now, before someone really got hurt.

thirty

David

Once Farzan left the table, David was able to redirect the conversation to his dad and Deb, and luckily for David, once you got Christopher Curtis telling a story, you could sit back and relax.

And David needed to sit back, because his heart was hammering in his chest. His cold chest, because he couldn't stop hearing how Farzan had answered no when asked if they were boyfriends.

Why did it make him feel cold? They *weren't* boyfriends. Yeah, David had panicked and said yes, because he didn't exactly want to talk about being fuck buddies in front of his dad, and he didn't think Farzan wanted to in front of his mom, either. Talking about queer relationships, or situationships even, was always awkward with straight people, even ones who loved you unconditionally, as David's dad did.

Still, it had been nice, cozying up in the booth. For a second, David could imagine they were on a double date. A *real* date. His cheek tingled where Farzan had kissed him before getting up.

But he couldn't think about that now. He needed his wits about him. He'd polished off his glass of wine and switched to water—he never drank more than one glass if he was driving, even though, after all these years, he could probably tolerate more before getting anywhere near drunk. Better safe than sorry, always.

So instead, he stuffed his face with the amazing food in front of him. As good as Farzan's stew had been, these kabobs… holy fuck. He wondered if he could weasel the recipe out of Farzan, if Brayan could make anything even remotely similar, because wow. His mouth was watering in overdrive. Savory, umami, just the right amount of spice, a little sweetness from the sumac Deb had him sprinkle on top. He'd never even tasted sumac before, at least not that he could remember. All he knew about it was that there was a poisonous version you were supposed to avoid, like poison ivy and poison oak, even though he was pretty sure there was no poison sumac in Missouri.

Come to think of it, he'd only ever seen poison ivy, though thankfully he'd never actually gotten any on himself.

David ate way too much, in between bouts of laughter (usually courtesy of Deb at his dad's expense), stories about Deb's daughters (both recent college grads, looking for jobs, and godspeed to them), and questions about his upcoming test.

"I think it's amazing you're pursuing your dream," Deb said. "Not too many people are brave enough to do that."

David shrugged. "I don't know if it was bravery or desperation. If I'd stayed at my old job I would've been a soulless, miserable husk by now."

"Mm. You raised your son right," Deb said, resting a hand on Christopher's arm.

"Me and his mom certainly did our best, but still, I don't know how he turned out so great."

David's chest warmed, but his father frowned.

"What are you going to do about this job offer, though? If your boyfriend already owns this place. It can't be that easy for him to come with you."

"Ah." There it was: the hole in their little fiction.

The angry moon, hovering ominously in the sky, waiting to crash down on them.

If only there really was an ocarina song that could sort out his and Farzan's problems.

"We haven't figured that out yet," David finally said.

He had, of course: David was going to LA, and Farzan was staying here. This opportunity was too good to pass up. He'd miss fucking Farzan—miss hanging out with him, too, honestly—but there were plenty of queer men in LA. He'd have plenty of options. Even if the thought made his throat squeeze.

He'd gotten lucky with Farzan, a good friend and a good fuck.

Luck like that didn't come around twice.

"Ah, don't be sad," Deb said. "If you love each other, you'll work it out. I know you will. Now, who wants dessert?"

David did his best, but he didn't manage to grab the check before his dad. He did, however, see that Farzan had given them a steep discount.

As Christopher helped Deb with her coat, David collected the huge container of leftovers and tried not to groan at the pressure in his stomach. He hadn't really had room for dessert, but the rosewater sorbet had sounded too good to pass up. He'd have to ask Farzan how he made it.

As they made for the door, Farzan's mother said, "Wait! I'll go get him so you can say goodbye."

"Oh, you don't . . ." David started, but she was already gone, her pumps clopping on the floor. It couldn't have been more than a minute before she dragged Farzan back with her. He had a towel over his shoulder and his sleeves rolled up, and David remembered tracing the cords of his forearms with his thumbs as they curled up on the couch.

"So nice meeting you," Farzan's mom said, pulling David in to air kiss him on both cheeks.

"You too." She had the same eyes as her son, brown and rich and heavy-lidded. Bedroom eyes.

If David wasn't so stuffed, he might've suggested he and Farzan go for a quickie somewhere, even in his car in a dark corner of the parking lot like horny teenagers, but he honestly couldn't contemplate sex right now. All he wanted to do was roll into his bed and pass out.

Farzan walked them out, hunching his shoulders up against the drizzle that had started falling. David offered his arm to Deb and helped her back into his dad's car.

"Thank you for joining us," Deb said to David, softly, so his dad couldn't hear. "He might not have acted like it, but Chris was pretty nervous. I think he was worried you wouldn't approve of me."

David grinned wide.

"Well, I do."

"Thank you. And speaking of..." She nodded toward Farzan, hovering outside the door. "He seems like a keeper."

David followed her gaze and swallowed away the food-laden butterflies trying to flutter in his stomach. "Yeah. He does."

Once the SUV pulled away, David joined Farzan beside the door, waving goodbye. There was no awning, but at least the building itself blocked some of the rain.

"Hey," David said, bumping Farzan's elbow. "Sorry for ambushing you like that. I didn't know Deb was going to bring us here tonight."

"It's fine," Farzan said stiffly.

David did his best not to bristle. It wasn't his fault (well, maybe a little bit for not checking the map more closely), but he hadn't done any of this on purpose.

The problem was he kept hearing Farzan saying no in his head. "Still, you didn't have to throw me under the bus in front of our parents."

"So lying to them was the better choice?" Farzan crossed his arms and shifted out of view of the windows. "You made it abundantly clear that this was never going to be anything serious. Just friends with benefits. Which is a far cry from boyfriends."

David rolled his eyes. "Oh, did you want me to tell your mom we were fuck buddies instead?"

Farzan looked away, but his lip quivered and his ears were turning red.

Shit. That was a dick thing to say. What was wrong with him?

"I'm sorry." He reached for Farzan's face, but Farzan leaned away.

David's insides went colder than the rain.

"I can't do this anymore," Farzan said.

"What?" David croaked. "Why?"

And why did it hurt so much?

Farzan bit his lip and shook his head. The rain was picking up, and David couldn't tell if those were tears at the end of Farzan's eyelashes or raindrops.

He blinked away the burning in his own eyes. It couldn't just . . . end, could it?

They had a real connection. Didn't Farzan feel it? It wasn't just about all the wine they'd shared, or the flash cards and movies, or even the best sex of David's life. It was about kissing and cuddling, smiling and laughing. It was about feeling exactly right in someone's arms.

Fuck.

He'd walked right into it, hadn't he? He'd gone and caught feelings. And he wasn't ready to let Farzan go, not if he could help it.

"I don't want this to end," David finally said.

"Don't you get it?" Farzan snapped. "I like you. I more than like you. I can't do casual. Not anymore."

"Well, I more than like you, too!" David snapped back. "It's not casual for me, either!"

Farzan blinked at him, mouth hanging open. A raindrop slid off the end of his nose.

"Maybe it hasn't been for a while," David finally admitted.

Maybe it had never been in the first place. Because no matter what he told himself, from the moment David saw Farzan sitting in Aspire, he'd wanted him.

Not that he could say that aloud, before. But now?

He had to get this right.

"I like you, Farzan. I've liked you since the moment I met you and thought you were a restaurant critic."

Farzan gave a wobbly sort of smile; yeah, their meeting had been a little unconventional, but it was funny and would make a good story some day.

It *already* made a good story. And David didn't want it to end just yet.

"And I called you my boyfriend because I wanted to. Because it felt true." He stepped closer, bracketing Farzan's legs with his. Farzan gave a little shiver, blinking hard.

"Really?"

"Really." David leaned in. "You're smart and you're sexy and you're kind, and whenever we're together, I'm happy. It's been so long, I think I'd forgotten what it felt like. Until I met you."

Farzan's eyes softened. David wanted to drown in them.

But then Farzan bit his lower lip, and David's gaze was drawn there, and he wished it was his lips against Farzan's mouth, his teeth nibbling on the soft skin there.

But Farzan still hadn't spoken.

"Are you . . ." David swallowed. "What are you thinking?"

Farzan blinked, sending raindrops cascading down his cheeks like tears. Or were they actual tears?

Had David messed this up, ruined things beyond repair? Was this too little, too late?

But slowly, Farzan's lips curled up, a smile dawning on his perfect face.

"I'm happy too," he said, and David's chest soared. Literally soared. He thought it was just an expression, but that's what it felt like: his heart suddenly shooting skyward, through the clouds, out into space, until it shone like a star.

David brushed his wet nose against Farzan's, oh so gently, and Farzan tilted his head so their lips met. Despite the cold rain, the contact warmed David all over. The sweet movements of Farzan's lips drew him in. He kissed, and kissed, until he was interrupted by the revenge of dinner.

He broke off the kiss, clamped his lips shut and turned away, covering his mouth with the back of his hand, but the burp reverberated through his chest.

Farzan snorted. "Glad it's not me this time."

"I shouldn't have had dessert." David pressed his forehead back against Farzan's. He needed the contact to ground him. Otherwise he might float away. "But that sorbet was so good."

"Yeah?"

"Yeah. Everything was amazing. Not that I'm surprised." He stood up straighter so he could rest his hands on Farzan's ass. "So. What do you say? Boyfriends? For real?"

Farzan's smile dimmed. He pulled away, hugged himself tight.

"But you're leaving."

"I know," David said softly. "But that's months away. And I still have to pass my test, anyway."

"You're going to pass," Farzan said. "You've studied way too hard."

"Thanks." David moved in close again, rested his hands on Farzan's hips. Nothing had ever felt so right. But Farzan wasn't wrong.

He didn't have any answers about the future. All he knew was he wanted Farzan.

David brushed a strand of wet hair off Farzan's forehead. Farzan shivered, at the touch or the cold, David couldn't be sure.

He hoped it was the former.

"But can't we enjoy this for now? Who knows what the future will bring."

Farzan finally looked at him again. Really looked.

"So what do you say?" David held his breath.

Farzan swallowed. And then, finally, he nodded. "Boyfriends. For real. For as long as we have."

It was David's turn to smile, a smile so big he thought his heart was trying to escape out his mouth, but it didn't have the chance. Farzan leaned in, smashing his lips over David's, cupping David's face in his hands, tracing the fresh slit in his eyebrow with his thumb. David sighed into the kiss, pressed Farzan against the wall, gripped his hips tighter.

He was just about to suggest they go make out in his car when the door to Shiraz Bistro swung open, setting off an electronic chime and letting out a burst of warmth. David stepped back to see Farzan's mom watching them with a smirk on her face.

"Ah. Maman." Farzan's voice cracked. He cleared his throat. "Everything all right?"

"Everything's fine," she said.

Farzan swallowed. "I better get back to the kitchen."

But he leaned in and kissed David one more time before sliding away, whipping the towel off his shoulder to casually drape it in front of his groin.

"See you," David said, watching him go.

Persis winked at him and followed her son inside. David let himself into his car. While it warmed up, he ran his fingertips across his lips. His cheeks hurt from smiling so much.

Boyfriends.

Yeah. They were boyfriends now.

thirty-one

Farzan

"Boyfriends?" Arya gasped, squeezing his cardboard cup so hard the lid popped off, sloshing steaming herbal tea over his hand. He hissed and shook it off. "Shit."

Ramin handed Arya a couple napkins, then grabbed more to mop up the table. They were in the very back of Farzan's favorite coffee shop in the River Market.

Well, ex-favorite. It had been his favorite, until a bigger (still local) coffee shop had taken over, and the vibe was still great, but the coffee had gone downhill.

Still, it was walkable from his apartment, and easy enough for Arya and Ramin to get to over a lunch break.

"Boyfriends," Farzan said, dumping two packets of sugar into his espresso. He didn't used to need any, because the old owners had made a darker, rounder roast. This one was sharp and bitter. "For real."

"That's good, right?" Ramin said, sipping his own tea. One good thing about the shop—it had decent Darjeeling. "I mean...how do you feel about it?"

Farzan sipped at his espresso, trying to cover up what he knew was a goofy smile. "Good."

"That's it?" Arya said. "Just 'good'?"

"I mean, I like him. A lot." Farzan felt his smile turning uncertain. "But I'd be lying if I said I wasn't kind of nervous about the future."

"I get that." Ramin's mouth twisted back and forth. "You know you can...I mean...I'd miss you—*we'd* miss you—but if you wanted to follow him to California or wherever..."

"What he's trying to say is," Arya interjected, "we want you to be happy. Always. Even if it means leaving Kansas City."

But Farzan shook his head. He loved his friends for that, but he couldn't leave them. Or his family. Or the restaurant he'd just taken over.

"You guys don't have to worry about that," he said. "You're stuck with me."

Ramin grinned, and Arya relaxed into his chair, slinging his free arm over the back and resting a knee against the table. As a gay man, Arya had always taken his *sitting in chairs weird* duties extremely seriously.

"But for now...I guess we're going to try to enjoy it. The being together, I mean. For real."

"Aww," Arya cooed. "Look at you. Finally locked down a permanent supply of Vitamin D."

Farzan scoffed and rolled his eyes. Ramin swatted at Arya's shoulder, but Arya ignored him.

"Hey. You know what this means?" he asked.

Farzan narrowed his eyes. "What?"

"Now that kickball season is over, I'm putting together a volleyball crew. You can ask David!"

Farzan laughed. "What makes you think *I'm* doing it?"

Arya straightened up and leveled Farzan with an intense look. "Dude. You can't leave me hanging. Todd already backed out."

Todd's lease was up at the end of the month, so he and Ramin had been busy packing and moving. Much too busy for a volleyball league.

"Sorry," Ramin muttered, but Arya waved his hand.

"It's fine, I get it," he said. "I'm happy for you. You know that, right?"

Farzan carefully avoided Arya's eyes. Like him, Arya also wanted Ramin to be happy, no matter what.

Also like him, Arya only gave Todd a B-minus. But Ramin loved him.

"I know." Ramin smiled this wistful, sweet smile that made Farzan forgive Todd for his terrible taste in music. Any man who made Ramin that happy was worth it, no matter his flaws.

Arya turned back to Farzan. "Anyway, we only need six players. So what do you say?"

"Send me the schedule and I'll think about it."

"What about David?"

"I'll think about telling him, too," Farzan said, though truth be told, he wouldn't mind the chance to get sweaty with David more often. Especially if they could have more sweaty sex after.

"Fine," Arya grumbled and sipped his tea. "Hey. Did I tell you about this guy I met last weekend?"

"You didn't, and you don't need to," Ramin teased, but he leaned in anyway.

Arya's hookup stories were always chaotic and hilarious.

"Okay, so first of all, his profile pic was a stuffed animal, which you'd think would be a turnoff, but he'd lit it just right and I'll be damned if that Build-A-Bear didn't look weirdly sexy..."

Farzan ran a hand through his hair and sighed. He wanted to bang his head on his desk, but it was too full of paper. And what was it with bills always coming on Tuesdays?

It wasn't the money. The bistro was doing fine, it stayed full most nights—hell, they usually had to turn away guests on the weekends. It was the tedium. And the gnawing anxiety that if he missed one piece of paper, the whole thing would come crashing down around him. He knew it wouldn't, but still.

Why couldn't everything be on autopay, like his bills at home?

The more time he spent at Shiraz Bistro, the more he admired his mom, who'd seemed to juggle the endless stream of paperwork and to-do lists and little annoyances with ease. Farzan felt like he was constantly treading water, only a few to-dos away from drowning. Some days he barely had time to get into the kitchen.

Farzan paused his music (the *Final Fantasy X-2* soundtrack, and he would hear no blasphemy about either the soundtrack or the game itself, which was a masterpiece) when he heard thumping. There it was again. He stood and groaned; he'd been slouched over his desk too long.

The mail carrier was at the front door with a few small parcels. A couple of the staff had taken to having packages delivered to Shiraz Bistro, since most lived in apartments with shoddy mail security. (Including Farzan, after all the packages he'd had stolen from the mail room at home.)

"Thanks," Farzan said to the postal worker. As he stretched and enjoyed the sun on his face—he'd definitely been inside for too long—he glanced right at the Trans' place and froze at the new sign on the window.

GOING OUT OF BUSINESS

Farzan blinked, just in case it was a stress-induced hallucination, but nope, it was still there.

The Trans were closing their place?

Were they sick? Retiring? Selling? Moving?

Had they colluded with his parents to uproot all his childhood haunts in one fell swoop?

The door to their salon swung open, the scent of nail polish and citrus scrubs reminding him how bad his cuticles were these days. Even at one o'clock on a Tuesday, there were folks inside, one at the pedicure station and two getting manicures. Mrs. Tran was at the counter, her blue plastic glasses pushed up into her dark hair.

"Farzan!" She smiled when she saw him. She had bags under her eyes that Farzan didn't remember from when he was a kid, and a few streaks of gray at her temples, but her smile was every bit as warm as it had ever been. "You need a mani-pedi?"

Yes, but he didn't have time right now.

"I saw the sign. You're closing?"

She nodded. "Retiring. We're going to move to Denver to be closer to our grandkids."

"Wow. Uh, congratulations, then."

"Thank you. How are your mom and dad? They keeping busy?"

"Doing okay. My brother's getting married next year, so they have plenty to do."

"Little Navid? Wow!" A wistful smile crossed her face. "I remember when he used to run around the restaurant angry and naked."

Farzan choked on a laugh, so hard he had to thump his sternum before he could breathe normally. The incident in question—spurred by a tantrum after their mom had discovered Navid eating sugar cubes out of the little silver bowls on the tables—had only happened once, but it had taken on a life of its own in their family lore and the communal memory. It happened on a Saturday night, and the restaurant had been full at the time.

Farzan made a mental note to mention it in his best man speech.

Well, maybe. He didn't want to embarrass Navid, but it was a cute story, and after all, weren't older brothers supposed to tease their younger siblings, at least a little? Maybe he'd better run it by Gina to be on the safe side.

Farzan cleared his throat. "Yeah. Hard to believe. So what are you doing with the place?"

"We've found someone to buy most of the equipment," she said. "And we're selling the space. It's too much work leasing it, especially from out of state."

"Yeah." But Farzan was already imagining something different.

With the extra space, he could expand Shiraz Bistro's kitchen: a bigger grill, more prep stations, and wider aisles so they wouldn't have to dance around each other as they worked. Not to mention a bigger dining room, so they could do more covers per night, maybe hold larger parties or do events, too.

It would be a lot of work, but it felt like a sign. Like this was what he was supposed to be doing.

He wasn't just keeping Shiraz Bistro going; he could make it better than ever.

"Hey. Who's your real estate agent?"

thirty-two

David

> **Farzan**
> Random question
> What do you know about real estate?

> **David**
> Some...why?

> **Farzan**
> Tell you when I see you
> Soon?

David smiled and pressed his phone against his chest.

Yeah, they'd see each other soon.

"Boyfriends," he sighed.

David couldn't quite believe it. But it felt right, as he said it.

Boyfriends. The last thing he'd expected when he and Farzan had fought outside Shiraz Bistro. Did that make it their first fight? David wasn't exactly hoping to argue more, but still, the aftermath had been hard to beat. The only thing that would've made it better was makeup sex.

But they hadn't had any makeup sex. They'd barely seen each other since, with both their schedules so full. David was half-tempted to show up at Shiraz Bistro after closing to see if Farzan wanted to hook up in one of the booths—or maybe on top of his desk, health and safety be damned.

It had been a long time since David had craved someone the way he craved Farzan. Dreamed about his lips. Ached for the next time they could be together.

Ah, shit, he had it bad, didn't he? Exactly what he told himself wouldn't happen. Exactly what he'd warned Farzan not to do.

But here they were. Boyfriends. And David missed his.

> **David**
> Yes please
> I miss you

David hit send before he could talk himself out of it. *I miss you* wasn't too clingy. It was a normal thing to say to your boyfriend (his boyfriend!) when you hadn't seen each other for several days.

He slid his phone into his pocket and grabbed the black plastic tub he used for glass recycling. The city would take everything else, but not glass; thankfully, Ripple Glass had one of their big purple recycling bins on the way to Aspire.

He stuck the tub in his trunk. The worst part of recycling day was hearing the constant clanking of the bottles as he drove, and the alarming clash if he hit a pothole. As he headed back inside to get ready for work, his phone buzzed.

He smiled to himself. That last message must have worked better than he thought.

"Hey, handsome," he said. "Miss me too?"

"Handsome?" Ayesha's voice was dry and dubious. "And I *do* miss you, which you would know if you ever answered any of my texts."

"Ah, shit," David said, guilt setting his ears aflame. "I'm sorry, Ayesha. Life's been . . ."

"Hectic? Busy? Chaotic?" He couldn't see her, but he could just picture an eyebrow arching. "When is it ever not?"

"Yeah."

"So, handsome, huh? You seeing someone?"

"Maaaaaybe," he said, reaching for a tissue on the kitchen counter. The weather had turned cool and crisp, and even the short walk to his car and back had given him the sniffles. "We made it official a few days ago. That's why I didn't text you back."

"Which time?"

He deserved that.

"Last Friday. I was about to text you when my dad showed up with his new girlfriend."

"New girlfriend? Wait, what does that have to do with you seeing someone?"

"It's a long story." David wasn't sure, but he thought he heard Ayesha huff a breath. She'd never been one for long stories. And he had quite a few to share, didn't he? Plus he hadn't even asked about her. "It doesn't matter. How are you? How's Janine and the kids? How's Winnie?"

Winnie was Ayesha's snow-white pit bull. He remembered her from when she was a puppy; he'd been the designated dog-sitter whenever Ayesha needed someone.

"Winnie is spoiled rotten," Ayesha said. "One of the boys is definitely feeding her under the table. Actually, that might be Janine."

David chuckled and relaxed onto his couch, clearing his throat. His allergies had been acting up the last couple days. Why was it that he'd gone his whole life without any issues, but as soon as he hit thirty-seven, he was suddenly allergic to air?

He blew his nose again.

"Didn't little Micah have a birthday?"

"Next week. Six years already."

David whistled. Was it really? "Wish him happy birthday for me."

"I will." Ayesha went quiet for a long moment, so long David looked at his phone to make sure they hadn't disconnected.

"A? You there?"

"Yeah, I'm here." She sighed. "Are we good?"

"What? Why wouldn't we be?"

"You literally never call me. I'm always the one that calls you. I text and text and you never text back. Or when you do, it's one sentence. And today, you clearly thought I was someone else when you answered."

David sniffled—not because he was upset but because his damn nose kept running.

Granted, he *was* upset. Upset and ashamed.

Ayesha was one of his oldest friends. Yeah, she was still working at the job that had threatened to devour his soul, and yeah, she was five hundred miles away and had a whole family back there. But she was also the one who'd checked up on him at JPMorgan, made sure he knew the ropes and who was safe and who was a walking, talking Am-I-the-Asshole post. Who would listen to him and never gaslight him when he complained about microaggressions.

Fuck, he missed her. He'd been so focused on his test he hadn't let himself realize how much. He grabbed another Kleenex, blew his nose, and cleared his throat.

"You're right," he said softly.

"What?"

"I said, you're right. I've had my head up my ass. I've been putting everything I have into this test, but that's no excuse for not holding up my end of our friendship. I'm sorry. Really."

Ayesha didn't respond.

"Ayesha?"

"I'm here," she said. "Just making a note in my diary. *October 22nd… David Curtis said I was right.*"

"You're a brat."

"And you love me."

"Yeah, I do," David said with a sigh. He cleared his throat.

"Good. I forgive you. This time."

"There won't be a next, A."

"Just answer my texts, okay?"

David nodded, even though she couldn't see him. "I will. Promise."

"Good. Now tell me about this new man of yours. If he's got you out here admitting your faults and making apologies, he's got to be some kind of miracle worker."

"He's really special."

"So what's his name?"

David blew his nose again and sighed. As the afternoon wore on, it had become increasingly clear he wasn't having allergies. He had a cold.

A fucking cold.

He called Jeri to let her know.

"See, this is what you get for working too hard," she said. "Your body's not giving you a choice about getting rest."

"I get plenty of rest." Five hours a night wasn't that bad.

"Ugh, you sound horrible."

David sighed. His throat was sore, too, and his voice had gotten hoarse from talking with Ayesha for over an hour.

He couldn't remember the last time he'd talked to someone who wasn't Farzan for so long. Would've kept talking, too, except she had to go collect Micah from kindergarten.

"Get some rest, okay? Let me know if you need anything."

"I will. Sorry, Jeri."

"Don't be sorry. Just be well. Okay?"

"Okay. Thanks."

David hated being sick. His body wasn't built for long hours of rest: he needed to be doing things. Being sick was boring.

Still, more time at home meant more time for studying. He couldn't practice his tastings, not with his sinuses clogged, but Mount Flash Card still towered in the corner of the living room, threatening to blow its top off.

He grabbed a handful of note cards about the wines of Eastern Europe—from Slovenian Cabernet to Hungarian Tokaji—and leaned back on the couch, pulling the fuzzy blanket into his lap. He wasn't cold, but the blanket was cozy.

His phone buzzed again; this time he made sure to look at it before answering. It was a text from Farzan.

> **Farzan**
> Miss you too

David smiled so hard his jawbone popped, and warmth that had nothing to do with the cozy blanket flushed his skin.

> **Farzan**
> Sorry, was making kabob
> What are you up to?

> **David**
> Just chilling at home.
> Guess who has a cold?
> You feeling okay?

> **Farzan**
> I'm good. You want some company?

> **David**
> You don't have to

Farzan
I want to

David was tempted to say no. To tell Farzan he'd be fine. That he didn't feel like having any company. That he just wanted to sleep.

But no. He wanted to see Farzan.

David
Okay

thirty-three

Farzan

For whatever reason, Farzan had gotten sick a lot as a child. All through elementary and middle school, it seemed like he'd gotten an ear infection once a month, on top of the usual other complaints: several bouts with strep throat, one particularly nasty stomach flu in third grade, and plenty of colds.

And every time he got sick, his mom would stay home and take care of him, making one of the few dishes she was actually good at, ash-e reshteh, a thick, herby soup with thin noodles. Even now, as an adult, whenever he felt sick, he'd make it for himself.

He had no idea if David would like it—he and David hadn't actually talked too much about food preferences—but still, he'd swung by the Persian grocery store on the way to David's house.

David was quick to answer the doorbell, dressed in the softest-looking pink hoodie Farzan had ever seen, and another pair of those damned sweatpants. Farzan did his best to ignore the swish, swish, swish of David's dick in them as he stepped back and Farzan kicked off his shoes.

"What's all this?"

"I was going to make you soup." He held up his bags.

"You don't have to do that," David said, giving a loud sniff. His voice was hoarse, and he had white Kleenex dust powdering the edges of his chapped nostrils and caught in his stubble, but he seemed in good spirits. "I have a frozen pizza we can eat."

"I want to," Farzan said. He hated the thought of David wolfing down pizza when he was sick. "Unless you don't like soup? Or beans? Or herbs?"

"If you're cooking, I know I'll like it," David said, and he looked so sincere and miserable and cute in his pink hoodie, Farzan wanted to just cuddle up with him.

But soup came first.

"You go relax. Let me take care of it."

Instead of going to the couch, though, David followed Farzan into the kitchen.

"I got it," Farzan insisted. "You can rest."

"I'm tired of resting," David said with a shrug. "Besides, I'd like to watch you cook."

Farzan wasn't sure why that sent tingles dancing across his skin. David had seen every inch of him at this point. But watching him cook? That felt . . . weirdly intimate.

David gave Farzan directions around the kitchen—pointing out pots and pans and cutting boards and colanders—as he got to work. He set a pot of water on the stove to boil. He rinsed and drained the chickpeas, red pearl beans, and lentils; while they cooked, he chopped an onion and got it caramelizing in one of David's smaller sauté pans.

"What's that?"

"What's what?" Farzan pulled the leaves off a stalk of parsley and added them to the colander.

"You're humming."

"I am?" Farzan thought back. "Oh. You ever play *Final Fantasy X*?"

"Of course. Bawled my eyes out at the ending."

"Right? Anyway, it's 'Suteki Da Ne' from the soundtrack."

"Ah. Thought it sounded familiar. You have a nice voice."

Farzan hid his smile. "I'm not much of a singer."

"Take the compliment, Farzan."

Farzan blushed and nodded. When had he become such a blusher? But it was like David knew just what to say to make him feel like a shy teenager.

Farzan gave the onions a stir and got to chopping the herbs. He knew a lot of Iranians used food processors for this part—they did at Shiraz Bistro too, of course, a necessity for the quantities they made. But his mom had always chopped her herbs by hand, so that's what Farzan did, too.

As the soup came together, David edged closer, still keeping his distance but leaning against the counter, ankles crossed in a way that made the bulge in his sweatpants even more alluring.

"My eyes are up here," David teased.

"You know I can't resist you in those sweats."

"No funny business. I don't want to get you sick."

Honestly, Farzan was half-tempted to risk it. He and David hadn't had the chance to fool around since the kickball game, and that was weeks ago now. Work had kept them both busy. They hadn't even gotten to celebrate their official boyfriend status.

"Fine, no funny business, but you can't stop me admiring."

David ducked his head and coughed into his fist. "You sure you don't mind doing all this?"

"I like cooking." Farzan began breaking the reshteh—long, thin flat noodles a bit like linguine—into the soup. It was just right, thick and aromatic and vibrant green. "I like cooking for you."

David's smile warmed Farzan even more thoroughly than the heat from the stovetop.

When the noodles were cooked through, Farzan added the kashk and checked the taste. It was pretty good: not his best batch ever, but he wasn't in his own kitchen, and he'd had to use canned beans instead of soaking his own overnight. He ladled a bowlful for David and drizzled a bit more kashk on top, along with a few crispy onions.

David cupped the bowl in both hands, bringing it up to inhale the steam.

"This looks amazing," he said. "Thank you."

"You're welcome. It'll keep getting better over the next few days, too." Farzan dropped the last of his dirty dishes into the sink. "I can clean these up and get out of your hair."

"What? You're not going to stay?"

"I didn't want to assume..."

"You should."

Farzan cocked his head. *Should what?*

"Assume I want you to stay," David said, voice low and scratchy. "Always."

Always? Farzan didn't know what to make of that. Was David feverish? They'd just decided to make their relationship official, after all, and even so, they hadn't really settled on what that meant.

"Come on. Grab a bowl. Weren't you going to tell me something?"

Farzan looked down, wracking his brain. What was he supposed to tell David?

"Something about real estate?" David said.

"Oh, yeah." Farzan wished he had some nice, crunchy noon-e barbari to dunk in his ash, but bread took way too long to make on short notice.

David wrapped a blanket around himself and took one end of the couch, leaning away from Farzan and blowing on his soup to cool it with every spoonful. Farzan took the opposite side.

"So what's up?"

David looked so cozy and cute, Farzan couldn't stand it. He wanted to lean across, take the bowl out of David's hands, and smother him in kisses. But David was sick, so he had to settle for looking.

"Did you see that nail salon next to Shiraz Bistro when you came? It was probably closed."

"Yeah?"

"So, the owners—the Trans—are retiring and moving to Colorado. And I kind of want to buy their side of the building. Expand the restaurant. We could have an event space, and more tables obviously, a bigger kitchen..."

David's eyebrows raised. "That's not a bad idea, necessarily, but..."

"But?" Farzan's shoulders fell. He kind of wanted David to tell him it was a brilliant idea and he should plow forward with it.

"This business is weird. Financing can be hard to find. But if your fundamentals are good...good cash flow, decent covers per night, and a bit of liquidity...you know, the right numbers to show to a bank. I assume you'd be financing this?"

"I don't even know..." Farzan sighed. "I still rent my apartment. I've never bought any real estate before."

Farzan stared into his soup, afraid to look up and see derision in David's eyes. David clearly had his shit together. He probably understood what the fuck escrow was. Farzan had had it explained to him, several times, by both his siblings and much more patiently by Ramin, but it never really stuck.

But David simply said, "We all start somewhere," and launched into explaining the things Farzan needed to pull together before talking to the bank. He paused regularly—to eat more soup, and to give Farzan time to take notes on his phone—but he never once sounded annoyed, even when Farzan interrupted to ask questions.

David took him seriously.

Farzan barely took himself seriously some days. But David didn't seem to doubt Farzan could pull this all off. That of course the bank would say yes. That the restaurant would succeed.

Farzan hadn't even told Ramin and Arya about his plans for expansion yet. Or maybe *hopes* was a better word. Farzan wasn't sure why he'd asked David first.

Except David was his boyfriend.

David believed in him.

And he'd never admitted how badly he needed that.

By the time David finished, both their soups had gone cold, and David's voice sounded even scratchier.

"Hey. Sorry. I didn't mean to wear you out," Farzan said, standing to get David a fresh bowl.

"You didn't," David said. His eyebrows danced. "I wouldn't mind it if you did, though."

Farzan rolled his eyes, but he smiled. "No sex until you're feeling better."

David puffed out his lower lip. As far as pouts went, it was hilarious and ineffective and so adorable, Farzan wanted to kiss it right off his face. But David was still sick.

Farzan came back with fresh soup and a glass of water.

"Thanks." David took the soup and snuggled deeper into his blankets.

"Thank you," Farzan said. "I can clean up and head out."

"Wait," David said. "You want to watch a movie or something?"

"You don't mind?"

"Nah. When I was a kid, me and my mom would always watch the Muppets."

"I love the Muppets."

"Yeah?" David grabbed the remote and scrolled through movies until he found *The Muppet Movie*. The original one. "Want to watch?"

Farzan flopped back onto the couch.

"Sure."

David fell asleep midway through the movie, his soup bowl flopping sideways onto his lap. Thankfully it was empty. Farzan collected it as quietly as he could and tucked the blanket in around him more tightly. David looked so peaceful as he dozed, his eyelashes brushing his cheeks, his nostrils flaring ever so slightly as he breathed through his stuffy nose.

Tonight had been . . . perfect. Weirdly perfect. Farzan couldn't explain it to himself if he tried. But this—cooking and watching a movie, just being together—was maybe the most fun he'd ever had. Taking care of David. Making him soup. Laughing and joking and talking as the evening waned.

Scenarios spun out in his imagination, of more nights spent like this:

coming home to David holding a glass of wine, cozying up together to watch a movie. Or David coming home to him, with dinner on the stove, but it would go cold because they'd kiss hello and end up in the bedroom, or on the couch, or anywhere really, because every time they touched it was electric.

Farzan could get used to this. Even if *this* was just making soup for David when he was sick and watching the Muppets. His heart squeezed. *This* had a time limit. What was he supposed to do when David moved away?

The doorbell interrupted Farzan's spiral before it could get properly started. He shook himself and tried to get up without disturbing David, who muttered and wiped at his eyes with the back of his hand.

"I'll get it," Farzan said. "You relax."

"Probably UPS or something," David said into the couch.

But when Farzan opened the door, it wasn't a UPS driver. It was an older Black woman, with David's beautiful nose and upturned eyes, and an enormous soup pot gripped tightly to her chest.

"Hello," she said, eyeing Farzan up and down, and he felt the weight of her judgment on his skin. But then she smiled, and it was easy to see where David got his smile from. "You must be the boyfriend."

"Farzan," he said, stepping back. "Can I take that?"

While he carried the pot—it smelled rich and hearty, probably chicken noodle—David's mom (she had to be) went to say hello to her son, pressing the back of her hand to his forehead.

"You feeling any better, baby?"

"Hey, Momma," he said, voice sandy with sleep. Farzan shivered, remembering the only time they'd actually gotten to sleep together, curled up in Farzan's bed their first night together. David had sounded just like that when he woke up the next morning. "You didn't have to come."

"Apparently I didn't. Looks like your man already took good care of you."

"Oh, shit." David looked past his mom and met Farzan's eyes. He gestured back toward Farzan. "Momma, this is Farzan. My boyfriend. Farzan, my mom, Kathleen."

"We've met," Kathleen teased, but she shot Farzan another soft smile that had Farzan's ears burning. He retreated to the kitchen to let David and his mom have a moment, but Kathleen followed him, looking into the pot of ash and giving an approving nod.

"If I'd known you were here I would've let you two alone," she said. "He didn't tell me you were such a good cook."

"Ah, well..."

"It's sweet of you to take care of him." She leaned in and kissed Farzan on the cheek. The burning in his ears was spreading across his face.

"He didn't tell me how handsome you were, either." She winked. "So what's in this soup?"

Farzan explained to her, while they divvied up both pots of soup into David's collection of storage containers and stacked them in the fridge. Farzan made for the sink to get started on the dishes, but Kathleen shooed him off with a hand towel.

"You go relax. I got this."

"I really don't mind."

"I know you don't," she said. "David's always been a good judge of character."

Farzan didn't know what to say to that. So he slipped back into the living room. David was dozing again, snuggled up in his blanket, and Farzan wanted to wrap himself around David, nestle in and smell the sweet mixture his cologne and moisturizer made at the crook of his neck.

But instead, he lowered himself onto the couch. David peered at him, blinking slowly, with a soft grin.

"So. You survived meeting my mom. We've got to stop springing our parents on each other."

Farzan snorted. "Turnabout is fair play?"

"She likes you. I can tell."

"Yeah?"

"I like you too." David shifted to rest his head against the back of the couch, looking right at Farzan. "I like you a lot."

"Me too." Farzan was tempted to lean in and kiss David, sickness be damned, but then David's face scrunched up and he sneezed into the crook of his elbow.

Probably safest to keep his distance for now.

Instead, he asked, "Want me to make you some tea?"

thirty-four

Farzan

"A w," Ramin said, reaching for his mimosa. "That's sweet."

Farzan shrugged and cut his French toast. "Like you wouldn't do the same for Todd."

Todd grinned, but Ramin blushed. "Maybe. I'm not as good a cook as you, though."

"Don't worry, honey. I make a mean grilled cheese sandwich. And canned tomato soup." Todd leaned in and kissed Ramin on the lips, which only made Ramin's dimples deepen and his blush darken.

"No PDA at brunch!" Arya said, tossing a sugar packet. They were all seated on the patio of a spot Arya had found for them in the West Bottoms, not in the strip of restaurants and bars near the American Royal, but on a little side street close to the river, nestled between a warehouse and an auto-repair shop. The mimosas were bottomless, and the French toast was excellent.

They used to brunch all the time, when they were all in their twenties, before they had busy lives, stressful jobs, or, in Ramin's case, a live-in boyfriend.

"Is that a rule?" Todd asked.

"It is now," Arya said.

Truth was, brunch was sacrosanct. They didn't get to do it very often, and when they did, it used to be just the three of them. But things were serious with Todd now. Moved-in-together serious. They couldn't leave him out, but now they had to figure out how all this worked.

If Farzan and David got that serious, he'd want to bring David with him, too.

"You just made that up," Todd teased, but Ramin rested a hand on Todd's.

"Iranians don't do PDA," he said. "Even the straight ones."

"All right, all right," Todd said. "I'm just glad I finally rated an invite."

"You're practically family now," Farzan said, before Arya could get another dig in. For friends—teammates—they certainly liked to snipe at each other.

Arya opened his mouth anyway, but Ramin cut him off too.

"So David's doing better now?"

"Yeah, it was just a twenty-four hour cold. He's all better."

"I hope he thanked you appropriately." Arya stabbed a breakfast potato on his fork and brought it to his lips, licking the spud lasciviously.

Farzan rolled his eyes but kept his mouth shut. David might have indicated he wanted to do something a little special and sexy, but Farzan didn't need any thanks. He was glad to take care of David.

He'd still take a little sex, though. They *still* hadn't gotten a chance for a repeat of their postgame session. Juggling two schedules in the service industry, plus David's studying and Farzan's work on the restaurant, made it hard to find time to fuck. Farzan was the boss, and technically could take time off whenever he wanted, but he'd already missed a whole day taking care of David. He needed to show everyone he was dedicated.

"Any news on the Trans' place?" Ramin asked, gracefully diverting the conversation away from dick.

"No. I'm still pulling my numbers together." Farzan ran a hand through his hair. He'd finally explained his plan to Arya and Ramin, and both thought it was a good idea too. "Plus we're working on revamping the menu for winter. And our produce distributor was late on our last two orders, so now I'm fighting with them."

Todd frowned. "You can't call someone about it?"

Farzan shook his head. "Already did. I've never left so many voicemails in my life." He grabbed his mimosa and slouched in his chair. "Some days I really love what I do. Others I just...don't get how my parents did it for all those years."

"Well, there were two of them, and there's only one of you," Ramin pointed out. "You're only human."

"Yeah." Arya sipped at his herbal tea. "When's the last time you actually took a day off?"

"We're closed every Monday."

"Not what I asked."

"And I took care of David."

"That's a sick day, then."

"I wasn't sick!"

"But you were taking care of someone," Ramin said. "And last Monday when I talked to you, you were doing a spreadsheet, so you can't act like you take Mondays off either."

Farzan bit his lip. Arya and Ramin rarely ganged up on him, but when they did, well...

"Listen, I'm fine. I can handle it. And besides, I am taking tomorrow off. Purely for fun."

He and David had juggled their schedules to get a day off together. On a Saturday, no less. They were going to spend the whole day together. Preferably without clothes.

Farzan's thoughts must've shown on his face, though, because Arya's eyes lit up.

"Are you shitting me? You made a dick appointment on a workday?"

Across from Arya, Todd started coughing, choking on his mimosa. Ramin rubbed his back until he stopped, but the damage was done: several of the other tables were definitely staring at them, and Farzan's face felt hotter than the Cholula Todd kept smothering on his eggs Benedict.

"We're just hanging out," Farzan lied.

"Damn, dude. Good for you." Arya raised his flute and toasted Farzan. "Get it."

Farzan clinked his flute and sipped, trying hard not to laugh. There was one surefire way to get Arya off his back, though.

"So what about you? What's new at work?"

Arya groaned. "Ugh. Did I ever tell you how much I hate working with dogs? Playing with them, great. Trying to get them to hit a mark on stage? Nightmare."

"Hey, you." David answered the door in those sweats that Farzan liked so much and a rose-pink Henley that looked stunning against the sapphire undertones of his skin.

Farzan wanted to devour him on the spot.

"Hey." He stepped inside, and before he could get his shoes off, David had swept him into a kiss, nearly knocking over the coat rack in the process. "I missed you."

"I missed you," David breathed between kisses. "Thanks for coming over."

"Thanks for asking me."

David growled, his hands sliding down to Farzan's waist. "Fuck, I've been wanting this all week. I need you."

"Yeah?" Farzan's eyes rolled as David sucked the cord on the side of his neck hard enough that he'd definitely have a hickey, but he didn't care. He needed David, too. It had been a week of texts and FaceTimes, but those had always been quick, late at night, never enough for more than a "Hey, I miss you."

Farzan had his favorite dildo on the nightstand, just in case he could talk David into some phone sex, but all the yawning made it clear that wasn't in the cards.

"I'm dying here," David said against Farzan's skin.

"You don't want to go through your flash cards again?" Farzan teased.

David growled in protest. "Or I was thinking, we could play a little game. You try to get through your blind tasting, while I'm between your legs, and if I make you come before you name all six wines, I get a prize."

"That sounds more like I get the prize."

Farzan shrugged. He hadn't thought that through too well, to be honest; he just had this really hot vision of himself sucking David off while David tried to ignore him and taste wines.

"Whatever. You know what I mean."

"I do know what you mean. But we're not doing that tonight." David pressed his lips to Farzan's, suddenly soft and so tender Farzan shuddered. "Tonight, you're gonna fuck me into next month."

November was only a few days away, so that order wasn't quite as tall as it could have been, but Farzan was definitely excited to try. His dick surged in his joggers, which he'd worn in a vain attempt to level the playing field, but the things David's sweatpants did defied modern science. Farzan's dickprint in his joggers just couldn't compare.

Still, David seemed to like them, trailing his fingers along Farzan's waistband.

"Commando, huh?" he whispered.

"Seemed only fair."

David chuckled, a warm, throaty thing that made Farzan's hairs stand up and his ass clench. His core was heating up, heart hammering out a beat in time with each kiss. He ran his hands through David's soft hair, carefully caressing his scalp without messing up his twists. David pulled him closer, dragged him slowly, inexorably toward the living room, which seemed like a decent layover on the way to the bedroom. They tumbled onto the couch, Farzan on top of David, chest to chest and cock to cock.

"I can't believe I've waited this long for you to fuck me," David whispered. "I must be getting sentimental if I picked the Muppets over this."

"Hey. Don't knock the Muppets." Farzan refused to hear any slander against them.

"Never," David agreed, bucking his hips up to grind against Farzan.

Farzan relished the pressure, the softness of David's sweats, the hard, hot steel beneath.

"Besides. You were sick."

"I'm all better now."

Farzan ground himself downward, pressing David into the couch, savoring the way his breath hitched.

"Good." Farzan angled his mouth over David's, slipped his hand under David's shirt. Warm, smooth skin met him, strong muscle, soft hair, and there, pebbled and ready, David's nipple. Farzan rolled it with his thumb, captured David's gasp of pleasure between their lips. He twisted it, gently at first, and David let out a warm, throaty chuckle. But when he twisted harder, David laughed, hard, breaking the kiss and nearly throwing Farzan off the couch.

"Shit. Sorry," Farzan said, dragging himself back over David. "You okay?"

"Yeah, just...the twisting is a little much."

"Sorry."

"Don't worry. I'll give you a purple nurple of your own later."

"Oh yeah?"

"Yeah." David slid his hands down the back of Farzan's joggers, combing the hair on his cheeks with his fingers. "God, you feel so good."

David massaged Farzan's ass gently, as Farzan ground their cocks together and kissed every part of David's face, from his lips to his jaw to his nose to that sexy little slit in his eyebrow. "This is from your barber, right? You didn't hurt yourself when I wasn't paying attention."

David laughed. "Yeah, it's from my lineup."

"Okay, good. You're not allowed to hurt yourself."

"Noted." David rolled his hips against Farzan. "I'm gonna get hurt from blue balls if you keep teasing me like this, though."

Farzan slipped his hand out of David's shirt and moved for his waistband, kissing David hard. Kissing his boyfriend hard. He couldn't stop smiling through the kissing, even when the doorbell went off.

Farzan shifted, but David growled and kept his hands on Farzan's ass. "Ignore it. It's just UPS or some shit."

"What if they need a signature?"

"They can come back later. I'm busy." David's smile turned devilish. "And so are you."

This time, when their lips met, it was David who took control, sucking Farzan's tongue so hard he thought it might rip off. Farzan's hand finally made it beneath David's waistband, found his cock warm and wet and ready. Farzan teased David with light touches, playing with his foreskin, scraping his fingernails gently against David's balls, enjoying the way David shivered beneath him.

Farzan shifted to get a better angle to pull David out of his sweats, but before he could, the doorbell rang again, three times in a row.

David groaned in frustration. "Ignore it."

"They sound a little impatient."

"I'm impatient!" David insisted, his voice hitching into a whine. "Please, Farzan."

Farzan had never seen David like this. When David had fucked him, he was all cockiness and dirty talk. But now, he was letting Farzan take control, voicing his need, begging.

Farzan liked it when David begged.

His heart was beating double-time. "I like you like this. All desperate beneath me. You're beautiful."

David's smile was so radiant, he couldn't hold the glower he tried shooting Farzan.

Farzan gave David's cock a long, lingering stroke.

"Fuck yeah, play with my cock," David muttered.

"Yeah?"

"I love your hands on me."

"I love—"

BANG.

Farzan jumped, yanking way too hard on David's dick.

"Jesus!" David gasped.

"Sorry!"

But David wasn't looking at Farzan, he was looking out the living room window. In their haste to touch each other, they'd forgotten to close the curtains, and now someone stood outside, doubled over in laughter, held up by a hand against the window.

"Rhett!"

Farzan rolled off David, keeping his back to the window, and helped David get as decent as possible. The fright and surprise had deflated Farzan's dick and had done the same to David's. He arranged himself in his joggers and figured that was as good as it was going to get.

Fuck, how much had Rhett seen?

With a frown that didn't reach his eyes, David gestured for Rhett to go to the door. Once he did, David turned back to Farzan.

"I can't believe this."

"It's fine." Farzan leaned in for one last kiss. "To be continued?"

"It fucking better be."

thirty-five

David

"You don't have to go."

"I know, but I should," Farzan said. "This sounds important."

"You could hang out with us." David zipped up his jeans.

"Dressed like this?"

"Fair point. Maybe it's time to start leaving some clothes at my place."

Farzan laughed. "Maybe."

But the laughter didn't light up Farzan's face the way it usually did. David's stomach turned.

"What?" he asked, threading his fingers through Farzan's.

"Just..." Farzan swallowed, showing off the hickey David had given him. "It kind of hit me. How real this is all getting. You moving away."

"We're just talking," David said. His test was more than six weeks away. They still had plenty of time. "Nothing's certain. Rhett's a friend. I haven't seen him in forever."

A friend who had showed up unannounced—David had double-checked both the group chat and his regular texts with Rhett, and he definitely hadn't missed anything. But Rhett was an agent of chaos.

"All the more reason to catch up," Farzan said. "I'll be fine."

David stifled a growl. Today was supposed to be for him and Farzan. He'd cleared his schedule, gotten Farzan to clear his. He had a bottle of Paul Pernot Puligny-Montrachet, one of his favorite white Burgundies, chilling in the fridge. A carryout order from his favorite Thai restaurant all queued up and ready to go at the proper time—namely after Farzan fucked his brains out.

Now he had to go talk business instead.

"Hey. Join us for dinner after?"

"I don't..."

"Meet us at Aspire? Seven o'clock?" If he and Farzan couldn't spend the day together, at least they could have dinner. "I met your friends at kickball. Why not spend some time with one of mine?"

Farzan bit his lip but finally nodded, giving that soft little smile that was David's favorite.

David's stomach finally righted itself. "Okay. I'll walk you out."

"See you tonight," Farzan said at the door. "Nice meeting you, Rhett."

"You too! What's tonight?"

"Dinner. Assuming you behave," he warned Rhett, but with no heat. Like he'd ditch his friend in the city. Granted, Rhett probably had about a dozen places he wanted to check out anyway. As far as David knew, Rhett had never tasted Kansas City barbecue, which meant his life was sorely lacking. "See you tonight."

He stole a quick kiss from Farzan, stood in the door to watch him make the short walk to his car. What was the old saying? *I hate to see you go, but I love to watch you leave.* Farzan's ass looked incredible in those joggers. Plain black ones, with the white stripes on the sides. David had been ready to peel Farzan out of them when Rhett interrupted.

"You have got it so bad," Rhett said behind him. "I have never seen you smile like that."

David rolled his eyes and shut the door, glowering down at Rhett, who stood a good head shorter than him. It was a bit challenging because

Rhett had grown a patchy beard and it wasn't trimmed quite evenly. David felt the corner of his lip quirking upward against his will.

"What?" Rhett finally asked. "Do I have something on my face?"

"Your beard is uneven."

"Really? Shit." Rhett felt at his chin.

"Can I give you a hand before we head out?" David gestured toward the bathroom.

"You don't mind?"

"You know I got you."

David grabbed the rubbing alcohol, sanitized his clippers, and had Rhett sit on the counter with a towel on his lap.

"The beard does suit you," David said as he worked. It was the same vivid red as Rhett's hair and helped show off the angle of his jaw.

"Four years on T this past summer," Rhett said as David evened out his sideburns. "Figured it was time to try. Didn't know how much maintenance went into it, though."

David chuckled. "This is where a good barber comes in handy. You know how often I used to fuck mine up?"

"I like this look on you, though." Rhett gestured to David's jaw.

He used to keep a neat beard, but he'd switched to a three-day scruff look when he moved. Kansas City summers were miserable with a beard.

"Thanks. How do you like it?" He got out of the way for Rhett to look in the mirror.

"It's fire."

David snorted.

"No pun intended."

"Sure." David handed Rhett a towel as he rinsed off his face. "So. Ready to see the city?"

They took the long way, cutting south so they could take Westport Road to Main before following that all the way to the Liberty Memorial and Union Station. As David drove, Rhett caught him up on everything happening in LA: backers falling in line, the renovations of the kitchen, getting to join in the tastings as Shyla developed the menu.

After Union Station, David drove them around Crown Center, then headed north to swing through the Crossroads, past the Kauffman Center and Convention Center and toward the River Market.

"There's so little traffic," Rhett said, even as David swore under his breath when they caught another red light after getting stuck behind the streetcar. Still, Rhett was right, it was way better than Chicago had been. And as for LA...

"What's your commute like?" David asked, pulling off onto Delaware. He hadn't exactly meant to drive the route to Farzan's apartment, but it was a good way to see the downtown core.

"Ugh." Rhett swiped his hand over his face. "Hour to an hour and a half, usually. Sometimes two."

"Shit, really? Where're you at?"

"Little place in Claremont."

David shook his head, trying to picture LA in his mind, but he'd only visited once, when he was in his twenties, and he hadn't strayed too far from WeHo. He couldn't imagine spending hours in the car every day. He didn't like podcasts enough.

Kansas City had spoiled him. He could be at work in fifteen minutes, most days, and it never took him more than thirty, even if he somehow hit roadwork or rush hour. That would take some getting used to.

"Hey, you know any good coffee shops around here? I could use some caffeine. You would not believe how early I had to wake up to get to LAX."

Despite David's best intentions, they ended up spending hours at the coffee shop, catching up, talking about Shyla's restaurant and Rhett's life as an Angeleno. Seven o'clock crept up on them as the sun set and Kansas City did its thing where the temperature plummeted twenty degrees in less than an hour. A stiff wind carrying the scent of fresh snow nearly bowled them over as they ran for David's car to make the short drive to Aspire.

Farzan was already seated at a high-top in the corner when they arrived, sipping a glass of red wine and chatting with Kyra.

Now that was dangerous.

Farzan spotted him and waved, which meant Kyra saw him, too, and Rhett. Her eyes went wide.

"Are you shitting me?" she said, looking from Farzan to Rhett and then to David. "You know two whole people outside work? This is a scam, right? You guys are paid actors?"

Farzan grinned into his wine, but Rhett laughed.

"Are you kidding? He couldn't afford me." He offered Kyra his hand and they both shook, cementing an unholy alliance David might not live to regret. "And I know it sounds like fake news, but he's actually an old friend of mine."

"Technically, *you're* an old friend of *mine!*" David said, tossing his jacket across the seat back and sitting next to Farzan. "Hey, babe."

Farzan's cheek was warm and firm as he kissed it; when he leaned back, Farzan was grinning at him.

"What?"

"Nothing, babe."

David blinked. He had called Farzan babe first, hadn't he?

It felt . . . good. A little weird, yeah, but something to grow into. David mirrored Farzan's own smile.

"Okay, I take everything back," Kyra interrupted. "This is awkward and embarrassing for all of us. I liked it better when you were an introvert."

"Oh, he's still an introvert," Rhett interrupted. "That's why he needs extroverts to make him leave the house."

Kyra snorted. "You all need anything?"

"What're you drinking?" David asked, eyeing Farzan's glass. "Mind if I taste?"

Farzan slid it across the table; David recognized it at first sniff. He knew that burst of fruit well. "Oh, the Dashe." Dashe Les Enfants Terribles. "A bottle to share?"

"You're the wino," Rhett said.

"I took the streetcar," Farzan added. "I'm good if you are."

"Perfect. I'll grab it and some glasses," Kyra said.

"And some fries, if it's not too much trouble?" Farzan called.

"For David's boo? No trouble at all." Kyra winked conspiratorially at Farzan.

David groaned as she finally left them. "Why did I agree to bring you here?"

"Because you're a glutton for punishment," Rhett said. "So, Farzan. How'd you and David meet?"

Farzan's eyes went wide. "Well... we met here, actually."

Rhett clutched imaginary pearls. "A workplace romance? Scandal!"

As Farzan and David took turns telling the story—not the *whole* story, but close enough—Kyra brought their wine and fries.

"Well, you're doing something right," Rhett said. "I've known David for five years and I've never seen him smile this much. Are you coming to LA with him?"

It was a subtle thing, the way Farzan's smile turned brittle. Maybe David wouldn't have caught it if he wasn't so addicted to Farzan's face. The way his lips curled around his words, the way his eyes crinkled up when he was trying to suppress laughter.

"We're still figuring that part out," David finally said, once it was clear Farzan wasn't going to answer. Farzan nodded, but for some reason David wanted more than that. Annoyance gripped his windpipe. But what was he expecting? For Farzan to just say yes?

He had a life here, family, he was trying to expand his restaurant. Living his dream. How could he begrudge Farzan for not wanting to give that up for him? Besides, there were probably a million Iranian restaurants in LA. Not like he could just open up a new one in one of the most expensive cities in the country.

"Well, you should come," Rhett said. "You're the first thing in a long while that David's talked about other than wine."

Farzan blushed at that.

"Come on, man," David said, but Rhett kept going.

"Seriously. You know I was surprised when he answered my call about the job? He never answers the phone. Too busy studying. Making his dream come true."

"And what's wrong with that?" David asked.

"Nothing! Hell, I'm doing the same, though with way less flash cards."

"You know about the flash cards?" Farzan asked.

"Oh, yeah, I used to help him study for his advanced somm back in Chicago. The only time he'd hang out. Not to go out for a drink or help a friend move apartments or even go to Pride."

"I've gotten better about that," David said into his wine. If he'd known he was going to get roasted, he would never have brought Rhett and Farzan into each other's orbits. "I mean, I played kickball with Farzan's team just a couple weeks ago."

David caught Farzan blushing, no doubt remembering the postgame.

"I'm just saying," Rhett said. "I don't think I know a single person in the world more driven than you. When you want something, you go for it, and you don't let anything stop you. That's why I called you, man. Shyla wants this restaurant to be something special. She only wants the best. People who are gonna give two hundred percent to make it happen. And that's you."

Rhett raised his glass. "To the hardest-working guy I know."

David clinked with Rhett and with Farzan, who said, "To David."

"Okay, but seriously," David said, once they'd all drank. "Enough about me. What's new with you? What's LA like?"

Rhett launched into an epic about his struggles finding an apartment, which led to a story about discovering the wrong tables had arrived at the restaurant, and then to a passive-aggressive fight with an independent contractor about gas lines for the kitchen.

Farzan laughed at all the right spots—Rhett was an impeccable storyteller—but there was a tightness around his eyes, too, and he clenched the stem of his wineglass so hard David was worried it might snap.

When Rhett excused himself to visit the bathroom, David leaned in, rubbed his thumb against the back of Farzan's hand.

"You okay, babe?"

Farzan nodded, but his face was like a cork about to crumble.

"What's wrong?"

"Nothing." Farzan cleared his throat and straightened in his chair, though his shoulders still hovered by his ears. "Sorry. I guess all this talk about your new restaurant is making me think about all I've still got to do at the bistro."

David pursed his lips. Yeah, maybe it was, but he could tell it was more than that.

"It's starting to feel real, huh?" he said. "Expanding the place?"

"Still need to get a loan," Farzan said. "But yeah, I guess. You?"

"Me what?"

"Your test. Your move. Is it feeling real too?"

"I don't even know." David rubbed his jaw. "Yesterday marked seven weeks out. So I feel like it should be feeling real, but it's still not. I've been preparing for so long, I don't know if it'll feel real until I'm in front of the judges."

"You'll do great." Farzan gave him a real smile then, squeezing his hand.

"Most people don't pass their first time," David muttered.

It wouldn't be the worst thing, either, if he didn't pass. If he spent another year at Aspire. Another year with Farzan.

Except Rhett said he pretty much had the job either way. He couldn't give that up. It was everything he'd been working for.

"You're not most people," Farzan told him. "You're David Fucking Curtis. You got this."

David laughed, pulling Farzan's hand close to kiss his palm, as joy warmed his belly and chest.

"You two are too adorable," Rhett said, flopping into his seat again and fixing Farzan with a look. "You must really be something special if you got this guy to abandon his too-busy-for-a-relationship ways."

David kept a grip on Farzan's hand. Farzan was sweet, and kind, and hardworking, and fucking sexy. He came alive when he met Farzan. Wasn't there some way to have both—to chase his dreams and keep his man?

For Farzan, he'd have to try.

thirty-six

Farzan

So you're the one who's trying to steal David, huh?" A short woman with boulder shoulders asked, doing her level best to glare at Rhett as they got their coats on at the door.

"Only after you stole him from me," Rhett teased back. "Jeri, right?"

So this was the mysterious Jeri. Farzan hung back and let them tease each other. David's hand was warm against the small of his back.

David leaned in to whisper, "Sorry."

"What for?"

"For all this. I really did want to spend the day with you."

"It's fine," Farzan said. "This was important."

"So are you."

Farzan's chest gave a painful squeeze at that.

Because yeah, he and David had apparently moved into pet-names territory, but when it came down to it, David's dreams were bigger than Farzan. Bigger than Kansas City. And today had been a painful reminder that despite what they told each other, about figuring out the future when it came, there wasn't really going to be a choice to make.

David had a brilliant career ahead of him. He'd probably become the most famous sommelier in the United States. He'd pour wine for rich assholes that made more money in an hour than Farzan would in his lifetime. He'd go to fancy parties and travel the world and be featured in wine magazines and websites.

Farzan wasn't jealous of all that; he didn't want it. He wanted his restaurant to succeed. He wanted to prove to his parents he could do it. That he wasn't a fuckup.

He wanted to hang out with his best friends and not be the one who hadn't made anything of his life. To go to family dinners and not be reminded what a failure he was.

He didn't want to prove himself to strangers. Just to the people he loved.

Jeri and Rhett finished bickering, and Jeri turned her gaze to Farzan, her gray-green eyes kind. "And you must be Farzan. I've been wanting to meet the guy who put a smile on David's face."

"Jeri," David pleaded, but she waved him off.

"You must be a good influence on him, if you're getting him to leave the house and not work. Though this barely counts."

Farzan chuckled. "I don't know about that, but I do like spending time with him."

David's hand shifted to the side of Farzan's waist, giving a soft squeeze and pulling Farzan in a little closer. "It's nice to finally meet you. David's told me how great you are."

"He's pretty great himself," Jeri said. "The hardest worker I know. And a good friend. When he gets his head out of his ass."

"Hey!"

But Jeri's gaze softened. "I knew him when he was a scrawny college kid—"

"Oh my god, you were a twink?!" Rhett said, but Jeri ignored him.

"And I've never met anyone as passionate as him. When he wants something, he goes after it with his whole heart."

Jeri held Farzan's eyes, like she was trying to say something more. But Farzan already knew that. He'd seen how driven David was, how passionate he was with each tasting, how diligently he studied his flash cards.

David had big dreams. And Farzan would never forgive himself if he stood in David's way. Even if that meant they'd have to say goodbye.

All he could do was enjoy this while it lasted.

"Thanks again," Rhett said from the back as David drove down Grand toward River Market.

He'd insisted on driving Farzan home, even though he lived on the streetcar line. But the wind had turned biting, and Farzan didn't mind.

"But seriously, dude, I didn't come here for you to buy me free food. I hope you know that."

David laughed and glanced at Rhett in the mirror. "It's all good. You can buy the barbecue tomorrow."

"Oh?" Farzan turned to look over his seat. "Where are you going?"

"We're doing a full tour," David said before Rhett could answer. "Q39, Joe's, Slaps. You know, the greats."

Farzan's mouth watered, but his stomach gave an uncomfortable clench as he imagined just how much meat that would entail. Delicious meat, but still.

"I'm going to be in a food coma on the way home," Rhett said. "And I will regret nothing."

"Your neighbors on the flight might," David muttered.

"Speaking of which," Rhett said. "When are you coming to visit me?"

"What?" David asked.

Farzan went cold, despite the seat warmer keeping his ass toasty.

"You should come out to LA, see the restaurant—well, what there is— check out apartments and stuff. You can crash with me. I'll even let you interrupt me having a little afternoon delight."

David snorted. "All right, I'll check my schedule." He glanced at Farzan. "You want to come with? A little getaway?"

"Can't," Farzan said automatically.

This whole thing was difficult enough. But going to see what David's new life was going to look like? That felt like a stab to the chest.

"Thanks, though."

David shrugged, but his lips pursed. He didn't really want Farzan to go, though, did he? What did he expect Farzan to do? Admire his fancy new restaurant? Faint at the rent prices?

Farzan hugged himself.

"You cold, babe?" David turned the heat up, even though they were blocks away.

"I'm all right."

Rhett filled the rest of the ride with a litany of places David needed to try when he came to LA. Farzan hugged himself tighter.

Finally they pulled up to his apartment.

"Thanks," Farzan said, unbuckling his seat belt, but David grabbed his hand.

"Hey." He stroked the top of Farzan's hand with his thumb. "Thank you."

"Ugh, you two are so cute I can't stand it," Rhett said. "David, you get out and kiss him good night. I'll circle the block or something."

"What?" David asked, but Rhett had already leapt out of the car and yanked David's door open.

"Come on."

Farzan laughed and let himself out, tugging his jacket tighter. Rhett pulled away—probably faster than he should have—and Farzan drew David under the awning.

"He's..." Farzan wasn't sure what to say.

"Yup," David agreed anyway. And then he looked at Farzan, really looked at him, and Farzan felt trapped against the door frame. His chest tightened, and he tried to breathe.

"Hey," David said softly, stepping closer, resting his forehead against Farzan's. "We're going to figure it out. I promise."

But Farzan shook his head. "It's okay. I want you to be happy. You know that, right?"

"I do." David kissed him, soft and tender. "You make me happy too."

Farzan's heart thundered.

David made him happy, too. But what were they supposed to do?

"Just don't give up on us." It was like David could read his mind. "Please?"

David kissed him again, kissed him harder, and Farzan gave in. He took control, pushing David back so it was him pressed against the awning, with Farzan's tongue plundering his mouth.

They'd make this work. They'd figure things out.

Farzan wouldn't fuck this up.

thirty-seven

Farzan

"Azizam, what's all this?" Persis asked, thumbing through the stack of papers at the corner of Farzan's desk. With her free hand, she sipped her tea, a piece of rock sugar tucked between her cheek and teeth like a chipmunk hoarding nuts for winter.

"Financials." Farzan ran his hand through his hair. He needed a haircut, and a shave too, for that matter; his scruff had become a full-on shaggy beard. When had he gotten so much gray in his chin? If he grew it out he'd look like the six-fingered man from *The Princess Bride*. The last thing he needed was Inigo Montoya busting down the door of Shiraz Bistro looking for vengeance for his slain father.

"For the bistro?"

Farzan turned down his *Chrono Trigger* playlist. "Yeah. I've got a meeting with the bank in a couple weeks."

"The bank? What for? Are you in trouble?" Persis began thumbing through the papers more rapidly. "You know, if you need help, you can ask us. I know you don't like asking, but..."

"Nothing's wrong," Farzan insisted, gently easing the papers out of his mom's hand. "I'm getting a loan to buy the Trans' place next door. That way we can expand the bistro."

"Expand?" Persis's eyes went wide. "Are you sure? You know this business can be unpredictable."

Farzan was well aware. He'd lived through enough recessions and scares about the mortgage and worries about college funds to know just how much uncertainty was involved. But he'd been over it from every angle with David. And David thought it made sense.

"I know," he said, straightening in his chair. "And I do know. But with more space, we can host events, get more covers per night, and expand the kitchen so we're not always bumping elbows."

Not to mention he could finally keep the extra cleaning supplies somewhere other than his office.

"If you say so." Persis didn't sound convinced. Farzan tried not to take it personally. His parents had run the bistro for decades, after all, and had a wealth of experience. Yet his mom still always seemed to think the world was going to come crashing down around him.

Just once, it would be nice if she could believe in him. The way David did.

He didn't say that, though. He shrugged, gritted his teeth, and kept at his spreadsheets. After the third time their online reservation system fucked up, he'd talked it over with Patricia and the other hosts and decided it was time to switch over to a bigger (and more stable) one. But that meant switching over all the existing reservations already in the system, which was tedious because he couldn't just export a list like a normal app. And it meant a higher monthly fee, which meant he had to go back and adjust all the financials for the bank. His mom didn't get any of that.

Yeah, his parents knew how to run a restaurant, but sometimes it felt like they were still running it like it was the nineties. The 1990s, he mentally corrected, because Chase liked to tease him that some of their staff weren't even born when the nineties ended. Last year, when he was subbing for a history class, a sixth grader had looked at a date on the board and gasped, "The 1000s?" When did he get so old?

As if to remind him, his shoulder twinged. He'd been slouched over his computer too long.

"You look tired, maman," Persis said softly. "Are you sleeping?"

"Yeah." Farzan stood and rubbed his neck. "What about you? How'd your doctor appointment go?"

Farzan's parents were supposed to text him after his mom's latest cardiology appointment but had conveniently "forgotten."

"Fine. Maheen agrees everything looks good."

So not forgotten. They'd just skipped him and gone to the family doctor instead.

"I promise you don't have to worry."

"I can't help it."

"Oh, my son." Persis set her tea down and wrapped Farzan in a hug. When he was growing up, her hugs had always been bone-crushing. When had they gotten tender? "Everything will be all right. I promise."

"I just worry about you."

"I know. You don't have to take care of me, though. That's my job."

Farzan wasn't convinced. But Persis rubbed her thumb along his jaw. "You need a shave, maman. How is your boyfriend supposed to kiss you through all this? You can't hide your handsome face."

Farzan snorted. "David has stubble too."

"Hmm, but his is neater. When are we going to see him again?"

"You know he works at a restaurant too. It's hard to find time."

"Well, your sister's hosting a dinner Saturday. Can he get off in time?"

"Saturday? Maybe, but I can't—"

"Sure you can."

Farzan bit his lip. He couldn't tell his mom he'd already taken last Saturday off for a canceled dick appointment. So had David.

Plus David was leaving for LA on Tuesday.

Leaving for a visit, Farzan reminded himself, but that didn't help the dread in his stomach much.

"I'll ask David," he finally said. "And see how busy we're looking that night. No promises, though."

"Good. I'll see you both there," Persis said, ignoring everything Farzan just told her.

She slurped the last of her tea. Farzan followed her out, taking her cup and setting it in the dishwasher.

"I love you, azizam," she said as he held her coat for her. "I only want you to be happy. You know that, don't you?"

"I know, Maman. I love you too. See you soon."

He kissed his mom on both cheeks and let her out, waving as she drove off.

Farzan stood at the door, enjoying a bit of sunshine through the windows and rolling out his neck until a shout of "Fuck fuck fuck!" from the kitchen grabbed his attention.

He spun around. "What was that?"

"Nothing..." Spencer called.

And then: "We have any spare skewers?"

Farzan sighed. They bought new skewers every month, but sometimes they needed to be replaced early. "I'll get some."

Farzan was still getting dressed when David knocked on his door. He left his shirt unbuttoned and ran to let him in.

"Hey, you." David's smile was luminous. "You got a haircut."

Farzan had finally managed a trim and a shave, too, but his stubble had already come back.

"Yeah." Farzan pulled David into his apartment and let the door close behind him. "I missed you."

He pressed his lips to David's; he tasted like mint and orange and vanilla, smelled like vetiver and amber and heaven. He could feel David's smile against him.

"I missed you too, babe." The last week had been intense for both of them. Taking a Saturday off was hard in the restaurant business; taking two in a row was basically asking for fate to knock you on your ass. Farzan's to-do list was going to murder him.

Still, now that David was in front of him, all Farzan wanted to do was drag him to the bedroom. They weren't due at Maheen's for another half hour, and that was before taking Persian Standard Time into account, but David looked perfect, in dark-wash jeans and an emerald V-neck sweater so soft Farzan wanted to rub his face against it. They couldn't risk showing up looking freshly fucked.

But damn was it tempting.

"This is a great color on you," Farzan said instead, following the V of the collar, letting the pads of his fingers trace David's collarbone. "You look perfect."

"Mm, so do you," David said, running his hand through Farzan's exposed chest hair. "You sure we don't have time for a quickie?"

"I wish." But Farzan was so nervous, his arms quivered as he rested them at David's waist. He wasn't a hundred percent certain he could even get hard right now. "But I better get ready and go."

David pouted. "Fine. But what about after?"

Farzan waggled his eyebrows as he backed into his bedroom. Once he was dressed, he grabbed the glass container of sholezard—sweet saffron rice pudding, decorated with almond slivers and pistachio crumbles and cinnamon in the shape of a flower—out of the fridge, slipped his shoes on, kissed David one last time. "Let's go."

Farzan offered to drive, but David insisted. "Sorry, but I get carsick if I'm the passenger."

"All good with me."

As soon as they were on the road, David laid his hand on the console, palm up, and Farzan wound their fingers together. "Thanks for coming tonight. I know you're busy."

"Hey. Not too busy for something this important."

"My family's going to love you."

Farzan bit his lip as soon as he said it. They hadn't even said *I love you* to each other, so why had he stuck his foot in his mouth and said that about his family?

But David just shrugged. "If not, I brought some wine to bribe them."

"I hope it's nothing special. My parents still think wine shouldn't cost more than ten dollars a bottle."

"Shit, really?"

"Really really."

David sighed. "Inflation's a bitch. There used to be tons of bottles under ten dollars that were amazing. Now you've got to go to fifteen for most of them."

They made it onto I-35, heading south toward Leawood. David clicked his thumb on the steering wheel, turning up the music just a bit. Farzan recognized the piano right away.

"*Howl's Moving Castle?*"

"Yeah. You mind?"

"I love Joe Hisaishi."

"Okay. Best Ghibli film. Go."

"Ugh." Farzan frowned. "Okay, but best and favorite are separate, right?"

David laughed. "If you insist. Best and favorite then."

"Okay, favorite is *Castle in the Sky* because I used to have a huge crush on James Van Der Beek and I liked the robots. Best is *Princess Mononoke*."

David gasped. "First off, we need to have a serious talk about dubs versus subs."

"Verses? Subs?" Farzan teased. "Sounds kinky."

David shot Farzan a fleeting side-eye before turning back to the road.

"As I was saying...Second, *Princess Mononoke* over *Spirited Away*? That's slander."

"Okay, listen, I love *Spirited Away*, and I know it won an Oscar and everything, but I think *Princess Mononoke* most powerfully captures the environmentalism, spirituality, *and* coming-of-age themes that make Studio Ghibli so powerful, and *Spirited Away* does the second two exquisitely but not the first."

"You don't think the whole river-polluted-by-junk was environmental enough?"

"I didn't say it didn't do them, I just think that was a bit overly simplistic compared to *Mononoke*..."

David kept up a lively argument as they drove, sometimes making good points, sometimes clearly arguing just for the sake of getting Farzan riled up, and sometimes only trying to make Farzan laugh. But before Farzan knew it, David's phone interrupted the music to announce that their destination was on the right.

"Should I pull into the driveway or stay on the street?"

"Street," Farzan said. "Unless you like taking your life into your own hands."

"All right..." David said, pulling up in front of Maheen's house. As Farzan got out, cradling the sholezard, David grabbed a little wine tote from the back, filled with six bottles.

Farzan blinked. That was a lot of wine for the eight of them.

"Don't worry, I don't expect us to drink it all. I wasn't sure what everyone liked. Plus what if I only brought one and it was corked?"

"I promise you, my family wouldn't notice if it tasted like a handful of coins."

"Ugh, handful of coins? That's a good one."

Farzan chuckled and led David toward the door, pointing out the driveway to their left, which sloped steeply downward before turning into the house's basement garage.

"Oh damn," David said. "That must be fun in the winter."

"I don't know how they do it."

Farzan paused in front of the door, his hands full. Sure, he could've shifted the sholezard to just one hand so he could ring the doorbell, but now that he was here, his heart was in his throat. Not because of David—how could anyone not like David?—but because this was how he always felt at family gatherings. Like he was waiting for the other shoe to drop.

No, not just a shoe. For the sky to open up and rain down loafers upon him, like the newscaster from the Muppets.

And he knew it made no sense. He loved his family with his whole heart. And he knew his family loved him. He knew if he ever needed anything—*anything*—a hundred pairs of hands would be ready and waiting to offer it.

But if comparison was the thief of joy, then the Alavi family was full of master thieves.

David rested a hand on his lower back. He stepped closer, wrapping Farzan in his scent and warmth, and Farzan's shoulders unhitched.

"Okay," he said, taking a deep breath. "Let's do this."

thirty-eight

David

Both of David's parents were loud and opinionated, as were his aunties and uncles. Many a holiday gathering had left David convinced he was going to suffer permanent hearing loss. He'd even contemplated ear plugs, but so far all the ones he'd found were bright orange and way too likely to stand out.

The Alavi family could put the Curtises to shame.

As soon as the door swung open, a wall of noise slammed against him. Persian music—he recognized the syncopated beat from Shiraz Bistro—provided background to a host of loud voices arguing, in both English and Persian, and no one seemed to notice the two new guests.

Farzan turned back with a small smile and a *what can you do* shrug. Despite the trepidation he'd shown outside, he seemed genuinely happy to see his family.

Farzan directed David to the row of shoes by the door; David had worn his newest pair of sneakers, shining birds of paradise against a deep green field, with white soles and toecaps, and he had to set down his wine and fight to get them off, because they were high-tops and needed a tiny bit of breaking in.

He had a feeling going into this that Farzan's sister's house was shoes-off, but he couldn't resist showing them off, and was gratified when Farzan said "I love those."

David beamed at him, kissed him on his nose. "Thanks for inviting me."

"Are you kidding? It was either that or flee the country, change my name, and go work in an oil field in Manitoba."

"Why Manitoba?"

Farzan shrugged. "I don't know. Sounds gay."

"You..."

Before David could tease Farzan anymore, a woman appeared at the end of the hall. She looked a bit younger than Farzan, but they shared the same chin and nose and endlessly kind brown eyes.

And when she smiled, it was Farzan's smile.

"Farzan!" She pulled her brother into a hug. "And you must be David."

"Nice to meet you," David said, offering a hand, but she pulled him into a hug and kissed both his cheeks. She smelled like jasmine and strawberries. "Maheen, right?"

She nodded, backing away but holding onto his arm as she looked him up and down. She turned to Farzan and stage whispered, "He's handsome."

"I know." Farzan linked his arm through David's. "You need help in the kitchen?"

"God, yes." She practically dragged Farzan into the house; David kept close, because meeting Farzan's family had seemed like a fine idea—Farzan had met his parents, after all—but now, meeting all of them at once, David wondered what exactly he'd gotten himself into.

The kitchen was huge and modern, anchored by a granite-topped island with a sink and ample prep space. An induction stovetop, convection oven, and slate gray cabinetry lined the walls. Farzan's father, who had a severe-looking nose but a friendly smile, was already at the stove, stirring a pot of something that smelled sweet and savory and sour.

"Baba, this is David. David, my father, Firouz."

"Nice to meet you, David. Farzan, can you check the rice? And the kufteh?"

Farzan licked his thumb and tapped it against one of the pots on the stove, frowned and turned the heat up a tad, then pulled the lid off a sauté pan filled with enormous meatballs. He dipped a spoon into the simmering sauce, puckered his lips as he tasted, and rummaged through the spice cabinet.

It was like seeing double: Farzan and his dad moved the exact same way in the kitchen, from the little head bobs as they stirred, to the way they pursed their lips, and even the way they banged the spoon against the edge of a pot.

Farzan was in his element. David had gotten glimpses of Farzan cooking before, when he'd made soup, but David had been sick and foggy. Now, though, well. His mom always said there was nothing sexier than a man who could cook, and she was right.

He wasn't just sexy, though. Farzan was freer, somehow. Confident and poised and happy. It was beautiful to witness.

Farzan caught David smiling.

"What?"

"Nothing." No need to get all mushy in front of Farzan's family. "Where should I put the wine? And should your sho . . . your rice pudding go in the fridge?"

"Sholezard, and yes please. You can leave the wine on the counter next to the doogh. Open one if you like. Gimme a second."

"Doog?" David couldn't quite make the sound Farzan had made, an unfamiliar consonant that sounded alarmingly like Farzan was choking.

David shook the thought off.

"Doogh," Farzan repeated, emphasizing the sound, but that just made David's dick twinge in his pants, remembering when Farzan made that sound around him. "The big white bottles."

"Gotcha."

David put away the sholezard, stood up the wine where Farzan indicated, next to a pair of two-liter bottles filled with a fizzy white liquid.

"It's like a carbonated yogurt drink," Farzan explained. "It's not for everyone."

"Hm." It sounded sus, but David wouldn't mind trying it.

He cracked open a screw-top Oregon Pinot and filled a pair of stemless glasses.

Farzan kissed his dad on the cheek, wiped his hands on a towel, and took the offered glass. "Thanks. Come on, let's meet everyone else."

Farzan dragged David into the living room, where the rest of his family was gathered: his mother; his younger brother, Navid, and Navid's fiancé, Gina; and Maheen with her husband, Tomás. They were loudly discussing Sporting KC's performance in the playoffs, but stopped as soon as they saw David.

David had heard of being love-bombed before, and he'd always associated it with cults, but he wasn't sure what else to call being suddenly surrounded by Farzan's family, exchanging hugs and cheek kisses and hasty greetings with five people all at once.

"Let him breathe," Farzan said, laughing and pulling David aside. "He'll be here all night."

"Can you blame us?" Maheen said. "You know the last time you brought a boyfriend around to meet us?"

"Jason, right?" Navid said, elbowing Farzan in the side.

Farzan's lips pressed together, and his brow knit, but Navid kept going. "God, I don't miss that guy."

"Aw, he wasn't that bad," Maheen said. "He was cute at least. Though not as cute as you," she said to David.

"No, he wasn't that bad up until the whole cheating thing," Navid said darkly.

David nearly spat his wine out, but poor Farzan looked like he wanted to dive into his glass and drown in it. He took a huge gulp and shook his head.

"Oh, wait, there was Sean too," Maheen said.

"Sean!" Persis shouted from the couch. "Don't mention that pedar sag in here. I can't believe I spent all day making noon-e panjereh for him."

Farzan's shoulders were creeping up toward his ears again. David grabbed his shoulder and squeezed. "Hey," he whispered. "It's all good. I don't care about your exes."

Farzan shook his head and finished his glass, then stared at it.

"Want me to grab you more?"

"Yeah. Thanks."

"Anyone else want some wine?" David asked.

"I'll grab some." Tomás followed David to the kitchen. "What is it?"

"Oregon Pinot."

Firouz was humming to himself at the stove while David topped up Farzan's glass and poured another for Tomás. "Want me to pour one for Maheen?"

Tomás bit his full bottom lip and shook his head. He was handsome, with bronze skin, bowed lips, ink-black hair cut short and stylish, and a nose just crooked enough to make him look a bit roguish. "Nah, just me."

"All right."

"I know it can be overwhelming. I remember the first time I met everyone. Just keep breathing."

"Thanks."

"David," Firouz called from the stove. "Could you pour me one, too?"

"Sure, Mr. Alavi."

"Please. Firouz."

Tomás retreated to the living room while David passed another glass to Firouz.

"So," he said, pulling out his wooden spoon and swiping a finger across the back to taste. He grabbed the pepper mill and gave it a few good cranks. "I heard Persis knows your stepmom?"

"Dad's girlfriend," David said. "They just started dating."

"Ah. But you took them to Shiraz Bistro?"

"Yeah. Well, they took me. Deb really likes it."

"You know, me and Persis were going to close it, but Farzan said he wanted to take it over. I didn't want to let him at first, but now..."

Firouz swirled his wine and sipped.

"This is good."

"Cheers." David clinked glasses. "But now?"

"Ah, well." Firouz ran a thumb over his mustache; it was gray and bushy and only a little bit out of control. "My son has so much to offer the world, but sometimes I think every time he's reached out, the world has bitten his hand. I just want him to be happy. Successful. Have a good life."

"Yeah." David didn't know what else to say. How much of this had Firouz ever said out loud to his son?

"Now he wants to expand the bistro, make an event space, make a bigger kitchen . . . It's a lot of change. I just don't want it to bite him again."

"He knows what he's doing," David said. "I've seen his plans. They're good."

Firouz nodded. "You know, growing up he was always looking out for his siblings. Helping take care of them. Now he's taking care of the restaurant. His mother and I never wanted him stuck following in our footsteps. He always had all these dreams, but now . . ."

Firouz sighed wistfully, looking toward the ceiling. In that moment he looked so much like his son, David ached just a tiny bit.

"Well, like I said. We came to this country because we wanted our kids to have it better than we did. To be happy."

Firouz sipped his wine, but he gave David an appraising look over the rim.

David straightened up, but Firouz's eyes crinkled in the corners. Like he liked what he saw.

"And I think he is," Firouz said. "When he's with you."

David grinned into his own wineglass. "I'm happy with him, too."

"Well of course you are. My son's pretty great. Now, you mind telling everyone dinner is ready? You might have to shout."

David chuckled and patted Firouz on the shoulder.

"Sure thing."

thirty-nine

Farzan

What was taking David so long? Farzan desperately needed more wine. Not to get drunk—no way was he getting drunk in front of his family—but a light buzz would certainly take the edge off the constant stream of backhanded compliments.

Then again, maybe David had picked exactly the right time to retreat to the kitchen, as the trip through Farzan's dating history was nearly to Brandon (fucking *Brandon*). Farzan had tried to swear off white guys after that, but he lived in Kansas City. That was like eighty percent of the dating pool.

Tomás returned from the kitchen, and Farzan waited for David to follow, but no: he hung back. Farzan pondered following, in case David had gotten trapped in conversation with his dad, but then he noticed Tomás only had a single glass of wine, and when he sat down Maheen didn't even take a sip. Curious: Maheen loved red wine.

More curious still, Farzan could've sworn her hand went to cradle her stomach for the briefest of seconds.

Wait. Was tonight some sort of pregnancy announcement?

That was . . .

Farzan didn't know what he was feeling. Joy for Maheen and Tomás.

Excitement for the new addition to their family. Anticipation, because he was going to be a great guncle. (He'd spoil that kid rotten.) Relief, because his mom would finally have grandbabies. Dread, because he did not need another reminder of all the ways he'd let his family down.

And shame. Because if Maheen *was* pregnant, this was supposed to be a happy night, not one for him to wallow in self-pity.

He kept his eyes on Maheen as Navid and Gina talked wedding venues with his mom, Maheen occasionally interjecting, until David finally returned.

"Hey, everyone!" he said, cutting through the chatter. Farzan's chest fluttered at the way his voice boomed. It reminded him of the way he'd called out plays during their kickball game, which reminded him of after the game, which…

Nope, not thinking of that during family dinner.

But damn. David's voice always did that to him.

"Dinner's ready."

What followed was typical Alavi family chaos. Maheen and Tomás's dining room table only had room for six, but they all crowded around it anyway, after a solid minute of all five Alavis taarofing about who would sit on the two brown metal folding chairs. In the end, Farzan and Navid won (if getting to sit on hard metal counted as a win), and Farzan scooted his chair in next to David.

The table was laden with food: a platter of rice, its tahdig top golden and gleaming; rich brown fesenjan, still steaming; verdant green wedges of kookoo sabzi, filling the air with the scent of sharp herbs; and of course, Firouz's famous kufteh, meatballs stuffed with dates and swimming in a sauce the color of the summer sun.

All that, plus two baskets of warm flatbread, two more baskets filled with fresh herbs, a platter of huge chunks of feta cheese, bowls of almonds and pistachios and three kinds of torshi.

"Here, try this," Farzan said, spooning a bit of lemon torshi onto David's plate. "Pickled lemons."

Farzan had helped his mom prep the batch, slicing a hundred fresh lemons into thin wedges, ten fresh jalapeños into slices, and jarring them with lemon juice and olive oil and his mom's pickling spices, before aging them for three months.

David took a tiny taste, his lips puckering. "Hm. Good. It's got something...hmm. I taste turmeric and white pepper but there's also this herbal..."

David's tongue danced against his lips in a way that was somehow both endearing and slightly erotic.

"Golpar. I always forget the English name."

"Hogweed," Maheen said around a mouthful of bread.

"Right. And black caraway."

"Wow."

While the family talked over each other, Farzan explained each dish to David, and David added a little bit of everything to his plate.

"You can take more than that," Persis said, trying to force another huge meatball onto David's plate, but he held up his hands.

"I want to make sure I have room to try everything."

"Maman, he doesn't know how to taarof," Farzan said. "I'll take care of him, don't worry."

"All right," Persis said, returning the meatball to the bowl, as Firouz sat up straighter.

"Oh, David, did you have doogh when you came to the bistro?"

David shook his head.

"Baba..." Farzan pleaded. The Doogh Test was cruel and unfair to spring on someone the first time you had them over. Wait until the third time, at least.

"You should try it. It's very good for digestion."

"All right."

"You don't have to," Farzan said. "I don't like it myself."

"Nah, I'm curious."

Firouz poured a small glass of the sparkling yogurt drink and passed it over. David studied it like it was a fine wine—the fizz rising to the surface, the larger bubbles clinging to the sides of the glass, the viscosity as he swirled it. He took a small sip, blinked fast.

"Interesting," he said. "It's a little salty."

"That's what he said," Farzan murmured before he could stop himself. David snorted and shot him a look, but Farzan feigned innocence.

"You're a menace," David whispered, but he rested his hand on Farzan's knee, rubbing little circles with his thumb.

"You like that about me."

"I really do."

Farzan bit his lip. He wanted to kiss David so bad, but his family didn't go for PDA. He could probably count on one hand the number of times he'd seen his parents kiss on the mouth. And certainly never around a dinner table.

"What?" David asked. He licked the side of his mouth where a bit of juice from the lemon torshi had leaked.

"Nothing," Farzan said. "You need some wine to get the taste of doogh out of your mouth?"

"Nah, I'm good."

"Okay. Anyone else need wine?" Farzan asked the table. Firouz held out his glass, and Gina pushed hers closer. "Maheen? You sure you don't want any?"

Maheen shook her head, and her hand went to her belly again, and fuck. She saw Farzan clocking the motion, met his eyes, and gave the softest of smiles. It was something shy and proud and awestruck. No wonder people said you glowed when you were pregnant.

Farzan smiled back. Holy shit. He was going to be a guncle!

Maheen nodded at him, eyes full of intention, and reached for Tomás's hand. This was it then.

Farzan inspected everyone's glasses to make sure they had a little bit of wine to toast. He poured a small splash in David's.

"But—" David said, but Farzan quieted him with a look, then winked at Maheen.

"Actually." Maheen cleared her throat. "There's something Tomás and I wanted to tell you all."

"Oh my god!" Persis shouted, nearly knocking over her wineglass. Only Navid's quick reflexes saved it. "Are you having a baby?"

Farzan held his breath until his sister finally nodded.

"Eyyy!" Firouz shouted.

And then everyone was talking all at once: asking when they knew, and how far along Maheen was, and had they thought about names, and did they hope for any particular gender.

Farzan cleared his throat. "Hey. To the new parents."

"Beh salamati!" his family cried, and they went around clinking glasses. Farzan saved David for last, holding his eyes the longest before sipping, staring at David's pink lips.

It felt so right, his shoulders pressed against David's, surrounded by his loud, complicated, argumentative family. David had folded right in, like he'd always been there.

"We're just grateful the baby is going to have such a great family," Tomás said, resting his hand on top of Maheen's. "The best uncles a kid could have. And a soon-to-be aunt, too."

Across the table, Gina ducked her head and smiled into her wineglass, while Navid rested a hand on her back.

"Okay, but Farzan's going to do the heavy lifting," he said. "He's the one that's good with kids."

Farzan's mom nodded, reaching for the spoon to grab another kufteh. "Always has been. You know he used to sing his little siblings to sleep?" she asked David.

David's eyebrows raised.

"Maman..."

"What? It's true," Persis said.

"He does have a great voice," David agreed.

"Not you too," Farzan muttered, resting a hand on David's thigh, but David only grinned at him.

Persis kept going. "I'm sad he gave up teaching. He was good at it."

"He won teacher of the year his second year," Navid added.

Farzan's ears began to ring. Not this again.

"Can we not—" Farzan began, but Maheen cut him off.

"You really were great."

"I just wish you'd stuck with it," Persis said.

"I was miserable, Maman."

"More miserable than you were in retail?" Maheen asked. "Or that snooty restaurant on the Plaza?"

His family had never gotten over him working at a fine dining place on the Plaza instead of waiting tables at Shiraz Bistro in college. But he made double or even triple some nights in tips.

"Or there was the real estate thing," Persis reminded him.

Extremely unhelpfully, because Farzan had worked hard for that license only to find out he hated selling houses.

"At least the translation job let him use his Farsi," Navid muttered. He'd always been a little annoyed their parents taught Farzan more than him and Maheen.

Farzan had liked the translation thing, but it had been more a gig than a job, never enough work to actually make ends meet. If he'd been fluent in Arabic instead, maybe he could've gotten something better going.

Instead, he'd cobbled together what income he could, picking up substitute shifts to supplement the translating. Subbing was consistent, especially when there was a big shortage in Missouri. And subbing let him leave school at school, instead of taking it home with him, like he had when he was teaching full-time.

"So he's tried lots of things." David swirled the last bit of wine in his glass. "I think that's pretty cool."

"Thanks." Farzan gave David's thigh another squeeze, his chest warmed through.

David got him. He *had* tried lots of things. His path had never been linear, but that didn't mean it was a bad path. He was happy and healthy. He had the best friends in the world. He had a boyfriend. He had a restaurant. He was more than his failures and detours. He wasn't just some fuckup.

"But after all those years growing up, wanting to be a teacher, to just—"

Farzan put down his fork and cut her off.

"You know, I'm not the only teacher to burn out on the job. Lots of us have. That doesn't make me a failure. And yeah, it took me a while to figure things out after. Excuse me for not wanting to be miserable going to work every day."

"We don't think—" Persis began, but now that Farzan was going he couldn't stop.

"And you know what? I'm good at running the restaurant. I'm proud of it. It's a pillar of our community. It's keeping lots of people employed. And when we expand it, it's going to be better than ever. And I never could've done any of that if I'd kept teaching. So."

Everyone at the table stared at him. He felt like he'd run a race. Or maybe been flattened by a truck. He took a deep breath and grabbed his wineglass.

But David took his hand off Farzan's leg and laid it atop Farzan's hand instead. David's thumb traced little lines along the tendons, and Farzan tried to unclench his jaw.

"We're very proud of you," Firouz finally said. "We didn't ever want you to feel like you had to take over the restaurant for us. But if it makes you happy, that's all that matters." He raised his glass. "My son, the restaurateur."

His mom and siblings raised their glasses. David raised his, too, eyes sparkling.

"Thanks," Farzan muttered.

Everyone went back to their food, spoons and forks clinking in the awkward silence, until Gina finally said, "Anyone catch the Chiefs game?"

That got Tomás talking, and Persis, too, who had strong opinions about the Chiefs' new defensive line, whatever that meant.

Farzan breathed deeply and grabbed his fork. But before he could take another bite, David's mouth was at his ear. The hairs on the back of

Farzan's neck stood up at the warmth and proximity, the sweet vetiver of David's cologne.

God, how could David do that to him with just a breath?

"I'm proud of you too," he whispered.

"Hey. Can I talk to you for a moment?" Maheen asked as Farzan portioned the leftover rice into glass containers. Farzan had gotten them for Maheen and Tomás as a housewarming gift, in the hopes they'd use them instead of collecting leftover plastic containers the way their parents did.

Farzan had visceral memories of old Cool Whip containers stacked higher than Everest in the refrigerator when they were kids, their insides stained yellow from saffron and turmeric. How many microplastics had he eaten growing up?

Farzan popped a lid on. "Sure."

"First off..." Maheen tucked a strand of curly hair behind her ear. "I wanted to say sorry. If I ever made you feel like shit, about your jobs or your boyfriends or anything. You're my brother, and I love you, and I've always looked up to you."

In the moment, it had felt right, saying what he said to his family. Bad enough they'd brought up his dating history, but diving into his job history too? That was rough. Yet now that he'd said his piece, he was tired of all the awkward apologies.

"And I wanted to ask you something in private. Well, me and Tomás wanted to ask you, but he's keeping everyone occupied."

Maheen rested her hands on her belly again.

Even if she made fun of him for his historically bad taste in men (though that had finally improved), there wasn't a thing in the world he wouldn't do for his sister.

"Okay?"

"Tomás's family has a tradition."

Farzan nodded. They were Catholic; they had lots of traditions. Maheen and Tomás had been married in the gold-domed Cathedral of the Immaculate Conception downtown. Farzan had never been to a proper Catholic wedding before, with all the sitting and standing and kneeling. It was a beautiful ceremony, though, and Maheen and Tomás had smiled so bright that day.

Maheen chewed on her lip. "Anyway, whenever a baby's born, they always ask one of the uncles to be the godfather."

Farzan nodded. "Makes sense."

"Well, the two of us talked it over, and we'd like it to be you."

Farzan's brain ground to a halt.

"You don't have to say yes," Maheen said, when Farzan kept quiet. "And you don't have to decide right now."

"But doesn't a godparent need to be Catholic?"

Farzan was about as far from it as one could be. The Alavi family had been more or less irreligious for as long as he could remember: His father had come from a Muslim family, while his mother had come from a Zoroastrian one. Neither had really practiced, though, and they'd let Farzan and his siblings find their own relationship with religion. Which in Farzan's case had been "no thank you please."

"Well, normally yes," Maheen said. "But Tomás's church is a little more progressive on that front. And it would mean a lot, to both of us, if you would accept. You've always taken care of me, and Navid too, and I know you'll be an amazing uncle, but this makes things sort of…" Maheen's voice trailed off to a whisper. "Official? If anything were to happen to us."

Even though he was flat-footed, and a little buzzed, and still kind of annoyed at basically everyone in his family right now, his heart flooded over with warmth. With love for the tiny new Alavi growing in his sister's womb.

With love for his sister and Tomás, too.

Tears prickled his eyes, streaking down his cheeks when he smiled.

"Yeah. Of course I will. I'd be honored."

forty

David

"That was masterful," David said once they were safely in the car and on the road.

Farzan chuckled. "What? Watching me and my family argue?"

"Watching you remind them how amazing you are." David stopped at a red light.

Farzan shook his head, but David gently trapped his chin with his hand.

"I don't drink carbonated dairy for just anyone, you know." David waggled his eyebrows, trying to get a smile out of Farzan, but he just bit his lip and looked away. The street lights streaming in through the windshield burnished his skin. He was luminous, outshining the moon and the sun and the stars.

David swallowed and turned back to the road as the light turned green. If he thought about Farzan's perfect face too much, he'd crash. He reached for the music, but Farzan stopped him.

"Maheen asked me something. While you were in the other room."

"Oh?"

"Yeah." Farzan was quiet for a long moment. "She asked if I would be the baby's godfather."

David whistled, low and slow. That was a big deal, right? "What'd you say?"

"I said yes."

"Wow."

"Yeah." David caught a shrug out of the corner of his eye. "She said she was sorry, too. For making me feel like a fuckup."

"That's good."

"I just..." Farzan blew out a breath. "Families are weird. All that teasing, but then *hey, look after my baby*. I don't know."

"Maybe they see you more than you think," David said. "Maybe the teasing is how they show their love."

"Maybe." Farzan sighed and rested a hand on David's thigh. "Thank you for coming with me tonight. It meant a lot."

"Thanks for inviting me." It meant a lot to David, too.

More than he was ready to think about.

Farzan's fingertips lightly stroked David's inner thigh, sending sparks straight to his dick.

He didn't let himself speed, even though what blood wasn't heading toward his cock was turning his foot to lead. But, fuck, he wished they were already back at Farzan's place.

David didn't even wait for them to get their shoes off.

As soon as Farzan clicked on the light in his apartment, and the door swung shut behind them, David spun Farzan around and pinned him against the wall.

David cut his laugh off with a kiss, pressing their chests together, grinding his hips against Farzan's. God, he wanted him.

Farzan returned the kiss, hands going to David's back, practically clawing at his sweater. It seemed David needed to invest in more sweaters, if this was the reaction they got.

When Farzan broke the kiss they were both breathing heavily, foreheads together.

"So," David said. "You're gonna be a godfather."

Farzan snorted. "That child is going to be so spoiled."

"Yeah?"

"Mm-hmm." Farzan's hands went up and down David's back, tracing lines down the tender muscles alongside his spine. David dug his own hands into Farzan's hips, pressing the length of his erection against the warm hardness of Farzan's.

"Maybe you and me should have a baby of our own."

Farzan snorted.

"We just had that big meal!"

"*You* had a big meal. I, on the other hand, prepped this afternoon."

"What, really?"

"There's a reason I didn't let you give me too much." And David's stomach felt fine.

Besides, he couldn't stand being here with Farzan—this self-assured Farzan who'd stood up to his whole family in grand style—and not finally get fucked.

"So. You wanna put a baby in me?"

Farzan's nostrils flared, a sharp intake of breath. His cock flexed against David's, evident even through two layers of jeans.

"There's, uh, prep stuff under the bathroom sink. If you need to freshen up or anything."

David felt fine, but a little freshening up never hurt anyone. Though that would mean leaving the circle of Farzan's arms. The haze of his cologne. The taste of wine and pomegranate on his ruby-stained lips.

David groaned, pressed one last kiss against Farzan, released him and took two steps toward the bathroom, but as soon as he hit the hardwood his shoes squeaked.

"Fuck!"

He bent over to untie them, just enough to yank them off. As he did, Farzan gave his ass a smack.

He straightened up, staring at Farzan, who immediately looked guilty. "Sorry. I should've asked."

"Asked me if you could smack my ass like a drum? Like in the song?"

Farzan giggled, a sound so light and unexpected David started laughing too, which made getting his shoes off a struggle, but he finally managed it.

"Okay. I won't be long."

Farzan's voice was molten lava. "I'll be waiting."

David stepped out of the bathroom, still in his undershirt and trunks, his favorite black Savage X Fenty ones with the mesh side panels. If Farzan liked his blue sweats, David couldn't wait to see his reaction to these.

The bathroom was a bit chilly, but a space heater hummed in the far corner of the bedroom.

"Sorry," Farzan said. "The bedroom always..."

He sat on the corner of the bed, still in his own shirt and underwear—solid lime green ones with silver trim—and David couldn't wait to peel them off him. Farzan was halfway through pulling off a sock when he saw David and his jaw dropped.

David always thought that was a euphemism, but nope. Farzan looked like a Christmas nutcracker as he stared at David's underwear. David flexed his dick—still mostly soft—to make the front of his underwear twitch, and he could swear Farzan's mouth opened just a little bit more.

Mission accomplished.

"My eyes are up here," David teased, and relished the blush that stole over Farzan's face.

"Sorry. Those are..."

"Better than sweatpants?"

"A million times." Farzan stood and pulled David toward him. "Is it warm enough? My bedroom's always cold."

"Yeah?" David ran his hands up and down Farzan's arms, feeling the gooseflesh, the coarse hair. "My place in Chicago was like that. But I know how we can keep warm."

David planted his mouth on the cord of Farzan's neck.

"Mmm," Farzan purred. He ran his hands under the hem of David's undershirt, pulled it up so David had to break the kiss and remove it. David returned the favor, pulling off Farzan's shirt. It left his hair messy and wild, and David ran his fingers through the silken strands. He rested his palms against Farzan's jaw, the stubble prickling in the best way.

But before David could pull Farzan into another kiss, Farzan had taken his arms and forced him gently toward the bed. With a playful shove, Farzan knocked him onto the towels already laid out. David laughed and got up to his knees, tugging Farzan closer so he could reach his mouth again.

Farzan tasted like wine and flowers and sugar. They'd had dessert after dinner—Farzan's rice pudding had been the star—but that hadn't been nearly as sweet as Farzan's mouth. David kissed slowly, oh so slowly, savoring every bit of warmth, every little moan Farzan let out, until with a frustrated, muffled cry, Farzan forced him back onto the bed.

"Too many clothes," Farzan muttered, tugging at David's waistband. David lifted his hips as Farzan slid his trunks off. His cock, already hot and leaking, barely had time to slap against his stomach before Farzan leaned down and took him in his mouth.

He ground his hips in time with Farzan's motions, eyelids fluttering as his skin came alive with sensation and his blood began to boil. When Farzan gently nibbled on his foreskin, he arched his back so hard it actually popped.

Farzan's mouth opened wide in surprise as David fell back on the bed. "You okay?"

"Yeah. Guess I can skip the chiropractor."

Farzan shook his head and nuzzled back between David's thighs, tonguing his balls, but David was already feeling overstimulated and he still hadn't gotten to touch Farzan. It wasn't fair.

David sat up. "Now you're wearing too many clothes."

Farzan sat back on his heels and reached for his waistband, but David stopped him.

"Let me."

David shifted so he could get his hands on Farzan's hips, yanking the underwear off. Farzan kicked them into the distance, narrowly missing the space heater.

"Oops."

David smirked. "The fire's supposed to be up here."

Farzan's eyes flashed hungrily as he peeled off his other sock and let it fall. He brought his hands up to David's sides, tracing his ribs, curving around to the back. Grazing down his spine until they found the curve of his ass, before dipping lower and teasing his hole.

David's muscle puckered up involuntarily. Farzan's fingers were still cold.

"Sorry. I've got warming lube."

"Mm." David didn't care if it was warming or numbing or flavored. He needed Farzan. Needed to feel every bit of him. Needed to feel claimed. His skin was on fire, despite the room's chill; his core was even hotter. "It's all good."

Farzan leaned over to the cabinet, grabbed the bottle and clicked it open. His lips stayed joined to David's, their tongues dueling, while his slick fingers found David's smooth ring once again. David relaxed against the warm, wet pressure, breathing hard into Farzan's mouth as Farzan gently probed him.

Sparks ignited along his nerves, deep within. As Farzan teased him, stretched him, pressed against his prostate, fireworks burst deep within, behind David's eyes, exploded out of him in hot, fast breaths.

"Please," he murmured, mouth clumsy against Farzan's, the pleasure too intense for him to concentrate on the kissing. His mouth hung open, pressed against the meat of Farzan's neck, as those fingers worked their magic. Electricity shot along his core as he relaxed, then tensed, then relaxed even more.

"Fuck, you've got talented fingers," David muttered, licking at Farzan's skin, inhaling the citrusy scent of him, enjoying the texture of the goosebumps he raised at every whisper into Farzan's ear. "I need you in me. I need you to fuck my brains out."

"I like your brains," Farzan murmured, adding another finger, and David's breath hitched at the fullness.

"Brains are overrated," David groaned. He was coming unraveled, every part of him ready to fly apart at the seams, and still, *still*, Farzan hadn't fucked him yet.

Somehow he found the strength in his limbs to spin them around. Farzan's fingers slipped out of him as he pushed Farzan back onto the bed and straddled him.

"I told you. I need you in me," he growled. "Condom?"

Farzan's pupils were dilated, his warm eyes glazed over with lust, as he gestured to the side of the bed. They must've gotten bounced off.

David growled, leaned over the bed and grabbed the packets. He opened one up, rolled it down Farzan's firm length, and added more lube. Leaned forward, so his face hovered right above Farzan's, breathing hard as he got the angle right and lowered himself down.

"Fuck," David groaned. Farzan's cock filled him perfectly, warmth pressing against his inner walls, the angle just right to get more pressure against his prostate. "Fuck."

He shivered, clenching up around Farzan, which got a shiver from below in response.

"You feel amazing," Farzan whispered, hands sliding up David's stomach to cup his pecs. "You're beautiful."

"You are." David leaned down to kiss Farzan, and Farzan rocked beneath him, thrusting slowly, making David see stars. "Oh, babe..."

He sat back up, so he could ride Farzan properly, gazing down into his liquid eyes, his bowed lips, his perfect face. How had he waited so long for this?

How had he never known how good it could be?

Well, he had himself to blame for that, didn't he? He told himself he only did casual. Told himself life was too busy to be with anyone for more than a quick fuck. Told himself that anything else would be a distraction.

But he was wrong. Farzan wasn't a distraction. He was a revelation. A gift. He turned everything brighter. Made every sip of wine sweeter. Made every rough day easier to bear.

David came alive with Farzan.

And he'd known, deep down, from the moment he laid eyes on Farzan, he was flirting with danger. But he'd been too stubborn to admit it. Too scared to.

David had been in love before. But never like this. He'd never felt the slow, inexorable slide toward someone, the snowflake that became an avalanche. The inevitable realization that life made more sense when shared with someone you cared about.

Someone you loved.

Fuck, he loved Farzan. Loved his kindness, his passion, his shy smiles and intense gazes.

And fuck, was he gazing up at David intensely now, driving his hips up with increasing vigor, threatening to unmake David.

But he was already unmade.

Fuck.

forty-one

Farzan

"**F**uck," David grunted again, as Farzan scooted his feet closer to get a better angle. "Fuck."

Farzan wasn't used to being ridden like this—it had never been his favorite position—but he might have to reevaluate his preferences. Because David on top of him, breathless and speechless (the repeated cries of "Fuck!" didn't count), dark brown skin glowing in the bedroom light, was a revelation. Muscles heaving, cock swaying in time, the smell of sweat and vetiver permeating everything, leaving Farzan drunk on David, David, David.

He was sweating now too, beads streaking down his temples, tickling his neck as they fell onto the towels below, and fuck, he should've turned the space heater down a bit, but he wasn't going to stop. He'd rather die than stop his thrusts, give up the hot squeeze of David around him, the warm weight against his hips. He craned his neck upward for another kiss, but the action adjusted the tilt of his hips. David's back arched and his head fell back with another cry of "Fuck!"

David unmoored was the most beautiful thing Farzan had seen in his entire life. He reached up, ran his hands along David's sides, grazing the soft hair in his armpits, tracing the muscles of his arms. David leaned forward suddenly, hands digging into Farzan's pecs, ripping out a few strands of his chest hair, but he didn't even care, because David was closer now, close enough to kiss again, to let their lips collide and their tongues dance and their breaths mingle.

Farzan was hot everywhere. It was dark outside, and his blackout curtains were drawn, but he wouldn't be surprised if his neighbors could see the glow. He had a sun inside him, threatening to burn him, consume him, and he didn't care.

Let it burn.

"Fuck," David groaned right into Farzan's mouth, and he clenched up at the same time, and fuck indeed, because Farzan was getting close. He let go of David's sides, gripped David's neck with his left hand and David's cock with his right to start stroking.

"Are you getting close?" Farzan whispered against the corner of David's mouth.

"Uh-huh," David breathed, and Farzan relished the sound. Usually David was all flirting, dirty talk, cocky promises he always delivered on. But now, he was just wordless, breathless need.

Farzan had never seen anything so sexy.

"You want me to make you come?" he asked, voice low.

"Fuck. Yes."

Farzan tightened his grip, and David tightened his ass so hard Farzan thought his dick might snap off, but the sensation sent a lightning bolt right up his spine.

"I've got you, David," Farzan said. "Come for me, babe."

And then with another drawn out "Fuck!" David did, ass pulsing around Farzan's dick, warm white ropes in Farzan's chest hair, and Farzan couldn't last either as he broke apart, hips losing their rhythm, legs shaking until they gave out and he collapsed back against the bed, David stringless on top of him.

He panted hard, chest threatening to throw David right off him, but David was still connected to him. His eyes fluttered open, deep pools of brown the color of rain-soaked earth, long lashes like butterfly wings against Farzan's cheeks as he levered up so he was looking down at Farzan nose to nose.

"Hey, you," he said, voice low and rich as Cabernet, and kissed Farzan on the nose.

"Hey yourself."

David hummed as he kissed Farzan again. "That was epic."

"Yeah? Did I fuck your brains out?"

"Yup. They're in your chest hair. Better clean them off before it dries."

Farzan snorted a laugh so hard, he nearly bucked David off him.

"Okay. Sorry. Let me clean you up, babe." David kissed his nose, his lips, and then gingerly rolled off as Farzan held the condom in place.

"Nuh-uh. Let me take care of you." He kissed David's shoulder. His skin was so hot it nearly burned his lips. "Just relax."

Farzan scooted off the bed and scurried to the bathroom, got rid of the condom and peed, then came back with a soft, warm wet cloth. He tenderly cleaned up David, leaning in occasionally to kiss his nipple or goose his belly button, which got a wild, flailing giggle. He hadn't known David was ticklish there; every time they were together, he discovered something new about his boyfriend's body.

He hoped he never ran out of discoveries.

Once he'd cleaned himself off as well, he came back, turned the space heater off before they melted, tossed the towels and slid into bed.

David's eyes were glassy, his lips curled into a contented smile. As Farzan settled, David rolled onto his side, facing away, then backed against Farzan. Farzan wrapped his arms around David, spooning until their breaths synced up.

His body was still buzzing, nerves lit up like the Plaza lights at Christmastime, skin prickling despite the warm bed and the warmer man pressed up against him. Everything went quiet inside him.

And then, in the darkness, so low Farzan could've pretended not to hear it:

"I love you."

Farzan's chest cracked open.

He'd been fighting it—might as well fight the tide—but there was no denying it.

He loved David, too.

Farzan Alavi. Thirty-seven years old, restaurateur, and in love with David Curtis.

How had he let this happen?

How could it have turned out any other way?

David was beautiful, and kind, and funny, and passionate. He had big dreams, and he worked hard to make them happen. He shone like a star, and Farzan's heart had been trapped by his gravity. You couldn't fight physics.

Farzan didn't want to.

"I love you," he whispered back, and felt David relax against him, the long, slow exhale.

Farzan held David tight, laid kisses along his back and shoulder, nuzzled that soft spot behind his ear.

Farzan was in love.

Fuck.

forty-two

David

David would've spotted Rhett's red hair, even if the owner of said hair hadn't been flailing his arm out the driver's side window like a Muppet.

David tossed his carry-on and backpack into the trunk, then hopped into Rhett's extremely clean Prius. Back in Chicago, Rhett's terrible old Corolla had been the butt of many jokes for the amount of crumbs and plastic wrappers littering the floor, not to mention the fact that different parts kept breaking down. David and the other waiters used to joke that one day Rhett would pull up to Millennium with the steering wheel clutched in his hands, hovering in mid-air on the driver's seat, as the rest of the car had fallen apart around him cartoon style.

"Who are you and what have you done with Rhett Donnelly?" David asked as he buckled his seat belt.

Rhett flicked the dangling vanilla air freshener. "New city, new car. You know they never have to salt the streets here? I bet the undercarriage is sparkling."

David rolled his eyes, but he couldn't stop himself smiling. "Thanks for having me out here."

"Don't thank me. Shyla bought the tickets. She said to say sorry she couldn't be here. She's in New York this week."

David shrugged. There'd be plenty of time for that. Right now, he just wanted to see the city.

As Rhett joined the endless line of cars trying to escape LAX, David pulled out his phone.

> **David**
> Made it safe and sound!
> In the car with Rhett now
> Love you

> **Farzan**
> That doesn't sound safe OR sound
> Say hi to Rhett
> Love you

David pressed his phone screen against his heart. He was such a goner.

"Did you do an edible on the plane?" Rhett asked. "Drink too much wine at the Sky Club? You know being on a plane gets you drunk faster."

"I'm pretty sure that's a myth," David said. "And no."

"Then why are you smiling like that?" Rhett eyed David at yet another stoplight.

Good lord, if they were back in Kansas City, they'd already be on the highway by now.

"I'm not," David insisted. "Just letting Farzan know I landed."

"Ahhhhh." Rhett's whole face softened. "You look happy."

"I told him I love him," David blurted out.

"Holy fuck!" Rhett cried. Thankfully they were still stopped; David had visions of Rhett swerving across lanes, his reaction was so loud. "Are you serious?"

David nodded.

"And?"

"And what?"

"Did he say it back?"

David bit his lip but nodded. His cheek muscles were getting strained from how much he'd been smiling the last two days.

He loved Farzan.

And Farzan loved him.

Fuck, what was he going to do?

Long distance would suck, but they could make something work. And some small, unrealistic part of him still wanted to ask Farzan to come with him. He knew Farzan wouldn't, couldn't, not with Shiraz Bistro and all his family there, but David couldn't help imagining their life in California. Sunshine and palm trees and sunsets at the beach. A little condo they could share.

They finally (finally!) made it onto the highway. David could see the synapses firing behind Rhett's eyes as he processed the news.

"I'm really happy for you," he finally said, voice a tiny bit pinched.

"Yeah? Then why do you sound like I kidnapped your dog?"

"First of all, you know Titus is too lazy to get kidnapped. And the LA weather has made him even lazier."

David snorted. Titus was Rhett's dog. He didn't know how long Chihuahua mixes were supposed to live, but Titus had to be pushing twenty-five. All dogs were good dogs, but that didn't mean all dogs were *cute* dogs. Titus always looked like he was getting ready to eat your shoes and then vomit them back up. Which he had only done to Rhett a few times. Four, maybe five.

Last year.

"Second," Rhett continued. "I'm not going to say I'm jealous, but I am willing to admit my dating life has taken a hit since moving here."

"You? Really?" Back in Chicago, Rhett was famous for the never-ending parade of pole and hole that always had him mired in some drama and nearly late for a shift.

Rhett shrugged. "I'm getting older. And it turns out managing a new restaurant is an exercise in frustration."

"Sorry," David said.

"Don't be. Soon you'll be in the shit right with me. Misery loves company and all that."

David didn't know what to say to that. Yeah, he'd be glad to help, and yeah, he knew it would be a lot of stress, getting Shyla's place up and running, building a list that would put their wine program on the map.

But he was going to miss how chill everything was at Aspire. How his colleagues did their jobs with a smile. How Jeri teased him but was always happy to see him. How she and Kyra had bullied him into having a social life again, meager though it was.

This was the job, though. This was what he'd signed up for, worked toward, sacrificed for.

"Okay. You want lunch first, or you want to go see the restaurant?"

David's body wanted lunch, but it was barely past ten a.m. on the West Coast. "Restaurant first."

"Great." Rhett turned on his blinker. "After lunch we can drive around the valley so you can get some ideas about where you want to live. Or you can always rent in my building. Pretty sure I get a referral, actually. Titus needs a new dog bed."

David laughed. "What, are there no bridges for him to hide under?"

"Are you calling my dog a troll? I'll have you know, if he's any mythical being, he's a dronkey."

"Like those things from *Shrek*?"

"Exactly." Rhett nodded once, sharply. "Now don't talk to me. I have to figure out how to get to the Ten from here."

forty-three

Farzan

I really think you've got it," Ramin said. He and Farzan were seated in the booth closest to the kitchen at Shiraz Bistro. It was still an hour before closing, but the crowd was dwindling, just a few late eaters and lingerers. Firouz had made good on his promise to join the card players at the table in the far corner.

"You think?" Farzan said, thumbing through the stack of papers on the table between them.

"I do."

Farzan's loan interview was tomorrow, and he was filled with the same weird anxiety he used to get before the first day of school, when he looked over his empty classroom, imagined it filled with students, and felt totally unprepared.

Unprepared and exhilarated.

He still missed it, sometimes.

But what he was doing now, at Shiraz Bistro, felt right. It felt like he finally knew where he was meant to be and what he was meant to be doing. It had just taken him a while to get there.

Farzan blew out a breath and ran a hand through his hair. "Okay. Thanks for doing this."

Ramin waved away his thanks.

"I mean it. I know you're busy."

"This is important to you," Ramin said. He'd spent the whole evening helping Farzan prepare for his interview, even though Tuesday was supposed to be his date night with Todd. "And Todd and I live together now. Every night is date night."

Ramin waggled his eyebrows in a very un-Ramin way. Farzan nearly spat out his tea. He pounded on his chest to stop himself coughing.

"Sorry," Ramin said, cheeks red. He rubbed at the tattoo on his left wrist. "I must be hanging around Arya too much."

"Ah, after twenty-seven years of friendship, he's finally rubbing off on you."

"Twenty-eight," Ramin corrected.

"Is it really?" Farzan blinked and did the mental math. "Shit. You're right."

Twenty-eight years. Wow.

"I'm happy for you," Farzan said.

Ramin smiled, deepening his dimples. Farzan loved seeing Ramin happy; he could tolerate Todd's eccentricities, if it meant his best friend would be happy. And, apparently, getting extremely regular dick.

"Thanks," Ramin said softly. "I'm happy for you too."

Farzan nodded and stared into his tea. "We said *I love you* on Saturday."

Ramin's face filled with wonder. Like he'd just witnessed the aurora borealis.

"That's amazing," he said. "I really like him. As a person. And I really like him for you, too." But Ramin's wonder seemed to dim. He bit his lip. "What are you going to do when he moves? Long distance?"

"I don't know. But we've got to figure it out soon," Farzan said. "He's in LA right now. Looking at the restaurant. Maybe apartment hunting, too."

Farzan's anxiety was back in full force; it felt like a raccoon was trying to claw its way out of his chest, *Alien*-style. He loved David. He wanted David. And he wanted to be enough to keep him here in Kansas City.

But he could never stand in the way of David's dream.

"I don't know," he said again. What else was there to say?

Farzan was nearly asleep when his phone buzzed with a message.

> **David**
> Finally back at Rhett's. You still up?

> **Farzan**
> Yeah. How was it?

His phone lit up with a FaceTime call.

"Hey, babe," David said. He was stretched out in a strange bed, shirtless, the curves of his dark skin gilded by the bedside lamp, his hair hidden beneath a plain black silk cap. "I missed you."

"I missed you too. How's LA?"

David looked past the phone's camera, like he was checking the door or something. "Promise not to say anything?"

"I promise."

David shook his head ruefully. "I don't get the In-N-Out hype. It was fine, don't get me wrong, but I didn't have a foodgasm or anything."

"Your secret is safe with me."

"Thanks. But Shyla's place is coming along. It's bigger than I expected."

"Oh? Not one of those two-table tasting menu kinds of places?"

"God, no. It's a little bigger than Aspire, I think."

"Oh, cool."

"Yeah." David scratched at his chest. The light made the valley between his pecs look particularly soft and pillowy. Farzan wished they were curled up together right now, so he could rest his head on David's chest and let him play with his hair.

David just kept looking at him.

"I miss you," David said softly.

"I miss you too."

"I can't stop thinking about what we did on Saturday."

"What? Yelling at my family?" Farzan teased.

"That was amazing," David said. He adjusted the phone, and suddenly Farzan could see his shoulder tensing and releasing, tensing and releasing. "But that's not what I'm thinking of."

David switched to his rear camera; after a brief, blurry transition, Farzan was confronted with David's hand, languidly stroking his dick, the brown head revealed and hidden over and over.

Farzan's mouth went dry, like he'd drunk a glass of Bordeaux.

"Fuck," he muttered.

Suddenly David switched back to front view. "Shit, is this okay? I didn't even ask."

"Yeah, it's okay," Farzan said. He tried to swallow away the hoarseness in his voice. "You know I love your dick."

"Yeah you do." David's voice had gone liquid. "I can tell the way your eyes turn into little hearts every time they see it. Like an anime character."

"It's perfect," Farzan breathed.

"You gonna get off too? I need you to feel good with me."

"Okay." Farzan pushed his covers down.

He hadn't had phone sex in . . . god, he couldn't actually remember the last time. He dug in his bedside table for some lube; he'd grown to full attention as David switched back to the dick view.

"I wish this was you touching me," David said, low and sandy. "Your hand wrapped around me."

"Me too," Farzan breathed, imagining David was whispering into his ear, his breath stirring the fine hairs along Farzan's neck, his voice rumbling, resonating, making Farzan shiver.

Farzan's cock was warm, his balls too; he'd turned on his heated mattress pad to fight off the chill in his apartment. He lubed himself up, imagined it was David's hand on him. Imagined it was David's dick in his hand, hot and hard, midnight velvet. David's hands were always warm and smooth, except for this one little callus on his thumb, where he pressed against his wine key to cut the foil off a bottle.

God, he wished David was in his bed right now. He stroked faster, keeping time with David.

"Let me see you," David said, a soft plea.

Farzan loved when David growled, loved when he talked dirty, but he loved the pleading just as much. He switched his own camera around. "Uh. Is the lighting okay?"

Farzan could see himself just fine, but the only light in the room was the glow from his phone screen.

"Depends. Is your dick a boundless void?"

"Okay, okay." Farzan clicked on the bedside lamp.

"There it is," David said. "I want to taste it. Want to feel it in me."

"It's yours," Farzan muttered. "All yours."

"Yeah it is." But then David's hand stopped, and he went still.

"Everything okay?"

"Yeah," David said after a moment. "I think it's Rhett. Taking Titus out for a walk."

"Titus?"

"The world's ugliest dog."

Farzan huffed. "Really?"

"You haven't seen him. He's a little monster." David sighed. "At least he didn't try my door. It doesn't lock."

"Bet that's more of a show than he wants."

"We already gave him one. Remember?"

Farzan blushed; his cock was going soft. "How could I forget? At least he didn't see me when I was inside you."

David's cock flexed on the screen.

"Nuh-uh. He doesn't get to see you. You're all mine," David growled, and suddenly Farzan was achingly hard again. David's voice rippled through him, attenuated as it was by the phone's speakers; Farzan shivered, even though he was warm.

"Your beautiful face and your sexy body and your perfect cock."

"It's only for you," Farzan agreed. He gripped himself harder, imagining David's hand on him, David's lips against his neck, David's weight on top of him.

God, he missed David. This wasn't enough. He needed David back. He needed David with him.

"I'm getting close," David said through heavy breaths. "I need to nut so fucking bad."

Farzan hadn't been close, but hearing David—hearing him like *that*—well, suddenly he was ready.

"Me too."

He'd never get enough.

"I wish I was with you. Wish I could swallow you."

"Yeah," David grunted. "Your mouth is so fucking talented. That thing you do with your tongue...*fuck*."

The camera went shaky as David came, his heavy breaths and spurting cock sending Farzan over the edge, too. The pleasure built and built until it pulsed out of him, so hard he hit himself in the eye.

"Shit," he hissed. He hadn't done *that* in years, and fuck it burned, but the burning didn't matter when he was still coming, imagining he was wrapped in David's vetiver scent.

When he came back to earth, he stared at his phone; silvery stripes shimmered on the midnight skin of David's stomach. David switched back to his face view.

"That was good," David said, blinking slowly. But then his eyebrows furrowed as Farzan switched his view, too. "Shit, did you get yourself?"

"Yup." Farzan winced as he tried to wipe his face.

"Fuck, that's hot."

"It burns!"

"I'm sorry I'm not there to clean you off," David said. "I wish you were here with me."

"Me too," Farzan sighed. A hollow ache crept into his chest, wrapped around his heart. He didn't want to say goodbye.

"I'm sorry I can't be with you tomorrow. But we'll celebrate when I get in. Okay?"

"That's assuming we have something to celebrate," Farzan pointed out.

"We will. You'll do great, babe."

That ache eased a bit.

"I love you," David said. "I better let you get some rest."

"I love you. 'Night, babe."

David's smile was radiant.

"'Night."

forty-four

David

David looked around and realized there were no tissues on the nightstand. Could he make it across the hall to the bathroom?

The jangling of keys, the swing and thud of a door, and the *scritch-scritch* of demon nails on hardwood announced the return of Rhett. Shit.

David found a sock and used that to clean himself off. Despite the annoyance, his skin was still buzzing, his dick twitching with aftershocks. He couldn't remember the last time he'd had phone sex. It was good, but after getting fucked by Farzan, his own hand and a phone screen were a poor substitute. Not that it hadn't been hot—it had—but it wasn't enough. David wanted to feel Farzan's breath ghost across his skin; he wanted to reach out and run his fingers through Farzan's hair; he wanted to kiss that little spot behind his ear, nuzzle into the crook of his neck, cuddle up and just hold him. Be held.

He sighed, scratched his head through his bonnet. When had he gotten so sentimental?

His phone buzzed. For a second he thought it was Farzan again, but no, it was just an upgrade alert for his flight home. He swiped through to get his updated boarding pass, then found himself looking through the photos he'd taken today.

Goofy ones of Rhett absolutely drowning his beard in Animal-style sauce. A few artsy ones of the Hollywood sign, which Rhett had insisted on showing David. But mostly they were photos of Shyla's new restaurant. It was sleek: black granite floors and walls, white marble counters, mahogany tables getting installed in the booths, a glass-walled wine room that enclosed a private dining room, plus a roomy cellar in the basement.

It was perfect. Pristine. Sterile.

Nothing like Aspire, where there was too little room for everything. Where he was always shoving cases of wine into whatever cranny he could find. Where he was constantly shuffling bottles into and out of the orphan bin. Where Jeri would tease him, and Kyra would laugh at him, and Brayan would make him try the latest toppings on his seasonal flatbread. Where they'd taste a bottle before service every night, because Jeri wanted the entire team—from the dishwasher up to the chef—to share in the love and knowledge of wine.

Aspire had character. It had love etched in every tabletop, in every counter, in every tile. It might not be on track for a Michelin star, but it was full every night, with regulars and newcomers and parties.

And it was home. When had David started thinking of Kansas City as home again? Was it the brunches with his mother? Dinners with his dad, and now Deb, too? Was it a kickball game in Loose Park?

Was it when Farzan made him soup, and he fell asleep as they watched *The Muppet Movie* together?

Fuck. David had told himself Kansas City was just temporary. A stopping point on the way to bigger and better things. He hadn't meant to put down roots, hadn't realized how deep they'd dug until it was time to start yanking on them.

He'd spent years pursuing this dream. And now that it was in reach, all he could think about was a pair of warm brown eyes. A big nose and a sweet smile and a heart full of love for his family, for his community.

For David.

Fuck. *Fuck!*

When had Farzan become his new dream?

He came alive when he met Farzan. And now that he knew what that felt like, how could he go back? How could he let go of Farzan? How could he move away?

He couldn't. It was as simple as that.

He couldn't move to LA. Couldn't take Rhett's offer. Not if it meant leaving Farzan.

Not if it meant leaving his mom and dad. Not if it meant leaving Jeri and Kyra and all his friends at Aspire.

He had a lot of figuring out to do. He'd have to adjust his financial goals, that was for sure, and he probably couldn't buy his mom a house anymore. But maybe being around was good enough.

And he'd have to see if Jeri would let him stay on permanently. Not that he really thought she'd turn him down, but what if she had someone else lined up? Some other young somm ready to learn and grow, like David had?

And he needed to tell Farzan. His heart gave a weird squeeze. Why did that make him nervous? Farzan would be happy, right?

Farzan loved him.

But Farzan loved his drive, and his passion. Farzan loved the version of him that was moving on to bigger and better things. Not the version that settled.

Except it didn't feel like settling. It felt like choosing to be happy, for the first time in a long time.

Farzan would understand. David knew he would. He was worried for nothing.

Tomorrow he'd fly home to Kansas City, open his best bottle of Champagne, and he and Farzan would have two things to celebrate. (And then they'd make love. A lot.)

Everything was going to be perfect.

forty-five

Farzan

Denied?”

Farzan blinked at the loan officer across the desk from him: Daniel, a young Korean man with deep dimples, bowed lips, and a sharp suit. The top button of his dress shirt was unbuttoned, showing the sort of smooth, sculpted chest only twentysomethings with good genetics and plentiful gym access could pull off. Farzan only hated him a little bit.

Twenty-five, maybe twenty-six, young and hot and well established in a good career. If he hadn't been so damned nice, Farzan would've hated him more. But he'd walked Farzan through the whole loan process. Had thought Farzan was a good candidate. And now…

“What do you mean, denied? I thought things were looking good.”

“I thought so too,” Daniel said sadly. “But with the way things are right now, the bank is being very selective about small business loans, and restaurants always face an uphill battle.”

“But we've been around for nearly forty years,” Farzan said. “It's not like I'm some…some sort of pop-up diner.”

“I know.” Daniel ran a hand through his hair. It was stylishly cut, a little long and swoopy on the top.

Maybe Farzan should've cut his hair for this. Something short and professional, like Ramin's. The kind of haircut that let you walk into a law firm or accounting service or—well, a bank—holding a mug of coffee, yell at some interns, fill out some TPS reports, then call it a day and drive your imported European car back to your house in Brookside or Leawood or even Loch Lloyd.

"I'm really sorry, Mr. Alavi."

Farzan pressed his lips together and nodded. He didn't trust himself to speak, especially with the lump in his throat. He'd sound like a Muppet.

The bank's door let out an electronic chime that definitely didn't make him feel thankful. Neither did the stuffed turkey and fake cornucopia on the windowsill. The wind had picked up, blustering down Main Street, a frigid blast amplified by the wind tunnel effect that cut right through his puffy coat. The right cuff was beginning to fray, too.

A cold front had moved in, the nasty kind that Farzan associated with early February, not early November. He pulled his hat on tight to protect his ears, which were already burning from the cold. His smooth cheeks were beginning to chap, too.

He'd shaved—full-on shaved, not just trimmed—and for what? Nothing. Just a bunch of ingrown hairs in the morning, most likely.

Fuck.

He'd tried. He'd really tried.

He'd worked so fucking hard. Ran the numbers by David three times. Got Ramin's help jazzing up his little packet. Rehearsed his interview over and over.

Shiraz Bistro was a good, solid business. They were in the black. Farzan was running it just fine.

And it still wasn't enough. He wasn't enough.

David's plane was supposed to land this evening, and Farzan was picking him up. He'd get to hear all about the new restaurant David was going to be working at; about all the hot young gay folks David would be swimming in, once he moved to LA; about all the cool, successful people living their dreams and getting loans and being responsible adults, instead of fuckups.

Fuckups like Farzan.

Farzan loved David, loved him so much he thought his heart might explode. But David was going places. David was talented and passionate. He had dreams, dreams that were coming true.

Farzan's dreams had just turned to ash.

What was he supposed to do?

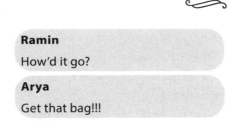

Ramin
How'd it go?

Arya
Get that bag!!!

Farzan stared at the group chat, throat squeezed shut. How could he tell his best friends he'd fucked up again?

He glared out at the cell phone lot. He'd turned his car off while he waited for David to text; the chill was starting to seep back in. The night sky was clear, but light pollution obscured everything except Orion, which was one of the two constellations Farzan actually knew how to find. (The other was the Big Dipper.)

His phone buzzed again.

Maman
Farzanjan can you grab me some rice next time you go to Costco?
Love and thank you

God. What was he going to tell his family? He'd talked himself up in front of all of them. Now they'd know he was a failure.

Well. They'd already known that, hadn't they? After the teaching thing. The real estate thing. The translating thing. After Jason and Sean and Omid and Brandon (fucking Brandon).

Farzan's eyes were burning. The air in the car was too close, despite the cold. He wanted to get out, stretch his legs, run across the parking lot, but being Iranian around an airport was already tricky enough. No need to piss off the TSA.

David
Here!

Farzan couldn't breathe. Was it too late to drive into the river? Or maybe take off for a new life in Manitoba after all, where there'd be no one around to disappoint except for caribou?

But he couldn't leave David stranded at KCI. He wiped his eyes, put on his best smile, and got ready to do battle in the pickup line.

"Hey, babe." David leaned across the center console to kiss Farzan's cheek, then buckled himself in. "Thanks for coming to get me."

"Sure!" Farzan knew his voice was too high, but he didn't know how to do this. "How was everything?"

"It was okay," David said as Farzan finally escaped the pickup zone and headed toward the first roundabout that would lead him out of the airport and toward the highway. "The weather was nice. It got cold here."

"Yeah. You warm enough?" Farzan's car didn't have seat heaters like David's fancy one did. Of course it didn't. He was a fuckup with a fucked-up car. "Let me know if you feel carsick."

"I'm good." David was wearing dark-wash jeans and a soft-looking cobalt sweater. Farzan wanted to run his fingers along David's shoulder. Wanted to snuggle his cheek into David's chest and feel the warmth. Smell David's cologne. But he was driving.

And he knew he couldn't. His heart hammered as he finally pulled onto I-29.

David was quiet as they drove, occasionally tugging at the wrists of his sweater, or nodding along to the music. Farzan turned up the *Chrono Cross* soundtrack he had playing. An old favorite.

He cleared his throat. "How's the new restaurant?"

"Hm? Oh." David shook himself off, like he'd been daydreaming about sunny skies and warm weather. He'd been gone two days and he already missed LA. Farzan couldn't blame him. His dream was in reach now, so close he could touch it. Coming back to Kansas City must've hurt.

"It was really cool. Sleek and modern and kind of minimalist, I guess."

"Cool." Farzan didn't know what to say. He couldn't compete with *sleek* and *modern*. He couldn't compete with nice weather, with hot sun-kissed people in fancy clothes.

He couldn't even get a small business loan.

David went quiet again, staring out as the Northland sped by.

God. He'd already checked out, hadn't he?

Farzan swallowed back a sigh. Or maybe it was his tears, threatening to return. David already had one foot out the door. They'd said, over and over, they'd figure things out when the time came.

Well now, it had.

And if Farzan had at least had some success to share, some good news, some promise for the future, he thought that might be enough to get David to stay. To at least ask. But now?

Now all he'd be doing was asking David to give up his dream. And for what? For the love of a fuckup.

They made the rest of the drive in a miserable, loaded silence. Farzan wished David would just rip off the bandage. Tell him it was over. Anything but this awful waiting.

It was getting dark when they pulled into David's driveway. Farzan's headlights lit the browning grass, the scraggly-looking shrubs that would no doubt bloom with color once summer came around. But David would be gone, and the house would be sold by then, and Farzan hoped the new owner appreciated hydrangeas or peonies or whatever kind of fucking flowers they were.

"Here we are," Farzan managed.

"Yeah." David swallowed. "You want to come inside? Have a glass of wine and talk?"

Talk.

No, Farzan didn't want to go inside for that. Better to do it right here, where he could make his escape with some shred of dignity.

He shook his head.

David's brows furrowed.

"Is something wrong?"

Farzan swallowed. His chest was too tight. His heart hurt, like a fist was squeezing it until it burst.

"Let's just get this over with," he finally said.

"Uh. What?"

"It's okay," Farzan said. "I'm a big boy. I knew this was coming."

"Knew what now?" David asked, cocking his head to the side. But he didn't have to put on the act. Farzan was strong enough to handle this.

It wasn't the first time a guy had broken up with him.

"We always said we'd figure things out when the time came. And it's time, isn't it?"

David shook his head. "What are you saying?"

"I'm saying it's okay." It wasn't okay. It would never be okay. But this was what was best for David. Farzan had to let him go. "I don't want some . . . some long, drawn-out thing, okay? I can't take it. So let's just end things now. Before this whole thing becomes even more painful."

David's eyes went wide. "*End* things? I don't understand."

"You're leaving," Farzan said. "I know it'll be a little while, but why dig the hole any deeper than it already is?"

"What if I wasn't?"

"Wasn't what?"

"What if I wasn't leaving?" David swallowed, slow, and for some reason that nearly broke Farzan. His eyes were burning. He pursed his lips and took a sharp breath.

"It's your dream, David. I'm not going to hold you back."

"What if it's not my dream?"

"It's literally all you've talked about for as long as I've known you." Why was David making this so hard? Didn't he get it?

Farzan was setting him free.

David tried to turn, but his seat belt was still buckled. He unlatched it and faced Farzan fully. "Why are you doing this? I thought we were happy. I thought we loved each other. You know how hard it was for me to say that? You know how long it's been since I loved someone?"

Every word felt like a corkscrew to Farzan's gut.

"It's been a long time for me, too," Farzan said. "But the longer we put it off, the worse it's going to hurt. So let's do ourselves both a favor and end it now."

"Something happened," David said. "We were happy last night, and now . . . fuck. Your interview was today. I meant to ask."

Farzan went quiet. He didn't want to get into this. Didn't want to admit it out loud.

"What happened?" David asked, gentle as a fall rain.

Farzan shook his head.

"What happened, babe?"

Babe. Farzan wasn't David's babe anymore.

"I didn't get it. All right? I fucked up. Again. Big surprise. But just because I'm a fuckup, it doesn't mean you are. You've got this whole big adventure ahead of you, and I won't be the one to hold you back."

"But I want you," David said, reaching for Farzan only to stop just short of touching him. "I love you."

"You say that now. But what happens in a year or two? When you're stuck in Kansas City, and you've got your master somm, and you're still pouring the same old bottles and living the same old life, and I'm dealing with the same old shit in the same old restaurant that I can't even afford to expand? It's better this way. For both of us."

Farzan didn't think he could survive if David stayed and ended up unhappy. If it was him that fucked up David's life.

"No, fuck that," David spat. He gripped at his twists. "I get to decide what's right for me. Not you. Yeah, you had a setback, that doesn't mean you just…just give up on everything. Give up on us! God, it's like every time things get hard for you, you just stop trying."

Farzan went cold.

David had been around his parents too much.

But they were right, weren't they?

"You're not a fuckup, Farzan. You're just allergic to your own happiness. Because if you'd stick with something and see it through, you'd know just how good it could be. But you never do."

It felt like David had punched him in the jaw. His whole face was numb. His body, too. His hands went slack around the steering wheel.

David was breathing hard, but he blinked and sat back. Like he couldn't believe what he'd just said.

"Farzan…"

"I think I should go," Farzan said. "You better get your suitcase."

Somehow Farzan found the trunk release.

David chewed on his lip, holding back something. More words they'd both regret.

Finally he shook his head and lurched out of the car.

Farzan waited until he saw David's front door close and the light turn on inside before he pulled away.

Why in the world did David's street have so many cars parked on the curbs? Farzan could barely navigate through his tears.

He hit West 39th and pulled into the first parking lot he could find. A little wine store, big red letters spelling THE WINE SELLER. Farzan pulled into the first empty spot he could find and let himself sob.

forty-six

David

David could barely hear Farzan's car pulling away over the sound of his own pulse, pounding in his ears. They felt full, like he was back on the plane, about to descend. Maybe he was. Maybe this was a nightmare. Maybe the cabin pressure had dropped, and he hadn't gotten his mask on in time, and his brain wasn't getting enough oxygen.

But his hand was cramping around the handle of his carry-on. He'd gripped it so tight, the logo had imprinted on his palm.

He let it go and swiped at his eyes.

What the hell had just happened?

He'd gotten off the plane anxious and excited. He'd missed Farzan. Just two days apart, and he couldn't stand it.

He spent the whole car ride working up his courage to tell Farzan the news: That he was staying here. That Kansas City was his home. That Farzan was his home.

And now it had all blown up.

David could barely breathe. He collapsed onto his couch, grabbed one of the decorative pillows his mom insisted on buying him, and hugged it to his chest.

How could he just end things like that? Farzan hadn't even given him a chance.

David's chest collapsed in on itself. He hugged the pillow tighter, cried harder.

He hadn't been fair, either. He shouldn't have said what he did to Farzan. He knew that wound ran deep. Knew it would hurt. He couldn't believe himself.

David hadn't expected their first fight as a couple—their first real fight—to be their only one. To be their last. But what could he do, if Farzan wouldn't even try?

His phone buzzed against his hip. He didn't want to talk to anyone, but shit, what if it was Farzan?

The phone got caught against the couch cushions as David fought to get it out of his pocket. But it wasn't Farzan.

It was his mom.

"Hey, Momma," he said, trying to keep his voice even, but he could tell it was throaty. "What's up?"

"Hey, baby," his mom said. "Did you make it home all right?"

"Yeah, I'm here now." David tried his best to sniff quietly. But his mom had to have heard it. "Just got in."

"Is Farzan with you?" she asked.

David went quiet. He couldn't stop crying.

"Oh, baby. What's wrong?"

David's mom joined him on the couch, two cups of chamomile in her hands. She passed one to David as she settled, adjusting the other, not-cried-on, decorative pillow behind her back.

David inhaled the steam slowly; his sinuses were clogged from crying, though the tears had finally abated—for now.

"Thanks," he said. His throat still felt like sandpaper. "You didn't have to come all this way."

"I know." Kathleen played with one of David's twists.

"I really love him, Momma."

"I can tell. I've never seen you smile the way you do with him."

"Then why..." David swallowed.

He didn't know how to say all the things he was feeling.

He wanted to stay here, but what would his mom think? She'd worked hard all her life, supported David as he built a future. What would she say if he threw it all away to stay home?

What would she say if she knew it was Farzan that made him want to stay, not her? Or at least, not just her. David didn't even know anymore. It was all tangled up: Farzan, Aspire, his mom and dad, Jeri and Kyra, even the goofballs he'd met at kickball. A life he hadn't let himself live, until Farzan had gotten under his skin.

What would his mom say if she knew a man had upended his future?

"He loves you, too," his mom said, when his voice failed him. "Loves you more than he loves himself, it sounds like."

"I know that's right," David muttered. That was the problem, wasn't it? Farzan didn't think much of himself. And David had only twisted that knife when they fought. "I don't know what to do, Momma."

"I don't either," she said with a sigh. "But I love you, baby."

"I love you, too." David hugged his mom with his chamomile-free hand. "I'm glad you're here."

"Me too," she said. "I'm gonna miss you when you move again."

David squeezed his mom tighter.

He didn't know what to do about Farzan, and he didn't know what to do about Rhett, either. Maybe it would be better if he did go. Got a fresh start, somewhere that wasn't full of heartache. His dream of making a life with Farzan had come crashing down; maybe he needed to let it go. Stick with the plan. Get his master somm and move to LA.

David swiped at his eyes again. His mom pulled him close and rubbed his back.

"It's going to be okay," she said. "It might not feel like it, but it will."

David nodded and let his mom hold him.

forty-seven

Farzan

Jarrod Pancake—yeah, that was his real name, and yeah, Farzan always referred to him by his full name, Jarrod Pancake—stared at him in the mirror.

"What're we doing today?" he asked. "The usual trim?"

"Not today." He held up his phone, with a picture of a simple, short haircut with a side part. It almost looked like Ramin's, now that he thought of it.

Well, Ramin had his shit together. Ramin was successful and happy and in a committed relationship and probably had a good credit score.

"Shit, you go through a breakup or something?" Jarrod Pancake said as he studied the picture.

Farzan stared into Jarrod Pancake's cornflower-blue eyes in the mirror. He was in his fifties, white and bald and a little fat, and Farzan had been coming to him to get his hair cut for the last fifteen years because he was the best. But he was also alarmingly direct and too damned perceptive.

"No comment," Farzan huffed.

"Oof. I feel you. Just be careful. Cut your hair for a man too much, you'll end up looking like me." Jarrod Pancake pointed at his shiny head, which finally got a small smile out of Farzan.

His cheeks were out of practice. He hadn't found much energy to smile lately.

In the nearly two weeks since he'd called things off with David, Farzan had filled the days with work. There was always something to do around the bistro: in fact, he was actually turning into a somewhat decent plumber, after having to fix the bathroom sink when it broke in the middle of service one night and they hadn't been able to get someone to come quickly enough.

Farzan's shirt had been drenched and his phone battery dead from all the videos he'd watched, but he'd fixed it.

His father had been impressed when he saw it.

He'd been less impressed when Farzan said he and David weren't together anymore, but Farzan hadn't been ready to talk about it. Or about the loan. He'd spent enough nights crying. He might've been a fuckup, but he had people counting on him and a job to do.

Farzan blinked when he realized Jarrod Pancake had asked him something as he sprayed down Farzan's hair.

"Come again?"

"He break your heart or you break his?"

"I don't know," he said, shifting uncomfortably.

Only...no. That wasn't true.

"I guess maybe I broke his," Farzan admitted as Jarrod Pancake combed and sectioned him. It had been for David's own good, though. So why did he still feel like shit?

"Oof." Jarrod Pancake began combing and sectioning. "You want a shave too?"

"I better." Farzan's scruff had turned into a scraggly beard, in that awkward stage of growth where there was no making it look good. He hadn't exactly been on top of his facial hair lately.

"All right. When I get done with you, you're going to be a new man."

He hoped so. He didn't much like the man he was now.

"Where do you want these?" Arya hoisted a green plastic laundry basket, its contents shrouded by a Persian tablecloth. His nails were painted alternating gold and silver.

"What are they?"

"Pies."

Farzan gestured to the small folding table against the dining room wall.

"Got it. What happened to your hair? Was Jarrod Pancake drunk or something?"

"I think it looks nice," Ramin said diplomatically as he held the door for Todd. "It'll take some getting used to, though."

While Arya put out the pies, Todd took Ramin's coat to hang, and Ramin thanked him with a little kiss on the cheek. Farzan tamped down his annoyance. It wasn't fair to be jealous or annoyed with Ramin, just because he was in a stable relationship and Farzan's had imploded.

No, not imploded. Farzan had taken it out back and shot it, like a rabid dog from one of those horrible books they'd had to read in elementary school.

Farzan grabbed a spoon to sample the gravy; it was his signature Spanish chorizo and sage gravy, smoky, with just a little bit of heat, and the sweetness of fresh sage running through it. It needed a bit more salt, though.

As he stirred, Ramin squeezed into the kitchen to give him a side hug, careful not to disturb the stove. They'd been doing Friendsgiving dinner for half their lives, now—ever since they all went away to college, really—but *Farzan does the cooking* was still one of the cardinal rules.

"How're you doing?" Ramin asked, voice low.

"I'm fine," Farzan said, careful to keep his voice neutral.

When Farzan finally told the group chat about the breakup, Ramin and Arya (and Todd) had come over with wine and pizza. And they'd both checked on him over the two weeks since.

But he was fine.

He and David had always had an expiration date. He'd known that going in. So really, he was okay. He'd been ready for it. It was better he'd ended it now, rather than waiting, when it would've hurt more.

And the loan had been a long shot, really. Ramin and Arya had offered to help Farzan find other banks, take another look at his numbers, see what he could change to make him a "more attractive candidate," whatever that meant, but Farzan was so tired of dealing with it.

"Hey." Ramin kept his hand on Farzan's back, leaning over the stove to smell the dressing: more chorizo and sage, plus apples and celery and parsnip and breadcrumbs made from his mom's noon-e barbari. "You know you can be honest with me."

"If this is about the haircut, don't worry. I just needed a change. I'm okay. Promise. Go worry about your boyfriend."

Farzan didn't mean to spit out the last word, but Ramin definitely caught it. His winter-green eyes softened.

"Okay." He gave Farzan another side hug before retreating back to the dining room. Soon Arya replaced him, holding two glasses of wine.

Farzan accepted his and took a sip.

"Mm."

"Smells good," Arya said. "Anything we can do?"

"Nah. We're almost ready."

"Uh-huh." Arya grabbed a spoon from the drawer and stole a taste of the dressing. "Mmmm."

"Hey! No samples."

"I was just making sure it wasn't burnt."

Farzan elbowed Arya away from the stove and faced him, taking another long sip of his wine. It was a good bottle: Domaine de la Vieux Telegraph La Crau. He'd been cellaring it for a few years—well, as much as you could call a little wooden wine rack in the back of his closet cellaring—waiting for a holiday to share it with his friends.

It was smooth, deep ruby in color, with hints of... was that Cherry Coke on the nose?

Farzan wondered what David would've made of it. But he wouldn't get to compare notes later. Share the other bottle still in his cellar.

He and David were done.

He bit his lip and turned back to the stove, blinking fast.

If Arya noticed, he didn't say anything.

"Right, okay," Arya said, leaning over the table. His cheeks were flushed a darker brown with all the wine they'd had, not to mention the enormous spread of food.

Maybe a whole turkey had been a little much for the four of them. Especially with all the sides. Farzan wasn't sure he had enough containers for all the leftovers.

"So we only need two more, right?"

"Right." Todd's cheeks were full-on red, and he was getting extremely handsy with Ramin, who kept laughing and gently shoving him away. "The biggest problem will be finding a decent goalie. How about it, honey?"

Ramin shook his head and made a show of swirling his wineglass intently.

"Come on, it'll be fun." Todd must've goosed Ramin under the table, because he jumped and laughed and swatted at Todd's chest.

"I'll be your cheerleader."

"Ugh." Arya groaned. "Farzan, you in?"

"Sure." Farzan liked soccer, liked it more than kickball to be honest. "As long as I don't have to be the goalie."

Arya sighed. "Fine, fine. Who else?"

Todd's head lolled, like his neck couldn't support the weight of his brain as it worked. "What about David?"

Ramin sat up straighter at that. Arya's mouth dropped open.

A pit opened up in Farzan's stomach.

Todd's eyes went wide. "Oh shit. I wasn't thinking."

"It's fine," Farzan said.

"I shouldn't have brought him up."

"I said it's fine," Farzan said. "He's moving, so that's a no."

"I'm really sorry."

"You don't need to be." Farzan was over it. He was fine. "Can we move on?"

"No, we can't," Arya said, and suddenly he didn't look so tipsy anymore. His brown eyes were hawklike as he stared Farzan down. "Are we ever going to talk about it?"

"Talk about what?" Farzan's neck started to burn. He reached for his water.

"You. Acting like you're fine with this. Moving around like a zombie, getting what is *clearly* a gay crisis haircut, and then telling us you're not heartbroken."

"I'm not!" Farzan knew he was protesting too much, but fuck, why couldn't his friends just leave him alone? He didn't want to talk about this.

"Farzan," Ramin said softly. Of everyone at the table he was the soberest, since he was the one driving. "I've known you forever. I have never seen you that happy with anyone before. And I've never seen you like...whatever this is."

"Whatever this is?" Farzan began, ready to argue, ready to get up and shout at Ramin and Arya and Todd for thinking they knew what he was going through. But one look at Ramin, his eyes so sad and loving, deflated all Farzan's anger, like a collapsed soufflé.

He fucking hated it when people felt sorry for him.

He fucking hated feeling sorry for himself.

"What does it matter anyway?" Farzan said, swallowing against the tide of sadness threatening to drown him. "He's better off without me."

"It matters because he made you happy, dude." Arya rested a hand on Farzan's back, squeezing his shoulder. "And you made him happy. We could all see it."

"But he's leaving!" Farzan said, heart hammering its way up toward his throat. "He's got big dreams to pursue. He's going somewhere. And what have I got to offer him? I can't even get a fucking small business loan."

"You only tried the once," Ramin said. "There are other ways—"

"Can we just *not*?" Farzan snapped.

He'd tried and he'd failed. It was like he was only allowed to want *so much*, and every time he reached for more—for a bigger Shiraz Bistro, for a life with David—the universe came along and smacked his hands.

David was wrong. He wasn't allergic to happiness.

But maybe happiness was allergic to him.

forty-eight

David

David was sweating in his jacket. Whose idea was it for the temperature to reach sixty-five degrees on Thanksgiving Day? Fucking climate change.

Growing up, David and his family would have Thanksgiving dinner, sleep off the food coma, do the dishes, and then head down to the Plaza to enjoy the Lighting Ceremony, when they'd throw the big switch and turn on the miles of Christmas lights lining the roofs of the shops and offices in Kansas City's fanciest shopping district.

David had always dreamed of getting to throw the big switch himself, and truth be told, there was still a tiny part of him that thought it would be fun.

After his parents divorced, Thanksgivings got a little more complicated, as he was juggled between families each year. And as his grandparents had passed away, as aunts and uncles and cousins moved—as David himself had moved—the day got smaller and smaller.

Now he was back, but his mom had found a new tradition, enjoying the meal with her church friends. David had gone along with her this year, a brittle smile pasted on his face as his mom's friends teased him about being too handsome to be single. His mom had given him a few sympathetic glances, but honestly? He was fine.

No Farzan meant no distractions. He was back on top of his flash cards and his tastings. The test was two weeks away.

He could taste it now. He was thirsty for it. Thirsty to prove himself, to pass this final hurdle, to show he had what it took. To finally hold his dream in his hands.

After the meal, David had gone home, spent a couple hours with his flash cards—today it was the seven valleys of Rioja—then met his dad and Deb for the Plaza lights.

"David?" Deb tugged him gently; the walk sign was on, and David had just been standing, thinking.

"Sorry. Just admiring the lights."

And they were beautiful: twinkling lines outlining the rooftops, high-lighting the Plaza's Spanish-inspired architecture. Yeah, J. C. Nichols had been a racist piece of shit, but the man knew how to build neighbor-hoods. Besides, he was long dead, yet David and his dad and Deb were here, strolling along and enjoying the lights for Christmas.

Deb smiled as they crossed Wyandotte, her arm nestled in the crook of Christopher's elbow. Both were dressed in their holiday finest, which meant that sweat beaded along their brows, too.

"Let's go see the fountain," David's dad said as they approached Mill Creek Park, the narrow strip of green at the Plaza's eastern edge. The huge fountain with its four horses and dolphin was still splashing merrily, not a single bit of ice built up along any of the spouts. A few parents had to keep their kids from splashing in it, the night was so warm.

"Let's take a picture!" Christopher pulled his phone out and turned to take a group selfie with the fountain in the background.

He snapped the picture—another terrible photo, slightly blurry from his hand shaking as he tapped the shutter, because no matter how many times David told his dad, he still wouldn't use the side buttons to trig-ger it.

"Perfect," he pronounced nonetheless.

"Lemme get one too, Dad." David snapped another picture with them actually smiling, though his dad was looking at the screen instead of the lens, as usual.

"How come yours always turn out better?" he grumbled, examining David's phone, but then he pressed his lips together. He pulled David away a few steps, so they could talk without Deb hearing.

Deb quirked an eyebrow, but just smiled and let them go.

"You doing okay, son?"

"What? Yeah. I'm good."

"Hmm." He stuffed his phone back into his pocket and stared at David.

Growing up, David had always spilled the beans when his dad stared at him that way. Like he knew every secret in the world.

David puffed up his cheeks and let out a breath. "I mean, yeah, it hurts sometimes."

Hurt so bad it was like someone had taken a corkscrew to his insides. A big, rusty winged one, the handles hollowing out his rib cage while the screw pulled his heart out through his chest.

The hurting was almost preferable to the anger, though. Anger at Farzan for ruining a good thing, for being a coward, for not even giving David a choice.

Anger at himself, too, for how he'd handled things. For the cruel things he'd said. For waiting so long to realize what it was he truly wanted. For not fighting harder.

Fuck, he was so in love, and he knew deep down it was real. The kind of love that would've aged like a perfect bottle of Bordeaux, growing deeper and more complex, smoothing off the rough edges, revealing new truths with every year it cellared.

And Farzan had thrown all that away.

"I'm gonna be okay, Dad," David said. "I'm just focusing on my test right now."

"You know there's more to life than work, right?"

David snorted.

His dad's eyebrows raised. "What's that for?"

"This from the man who never took a day off in his life."

Christopher opened his mouth, but—

"Not counting weekends or holidays."

His mouth snapped shut again as he considered. "Last year. I had that flu and stayed home the whole time."

That had been rough. David had been out of town, visiting wineries in Walla Walla, and had felt singularly useless not being able to do anything to help. Make his dad soup or something. Not that he was nearly as good a cook as Farzan.

Fuck, not thinking about him right now.

Christopher sighed. "I thought I had to," he said. "Your mom and I wanted you to know the value of hard work."

"And you did. I'm not criticizing you. I'm just saying, this is what it takes to chase my dreams. Sometimes there isn't time for anything else."

Christopher frowned then. He stepped closer and gently grasped David's arm.

"I spent a long time thinking that," he said. "But there's *always* time. If I had made time, maybe your mother and I . . . well. That's in the past. But, David. You made time for Farzan."

And look where it had gotten him.

Heartbroken and behind on his studying.

"You were blossoming with him. Blossoming in ways I'd always wanted for you. You were happy."

David had been happy. Every moment with Farzan had been colored with joy.

"Yeah, well, it wasn't enough in the end, was it?" He hated how small he felt.

"Sometimes nothing is," Christopher said softly. "But you have a big heart, son. Don't ever regret using it."

Yeah, a big heart. A big target in the center of his chest.

A big distraction from what he wanted out of life. Thought he wanted.

He'd get over Farzan. Whether he stayed here or moved to LA, there would be other guys. His life was finally getting started.

He was gonna be fine.

Just fine.

forty-nine

David

"All right." Jeri stared at him across the high-top in the corner they'd commandeered. The first real snow of the season had left them with a lighter crowd than usual for Sunday night, and with his test only five days away, he was practicing tasting as often as he could. "You know the drill. Six wines. Twenty-five minutes. Ready whenever you are."

David stared down the three whites and three reds, lined up like little soldiers, prepared for him to go to war. His spit bucket off to the side, a fresh picture of Reagan's face at the bottom.

He was ready for this. He was—

His phone buzzed in his pocket, but he ignored it.

He was going to smash this test.

He grabbed the first wine as Jeri started the timer on her phone. Tuned out the hubbub of Aspire all around him: Kyra's friendly voice as she seated a regular who lived in the condos across the street, the ringing of Dannon banging out a spoon on the rim of a saucepan.

There was only him and the wines.

Color, clarity, brightness. Body, acidity, tannins. Smells, tastes. Grape, region, producer, vintage. Move on to the next.

All three whites were California. He'd bet money on it. But statistically, that made no sense, right? There were so many wine regions across the globe. Was Jeri trying to fake him out?

The first red—Sonoma Pinot, it had to be, but four California wines in a row?

Was she teasing him about the offer from Rhett? He still hadn't given Rhett a firm answer. He knew he owed it to Rhett to say one way or another, but he honestly didn't know. Every night spent hunched over flash cards, every missed social engagement told him to say yes, that this is what his life had been building toward.

But every brunch with his mom, every service spent teasing Kyra, every night curled up with Farzan—it still hurt to remember, but it was the happiest he'd been—all told him to stay. To let himself be happy.

Maybe he was allergic to happiness too.

Shit, how much time was left? He skipped naming number four, reached for number five, but—Napa Cab, Stags Leap for sure, there was nothing else quite like it. So maybe four was Sonoma Pinot after all.

And number six, that was Paso Robles for sure, a Rhône blend, and—

"Fuck. These are all ones you've given me before, aren't they?"

Jeri's eyebrows raised, but otherwise she kept her face neutral as David went back through the reds, naming them off.

"You sure?" she asked, once he'd named number six—the same Saxum he'd tasted months ago.

"Positive."

She smirked. "Got them all."

"That was evil." David smirked right back. "I didn't think you had it in you."

"You've got to be ready for anything they throw at you. Maybe everything will be familiar. Maybe nothing will be. Have confidence in your tasting. Don't psych yourself out."

David's phone buzzed in his pocket again.

"You need to take that?"

"I can clean up first," David said, standing, but Jeri reached out and took his hand.

"I'm proud of you, you know."

"I know."

"And I don't mean for this. Well, not just for this."

David's brow furrowed.

"I know it hurts, what happened with Farzan. But I'm proud of you for putting yourself out there. It made me happy, seeing you happy."

David was not ready to cry on the job. He put on his winningest somm smile.

"Thanks, Jeri."

Jeri went back to the kitchen while David cleaned up. His phone buzzed again, but he would deal with it once he was done. It wasn't like the one person he wanted to hear from would be texting him anyway.

Every day, the ache lessened, but still. Still. He missed Farzan. Sometimes, after a long shift, he found himself turning left toward River Market instead of right, toward home. Wishing he could go curl up on Farzan's couch, split a bottle of wine, talk about their days, watch a movie or play a game. Make out, fall into bed.

But then he remembered their last fight. He remembered the years he'd spent preparing for the coming weekend. He couldn't afford to be distracted.

Focus.

He wiped his hands and reached into his pocket, but Kyra waved him down to help pick a bottle of Champagne for a couple celebrating their anniversary (he did his best not to be bitter), then he got stuck explaining orange wine to one of their regulars who'd never heard of it. And then a huge crowd of finance bros surged in right at ten o'clock, and he wound up behind the bar, pouring wine for Tonya while she managed a dozen cocktail orders.

His phone buzzed one last time, close to midnight, but there were people to tab out, and then he had to help close up, and might as well wait until he got home.

Thankfully, the streets had been thoroughly plowed and salted, though the wind was bitterly cold as he pulled up at home. He hung his suit and pulled on his favorite sweats. The ones Farzan had liked so much.

He had four texts and a missed call from Ayesha. Fuck, he'd been meaning to talk to her—when had he last?—but she was probably in bed.

Still, he shot her a text.

> **David**
> Hey, sorry. Just got home from work.
> You still up?
> If not, catch you tomorrow maybe?

David knew she was a night owl, but not as much of one anymore, not with two kids. He went to the kitchen and poured himself a glass of Burgundy he'd opened the night before. Nothing ever felt quite so warming as Burgundy: it called to mind warm stone hearths, boeuf bourguignon melting in his mouth, and a butane torch over the shell of a creme brûlée. Fleece blankets and snuggling with Farzan and—

To his surprise, his phone started ringing.

"Hey, Ayesha," he said, once her face appeared on the screen, rich brown catching the orange light of a floor lamp as she sprawled on her living room couch. A pink silk scarf covered her hair, which looked freshly braided. "Sorry I missed you earlier. Work was..."

Well, it hadn't even been that busy, but busy enough.

"Don't make this about work. You don't work twenty-four hours a day, do you? You could've answered my texts yesterday, or the day before. Or any number of times over the past month."

"I answered!"

"*I'm fine, how are you?* isn't much of an answer, David." She sighed, which led to a coughing fit; she reached for a tissue and covered her mouth.

"Shit, you okay?"

"I'm fine. Micah brought home a nasty cold from school. I've been sleeping on the couch so I don't wake up Janine."

"Oh damn, I'm sorry. I had one a while back...it only lasted a few days, but it was rough." And Farzan had taken care of him, too. He shoved the thought away. "Drink plenty of fluids."

"I've got two kids, this isn't my first rodeo," Ayesha muttered before coughing into her Kleenex. "They're both walking petri dishes."

"I bet. Hey, wasn't Nate's recital last week?"

"It was. I sent you the link."

"Shit. I haven't seen it yet. Everything's been..."

Well. Where to start.

"I'm sorry. I'll watch it as soon as I can. I've just been so stressed. My test is this week, you know?"

"I know. I also know you said you were going to do better."

"You're right. Shit. You're right. It's just..." Hot shamed welled up in David's chest, like mulled wine about to boil over. "I've been a mess lately. Between studying, and then the whole Farzan thing, my head's been in a weird place."

Ayesha pinched the bridge of her broad nose, and David couldn't tell if she was annoyed with him or trying to stop a sneeze. Eventually she let it go, and he figured it was the former.

"I get you're busy, David. And I get you're hurting. But you said you were going to do better. Then all of a sudden it's *Oh, I'm going to LA to look at my new restaurant. Oh, my boyfriend and I broke up. Oh, my test is almost here and I don't know a Riesling from a Rioja.*"

Like anyone could mix those two up. Riesling was a sweet white, Rioja a dry red, and—

"Then you just go radio silent again."

"I know," David said, hiding behind his wineglass. "I know. You're right. I'm sorry. It's just..."

It's just my heart is broken.

It's just I don't know what I'm doing.

It's just I don't know what I want anymore.

"I really loved him, A," he finally said. "I don't think I've ever loved someone like that. And I thought...I don't know. I thought we'd figure out how to make it work. But he didn't even want to try."

Ayesha was quiet. For a moment David worried the call had frozen, but Ayesha blinked. She still didn't say anything, though.

"Ayesha?" he asked.

"Yeah?"

He wasn't going to beg her to make him feel better. He wasn't sure how she could, anyway. "Just making sure you're still there."

"Mm-hmm." She blew her nose again. "You want to know what I think, or you want me to tell you it'll all work out?"

David didn't like the sound of that, but still: "What do you think?"

"It's pretty simple. What's more important to you: this job of yours or this man of yours?"

"He is," David said. "I was ready to give everything up. Stay here and be with him."

"And did you show him?"

"I told him."

"You told him when he was in the middle of dumping you."

"Ouch." But it was true.

"You spent your whole relationship with him—hell, you've spent the last ten years of your life—telling anyone who would listen about your big dreams. What did you expect to happen?"

David went quiet.

It wasn't like that. Was it?

Shit.

It was.

"I really messed up, A," David said. "I don't know. I didn't expect any of this to happen. I didn't expect..."

Didn't expect Farzan to become my new dream.

"What am I supposed to do?"

Ayesha let out the long-suffering sigh of someone who suddenly found herself dealing with an extra child. David tried not to be annoyed.

"Do you even know what it is you want?"

"Yeah, I—"

"Have you told Rhett?"

David went quiet again.

"Told your mom? Your dad? Have you told anyone? Or are you just hedging your bets?"

"It's not like that."

"As long as I've known you, you've gone for what you wanted without letting anything get in your way. So what's stopping you now?"

What *was* stopping him?

He didn't even know anymore.

"You're right," he said. "I'll talk to Rhett. Tell him I'm staying here."

"Mm. Well, that's a start." Ayesha's eyes softened. "You're the smartest guy I know. I'm sure you can figure out the rest."

David could.

He didn't know about smart—hard to feel that way when he was getting dressed down by his best friend—but he *was* capable of going after his dreams. He'd chased a lucrative career, and then a fulfilling one, and now . . . now it was time to chase Farzan.

He just had to figure out how. He wracked his brain, but it was too full of tasting grids and flash cards. He needed to be thoughtful.

He needed to talk to Rhett. To Jeri.

He needed to build the life he wanted here. *Show* Farzan that he was staying for himself. Prove that this is what he wanted, whether he passed his test or not.

(He still really wanted to, though.)

David nodded, sipped his wine, and sighed. "So what's up with you?"

"Oh, we're finally talking about me now?"

David snorted, but then he realized Ayesha wasn't laughing.

"You know you've only talked about yourself this whole time? You haven't asked me about work, or how Janine's doing, or my parents, or anything. Just you, you, you."

He stared at the couch. There was a small wine stain on it; he scratched at it with his fingernail.

"You're right."

God.

He was an asshole. He'd been focused on his test, focused on Farzan, focused on himself.

But he needed his friends. He always had. It just took him a while to get his head out of his ass and realize it.

"You're right, and I'm sorry. Tell me everything."

Ayesha snorted.

"What?"

"Where do I even start?"

"Well, how's work? Did you put in for that promotion?"

As Ayesha filled him in—first on work, then on some of their old friend group, then on Janine and Micah and Nate—David rolled off the couch and made himself a cup of herbal tea. The hot mug felt good in his hands; the steam rising off the tea felt even better in his sinuses.

"Hey. What do Nate and Micah want for Christmas?"

"I don't know about them, but their moms are partial to Sauvignon Blancs."

David laughed. His chest felt lighter.

Why didn't he talk to Ayesha more?

"Okay. I'll pick something nice. But seriously, what about the boys?"

"They're young, they won't remember if you get them LEGOs or stuffed animals."

"They won't remember me at all at this rate," David said. He hadn't even caught them on FaceTime in months; they were already in bed when he or Ayesha called. "Hey. Could I come visit you sometime?"

Ayesha finally smiled at that.

"How's February?" she asked.

David frowned. He didn't miss Chicago winters at all.

Ayesha laughed, though.

"Just kidding. Come in May or June. When the weather's nice and Micah's out of school."

"Okay."

"And in the meantime, just call me sometimes, okay?"

"I will. I really will. I promise."

"Good. And, David?"

"Yeah?"

"If you want him, go after him."

David grinned. Something fell away from him then, something he'd been carrying around for weeks. Maybe even longer. An old idea of who he had to be. What his life had to look like.

"I will."

fifty

Farzan

The lights were on in the Trans' place when Farzan pulled up to Shiraz Bistro.

The salon had been gutted, everything gone but the sinks. A FOR SALE sign still hung in the window. And inside, Farzan recognized their agent, showing around a couple of folks, who were nodding along with whatever she was saying.

What did it matter, anyway? He'd never be able to get a loan, never be able to make an offer. He could only hope his new neighbors wouldn't be assholes.

Farzan let himself in and headed to the kitchen. Chase had the week off—spending time with his family in the Ozarks—so Farzan was on rice duty. At least that was one thing he couldn't fuck up. He got the tah-dig started and headed to his office, where he found the papers from the Trans' real estate agent on his desk. For all the good they would do.

There was a knock on his door frame. "Hey, boss?" Elmira asked.

"Huh? Sorry." Farzan tossed the papers in the blue bin under his desk. "What's up?"

Elmira's lips twisted back and forth. "Uh... is everything okay?"

No, it wasn't, but he wasn't going to unload on the staff. "Yeah. Why?"

"Well, usually my paychecks go through overnight on Tuesdays, so they're in my account by Wednesday, but this morning there wasn't anything, and it still hasn't posted."

That was odd. Everyone who got direct deposit was, indeed, supposed to get paid Tuesday night.

"It definitely should've gone through . . . let me do some checking?"

"Sure. Thanks."

Farzan held in a sigh. The last thing he needed was a payroll problem. Everything was supposed to be automated, as long as he filled out all the forms Monday night and signed them and—

Fuck. Fuck!

He looked through his emails for the usual confirmation that payroll was being processed. It was always filtered and sorted without him doing much more than glance at it, but this time . . . nothing.

He'd fucked up. Big time.

It was his own fault. He'd been out running errands Monday and had accidentally driven right by Aspire. It wasn't like he could see inside, but that hadn't stopped heartache from consuming him the rest of the day. Plus the family group chat had been blowing up about Maheen's first ultrasound. And Ramin and Todd were asking about hosting everyone for Friendsmas, and that's just what Farzan needed, to look at a happy and successful couple as they cuddled and kissed and celebrated another holiday together while Farzan was alone. Again.

God. He really was a fuckup.

And now he had to get to the bank before they closed, so he could get them to run some checks for him. And oh how fun that would be, showing up asking them to help him fix his fuckup, as if they needed any more confirmation they'd been right to deny him a loan.

He grabbed his coat and keys and stepped out into the kitchen—only to be greeted by the scent of burning rice.

His tahdig!

He ran to the stove, killed the heat, grabbed a towel, and took the pot over to the sink to run it under cool water. As if that could undo the disaster.

There was no saving burned tahdig. There might not even be any saving of the pot itself. He didn't have time for this. He left the pot in the sink, hollered at Spencer to hold down the fort, and ran for his car.

The sky was a bright, uniform gray, and a light sleet was coming down, catching in his eyelashes, landing cold against the back of his neck where his hair used to protect him. He would need to invest in a hat until his hair grew back out. Or maybe it would all fall out from the stress and he'd be bald like Arya.

He shut himself in the car and turned it on to get the defroster going. He gripped the steering wheel and clenched his teeth, but he couldn't keep the sob in any longer.

Somehow the rice was the last straw. Because even when he'd been a total fuckup at everything else, he'd always been good at cooking. And now he'd ruined that, too.

His shoulders shook. Sadness swelled in his chest like a balloon that was finally about to burst. He wanted to break down, hug himself, hide in the car, and never show his face again. But he had a restaurant full of people counting on him.

He couldn't.

So he sniffled, and wiped his face, and pulled out of the parking lot.

He still had to make it to the bank. Sort out the payroll. Get through the night.

And then?

Well. He didn't know what came next. If he couldn't even cook tahdig, or get the paychecks done on time... if he couldn't make the restaurant valuable enough to expand, then what was he doing running it?

He was a fuckup. He'd always been a fuckup.

This was just the final proof.

fifty-one

Farzan

Farzan groaned and rolled over. His head was pounding.

Upon reflection, it probably hadn't been a good idea to drink an entire bottle of wine last night. But he'd gotten home after closing, anxious and frustrated, and when he was in a bad mood he liked to watch *Ratatouille* for some reason. But seeing all that French food made him want wine, so he'd opened a bottle of Chinon and ended up polishing it off by himself, crying when Remy's family came together to support him, when Colette came back to help Linguini, when the ending credits rolled and some lady sang in French.

Farzan was a fucking mess. And now he was a dehydrated, hungover mess, too. The pounding in his head was getting worse.

No. Not in his head.

Well, yes, in his head, but not only in his head. Someone was at the door.

Farzan ran his tongue across his teeth, fuzzy from last night because he'd been too drunk to brush them, and if his breath smelled as bad as his mouth tasted, then whoever was at the door was in for a rude awakening.

Farzan pulled on a shirt—he was still in last night's joggers, too—

and scratched at the back of his neck, where his hair was prickly as it grew in.

Before he reached the door, though, the deadbolt unlocked and it swung open, admitting a bald, bronze head.

"Farzan?" Arya called. "You here? You decent? You having some *alone time?*"

"You asshole," Farzan answered, stepping closer and pulling the door open.

It wasn't just Arya: Ramin was right behind him, clutching a white box from Doze Nuts, their favorite donut shop in the Northland. How a queer-owned donut shop with an extremely obvious double entendre for a name had survived for twelve years in Gladstone, of all places, Farzan didn't know, but he wouldn't look a gift horse (or gift donut) in the mouth.

"Did we wake you?" Ramin asked.

"Did you even sleep?" Arya knelt to untie his boots.

"Yes, I slept," Farzan said, taking the donuts so Ramin could deal with his own coat and shoes. "You're the night owl."

"Then why am I already dressed and you look a...you know. One of those wrinkly dogs. With purple teeth."

Ramin made a noise in the back of his throat, the kind he always made when trying to stop himself from laughing at Arya.

"Ugh." Farzan shoved the donut box back into Arya's hands and retreated to the bathroom. He showered quickly—one advantage of his new short hair was that it took no time at all to wash and dry—brushed his teeth, and pulled on a clean shirt and a different pair of joggers.

When he emerged, Ramin and Arya were sitting around Farzan's kitchen table, talking quietly. Ramin had a glass of amber tea in his hand—the pot was still steaming on the table—while Arya had a glass of reddish rooibos. The donut box still lay closed between them, though someone had pulled down three small plates.

"He lives!" Arya said as Farzan sat down. "And he doesn't smell like hot dog water anymore."

That time Ramin did laugh, nearly spitting his tea out.

"You do smell better," he admitted.

Farzan rolled his eyes. "Whatever. What are you guys doing here?"

"This is an intervention," Arya announced solemnly.

Farzan crossed his arms. "For what?"

"We're not sure," Arya admitted. "We'll figure that out as we go."

"You've barely answered the group chat," Ramin said. "And I heard... well, Todd went to get carryout the other night, and I guess he ran into Mr. Tran, and he said..."

Ramin's cheeks colored. He looked to Arya for help.

"He said you told him to go ahead and sell to someone else?"

Farzan's ears began to burn, the back of his neck, too.

But he couldn't ask them to keep holding out, hoping he'd get his shit together or find some other way to raise money. They couldn't put their lives on hold for him.

"What was I supposed to do?"

"You only tried one bank," Arya said. "You could—"

"What, go door to door, getting punched in the balls over and over because 'restaurants are a risky investment'? No thanks." Farzan reached for a red velvet donut. "Maybe my parents were right. Maybe I should've let the restaurant go. If I close down, they and the Trans can both sell, probably get more for the whole building anyway. I can go back to subbing or whatever."

He'd been thinking about it all night. Yeah, the expansion had fallen through, but now he was burning the rice, messing up people's paychecks. He was letting everyone down.

"You can't be serious," Arya said around a cherry-iced cake donut. Pink icing and sprinkles stuck to his lips. "That's the most ridiculous thing I've ever heard."

"Wait." Ramin rested a hand on Farzan's arm. "What do you mean, you don't want to do this anymore? Running the restaurant?"

Farzan massaged his temples. "I don't think I'm cut out for this."

"But..." Arya began.

Ramin cut him off. "You're joking, right? You know the bistro is doing better than it has in years? I've seen the numbers. That's not random. That's you. Your hard work."

"Yeah, but it's still not enough, is it?" Farzan said. "It'll never be enough. And I...I'm not good at it. You know last night I fucked up the payroll? Had to run back to the bank before they closed, the same bank that denied me a loan last month, and you know how fucking humiliating that was? To march in and ask them to do a rush job on checks because I'd messed up? It just confirmed to them they'd been right to say no in the first place."

Farzan's hand went to his hair, but it was too short to run his hands through.

Arya snorted as he clocked the motion. "That's what you get for having the Ramin haircut."

"Hey!" Ramin threw a donut hole at Arya. "I like it."

Arya arched an eyebrow. Ramin blushed and turned back to Farzan. "It's not really you, though."

"Whatever. It doesn't matter." Farzan stuffed half a glazed donut into his mouth, gulped down a mouthful of hot tea. Carbs were so good. They didn't solve anything, but at least his head felt a little better. "I should've known it would turn out this way. I always fuck everything up."

Ramin smacked the table so loud their tea glasses rattled.

"Dude—" Arya began, but Ramin cut him off.

"Don't you say that. That's my best friend you're talking about. You don't fuck everything up." His eyes were narrowed, brows drawn together.

"Yeah," Arya said. "Where's all this coming from? I thought you were happy."

"I was," Farzan said. "I felt like I was finally doing something right, you know? Something meaningful. But I don't know...every day it's just been getting worse. Like, it's fine when I'm in the kitchen, but it's not just being in the kitchen. It's spreadsheets and payroll and inventory and a thousand other things, and I'm not cut out for it."

No, that wasn't it. Farzan was cut out for it...mostly. He'd handled it. But...

"I hate it. It's exhausting. And now I barely even have time to do any cooking. You know I burned some tahdig yesterday? I don't burn tahdig! I just... I can't keep doing this."

Arya and Ramin stared at him.

Finally Ramin said, "You know... your dad hated all that stuff, too. That's why he stayed in the kitchen and let your mom deal with all of it."

"Yeah, and like..." Arya pressed his lips together. "Okay, don't tell your mom I said this, but she's just not as good a cook. She doesn't need to be, though. She's like a human calculator."

"So?" Farzan already knew all that. It's what made his parents such good partners.

"So you keep trying to do the job of two people at once," Ramin said. "Why not hire a manager so you can focus on being the chef? That's what you're passionate about."

"That's what you're *good* at," Arya pointed out. "And don't you dare call yourself a fuckup in the kitchen, or I will throw your best pot out the window."

"With what money? Yeah, we're doing okay, but not okay enough to just... suddenly hire a manager. At least, not with enough salary to get a good one. If I'd gotten the loan, maybe, but..."

"What if I bought in?" Ramin asked.

"What if you... what?"

"Hey, yeah, me too," Arya said. "We could be your partners."

"You two both have jobs."

"Fine, we can be your silent partners," Ramin said. "We bring the capital. You keep running the place."

"I can't take your money." Farzan knew Ramin had the resources—he'd gotten a decent inheritance from his parents, plus he was making good money at his job, especially after his latest promotion—but still. He never let friends and finances mix.

"You wouldn't be taking it," Ramin said. "We'd all benefit from the profits, right? We could draw up a contract and everything."

"Yeah. That could work," Arya said. "With the extra capital I bet you could buy the Trans' place *and* hire a manager to help you run everything."

"You guys don't get it!" Farzan said.

"Don't get what?" Arya asked.

"This was my family's legacy. I was supposed to be able to do it on my own."

Ramin said, "Your parents didn't do it on their own. They had each other. And they had our parents, too. Lots of people helped them. Hell, you helped them too, waiting tables when we were in high school. Don't you remember?"

"Yeah, but—"

"So why won't you let us—your best friends—support you? Why do you think you have to go it alone?"

"Because," Farzan said, but his throat constricted.

His friends were too good. He didn't know what he'd done to deserve them. That they'd just offer up money for the bistro without even blinking. Without considering all the ways it could go wrong.

"Because I couldn't stand it if the whole thing blows up and we weren't friends anymore. If it was my fault that your futures were ruined."

"Are you sure you're still talking about the bistro?" Ramin asked softly.

"What?" Farzan's neck started heating up again.

"I don't know, dude." Arya eyed Ramin's plate for a second before sliding a chocolate-frosted donut onto it. "That sounds a lot like what you said about David, too."

"I'm not . . . this has nothing to do with him."

"Maybe it's all part of the same problem, though." Ramin picked at his donut but fixed Farzan with his gaze. The morning light caught in his green eyes. "You're my best friend. You have been for most of my life. You've shown me—shown both of us—time and time again who you are. Someone we can count on. But you won't count on us to help you out. You didn't even give us the chance to say yes. And you didn't give David the chance, either."

"So what if I say yes? What if you both go in on the bistro and then it closes anyway? What if it's a huge disaster and all your savings are wiped out?"

"So what?" Arya said.

Farzan blinked at him.

"What if it does? Do you really think we're not strong enough to get past it? Do you think we'd stop being your friends if that happened?"

"Maybe," Farzan murmured.

Ramin shot Farzan the saddest look just then, and Farzan wanted to crawl into a hole. No one did *wounded* quite like Ramin. Something about his eyebrows.

"Let me ask you this," Arya said. "What do you actually want?"

"What?"

"Your future. You close your eyes and imagine it, what does it look like? What are you doing? *Who* are you doing?"

Ramin snorted and launched another donut hole. It bounced off Arya's forehead as Arya made his eyebrows dance.

The truth was, Farzan didn't even know. He'd long since stopped trying to envision a future, because every time he did, it blew up in his face. Being a teacher, or a real estate agent, or a translator. Being with Cliff or Jason or Sean or Omid or Brandon (fucking Brandon).

But then he thought about Arya and Ramin, sticking with him through thick and thin. Nearly thirty years of friendship and they were still going strong.

And yeah, his siblings were better off than he was, married or engaged or expecting. Fancy professionals who owned their own homes. But Navid had still asked him to be best man. Maheen had asked him to be her baby's godfather. Hell, his parents had signed over their restaurant to him. Maybe they did believe in him after all.

Fuck, what if David was right? What if he was allergic to his own happiness?

Farzan blinked. Swallowed away the nerves in his throat.

"I want to run the bistro," he finally said. "Be the chef. And yeah, maybe find a different manager. Expand it and make it a place where all the Iranians in town feel at home."

"We're with you," Ramin said. "Every step of the way."

Arya nodded.

"And...and I want David. I know it's selfish, and I know I messed everything up. But I want him anyway."

"It sounded like he wanted you too. Like maybe he was serious about staying. Making a life with you." Arya cocked a grin. "Maybe his dreams are Farzan-shaped."

Farzan ran a hand through his hair. It was still singularly unsatisfying. Why on earth did he cut it in the first place?

Oh yeah. Gay crisis.

"I really hurt him, though," Farzan said. "How am I supposed to face him again?"

"You are the best person I know," Ramin said.

"Hey!" Arya protested, though without any heat. "Okay, fine. Agreed."

Ramin cleared his throat. "As I was saying...I know you can figure it out. But if you need our help, we're here."

"Always," Arya agreed.

Farzan couldn't stop the smile spreading across his face like the dawn. He didn't know what he'd done to deserve such excellent friends.

But he wasn't going to doubt anymore.

"Okay. I love you guys." He took a deep breath. "I don't know what to do about David yet. But if you're serious about the bistro..."

"I am."

"Me too."

"Then I guess we better come up with a plan."

fifty-two

David

Somehow David expected Dallas to be warmer.

Granted, it was the middle of December, but in his mind Texas was always warm. Not today, though: it was actually snowing. Snowing! Big, fluffy flakes were twirling right outside his hotel room window.

He stared at them as he inhaled the steam from a mug of hot water.

His test was in two hours.

This was it: five years of studying (the last more intense than anything he'd done in his life), over two thousand flash cards and just as many bottles of wine (maybe more—he'd only started counting last year).

He was already dressed in his favorite suit, the blue and lavender plaid. He'd cleaned and polished and brushed his shoes: the black ones with gold floral print. He was even wearing his favorite pair of underwear.

Yeah, it was the same thing he'd been wearing when he met Farzan. But that had been one of the best days of his life. He just hadn't known it yet. And despite the heartache that had come since, he didn't regret it. In fact, it was only the beginning. Because he still wanted Farzan. And once he got back home, he'd find a way to tell him.

After talking to Ayesha last week, he'd thought about just showing up at Shiraz Bistro, or at Farzan's apartment, getting down on his knees and begging, but he didn't. Not because of pride—he'd easily give that up for Farzan—but because it didn't feel genuine. He needed to show Farzan that he was committed to building a life together. And part of that meant showing that he was staying in KC, regardless. He hadn't quite figured everything out yet. He had this damn test first.

For now, though, wearing his favorite suit—and with a fresh lineup— David felt like Farzan was with him. Wishing him luck. Despite the things they'd said, David knew Farzan wanted him to succeed. Wanted it bad enough to let David go.

But success wasn't worth it without the man you loved by your side.

David's phone chimed.

> **Ayesha**
> You got this!! 💪🍷

And beneath, a photo of her and Janine with their boys, all cheesing and giving him a thumbs-up.

David took a selfie to send back, smiling with the snow behind him. He was already looking forward to visiting next summer. And hey, it wasn't hard to get from KC to Chicago.

He got a few more texts as he watched the snow: his mom, his dad. Rhett.

> **Rhett**
> Good luck bud
> I'm proud of you

> **David**
> Thanks Rhett
> I'll come visit again soon, promise

> **Rhett**
> Bring your mans with you
> I could use another show 😉 😼

"Asshole," David said aloud. But he smiled.

Rhett had been more forgiving than David deserved, when he'd finally called and said no, he couldn't take the job. He wanted to stay in Kansas City. With his family, and his friends, and maybe, just maybe, with Farzan.

Rhett had understood, had even told David he would see about sending consulting gigs his way, ones where he'd travel for a week or two to help restaurants with their lists. David could do all that while staying on at Aspire. Living at home.

Being happy.

David sighed and rested his forehead against the cool window, staring out at the snow.

He could've been studying his flash cards one last time, or tasting a few more wines, but a strange calm had settled over him, dancing across his skin. He'd done the best he could to prepare. And he was going to do the best he could downstairs, when it was finally his turn. He was proud of himself.

He knew this wasn't the end for him, just the beginning. There was more to life than wine, and tests, and work. There were people he cared about.

A man in Kansas City he was determined to win back.

Next to all that, what did six little glasses of wine really matter?

"How're you feeling today, son?" the master somm across the table asked. He was an old white man, easily sixty-five and maybe pushing seventy, with the sort of tall snowy haircut that old white guys in suits seemed to favor.

"Feeling good," David said, though being called *son* by an old white man didn't exactly feel great. He'd dealt with worse, though. "Feeling ready."

"Good," the guy said. "Nothing to be nervous about. You've studied hard. You've practiced. And now here we are."

He set his phone on the table, the timer app already open.

"I'm sure you know how this goes. You've got twenty-five minutes. I'll start the clock when you pick up your first wine. Whenever you're ready." He gave a kindly smile, pale blue eyes twinkling. "Good luck."

David took a deep breath. Stared down the six wines in front of him, three whites and three reds, shining in the harsh light of the small hotel meeting room. Light jazz from the lobby filtered past the closed door.

Three whites. Three reds.

Twenty-five minutes.

He reached for the first wine and began.

fifty-three

Farzan

A ll right," Reza said, shuffling the papers from Arya over to Ramin. "Now you."

Ramin nodded, biting his lip as he signed with a black and gold fountain pen he'd gotten from work as a five-year gift. He signed his name with a flourish, then offered Farzan a warm smile. "Done."

"All you, then," Reza said.

Farzan swallowed away his fears. Ignored the sound effects running through the back of his head, ringing alarms like his hit points were low and he was about to get a game over.

This felt right.

This felt good.

This felt like a beginning.

Farzan signed his own name with a plain Bic from the mug on Reza's desk.

And then it was done.

"All set. Congrats, you three." He shook Farzan's hand, then Ramin's, then Arya's. "So about my lifetime discount..."

"What discount?" Arya sputtered.

"Should've read the fine print," Reza said, sliding their new partnership agreement into a folder. "Don't worry, I promise not to abuse it."

Arya laughed. "Fair enough."

"Seriously, though. I think this is great." Reza smiled. "I remember you guys growing up. The Three Musketeers. I can't believe it's taken this long for you to do something like this."

"More like the Three Must-o-teers," Arya said.

Ramin groaned at the terrible pun.

But a balloon swelled in Farzan's chest so fast, so fierce, he wanted to explode.

He loved these guys so much. He was lucky to have them in his life. And he was starting to admit that maybe they were lucky to have him, too.

"Okay, partners." Farzan threw his arms over his friends' shoulders. "I'm pretty sure Reza charges by the hour, so we better get out of here."

Reza chuckled. "Tell your parents I said hi."

"Will do."

"So going forward, I'll be transitioning more to a chef de cuisine role," Farzan said the next morning. "And we'll be looking for someone to take over as general manager. If any of you want to put your name in the hat for that, definitely do."

Farzan looked out over the staff of Shiraz Bistro, seated at the tables. Ramin and Arya hovered behind him, but they'd insisted this was his show.

"Also, I know this is a big change, but I...well, we...think this is what's best for the restaurant's future. For all of us. Any questions?"

Farzan waited, but no one spoke up. Not that he expected many qualms, but you never knew.

"All right. Well. Thanks all. Let's prep for service. Oh! And, Sheena, I've got something in the oven, but it should be done soon and out of the way."

"Got it."

As the kitchen staff filed back and the front-of-house team started setting the chairs and tables, Farzan retreated to the bar with Ramin and Arya.

"Good job, boss," Arya said.

Farzan rolled his eyes. "Come on."

"He's right, though," Ramin said. He slipped his phone out of his pocket to check the time. "Okay, we've got that meeting with the Trans and their agent. You sure you don't want to come?"

Farzan shook his head. "I've got some stuff to take care of here, and then . . . Well. David's test was yesterday, so he should be back today."

"Ah, so you're ditching work to go make some sort of grand romantic gesture?" Arya quirked an eyebrow. "A boom box outside his window? Oh, did he fly? Can you run through the airport to meet him?"

"I don't think the TSA likes that," Ramin pointed out.

"Maybe not grand," Farzan said. "But at least it'll be honest."

Arya grinned. "That's the best gesture of all. Good luck, dude."

"Whatever happens, we love you," Ramin said, pulling Farzan into a hug. "Go get your man."

Farzan nodded.

He didn't know if it would be enough. If he would be enough.

But he was willing to ask anyway.

The rest would be up to David.

fifty-four

David

"I haven't done this in a while..." Jeri muttered, peeling the foil and cage off a bottle of Champagne. She rotated it in her hand, felt for the seam with her thumb, and then, with one swift motion, ran a butter knife against it.

Brayan yelped and ducked as the top of the bottle—cork and all—sheared off and flew at him, disappearing into the corner of the restaurant. The clatter was immediately swallowed by the staff—David's friends—cheering.

"Here's to our new master sommelier, David Curtis!" Jeri cried. "Aspire's *permanent* wine director." Another whoop spread through the restaurant.

David's cheeks were about to pop off and float away like bubbles, he was smiling so much. Jeri poured, and Kyra passed out the flutes, starting with David.

"You did it," she said, pulling David into a one-armed hug, careful not to spill any Champagne. "I knew you could."

"Thanks, Kyra."

David more or less hadn't stopped smiling since last night when—after hours of waiting and pacing in the hotel lobby—he'd been summoned into a different meeting room, where the same old white man had waited for him.

The man had left him sweating as he looked over a folder for a painfully long while before meeting David's eyes and congratulating him.

David had nearly fallen to the floor with relief. And pride. He was even willing to (mostly) overlook being called *son* again as the guy shook his hand and helped him fix his new master somm pin on his lapel.

He'd smiled all the way through the reception after fielding questions about what was next for him. A winery? New York? San Francisco? A few people had already heard rumors about him and Shyla's new place. But he gave everyone the same answer: "I'm staying in Kansas City."

In fact, as soon as he'd gotten the news—before he even went to the reception—he'd called Jeri to tell her and asked to stay on.

"Like you even have to ask," she'd said, but her voice had sounded a little throaty on the phone, and she'd insisted on getting off because of a "bad connection."

And now here he was. Celebrating with the people who'd helped him, and cheered for him, and put up with him having his head up his ass some of the time. Okay, most of the time.

David was living his best life. It had just taken him a while to realize it.

"You need a top-up?" Jeri waggled another bottle of Champagne. Le Mesnil. The same one he'd served Farzan the night they met.

"I better not. I've got to head out soon."

"Oh really?" Jeri said. "What could be so important on the biggest night of your life? Could it be a certain fake food critic?"

"You're never going to let me live that down, are you?"

"I was willing to when I thought you were leaving me. But now that you're here to stay, yes, I will be teasing you endlessly about it."

David laughed and pulled Jeri into a hug, so fast she sloshed Champagne over them both. But David didn't care, and neither did she.

"Okay," she said, blinking fast, but David pretended not to see. "Go get your man."

He still didn't know exactly what he was going to say. He'd written speech after speech—those little note cards still came in handy, and he still had a thousand blank ones he had to get rid of somehow—but in the end he'd tossed them.

He'd spent the last ten years, even longer, trying to plan out his life. Thinking that if he worked hard enough, studied hard enough, he could reach his dreams. But this time, he was going to go with his heart and trust that the words he needed would be there.

He wove through the restaurant, giving out handshakes and high fives and hugs and fist bumps and so, so many *thank you*s before he finally reached the doorway. He grabbed his coat and started slipping it on as Kyra sidled up next to him.

"So. Gonna stay after all?"

"Yup." As David fussed with his zipper, Tonya swung by and slipped a twenty into Kyra's hand. "What was that? Did you take a bet on me?"

"I *won* a bet," Kyra said. "On me. I didn't want to have to train someone to replace you."

"You brat." But David pulled her into another hug.

"You going to go find your man?" she said when he released her.

"I am."

"Good. He seems like a keeper."

"He really is." David cleared his throat. "Okay. Bye."

He turned and pulled the door open—

And walked straight into a warm body coming through.

Instinctively, he reached out to steady them before they fell. His hands closed around the sleeves of a puffy coat.

And in that coat:

"Farzan?"

fifty-five

Farzan

Seeing David again had felt like plunging into an icy bath. Every nerve, every skin cell, every fiber of his being reacted.

Unfortunately, he also froze up, which meant he didn't get out of the way in time when David, still talking to Kyra over his shoulder, walked right into him.

Right away, David's strong hands steadied him, but it was too late for the cake he'd been holding, which was now smeared across his coat.

"Farzan," David said, and hearing his name across David's lips warmed him to the core.

"Hi."

Everything he'd had in his mind flew out his ear. Everything he wanted to say, everything he wanted to apologize for. Washed away as soon as he got a hit of David's cologne. Vetiver and home.

David looked good, too: fresh haircut, crisp slit in his eyebrow, and a smile that could melt a glacier. And on his lapel, a shiny new pin.

"You passed?"

"I passed." David was still smiling. At him?

Or from relief?

"Congratulations. I knew you could do it."

"Thanks." David's eyes strayed upward. "You cut your hair."

"Yeah." Farzan cleared his throat. "I kind of hate it."

"God, me too. But you're still the most beautiful man I've ever seen."

Farzan blushed. How could David still say something like that, after everything that happened? But the little flame of hope in Farzan's chest burned brighter as David looked down at Farzan's coat, then at the platter in his hands where a now-smushed cake sat.

"Shit! I'm sorry. Come inside, let me help you clean up..."

Farzan felt twenty pairs of eyes tracking them as David led him to a quiet corner, away from what was obviously a party. David took the ruined cake from him, swapped it for a black cloth napkin. Farzan took off his puffer coat and tried to rub out the crumbs and icing, while David studied the cake. His smile had gone wistful.

"What are you doing here?"

Farzan swallowed. He still couldn't remember his speech.

"I wanted to see you," he said. "I hope that was okay."

"I wanted to see you too," David said simply.

He was smiling still, despite all the ways Farzan had hurt him. All the ways Farzan had let him down.

"I came to tell you..." Farzan's voice shook, but he took a deep breath and steadied himself. "I'm sorry. I'm sorry for hurting you. I'm sorry for breaking up with you. And I'm sorry for trying to make your choices for you instead of trusting you. I was scared that if I asked you to stay, you would, and then you'd have to give up your dream, and I couldn't... I've had enough dreams blow up in my face. I didn't want that for you. But you get to be in charge of your life, not me. And I know you're moving away, and I know long distance can be hard, but I miss you. And I love you. And I want you back. If you'll have me."

Farzan clamped his mouth shut. He was rambling, he knew he was rambling.

But David's gaze had dropped to the cake in his hands.

"There's a hole in this cake," he said softly.

"Used to be, at least."

David chuckled. "I'm not, you know."

"Not what?"

"Not moving away."

"What?"

Farzan couldn't have heard right. David had passed his test. Had that shiny new pin. Had a million-watt smile and all his coworkers celebrating.

"What happened?"

"I turned down Rhett's offer. I'm staying here."

"But why?"

"Why? Because Kansas City is home. Because I'm happy here." David looked at him again, eyes shining in the lamplight. "Because you're here."

Farzan's heart cracked open. He thought he might start glowing from the light spilling out. But he had to be sure.

"I don't want you to stay for me," he said softly. "I'm not worth *that*."

"You are worth it," David said simply. "But I'm not staying for you. I'm staying for me. For what I want. In my career and in my life. I want you. I think I have since the moment we met."

Farzan took a shuddering breath. Was there a gas leak in here? His head felt light.

"But what about your dreams?"

"My dream doesn't mean a damn if I can't share it with you."

Heat prickled at the corners of Farzan's eyes.

He didn't come here to cry, damn it.

"Don't you remember when you came over and we watched *The Muppet Movie*?" David asked. "A dream gets better the more people you share it with."

Farzan snorted through his tears. "Okay, Kermit."

David grinned and stepped closer.

Farzan's body reacted immediately: the hair on his arms standing up, skin going all tingly. David's warmth and presence and scent overwhelmed him.

"I want you back, too," he said, threading his fingers through Farzan's. "I love you, Farzan. With all my heart."

Farzan shuddered as he tried not to cry. But he couldn't help it.

David smiled at him. Brought a warm hand up to thumb away his tears.

"Don't cry, babe."

"I'm happy," Farzan said.

He didn't think he'd ever been this happy in his entire life.

Farzan Alavi. In love.

Not such a fuckup after all.

"I'm happy too." David rested his forehead against Farzan's.

Farzan closed his eyes, breathed in the moment. He could've stayed there forever.

"For the love of god," came Kyra's voice to their side. "Would you two just kiss already?"

His eyes fluttered back open, but David was looking past him.

"You—" David began.

But he didn't finish, because Farzan smashed his mouth against David's.

David responded instantly, Kyra forgotten behind them, as he returned the kiss. Warmth filled Farzan from his toes to the top of his head. Joy sparkled in his belly, crackled along his hands, as he brought them up to cup David's jaw.

He kissed, and kissed, and kissed. And David kissed him back, humming in pleasure, lips vibrating against Farzan's, until all of a sudden he froze.

Farzan froze, too, opened his eyes to find David looking right at him, panic written across his face.

Right before a sudden, rumbling burp split them apart. Farzan tasted Champagne as he broke their kiss and started laughing.

"Oh my god," David groaned. "I'm sorry. It's the Champagne."

"It's okay," Farzan said. Before David could even cover his face, Farzan grabbed it and kissed him again. And again. And again.

"Ugh, I take it back," Kyra said. "Get a room, you two."

David chuckled and said, voice low and liquid so only Farzan could hear, "My place or yours?"

epilogue

Farzan

Six months later

Baby Safa was warm and soft, bundled up in Farzan's arms. Her tiny hands grasped and relaxed as she slept happily.

She was only two weeks old, and Farzan's niece, his goddaughter, had him wrapped around her little finger. She was perfect.

Farzan pressed a kiss to her forehead. She cooed but didn't wake. Did babies dream? What did they dream about?

What would little Safa's life bring to her? What dreams would she chase? Which ones would let her down? And which ones would turn out more amazing than she ever dared to imagine?

Farzan didn't know. All he knew was he'd support her through it all.

Ramin cleared his throat. He was dressed up, in a sharp gray suit, a green tie that matched his eyes, and a fresh haircut.

Farzan's own hair was still growing out; it was long enough now that his usual curl had come back, and he looked more like himself, but it would be another six months or so before it was back the way Farzan

liked it. The way David liked it, too: he'd whined, the first time he tried
to grab a handful of it and was thwarted.

The head Farzan was giving him at the time had made up for it, but
still.

"Sorry," Farzan said, blushing at the memory. "You need something?"

Ramin smiled at little Safa, dimples deep and eyes shining. "She's so
perfect," he whispered reverently.

"She is," Farzan murmured, pressing his lips to her head again.

Ramin straightened up. "Anyway. Arya says it's nearly time for your
speech. He also says if you ruin his schedule, he's going to murder you."

Farzan chuckled, bouncing Safa in his arms a few times.

"I can take her back to Maheen for you."

Farzan transferred the little bundle to Ramin, whose smile only shone
brighter as he looked down at her sleeping face. Of the three of them—
Farzan, Ramin, and Arya—Ramin was the one who most wanted kids of
his own. Farzan figured it wouldn't be long before he and Todd started
talking about marriage and adopting. Or surrogacy. Or who knows what.
And then Farzan would be a guncle twice over, because Ramin was as
much his brother as Navid was, and any kid of Ramin's would be surrounded with love. Just like baby Safa.

Farzan slipped out of the office—his new office, in the new, expanded
Shiraz Bistro. His old office had been taken over by the new general manager, but he still needed a place to decompress, to think over new recipes, to talk with Ramin and Arya about their plans for the future. It
was tucked into the corner of the expanded kitchen, across from the new
refrigerator.

The kitchen was humming with activity: Sheena kneeling in front of
the oven to keep an eye on a batch of kookoo, Spencer rotating skewers of
kabob over their new grill, Chase flicking water at the base of a pot of rice
to check the heat. The staff had already had their own celebration—at
Aspire, actually, last week—but today was for the community.

Their grand reopening.

Farzan emerged into a restaurant bustling with lively conversation, people shouting to be heard over the Persian music Reza was playing—apparently, when he wasn't lawyering, he was DJ Reza Bass—from a corner of the small dance floor set up in the expanded dining room.

Arya made a beeline for him, hooking his arm around Farzan's elbow and dragging him toward the bar.

"It's time for your speech." He was dressed up, too, in a shiny maroon suit with a pocket square the color of egg yolks and matching his nails.

"Do I have to?" Farzan muttered.

"You were already outvoted."

The only bad thing about being in business with his two best friends: they tended to gang up on him.

Only when they were right, but still.

Arya parked Farzan at the edge of the dance floor, grabbed the microphone from Reza, looked at it for a moment to check that it was on, then handed it to Farzan.

Farzan stared at the mic as Reza faded out the music. The crowd turned toward him.

Arya waved at him to start talking.

"Uh." Farzan cleared his throat. "Hi, folks. Thanks for coming tonight. Kheyli mamnoon."

In the middle of the crowd, a familiar whistle sounded.

Farzan fought a blush and kept going.

"It's an honor and a privilege to welcome you all back to the bigger, better Shiraz Bistro."

Someone—Farzan thought it might've been Navid—began clapping, which rapidly spread. He wasn't done, though.

"I just—I just want to thank everyone who got us here. My parents, who built this restaurant from the ground up, to share the cuisine of Iran with the metro area. To make a place where Iranians, where anyone, could feel at home." Farzan spotted his mom and dad in the crowd, smiling at him. "The amazing team here at Shiraz Bistro, who stuck through a change in leadership and an expansion and still somehow manage to put up with me, even when I blast video game music in the kitchen."

Most of them were still in said kitchen, but a few of the front of house staff had paused to listen to him.

"My new partners, of course. Ramin and Arya. My best friends. I never could've done this without them."

He glanced Arya's way. Ramin had sidled up beside him, his arm around Todd's waist.

"My boyfriend, David, who believed in me." He could just spot David over the crowd around the bar. Even though David had taken a week off work to visit his friend Ayesha in Chicago, he'd taken another week off just to help Farzan get ready for the reopening. Not only that, but he'd picked out the wines to serve, for tonight and for their updated wine list. "I love you, babe."

A chorus of *aww*s rippled through the crowd.

"And finally...all of you. Thank you for coming tonight to celebrate this place. Noosh-e jan!"

Navid let out a whoop, and the place broke into applause. Farzan smiled and waved and turned the mic over to Arya.

"Nice speech," Arya said. "But you could've spent a little longer on your more handsome partner, I think..." He pursed his lips and smiled with his eyes, like he was posing for a photo.

"Nah, Ramin doesn't like too much attention."

Arya pretended to be offended, but he couldn't hold the scowl for long before breaking into a laugh. He grabbed Farzan with one arm, yanked Ramin away from Todd with another, and pulled them all into a hug.

"You guys are the best," Farzan said over the music.

"You are," Ramin said.

"Now come on. Let's celebrate."

Farzan released his friends, only to find his parents waiting for him. His mom enveloped him in a hug, kissing both cheeks.

"We're so proud of you, Farzan-joon," she said. "So proud."

"And happy for you," Firouz added. "All we ever wanted is for you to be happy."

"I know, Baba. I am."

"Good."

"Oh! Deb!" Persis shouted, making a beeline for her friend, who was standing next to David's dad but talking to David's mom, sharing some joke that made Kathleen laugh so hard it could be heard over the music.

Farzan waved and pressed into the crowd, past Maheen and Tomás, who were swaying Safa to the music; past Navid, who was talking with Gina in a corner; past friends and strangers alike, all crowded in to celebrate.

"Pretty good turnout," Kyra said.

"I think so, boss."

Kyra swatted at him as they zigzagged toward the bar.

When they'd gotten their loan squared away—helped by the extra liquidity and collateral Ramin and Arya had been able to offer—finding a general manager had been first on Farzan's list. To his surprise, Kyra had applied—at David's urging.

And she was awesome at it. Better than Farzan had ever been. Better than his mom had been, to be honest.

"Here you go, babe." David handed Farzan a flute of Champagne. "Proud of you."

He leaned across the bar for a kiss, which Farzan returned. Perhaps a little too enthusiastically, since Kyra started making a retching sound.

"Ugh. You know I took this job to get away from you, right?"

"Mm-hmm." David passed her a Champagne flute, too. "If you really wanted to get away, you wouldn't work with my boyfriend."

"Whatever." She raised her glass and clinked it with Farzan's. Her face grew serious. "Thanks. Really. For giving me the chance."

"Are you kidding?" Farzan laughed. "Thank you for putting up with me."

Kyra's smile brightened, but then she gasped. "Hey. Is that who I think it is?"

She pointed at an older white man who'd just walked in the door, wearing a thin scarf despite the June heat.

"Who?" Farzan asked.

"Frank Allen. The *real* Frank Allen."

"The food critic?" Farzan asked.

"I think so. Looks like his profile picture."

David snorted. "You've got to be shitting me. You want to go say hi?"

"Nah," Farzan said. "I'll let our new manager do that."

Kyra arched an eyebrow. "You know I'll just bring him back to talk with our chef."

"Can't you stall him for a few minutes?"

Kyra looked between Farzan and David. She puffed up her cheeks and huffed. "Fine. I'll try."

"You're the best."

As she went to greet their newest guest, David stepped out from behind the bar, wrapped his arms around Farzan, and swayed to the music. Cedar and vetiver wrapped around Farzan like a snuggly blanket.

"Hey, you." David leaned down for another Champagne-tinged kiss.

"Hey." Farzan poked at David's master somm pin. "You know. Not many Persian restaurants can boast a wine list developed by a master sommelier."

"Oh yeah?" David rested his head against Farzan's. "Is that why you love me? For my wine?"

"I love you for that dick," Farzan muttered. "And those blue sweat-pants."

David snorted so hard, he nearly knocked Farzan over.

"Maybe I should've worn them tonight."

"Uh-uh. No one would've paid attention to my speech." Farzan pressed another kiss to David's cheek. "I love you because you're ambitious. And kind. And patient. And I love you because you make me believe in myself. You never give up on me. Even when I want to give up on myself."

David's eyes sparkled. "I love you too, babe. I love how you always take care of everyone around you. I love when you hum as you cook. I love when you cuddle up with me and we watch movies." David kissed him. "I love that you're my home."

Farzan set down his Champagne and wrapped his arms around David's neck, stepping lightly to sway to the music. Reza had switched to a classic Googoosh song.

"So," David whispered. "How does it feel?"

"How does it feel?" Farzan held David close. "It feels like a dream come true."

Acknowledgments

Just like a fine bottle of wine is the result of more than just a single vintner, a book is the result of more than just a single author. So cheers to everyone who helped make this one happen.

Cheers to Molly O'Neill, my agent, who didn't bat an eye when, after years of writing about teenagers finding themselves, I announced I wanted to write books about adults drinking wine and boning (and still finding themselves, I guess). And cheers to the entire Root Lit team, and Heather at Baror International, for all they do.

Cheers to Sam Brody, my editor, for helping me find the heart of this book, and for forgiving me for that one COVID brain-fog draft. Cheers to the entire team at Forever, especially Estelle for all the Muppet memes, plus Dana and Carolina. And cheers to the Sales Team, Marketing Team, Production Team, and all the countless people that helped shepherd my book from vine to bottle.

Cheers to Forouzan Safari for the stunning cover illustration, Daniela Medina for the gorgeous jacket design, Taylor Navis for the lovely interiors, and Anjuli Johnson and Lori Paximadis for the thoughtful copy edit. A day may come when I'll learn the difference between further and farther, but it is not this day.

Cheers to Jessica Brock, Kristin Dwyer and the Leo PR team, for helping get my book out into the world.

Cheers to Debbie Deuble Hill and the terrific folks at APA for being tireless champions of me and my work.

Cheers to Ronni Davis, Tessa Gratton, Tara Hudson, Lana Wood Johnson, Julie Murphy, Natalie C. Parker, Sierra Simone, and Julian Winters, for letting me talk your collective ears off about this book when I couldn't figure out what was supposed to happen next.

Cheers to all my friends, group chats, Discords, writing groups, and more. I used to be able to count all my friends on two hands and fit them into the acknowledgments. I count myself blessed and endlessly grateful that there are too many of you now.

Cheers to Tannin Wine Bar and Kitchen, the place where everybody knows my name. I didn't know that was really a thing before. And cheers especially to Barry, for taking the time to answer all my questions about life in the restaurant business.

Cheers to every bookseller and librarian who's ever put a copy of one of my books into the hands of a reader. And cheers to every reader who's found joy or hope or laughter or tears in the pages of one of my books.

Beh salamati!

YOUR BOOK CLUB RESOURCE

Visit **GCPClubCar.com** to sign up for the GCP Club Car newsletter, featuring exclusive promotions, info on other Club Car titles, and more.

Find us on
social media: **@ReadForeverPub**

Reading Group Guide

Questions for Discussion

1. Farzan, Ramin, and Arya's friendship is one of many trios we see in media: Kirk, Spock, and McCoy; Luke, Han, and Leia; Winifred, Mary, and Sarah. Why are trios so common in media? Are they common in your own life?

2. Farzan has been friends with Ramin and Arya for most of his life. Do you have any lifelong friends like that? What role do Ramin and Arya play in Farzan's life?

3. Unlike Farzan, David doesn't have many deep or lasting friendships, though over the course of the novel he opens up to Kyra and Jeri and reconnects with Ayesha and Rhett. How do those relationships affect him?

4. Farzan is an oldest child (of immigrants, no less), while David is an only child of divorced parents. How has this affected their outlooks, and how does it play into their relationships with others?

5. Farzan, David, and most of the characters are millennials. Are you a millennial? Did you identify with their mindsets? How did being a millennial affect the course of Farzan and David's relationship?

6. Farzan and David spend a lot of time feeling like they're behind and missing milestones for their ages, whether it be stable relationships or career status or homeownership. Have you ever felt that way? Are Farzan and David justified, or are they placing too much pressure on themselves?

7. Farzan is part of the Iranian diaspora, and his family's restaurant is an anchor for his community. What are the anchors of your community?

8. The Kansas City setting plays an important part in the novel, both as a backdrop for the characters' lives, and as a place to either be loved or escaped from. Have you ever been to Kansas City? Do you love your hometown, or have you ever wanted to escape?

9. Farzan and David first hook up under a case of mistaken identity, though it's quickly resolved. Does this satisfy the "mistaken identity" trope? Subvert it? What other tropes are included or subverted in the novel? What are your favorite tropes?

10. David's ambition is one of his driving motivators throughout the story, though he learns to temper it with his love for others. What are some of your own greatest ambitions? Did you achieve them? Or perhaps find out that your true ambition was something else entirely?

A Guide to Pairing Muppet Movies and Wines

First off, I feel like I should start with my usual caveat that, at the end of the day, your body is your business, as is what you put in it. I don't yuck other people's yums. Dairy with fish? Go for it. Wearing white after Labor Day? It doesn't harm anyone. White Zinfandel? I find it suspicious, but that's just me.

That being said, I *do* think magic can happen when you make the perfect pairing, whether that's in love or in Reese's Peanut Butter Cups or in wine and the Muppets. For the purposes of this pairing guide, I'll be sticking to theatrical releases, though of course there are *many* worthy inclusions that released direct to video or on television. (Foremost among them being *A Muppet Family Christmas*, which I would pair with a bottle of wine with holes in it, because the DVD is missing several songs they couldn't get the rights to and so the plot has holes in it too.)

And so, without further ado:

The Muppet Movie (1979): The one that started it all. Well, unless you count *The Muppet Show*. Or *Sam and Friends* before that. Or *Sesame Street*. Still, this is the Muppets' origin story, self-referentially mythologized. And if you can't find an amphora of three-thousand-year-old Greek wine, why not reach for something nonetheless tried-and-true and classic:

Bordeaux. Sleek and powerful and earthy, perfect for drinking under the stars or before having a shoot-out in a conveniently placed ghost town.

The Great Muppet Caper (1981): Yes, they're gonna be a movie! A mystery, in fact. A caper! It's right there in the title! This movie is vivacious, self-referential, and exciting. Just like Rhône blends from the Walla Walla Valley. Or skip a GSM (Grenache-Syrah-Mourvedre blend) and pick a single varietal, like a Syrah. Take a sip and enjoy that nightlife.

The Muppets Take Manhattan (1984): Full disclosure, this one's my favorite, probably because it's the one my dad's coworker recorded off TV onto a VHS cassette that got a lot of use in my childhood. This movie is romantic—not only in featuring a wedding between Kermit and Miss Piggy (*Muppets* creators can't seem to decide whether it's canon or not), but also in featuring the Muppets deeply in love with a dream of being on Broadway, and in love with each other, parting and then coming back together as so many of us do after college. This movie is delightful and comforting, and I can watch it any day. What could go better with it than rosé? Perhaps a nice Walla Walla rosé with crisp minerality. Look at us. Here we are.

The Muppet Christmas Carol (1992): The greatest Christmas movie of all time. The greatest Dickens adaptation of all time. The list of superlatives goes on and on. I watch this every Christmas Eve, of course—when there's only one more sleep. This movie is warm, and loving, and perfect, just like Bordeaux reds. Left Bank or Right Bank, you can't go wrong. Pinot Noir has the perfect spice to warm you on a cold December night.

Muppet Treasure Island (1996): An amazing adventure? Check. A guy who lives in a bear's finger? Check. A human main character whose voice inconveniently changed during filming? Check. Tim Curry at his most Tim Curry, unless you count that one video of him shouting "Space!"? Double check. You need a wine that can stand up to this movie, so reach no further than a nice Barolo. Those foggy tannins will put you in the perfect mood. Just remember, safety first, or Samuel Arrow might have you walk the plank.

Muppets from Space (1999): An often-overlooked contribution to the Muppets' oeuvre, but a delightful one nonetheless. While it's full of the usual Muppet hijinks, some delightful human cameos, and the occasional musical number, at its heart, this is a movie about searching for home, whether that's a place or a person or a feeling. Mendoza Malbec was one of the first wines I fell in love with, and they make me feel at home. I hope they'll make you feel at home, too.

The Muppets (2011): Not quite a reboot, but certainly a refresh, and one that ignores a few bits of continuity established on the TV shows and, in particular, 2002's made-for-TV *It's a Very Merry Muppet Christmas Movie*, insofar that it established the Muppet Theatre had been designated a historical landmark to thwart Joan Cusack turning it into a nightclub. Anyway! What could pair better than a new take on a classic wine—American Cabernet Sauvignon, in particular, one from Napa Valley. Whether it's valley floor or hillside, Stags Leap or Rutherford or Oakville, Napa Cabs are bold and full of character(s), just like this film.

Muppets Most Wanted (2014): This one doesn't seem to get nearly as much love as I think it deserves. The cameos? Amazing. Constantine the Frog, Kermit's doppelgänger? A classic villain. A trip across Europe? Honestly, that's what *I* want. And you know what else I want? A nice Marlborough Sauvignon Blanc from New Zealand. Approachable, well crafted, often underestimated yet never under-delicious. Zesty and sharp and fun. Just like the Muppets.

And there you have it: the ultimate guide to pairing wine and the Muppets. For the lovers, the drinkers, and you!

Cheers!

About the Author

ADIB KHORRAM is the author of *Darius the Great Is Not Okay*, which earned the William C. Morris Debut Award, the Asian/Pacific American Award for Young Adult Literature, a Boston Globe–Horn Book Honor, and was named one of *Time* magazine's 100 Best YA Novels of All Time. His novels *Darius the Great Deserves Better, Kiss & Tell*, and *The Breakup Lists*, as well as his picture books, *Seven Special Somethings: A Nowruz Story* and *Bijan Always Wins*, have garnered critical acclaim, starred reviews, and bestsellers.

When he isn't writing, you can find him playing his Fender Stratocaster, sipping a glass of Grignolino, or searching for the best french fries in Kansas City. (Just kidding. He's already found them.)

This is his first book for adults, and he had way too much fun writing it.

You can learn more at:

AdibKhorram.com
Instagram @AdibKhorram
TikTok @Adib.Khorram
Bluesky @AdibKhorram
Tumblr @AdibKhorram

YOUR
BOOK
CLUB
RESOURCE

VISIT
GCPClubCar.com

to sign up for the **GCP Club Car** newsletter, featuring exclusive promotions, info on other **Club Car** titles, and more.

**GRAND
CENTRAL**

FOREVER

TWELVE

LEGACY
LIT

balance